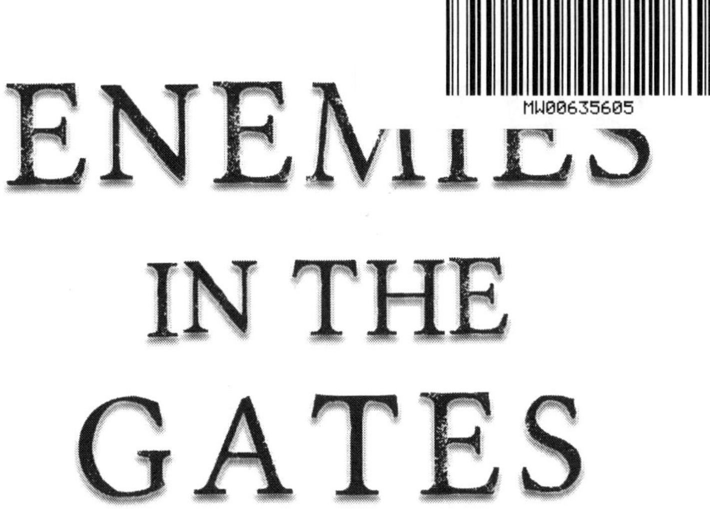

REDMOND CIVIL WAR ROMANCE SERIES

BOOK 3 ~ THIRD EDITION

T. NOVAN

TAYLOR RICKARD

AUSXIP PUBLISHING

Enemies In The Gates

Cover Design by Mary D. Brooks

Interior design by AUSXIP Media

Third Edition

ISBN: 978-0-6485709-7-4

Printed in the United States of America

Published by AUSXIP Publishing
Sydney, Australia

DEDICATION

Dedicated to the many readers who have supported us, welcomed us back after a long hiatus, and made bringing Charlie and Rebecca back to life easy.

Special thanks to the folks who have assisted us in preparing this manuscript, and especially to Kris Baldwin, for her focused service as the final proof editor.

—T. Novan and Taylor Rickard

HISTORICAL NOTES

This series of books started as a pair of short stories, but over time, it grew first into a book and then into a historical saga that explores the economic and social evolution of one family that, when completed, will reflect the times and stresses of the past hundred and fifty years of American history.

The Redmond family was founded by Charlie Redmond, a transgendered man who ran from an abusive father, took the identity of a man, and rose through the ranks of the Union Army to become a well-respected officer and achieve the rank of brigadier general.

In actuality, there were a number of women who served in both the Union and the Confederate armies. The highest rank that a woman rose to, that we know of, was a major under the command of Phillip Sheridan.

Wintering over in Culpeper, Virginia, a community that saw both southern and northern troops sweep through its lands repeatedly during the war, Charlie met Rebecca Gaines, a southern war widow and owner of what had once been one of the finest horse farms in Virginia.

These two survivors met, fell in love, and adopted a small horde of war orphans to begin what would become a strong family with a tradition of care and support for the community that would help Culpeper return to the successful farming area it once was.

But the trip to prosperity was not an easy one. The years immediately following the war were particularly hard in the southern states. There had been so much damage done to the land, especially in Virginia and Tennessee, where many of the major battles had been fought, that recovery was difficult. Labor resources were scarce, as many of the men had been killed in the war, and many of the Negro families had fled to the north after the war looking for work.

At the same time, the returning southern soldiers were still angry and resentful. For these men, the war had destroyed their way of life, their heritage, and their culture. The concept of freed blacks was alien, and the fact that colored men would work for a lesser wage, taking away jobs from poor white men, was a scourge. Yankees (carpetbaggers) and southern unionists (scallywags) were equally reviled. To add insult to injury, the southern states were not immediately reinstated to the Union. Instead, they were under military control, with the criminal courts, law enforcement and many other governmental functions under the control of the military or the Freedman's Bureau, which was established to help the blacks acclimate to their new status as free citizens.

It is from this roiling cauldron of resentment and anger that the Ku Klux Klan in Tennessee, the Crimson Shirts in South Carolina, and similar organizations around the south arose. The behaviors of some of the characters in this story are modeled on actual events across the south in those first few years after the war.

This resentment is exacerbated by the continued role of the military in the governance of the southern states. The line between civilian and criminal courts was blurred, and in many states, military rule continued to be the law of the land until the individual states were re-admitted to the Union.

On a lighter note, we observe the establishment of schools for both blacks and whites was a major theme of reconstruction activities. The local schools, such as that established in Culpeper, were popping up all over the south. In addition, Howard University was established in Washington DC as noted in this story and did include a medical degree as part of its curriculum.

One of our favorite historical aspects of this book within the Redmond Saga was the establishment of the relationship with the Schwarz family. The brothers moved to Baltimore from Germany, and the eldest brother, Henry, opened The Toy Bazaar in Baltimore as written. Younger brother F.A.O. Schwarz would open his famous store in New York later in the century. But The Toy Bazaar is not the only real store in our story. We have been meticulous in documenting real merchants, restaurants, taverns, and businesses in our presentation of these months and years after the war.

Robert E. Lee did indeed assume the management of Washington University (now Washington and Lee), and spent a good bit of time and energy canvassing the countryside and his many friends to raise money to elevate the quality of education offered by that institution. He was also an outspoken proponent of the effective reunion of the nation, and many of the words we have put into his mouth in this book were taken directly from his letters, articles, and testimony before Congress. Similarly, we have used General Grant's own words whenever possible.

Kate Warne was a noted detective among Alan Pinkerton's famed forces, and established an outstanding model for female detectives. Sadly, she died of pneumonia shortly after her time within our novel.

As ever, we have tried to represent the historical context accurately and realistically, drawing on a wide range of research resources. We particularly wish to thank the Historical Society of Culpeper for their documentation, and the owners of what is now called the Burgandine House, but was at that time the home of one Mrs. Allen, who did indeed make and sell the best moonshine in the region.

Taylor Rickard, December 2015

Dramatis Personae

(Historical characters are in italics)

The Redmond Household

General Charles "Charlie" Huger Redmond, US Army (Retired)
Rebecca Anne Randolph Gaines Redmond, his wife
Their children:
Darby Sweet Redmond
Suzanne Sweet Redmond
Emily Adams Redmond
Charles "Buddy" Huger Redmond II
Andrew Richard Adams Redmond
Their Staff and Household Servants
Albert Randolph, Rebecca's cousin and Redmond Stable's horse buyer
John Foxworth, family tutor
Tarent - ex trooper, farm manager/farrier
Rollins - stable boy, Tarent's apprentice
Robert Brooks, stable worker
Reg Washington, the butler and major domo
Sarah Coleman, the cook
Beulah Jones, the housekeeper
Lizbet Sessions, Rebecca's ladies maid, Beulah's niece, Tomas's fiancée
Tess Jones, the nursery maid and Beulah's younger sister
Ginnie, the wet nurse
Freddy, once the kitchen boy, now being trained as Darby's valet
Louis, Charlie's new valet and sometimes coach driver
Tomas Coleman, Charlie's old valet, now a med student
Ted, big farmhand

Big Ben, farm hand and BBQ pit master
Their Animals
Jack, Charlie's Horse
Shannon, Rebecca's horse
Tucker, Darby's horse
Peritas (Peri), Charlie's wolfhound
Feighlí, Rebecca's wolfhound
Sheridan, Charlie's cat
Madra, wolfhound who guards horses

Other Residents of Culpeper:

Reverend Edgar Vile, Church of England
Charlotte Redmond Vile, previously known as Lizzie Armstrong
Their children:
Edgar Charles Vile
Rebecca Elizabeth Vile
Dr. Tongzhi Xiang (Rex), member of Chinese Royal Family
Their Household Servants
Priscilla "Sissy," Charlotte's ladies maid, Lizbet's sister, and Beulah's niece
Japheth, houseman at manse
Deborah, housekeeper
Zipporah, the cook
Leah, the nursery maid.
Lt. Colonel Richard Polk, Provost of Culpeper County
Dr. Elizabeth Walker, his wife
Richard "Dickon" Polk II, their son
Their servants:
Ruth, their housekeeper
Nigel, Elizabeth's assistant
John "Jocko" Xavier Jackson, tavern owner

Esther White Jackson, his wife and tearoom owner
Roselle "Ro" Jackson, his niece
Duncan Nailer, carpenter and cabinet maker
Samantha Carter Nailer, his wife and Jeremiah's mother
Their son, Samuel Duncan Nailer
Jeremiah Carter, Samantha's son, leather worker
Mrs. Margaret Williams, widow of the previous minister
Mr. Edward Cooper, mercantile owner
Mrs. Grace Cooper, his wife
Rafe Johnstone, apothecary
Mayor Horace Frazier
Mrs. Missy Frazier, his wife
Miss Katherine Reynolds
Miss Mary Allison Simms
Henry Armistead, lumber mill owner
Mrs. Penelope Armistead, his wife
Nicholas Armistead, his son
James Armistead, his younger brother
George Randall, station master and telegraph operator
James Granville, blacksmith
Mrs. Laura Granville, his wife
Tom Granville, his son
Harold Kirtley, local farm owner.
Christopher Edward Rainey, carpenter
Alexander Fancher Raeburn, returning southern soldier
Frank Halliburton, banker
Ralph Hudnut, brick layer
Jimmy, black teamster
George, black teamster
Mrs. Allen, owner of a local tavern
Miss Eloise Langley, bank secretary
Annabelle Calvert, school teacher, Miss Reynolds cousin

Mr. Stevenson, the coppersmith and plumber
Mr. Butler, the well digger.
Master Sergeant Sean Cady, Dpty Provost, 1st military district.
Sergeant Max Frederick, Dpty Provost, 1st military district.
Miles Tolliver - black printer
Miss Dorothy Hunter - new dress maker
Lieutenant W. S. Chase - command of contingent of the 18th infantry sent to support orderly elections in Culpeper.
Reverend Warburton Addison
Ariel, his wife
Ainslie his son, age 1
Leslie his son, age 2.

Washington DC Residents:
Jerome Lord, attorney
Mrs. Amelia Lord, his wife
Miss Stella Lord, his oldest daughter
William Galloway, livery stable owner
Mrs. Galloway, his mother and Charlie's land lady
Geoffrey Galloway, his nephew
General Phillip Sheridan, Commander, Department of the Shenandoah
General Ulysses S. Grant, Commander, Army of the Potomac, later President of the United States
General Montgomery C. Meigs, Quartermaster General of the Army
President Andrew Johnson
Montgomery Blair, attorney
Morrison Waite, attorney
Oliver Wendell Holmes, attorney, clerk
Robert Todd Lincoln, attorney, clerk
Hugh Stevens - Washington Makeup artist.

Tribunal. Brigadier General Alfonse Mayberry, US Army Artillery.
Tribunal. Colonel Constantine Douglas, infantry
Tribunal. Colonel George Allenby, infantry

Richmond Residents

Major General John M. Schofield, commander of Military District Number One
Governor Francis H. Pierpont
Colonel Everett Salton
Lt. Colonel Trevor Veriton
Captain Jason Bailton
Captain Randall Lightborne

Other Characters

General Robert E. Lee, Provost, Washington College
Mary Lee, his wife
Alan Pinkerton, Detective
Kate Warne, Pinkerton detective and noted body guard.
Henry Schwarz, owner of The Toy Bazaar, older brother of FAO Schwarz
Caroline Schwarz, his wife

PROLOGUE

In the final days of the American Civil War, two very unique people came together to establish what would become a southern dynasty. Colonel Charles Huger Redmond brought his cavalry regiment, the 13th Pennsylvania, to the formerly bustling town of Culpeper, Virginia to establish winter headquarters that would allow for the protection of critical rail lines. In order to support his men and horses until the upcoming spring campaign, their winter encampment also required the taking over of lands owned by Confederate widow Rebecca Gaines.

Over the course of the winter, Charlie and Rebecca's relationship grows from one of cautious, mutual respect to something very different. As their unusual friendship grows, Colonel Redmond finds himself drawn not only to the land, but the woman as well. He makes a deal with the Widow Gaines to winter his men and horses on her property and she makes a deal for his personal protection during his stay.

Charlie is a charming gentleman, gentle, caring, and very appropriate, a very different kind of man from Rebecca's abusive husband. Though her husband had perished in November of 1863, at the Second Battle of Rappahannock Station, Rebecca finds it extremely difficult to come to terms with her growing feelings for this Union officer.

For his part, Charlie is alarmed to realize he is becoming romantically involved with the lovely southerner, for he hides a secret that, if discovered, would mean social disgrace and the end of a distinguished military career. Under the carefully crafted and protected military façade, Charlie is a woman.

Over the course of the winter, they find the courage to let their feelings blossom into a deep and abiding love. Before Charlie, who has now been elevated to the rank of brigadier general, and the 13th Pennsylvania are ordered back into the field of battle, they are married, in part so that Charlie can continue to protect and provide for Rebecca and for the two orphaned children, Emily and Andrew, they have taken in and plan to adopt.

The final months of the conflict in Virginia are brutal. Rebecca took in the waves of refugees, women and children who had been made homeless by the ravages of the war. One of these included the infant son of a notorious Washington prostitute and one of the conspirators who orchestrated President Lincoln's assassination, whom she adopted.

Charlie and his troops see battle after battle, as General Grant's forces push General Lee's struggling and poorly supplied troops back up the James River from Petersburg to Appomattox. The 13th Pennsylvania Cavalry manages to block trainloads of supplies from reaching General Lee at Appomattox, resulting in Charlie being terribly wounded, and the Army of Virginia being forced to surrender.

With the support of Dr. Elizabeth Walker, his regiment's physician, his batman Jocko Jackson, and medics Albert

Samuelson and Walt Whitman, Charlie's life is saved, but he is badly injured, with part of one hand missing and significant muscle loss in his right leg. After a frightening few weeks in the field hospital, they manage to return Charlie to Culpeper, where his recovery is a slow and painful process.

As the town of Culpeper begins to recover after the end of the war, several of Charlie's companions from the 13th Pennsylvania choose to join their leader and settle in the shattered town. Culpeper had once had a thriving population of fifteen hundred, but at the height of the war, after both the Union and Confederate troops had swept through it on multiple occasions, had been reduced to a burned out hulk with only 150 residents.

With the end of the war, men and families were slowly returning to their homes or what was left of them, and with the support of the handful of unionists, began the slow process of rebuilding. Elizabeth Walker, who married Charlie's second in command Richard Polk, settles in to be the town's only physician.

Several of Charlie's men had met women, either locals or refugees, and chose to join their former commander in supporting the town. There were a few people in Culpeper who supported the unionists; others were still angry and resentful. The reconstruction of the South had begun, and for Charlie, Rebecca and the residents of Culpeper, Virginia, the coming years would be an uphill battle.

Much of the south was still under military rule, and even those who were committed to restoring the economic and social well-being of their communities were faced with many challenges. These years also saw the creation of the Ku Klux Klan and organizations like them, who tried to repress the Negro community from finding a new place in the economy and political environments, through threats and even violence. Charlie and Rebecca face a community that is still barely functional, through both the damage done during the war and the anger and resentment that drive many of the recently returned confederate soldiers. The Redmond family faces many challenges, both personal and political as Culpeper struggles to find its place in the post-war world.

CHAPTER 1

Tuesday, January 29, 1867

It was a rare moment of quiet in the Redmond household. The children were either down for naps or off for afternoon studies. The only sounds in the parlor were the ticking of the mantle clock, the rustling of Charlie's newspaper, the clicking of Rebecca's knitting needles, and Feighlí snoring as the big dog lay sleeping by the fire. The knock on the door startled everyone. The dog growled as her head whipped up from the rug. Rebecca cursed when she dropped a stitch; Charlie chuckled and called, "Come in."

Reg opened the door and gestured their unexpected guest through. Ro Jackson smiled as she entered with her hat in one hand and a leash in the other. Attached to the end of the leash was an Irish wolfhound puppy. "Good afternoon, General. Mrs. Redmond. I have brought you a not so little gift."

As she moved across the room, Rebecca's wolfhound,

Feighlí, sat up; her thick tail immediately began thumping against the hearth rug. She was not only excited to see Ro, but the pup as well. Rebecca gave the command that released the big dog from her spot and she bounced to the smaller dog, which yelped and tried to hide behind her handler.

With a laugh, the young woman handed the leash to Charlie even as she gave Feighlí a loving scratch. "For you, General, the first Irish wolfhound pup born in America." She added with a wink, "To the best of my knowledge. My thanks to you for your help getting me started here in Culpeper. There has actually been quite a demand for my dogs. I had six pups in this litter and they are all spoken for. Including one for Colonel Polk and Dr. Walker, but I made sure you got the pick."

Charlie grinned and reached down to give the dog a good scratch. The big version was still trying to make friends with the smaller one, who was now content to try and hide behind the general's booted feet. "Thank you. He is a very handsome fellow. What is his name?"

"That will be up to you. I'll train him up for you, just like the others, but his name will be for you to choose."

The pup was already a one man dog and had dutifully fallen soundly asleep across his new human's feet, even as Feighlí continued to sniff and lick him.

Afternoon turned to evening, and the family gathered for an informal supper. The children delighted in playing with Feighlí and the newly named Peritas.

Charlie had decided on the name after he and Darby had spent most of dinner discussing Alexander the Great, as it had been the name of the great ruler's favorite dog. The children decided he would be called Peri.

Once supper was done, baths complete, games played and stories read, it was time for sleep. Mama and Papa were looking forward to it much more than the children, and after another forty minutes of multiple requests for one more story, kisses goodnight or a drink of water, they finally managed to break away and head for their bedroom.

Feighlí was in her normal spot at the top of the stairs right in front of the door, and Peri trailed along behind Charlie, looking nearly as worn out as the humans. At the door, the general gave the pup a scratch and told him to stay and lie down with Feighlí. Then he and Rebecca entered their room and closed the door behind them.

It took two seconds. Maybe three, and then the howling began.

Charlie's shoulders slumped. He turned and opened the door. Peri stopped howling immediately and looked up with eyes that the general could swear he saw tears in. Feighlí looked relieved the noise had stopped.

"Charlie, you are going to have to bring him in here. We cannot have him howling in the hall all night."

He nodded and gestured with his left hand. The smaller dog immediately jumped over the bigger one and scurried into the room. He moved to the fireplace and sat waiting patiently for whatever came next. Charlie sighed and closed the door.

As he sat down to take off his boots, Peri immediately threw himself over his feet. "Oh, dog, I am too tired for this tonight. You are very cute, but cute will only get you so far in this house. I should know; my cute rations ran out when the children all got here." He moved the dog off his feet and kicked off the short boots. The dog looked up, and then laid his head on the vacated footwear with a sigh.

Once the humans were settled into bed, and Charlie was about to blow out the candle on his night table, a little gray face and paws appeared on the edge of the bed. "Oh, no." Charlie shook his head and gave the pup and push back to the floor. "No way; the lady of the house is not going to let that happen in your lifetime or mine." He looked back at his wife, "Right?"

"Right."

He looked back to the dog. "Told you. Now lie down." After a minute or so of scratching, Peri lay down on floor next to the bed. Charlie rolled over and looked to Rebecca, who had a slightly annoyed smile on her face. At least it was a smile.

"You are still cute." She offered as a consolation when she snuggled closer to him. "Just not cute enough to justify a dog in our bed, especially a dog that will grow to the size of a pony." She wrapped her arm around his waist and kissed his jaw. "And I already let you have the damn cat."

He chuckled as her head came to rest on his shoulder. "You love Sheridan."

"Do not."

"Do too, and I can prove it." He kissed the top of her head as they settled down into the bed, pulling the covers nice and snug, to ward off the cold of the night.

"How so?" She purred, her face coming to rest near the hollow of his neck.

"You have to authorize the cream from the larder for him and you do it four times a week. You love my cat." He gave her a little tickle and kissed her good night before they both fell asleep.

~

Friday, February 1, 1867

Charlie was resting his brow on the palm of his right hand as he tried to read the documents Jerome had sent on for his approval. This was the absolute last item on his agenda for the night and he would be more than grateful when it was done. All he wanted was a cup of tea and a few minutes with Rebecca before he fell into what he was sure would be a coma-like state until morning.

He had not even reacted when the door to his office opened with a resounding crash. It was not until he felt the solid whack of the paper to the back of his head that he bothered to look up.

There before him was fury unleashed.

"Do you have any idea what you have done!?" Madam Fury inquired as she pulled back the paper, looking like she might go for another wallop to his cranium.

He ducked, bringing his good arm up, hoping to avoid another swat. "Apparently not!"

"Tomas proposed to Lizbet!"

"And this is bad why? I thought you liked it when people got married."

"Not when it happens to be the best lady's maid in three states! **My lady's maid**! Who intends to **join** her husband in **Washington** when he goes away to school!"

Charlie's eyes went wide.

To a southern lady of means like his wife, this was a **major** problem.

"Oh, shit!" He managed to stammer with appropriate reverence.

"Oh, shit is right, Charles Huger Redmond!" She pointed her paper at his nose and scowled. "Fix this! Fix this quickly!"

He shrugged, risking another smack from her rolled scroll of penance. "What do you suggest I do? I cannot forbid them to get married."

"I do not care. Fix it! Or you will find the sofa in my office a very lonely place."

He realized he was being threatened with banishment to the

basement. That was worse than the threat of the barn. At least he would have his horse for company in the barn.

This was a tidal wave in the ocean of calm that was his life. This was a major tactical error, worthy of Custer. He was not sure how to fix it, but one thing was certain--he had to do just that. Quickly.

Charlie rode Jack slowly across the property toward the little collection of houses. Over the course of a year they had managed to build six houses with another four planned. It was becoming a lovely little community, he mused as he rode down the path leading to the enclave.

All the cottages were being neatly kept and tended. Good size piles of firewood were scattered throughout the common area where each pair of houses shared a summer kitchen and an outhouse. Small gardens had been planted near the kitchen door of each home. Several chickens and a rooster or two ran around scratching and pecking the dirt between the houses. A few of the now locally known, infamous Redmond "fainting" goats that he raised on the farm wandered around.

He was glad to see the experiment was working for someone. He also noticed that while the free ranging goats would still show a bit of stiffness with a loud or unexpected noise, they did not fall over like the ones he kept penned. He suspected Rebecca would not take kindly to him letting his goats roam the farm at will. He would have to find another solution.

A handful of children were playing games with a few marbles and straw dolls when he stopped and dropped from Jack's back. Retrieving a small bag from his coat pocket, he walked slowly toward them.

The children stopped their games and all the little heads turned and smiled. They stood and dusted themselves off before approaching the tall man with their best bows and curtsies. They knew that he was very important. Their mamas and papas had told them more than once to be respectful when they saw him, but it was always easy to do with him because he was so kind.

"Mornin', Gen'l Charlie!" They all sang in chorus as they drew closer to him.

"Good morning, children." He smiled down to them. "Do any of you know where Miss Lizbet or Mr. Tomas might be this morning?"

One of the smaller girls lifted her hand, pointing at the first house to Charlie's left. "Lizbet is inside, sir."

"Thank you very much." He smiled as he opened the bag. "Now, I have something for each of you. Have you all been good?"

Seven little heads nodded all at once.

"You are sure? I am only allowed by Miss Rebecca to give treats to good children. You would not want me to get in trouble with Miss Rebecca, would you?"

Seven little heads shook vigorously. They most certainly did not want him in trouble with anyone. Whenever the general visited the houses, he always brought them something special. Last time it had been a carved toy for each of them. They loved it when he came to visit.

"All right then. Hold out your hands."

He smiled when they all lined up and waited as patiently as they were able while he put a small wrapped item in each tiny palm. The bundles held two horehound drops and a nickel. It was an enormous treat for these children who had so little no matter how hard he and Rebecca tried to make sure their parents had a good, well-paying job and a decent place to live.

Once the children were off with their prizes, he made his way to the little home and rapped on the kitchen door. It only took a few seconds for Lizbet to pull it open. She found him leaning against the house looking pitiful. She could not help but laugh; however, she recovered quickly.

"Yes, Gen'l Charlie?"

"First, let me say congratulations. I hope you and Tomas and I will be very happy together. Miss Rebecca has informed me that if you go, I go. And just so you know, I prefer my eggs over easy, coffee with a bit of sugar, and my toast burnt, and I am a complete baby when I get a cold."

The young woman began laughing again and stepped back from the door. "General Charlie, if you would like to come in for some coffee, I think I can explain."

He nodded, removing his hat and unbuttoning his greatcoat as he stepped inside the little home. It was warm and cozy and he was pleased to see Duncan and his men had done outstanding work.

There was nothing shoddy or unsafe in the structure. It was a million times better than the shacks in Slab Town, and even the little cobbled together houses in Sweetwater could not compare to what was quickly becoming known among both blacks and whites as Redmond Grove.

If you were of the black servant class in Culpeper, you hoped to work for the Redmonds to have a chance at one of the nice little houses. Of course, than meant being well trusted by the general and his wife and earning the spot.

Lizbet gestured for him to sit at the small kitchen table and she poured them both a cup of coffee. She slid a small dish of sugar in his direction but he did not take any of it.

"So." He lifted his cup. "What do I need to do to convince you not to leave Miss Rebecca?"

"I am not leaving Miss Rebecca. I am going to be with my future husband."

"Well, yes, you and I understand that. Miss Rebecca does not. Well, she does, but she trusts and relies on you so much, she does not want to understand it."

She nodded. "I promise you I will not leave before I have found a suitable replacement."

"I do not think she is going to find anyone suitable. I will make you a counter offer. If you would consider staying behind, I will pay for Tomas to come home every weekend, or I will make arrangements with Miss Rebecca for you to have weekends to go be with him. I will double your salary for the inconvenience of not being able to go to Washington full time, and I will pay for your wedding. You may have anything you desire. Anything."

He smiled very sincerely. "A woman's wedding day should be exactly what she wants. Please consider it. Talk it over with Tomas. Of all the things I have managed to do that annoy my wife, this is the most serious. I do believe I am in actual trouble, probably for the first time since I got married." He removed a pad and pencil from his pocket. "I am even prepared to give you my offer in writing."

Lizbet shook her head. "No, sir. There is no need for that. I would not insult you by asking you to do so. I will talk to Tomas tonight."

"Thank you." He patted her hand before standing to depart. "I do appreciate it. And we will certainly abide by whatever you decide is best for your family."

That evening, Tomas and Lizbet sat down at the table in the kitchen for a cup of tea before they retired for the night. She took his hand. "I had an interesting visit today."

"Oh? Who?" he asked.

"Gen'l Charlie. It seems that Miss 'Becca is not happy about us getting married."

Tomas looked very startled. This was not how he expected their mistress to respond.

"No, that is not quite right. She is very happy that you and I are to be married. What she is **not** happy about - **very** not happy about, is the idea of me going to Washington to live with you while you are in school."

The young man looked thoughtful as he nodded. "Ooohhh. And she does not believe we can find her a proper replacement for you."

"I suspect we could find the greatest lady's maid in the world and she would not be satisfied."

He laughed softly. "So, what did Gen'l Charlie want?"

"He wants me to stay here while you go to the university, and he has made us an extremely generous offer. He will double my salary, pay for you to come home on weekends or for me to go up to Washington, and he will pay for our wedding - anything we want. All of it."

Tomas took a deep breath. "He is willing to pay a lot of money to keep you around. Money we could use to start up a medical practice when I am done with school."

"I know, but it pains me to know you will be up there in Washington all alone during the week, with no one to cook for you or care for you."

"That is not exactly true. I will live in a boarding house that caters to students and provides meals as part of the cost. The general has already found several such places that I can pick from and he is paying the bill. And certainly during the week, I will have to spend as much of my time as possible studying when I am not actually in classes. Becoming a doctor is a complicated and difficult thing that takes a great deal of work. I am afraid you would be bored stiff hanging around waiting for me to find a few minutes of spare time."

"So you think we should take his offer?"

"Yes, dear heart. I do. Think about it. Between what you make, and the idea that I might be able to finish up more quickly if I focus on studying while I am in Washington, it could set us up for life. And we will be able to see each other every weekend and every holiday."

She nodded. "I think you are right. But I will miss you, sweetie."

"Just as much as you would miss me while you had to sit there and watch me study. Maybe less, since you would at least have something to do."

They touched their foreheads together and kissed tenderly. Tomas whispered, "You can tell her tomorrow." He took her hand and together they wandered off to their room to find sleep - eventually.

The stable boy who worked part time for the church was on hand to lead Charlie and Rebecca's horse and buggy to the small shed behind the manse as they made their way to the front door. It had been nearly three weeks since they had accompanied Edgar, Charlotte and Rex to Richmond for a very small and private wedding ceremony.

Once the newlyweds were off on their two week bridal excursion to whatever locations caught their attention, the rest of the wedding party had returned to Culpeper. Rex had borrowed Big Ben and a wagon and had gotten all of their belongings out of the house and into the manse. The time the newlyweds were away gave him just enough time to get the house unpacked and sorted. Now they were home and anxious to properly entertain their friends and show off their new home.

And show off they did. Duncan and Mr. Hudnut had done a splendid job of putting the building in order. The woodwork had the warm glow of well polished wood, the floors shone so brightly you could almost see yourself in them. Mrs. Williams's horrendous flocked flowers on the walls had been replaced with subtly colored and textured silk wall paper. The furnishings were a mix of French and Italian styles from the previous half century – elegant, slightly rococo, and lightly touched with gilt to set off the intricate carving of the frames. The only room that even somewhat resembled the old version was the office. Duncan had polished the wooden shelves until they shone, a large desk in dark wood graced the center of the room, and sturdy chairs in the Tudor style were arranged around the room.

After dinner, Rex headed up a detailed tour of the newly refurbished manse, with Edgar and Charlotte trailing along behind and smiling proudly.

The most impressive thing in the house was the new washing room. A large white enamel tub dominated the room, which was tiled in black and white marble. But most important, at least from Charlie's point of view, were the two taps that led into the tub, one of which was clearly marked "cold," the other was marked "hot."

"You have running hot water? How did you do it?" The general was jealous.

Rex smiled. "I would be happy to show you. The works are up in the attic, in addition to the gravity pump in the well."

Rebecca, looking rather annoyed, suggested, "Perhaps after we finish the tour, you two can climb up there." The idea of Charlie climbing a ladder to get into the attic was small satisfaction for the insanity she knew the new fangled water system was about to cause in their home.

Rcx understood exactly why she was being less than ecstatic over the water solution. He decided to side-step the issue by showing her the new cooking facilities. "Then let me show you what we have done to both the winter and summer kitchens."

They stepped into the winter kitchen, where Duncan and Hudnut had stripped everything down to bare walls and floor and started over. There was a large, deep sink with hot and cold water taps instead of the old hand pump. There were beautiful wooden cabinets with glass fronts so one could see where everything was. There was a lovely ice box, where things brought up from the cold room could be kept nice and cool until they were needed. And there was the brand-new, shiny Our Maine stove, with six burners in the top, and a small oven to compliment the two large ovens built into the fireplace walls. Beside the large stove was a second burner, designed specifically to support Rex's unique, flattened pans he called 'woks,' that would generate the very high heat he needed for his special style of cooking.

In the middle of the room was a large, tall table, topped with a butcher block, which could be used to prepare breads, meats and vegetables, yet still be convenient to the stoves and ovens.

Rebecca was in awe.

He grinned, proud of his design, and of Duncan and Hudnut's execution of it. But there was more. He knew the summer kitchen was a true work of art. "Shall we step outside? We have built an entirely new building out here."

They all walked out the back entrance, Rebecca eager to see the wonders Rex and Charlotte had commissioned, the gentlemen dutifully following.

The summer kitchen was a wonder. The new fireplace was large enough to spit roast a whole hog. There were four large ovens built into the walls of the fireplace, and an array of racks, hooks and spiders to support anything one might want to cook – either that or it was the rigging for a small ironworks.

In addition, there was another huge iron stove, and two more of Rex's special burners for the woks. A double sink sat under the windows on one side of the room, again with hot and cold running water. Pots of steel and copper, and various kitchen tools hung on hooks along one wall, while shelves, racks and bins lined the back wall to hold supplies.

Two more of the prep tables with butcher block tops stood in the middle of the room, one of which had a large marble slab inlaid in the middle to support baking and candy making activities. In addition, the room was structured to always ensure a cool breeze came through, and there was a fan system hanging from the ceiling to make the heat more tolerable.

Rebecca was drooling. Sarah would be in rapture at the sight of this kitchen.

Rex smiled. It was as if he had read the blonde woman's mind. "By the way, Sarah has already seen it. I asked her to come over and help me organize things while we were setting the kitchens up." His smile broadened. "She loves it and is truly envious."

Charlotte, Edgar and Rebecca retreated to the parlor, while Charlie and Rex, armed with lanterns, climbed up to the attic to have an in-depth discussion on the engineering of hot water delivery.

"I know what is going to happen," commented Rebecca as she prepared her coffee. "He is going to want to put wash rooms with hot running water into our place. Do you think I can negotiate for two new kitchens as well? And just so you know, I hate all of you."

Edgar and Charlotte broke into gales of laughter.

Monday, February 11, 1867

Charlie knew the moment he walked into the bank something was wrong. The tellers were doing their best to look very busy even though there was not a single customer, and Frank and Eloise were looking somewhere between scared and angry. As he drew closer to his office door, they both approached. "What?"

Frank lifted his chin, indicating something inside the office.

"We found it this morning when we came to open up." Eloise turned the knob and opened the door allowing her boss to go in first.

On his desk was a strong box from his bank. The same strong box stolen in the Christmas robbery. The lock had clearly been broken off of it, but other than that, it looked entirely intact.

"There is something inside," Frank offered quietly as he chewed his bottom lip with worry.

"I assume it is not a bomb?" Charlie glanced at them as he pushed the lid open. Inside he saw an envelope with his last name. He reached in and removed it; using a penknife fished from his pocket, he sliced it open. He removed a single slip of paper. In the same handwriting was a simple note:

Thank you for the generous donation.

The boys and I will put it to very good use.

N.B. Forrest

"Son of a bitch!" The explosion from the tall man within the little office rattled the windows and everyone in the bank.

Richard looked at the box on the desk and the note that had been sent back in it. "I suppose it is little consolation to know what actually happened."

Charlie looked at his friend with murderous eyes. "No," he growled. "I do not suppose it is!"

"Well, we know Forrest did not ride from Tennessee to rob your payroll. It had to have been sent to him."

"Who says you are not an investigator? You seem to be putting all the pieces together except the most important one. Like who in the hell gave it to him!" He was out of his chair, fists planted in the center of his desk, yelling by the time he got to his last words.

"I know, Charlie; I am sorry." Richard was contrite. "I wish there was more I could do. Raeburn and his men are using the shadows to their advantage. We cannot prove anything."

"Then we need to find someone who can follow shadows."

~

Friday, March 1, 1867

As it was a beautiful spring morning, and all of Charlie's business commitments for the week had been completed early, he wanted to invite his wife and eldest son for a ride around the farm. He needed to blow off some steam and he suspected it would do Rebecca and Darby a great deal of good as well.

Darby was more than happy to accept his father's invitation and they walked together toward the barn, where they knew Rebecca would be. She had her back to them when they arrived and Charlie gestured for his son to approach quietly. The boy loved that his papa was teaching him some of the silent communication he had used in the army and did just as he was instructed, sliding to the opposite side of the barn door. The older man stopped in the huge door and leaned against the frame. He gave Darby a wink and he did the same on the other side.

"Oh, Miss Rebecca?"

Charlie's voice was so light and full of mischief it made her laugh even before she turned around. When she got a look at them standing there looking like two sides of the same coin she could only smile and shake her head.

Today, they were even dressed alike; tall dark leather boots, dark trousers tucked into the boots, a crisp white shirt with suspenders, and a simple vest. Atop their heads, the same style of hat, the only difference being Darby's new hat seemed to be a shade or two darker gray than Charlie's old sun-bleached one. If his hair were darker, instead of brownish red, they would be the spitting image of each other.

"Yes?" She dusted her hands off on her britches and walked around the stall wall, desperately trying to hide the grin biting at her lips. "What can I do for you, fine gentlemen?"

"Ma'am." Charlie stood up straight and a split second later Darby did the same.

She was now finding it terribly difficult not to laugh out loud. They were just too adorable.

Darby offered, "Your gentlemen would very much like to invite you to go riding with us." At the same time they both removed their hats and gave a tiny bow.

"How can I say no to that?"

"Indeed," they both said with a slight nod of their heads as they replaced their hats in perfect unison.

She thought she would die of amusement. *Oh my God! He is becoming a little Charlie.* "Yes, gentlemen, I would be delighted to join you. However, I fully intend to ride in my work clothes, so as long as you are not ashamed to be seen with me."

"Never," Charlie said as he strode forward with that silly grin that was his very own. "I even have a lovely saddle that you will enjoy. It was a wedding gift from my men and I have never been able to use it. Shame to let it go to waste. I am sure if we find the right saddle pad, it will work beautifully for Shannon."

Rebecca turned to her son, who had apparently borrowed a cup of silly grin from his papa. *Do they stand in a mirror and practice this?* "Then let us go enjoy the morning, gentlemen." She offered Darby her right hand as her other arm wrapped around Charlie's waist. They moved as one toward the stalls holding their respective horses.

One of Mama and Papa's strictest rules was that everyone must be responsible for their own mount the majority of the time. Darby learned very quickly that occasionally it was alright to ask a groom to tack up a horse, but mostly they did their own. His parents expected a level of responsibility that he had never known before and he did everything he could to earn it.

They had placed his little black Morgan, named Tucker for the way he seemed to tuck and bow his head whenever Darby approached, right between Jack and Shannon. They knew the older, wiser animals would be able to teach the youngster how to be a trustworthy mount. It was the next best thing to having one of their offspring under their son.

It only took a few minutes to get all the horses ready to go. Rebecca was indeed impressed with the saddle Charlie had loaned her when she settled it on Shannon's back. He had been right--the proper pad made it fit as if it had been made for her and it would be a shame to allow it to sit in the tack room any longer. She could not wait to try it out. Riding astride was something she would only do in the safe and completely secure private company of her husband and son.

Rebecca on Shannon and Darby on Tucker had to stand and wait while Charlie let Jack do his normal 'I am out of my stall' dance. There was no way to get him to move until he was allowed to do it. They had discovered on one other outing that even riding away from him would not make him stop. So now, they just waited.

Charlie finally managed to get Jack on the move and the family was off down one of the well-worn paths that would lead them to the open fields they liked to race around in. Rebecca had learned on that same previous ride that having both of them on black horses trying to ride literal circles around her was a bit nauseating from time to time.

They rode for nearly an hour and then reluctantly Rebecca let them know she had to get back to work and they should find something productive to do as well. They laughed and agreed they had shirked their duties long enough. Well, almost long enough. Charlie challenged Darby to one more race.

Rebecca really did love watching these little contests. There was no way her son's little Tucker could ever beat Jack at anything and it was terribly funny watching Charlie trying to keep the big horse in check so the boy would gain more skill with his own animal.

She just shook her head and directed Shannon toward home. She knew her ornery boys would be behind her shortly. They knew better than to keep Mama waiting.

She had managed to get Shannon back in her stall and mostly brushed down before Darby led Tucker into the barn and the area that held the saddle racks. "Where is your father?"

"Helping a couple of Mr. Cooper's fellows who are on a delivery. They were trying to help Mr. Tarent wench a crate up to the loft of the storage building out back. A rope got twisted." The boy quickly untacked his horse and led him to his stall to brush him out. He did not want Mama irritated at him. Right now, Papa was in line for the oncoming conniption, and there was no way to try and make him the Powder Monkey. Papa was already holding the charge.

She closed her eyes and shook her head. "Charles Redmond…"

Darby looked over the back of his horse trying to gage her mood. "Mama?"

"Yes, sweetheart?"

"You are not really mad, are you?"

"No, no, I am not at all. Except maybe a little at your father; he knows better than to mess with…"

The sound of a panicked horse, the creaking of a wagon rolling and the yelling of men brought Darby and Rebecca to the back of the barn, where one of the farm's out buildings was located. It was the storage building where Charlie had been, according to Darby.

She saw immediately one man grabbing and calming the horse hitched to the wagon. It was clear something had spooked him and the wagon had moved unexpectedly. At the back end of the wagon the small cluster of men gathered around a prone form on the ground, and it made her sick at her stomach.

"Charlie!" She moved quickly and knelt down next to him. His eyes were closed, but he was breathing. He was also bleeding profusely from the top of his head. Blood was running freely onto the ground and down his face. "Someone get into town and get Doctor Walker or Mr. Rex!" She did not even look up to see who was on what horse. All that mattered to her was that she heard the hoof beats moving at a hard gallop before she had finished her command.

"Charlie?" She was careful not to move him as Tarent returned and dropped to his knees with a huge wad of cotton and some bandages. "Try not to move him too much."

"Aye, Ma'am, just want to get this bleeding stopped," he said gently as his hands worked quickly and efficiently to get a temporary bandage on Charlie's head. "I do not think it is as bad as it looks, Miss Rebecca. I am sure the hook caught him in the scalp when the wagon jerked out from under him. Scalp wounds look horrible but are usually not too bad. Like when a foal catches their nose on a barb or a briar. You know how those bleed, and usually it ain't nothin' but a scratch."

Rebecca knew he was trying to keep her calm and focused, and she appreciated the fact that her husband had managed to surround himself with such good friends. She was also relieved beyond measure when he groaned and lifted his hand to his head. "Lie still, darling. Someone has gone for Elizabeth. Just lie still until she gets here." She leaned over and managed to find a spot on his chin not covered in blood, and gave it a little kiss. "Thought we agreed to stop this bruised and bleeding thing."

She knew he could hear her when she felt him laugh, but that caused him to choke and cough and then she felt guilty. "I am sorry. Hold still, sweetheart, just hold still." She looked around and realized what horse and man were gone. "Your son and your horse have gone to get the cavalry."

His eyes opened and tracked directly to her. "You let Darby take Jack?"

"No, darling. Jack let Darby take Jack."

This made him laugh again, and then he groaned. "I need to sit up."

"Oh, no, please, humor me? Just lie still until Elizabeth gets here. I want to make sure nothing is broken."

He laid there for a moment, clearly taking inventory, and then he raised both his arms and flexed his thumbs and fingers. "Everything that is left seems to be working."

She tried hard not to laugh as she requested again, slightly exasperated "Charlie, please?"

Looking into her eyes, he remembered promising her he would do anything for her. He sighed. He had always thought that 'anything' would mean being her heroic and gallant knight in shining armor, who could and would rescue her from any threat, but apparently it really meant lying in the dirt for a half hour.

He put his arms down. "Could I at least have a blanket under my head?"

She moved around and put his head in her lap. "Better, old man?" She used the sleeve of her shirt to wipe away some of the blood from his face.

"Much. Thank you."

"Why in the name of the Good Lord did you think it was wise to get up on a wagon like that?"

"You told me to find something productive to do."

"Oh, yes, this is very productive. Well done."

"You are the one who will not let me up. Do not try to hang this on me."

When Rebecca knew she could not win an argument with reason and intellect she resorted to the one thing every southern woman knew worked with both their men and their children. "Hush."

Charlie chuckled from his spot on the ground.

Twenty minutes later, he was looking up into the very amused eyes of his friends. Elizabeth and Richard stood over him just shaking their heads.

"Can you get up?" Elizabeth quirked a brow. "Or are you using this as an excuse to lie around with your head in Rebecca's lap?"

He started to sputter a protest when his wife admitted it was her doing that he was still on the ground.

"Well, I think it is safe to get him up and into the house,

where I can have a look at that scalp wound. Richard, would you please help him get up?"

"Would not be the first time." The provost chuckled as he extended his hand.

Charlie groaned as his friend pulled him to his feet. "It probably will not be the last."

The general had been winded when he fell out of the wagon and the blood made things look far worse than they were, but as he started toward the house with his arm wrapped around Rebecca's shoulder, it was clear he was going to survive this particular mishap with very little collateral damage.

He stopped, looking at his eldest son, still mounted on Jack and looking very worried. "I am fine." He patted the boy's leg. "Thank you, Darby. Well done, lad. You are only one of a handful of people who can ride this horse. If Cousin Albert and I are unavailable to do it, I would be honored if you would look after Jack."

The big horse nodded his agreement and headed for the barn with Darby laughing as he jumped down from the great beast and walked with him.

CHAPTER 2

Monday, March 11, 1867

Darby threw his book bag over his shoulder. He was headed to meet his father at the bank. While most of the other children at the school were either walking home for lunch or had their lunches in bags, he would have lunch with Charlie at Jocko's before heading back to the farm. He only attended school in the morning; the afternoons were spent with John Foxworth, either in the classroom at home or in his father's library.

He understood why he had to go to the public school for at least part of the day. Mama and Papa had patiently explained the family, and by default on this issue he, must lead by example. If public school was good enough for him, it was good enough for everyone else. He did, however, wish he could spend more time with Mr. John. He learned so much more with the tutor than he did with Miss Calvert. She was a nice lady, but did not know anywhere near as many interesting facts as the tutor did.

As he walked outside and turned down the alley behind the school leading toward the bank, two of the bigger boys in the school were leaning against one of the buildings that backed onto the alley. They were waiting for him.

"So, Redmond? Gettin' out of school early, as usual?" Tom Granville, the blacksmith's son, growled.

"My da says it's 'cause you're a la-de-da son of a rich man who don't have to follow the same rules folks like us do." Nicholas Armistead gave him a poke in the shoulder for good measure.

"My pa says it's 'cause you think you be too good for folks like us." Tom nodded, tying to look wise and intimidating all at the same time.

By now the two of them were circling around Darby, poking at his shoulders and pulling on the straps of his book bag.

Tom sneered. "My da says your da is a nigger-loving scallywag who should get whas comin' to 'im."

"And you ain't no better. So we figure it's time for you to get whas comin' to you, too."

With that, Nicholas, the larger of the two boys, grabbed both of Darby's arms, twisting them behind him. Tom balled his fist up and delivered a hard cut directly to Darby's nose. The next blow was to his stomach, which made him double over. The boy continued to rain blows down on him, getting him in the ear, on the chin, and periodically in the torso when the boy behind him managed to pull him back upright by the hair of his head. At one point, Darby heard a nasty popping sound in one shoulder, followed by a searing pain.

The boys dropped him in the dust and walked off, laughing.

He pulled himself to his feet. His shoulder was so painful he could not move his arm. Blood was running down his face from his nose and down his jaw from his ear, which was ringing very annoyingly. He staggered down the alley, heading for Aunt Elizabeth and Uncle Richard's. They were closer than the bank, and he knew he needed Aunt Elizabeth's help more urgently than he needed Papa.

He got about a third of a block down the street headed for the infirmary when he ran into Nigel, Elizabeth's assistant.

"Good Lord, Master Darby! What happened to you?"

"I ran into a brick wall with fists. Will you help me get to Aunt Elizabeth?"

Nigel supported the boy as they walked down the street, deposited him in Elizabeth's treatment room, and then went to get the doctor.

She came in and took one look at the boy's face, then turned to Nigel and told him to go get General Charlie and Colonel Richard. "Well, young man. Would you like to tell me what happened?"

In a muffled voice, he tried to shrug off the attack. "Couple of the bigger boys decided that I needed a roughing up because I only go to school part time."

"Uh, huh," Elizabeth grunted as she started swabbing the blood and dirt off his face. She worked quietly for a few minutes, checking both his nose and his shoulder. "And they decided that breaking your nose and dislocating your shoulder would make you go to school full time?"

"Probably not. They probably hoped that it would make me not go to school at all."

She nodded. "This is going to hurt." She placed her thumbs on either side of his nose and pressed, popping it back into alignment, and then put a plaster across it to hold it in place. "So is this." She took his arm under her own, braced herself against his ribs and pulled. There was a nasty cracking, crunching sound as his shoulder slid back into alignment.

Once the shoulder slid back into place, Darby issued a loud, long, satisfied sigh. “Oh, that is so much better.”

She took a long bandage and strapped his arm into place, then hung it in a sling. “Keep it on for about a week. Come by and see me before you take it off.”

As Elizabeth was finishing up, both Richard and Charlie came charging into the office. Together, they looked at Darby and chorused, “Who did this?”

He mumbled, “A couple of guys from school.”

“That does it. You are not going back. I never liked the idea in the first place.” Charlie shook his head.

The boy pulled himself off the treatment table. “Papa.” He set his jaw. “Oh, yes, I am. I do not mean to be disrespectful or disagree with you, but since I am the one with the broken nose, black eyes and popped shoulder, I should be the one to say whether I go back or not. And I **am** going back.” He looked at his father through slitted eyes, whether because they were swollen or because he was being stubborn was debatable. “After all, **you** taught me that a Redmond does not run from trouble.”

Charlie looked at his son. This was the second time that Darby had managed to hoist him by his own petard. “Son, I really wish you would reconsider. If you go back, you are liable to get beaten up again.”

“If I do not go back, everything they said is true.”

“So what did they say?”

“They said I was just the son of a rich man who did not have to follow the same rules they did.”

His father thought for a moment. “What else did they say?”

Darby looked straight at him. “Just some other stupid stuff.”

Richard broke in at this point. “Who did this to you?”

“Just a couple of boys from school.”

“Which ones?”

The boy shrugged and shook his head.

His father offered, “Richard, there are only six children old enough to do this. Darby and Jeremiah. Two girls. And then there are the Granville and Armistead boys.” He turned to his son. “I assume that Jeremiah and the girls were not involved?” Darby shook his head as Charlie turned back to Richard. “So you have your answer.”

“I will talk with their parents.”

Darby’s head came up. “No, Uncle Richard. Please? That will only make things worse. Not only will I be the rich kid, I will also be a tattletale. Please, do not do that to me. Let me handle this, otherwise Aunt Elizabeth may as well just follow me around with fresh bandages. I will need them.”

“All right. I will let it go. This time. But if it happens again, I will do something,” Richard agreed, grudgingly. “I understand. Sometimes boys have to handle their differences without adults intervening.” He looked at Charlie, who was still fuming. “You understand, too. Right, Papa?”

He sighed. “Yes. I do not like it, but I understand. And you do not have to face Rebecca. Darby and I do.”

Elizabeth was watching this masculine exchange with some degree of amusement. “Well, young man, at least you can stay home for a few days and let your mother coddle you. I know she will take great pleasure in doing so.”

“Yes, Aunt Elizabeth.” He pulled his possessions together. “Papa, are you ready to go home?”

“Yes, son.”

As they started for the door, Darby asked, “Papa, do I have to be the powder monkey? I mean, since I am already injured…”

Elizabeth interjected, “What the hell is a powder monkey?”

Charlie had the grace to flush. “It is a navy term for the boys who haul gunpowder for the cannons. And a little bit of a game we play. When Rebecca gets upset, she tends to explode. The powder monkey takes the brunt of the initial explosion. We try to pass it off onto one another – rather a game of blame tag. If I see she is mad at me, I try to put the blame on him and vice versa. There are very strict rules." He explained it as a last resort, knowing they had just exposed the entire game and Rebecca would not be amused if Elizabeth ratted them out.

"Uh, huh." The doctor nodded. "You two have fun with that. And you do know what will happen to you both if she ever finds out about your little game?"

They nodded vigorously, knowing that they had unwittingly given Elizabeth an unspoken power over them.

She looked at her husband. "And you, sir. Do not even consider it."

Richard shook his head and smiled with a fake ruefulness. "I do not yet have enough troops to even consider such a deception. Some generals have all the luck."

Charlie and Darby rode home quietly, each working on what they would say to the family matriarch. As they neared the turn off to their driveway, they spoke at the same time.

"I think…" Darby offered.

"Perhaps…" Charlie started.

"You first, Papa."

"Perhaps I should break the news to her before she sees you, so she will know it is not as bad as it looks. I will be the powder monkey."

"I was going to suggest the same thing, sir. You can reassure her that I am going to be just fine. She has known you longer. She trusts you."

"You would hope so. I will try."

Charlie pulled the trap up in front of the house. Reg came out to take the buggy around to the stable for them. He climbed out, followed by his son.

The butler looked at the younger man. "Nice shiners, Master Darby. I will ask Sarah to bring you some raw meat for them."

"Thank you, Reg."

"Where is Miss Rebecca?" The general inquired quietly.

"I believe she is in the back parlor, sir."

Together, father and son walked into the house. Darby hung back in the hall, waiting for Sarah and trying to avoid Mama's explosion.

"Um, Rebecca, darling." Charlie knocked gently on the door of the back parlor.

She laid down the knitting she was doing and smiled up at her husband. He was home early. But as she heard the tone of his voice and the look on his face, her smile faded. "What has happened?"

"Well, dear, please do not get upset." He made his way into the room. "Darby got into a bit of a dust up at school. With a couple of the other boys. He is a little battered looking – nothing that you would not expect from an eleven-year-old boy – a school yard fight, you know. Elizabeth has already looked at him and patched him up. Richard knows about it and..." He had to stop to breathe. The information had rushed out of him like a runaway train with no brakes, going down a steep, snowy hill.

Rebecca looked at him, not saying a word for a moment, and then she calmly asked, "So, it was bad enough that Elizabeth had to look at him?"

He was shocked by her restraint. "Um, yes dear. He has a broken nose and a dislocated shoulder."

She sat there and nodded for a moment. "And what damage did he do to them?" She had memories of her brother coming home with black eyes, busted knuckles, and assorted other bangs and bruises.

"You will have to ask him, I am afraid."

Darby was peaking around the door, since he had not heard Mama explode. He stuck his head in. "Well, I am pretty sure their knuckles are badly bruised. And their shins have boot prints on them. I mean, they caught me by surprise, and there were two of them, and they were both bigger than me. But the good news is they knew it would take two of them to get me. I will make sure Jeremiah is with me from now on."

By now he was fully in the room. Rebecca looked at her son, standing there with two beautifully purple eyes, and a sling around his left arm, as well as the plaster across his nose.

Sarah came in right behind him, carrying a plate with a piece of raw steak on it. "Here, Master Darby." She then turned and escaped.

Rebecca pursed her lips. "You are not going back."

Her son smiled. "No ma'am. I will not go back for a few days. Aunt Elizabeth said I needed to stay home and rest."

"You are not going back at all," Rebecca stated flatly.

Charlie quietly sat down out of the line of fire. Darby just willingly stepped up to take the charge. The general lit a cigar and watched as his eleven-year-old son took on his mama. He had already been in the receiving end of Darby's determination; she did not stand a chance.

The boy smiled sweetly at his mother – or as sweetly as he could with the two black eyes and the nose plaster. "Oh, Mother, of course I have to go back. If I do not, those two are just going to make things worse for me in the long run. They will know they can successfully bully me, and then where will I be? I will never be able to go into town safely if I do not go back. And if I do not go back, who are they going to pick on next? Will it be

Jeremiah? Will it be the girls? No, Mother. I have to go back. I have to face them down. A Redmond does not run."

Rebecca looked at him for a long moment. Then she sighed. "All right. But I want you to get some lessons in self-defense. You need to learn how to handle these bullies. I do not like seeing my boys bruised and bleeding. Just ask your papa."

"Yes, Mama. Papa? Who do you think is best for me to learn from?"

"Well, Jocko and I can teach you to box and some basic street fighting. Duncan can probably show you some close combat techniques, which might be good for both you and Jeremiah. And I will ask the other gentlemen in town if they might have any other suggestions."

"That is all well and good." Rebecca rose and moved to her battered son giving him a closer appraisal. "But right now you are not suited for much more than finding a book in your father's library and retreating to a soft surface to rest. Let me know where you intend to roost and I will see to it Sarah sends a tray of treats."

Darby sighed with relief. This had not been nearly as bad as he and Papa had expected. "Yes, Mama. I love you."

"I love you too." She kissed him on the top of his head and sent him on his way. Once the door was closed she turned to Charlie and sighed. "You were right. We never should have sent him there. I did this to him." She could only remember with some degree of chagrin the fight she and Charlie had when she had insisted they send Darby to school. He had been against it and they had fought outright for an hour and bickered for another two days. The entire house had been on high alert until the worst passed. No one had ever seen them battle like that before.

Charlie was out of his chair instantly and had her in his arms before she could actually fall apart. "You did no such thing. This was a school yard tussle among young bucks jostling for position and power. It would have happened regardless of the location. If Darby did not go to school they would have just caught him in town one day, or after church. You know how boys are. Darby has a plan for handling it. We need to give him that opportunity."

~

Tuesday, March 19, 1867

Edgar stood at the drafting table with Jeremiah as the young man made a couple of quick sketches on his notepad. "Something like this, Reverend?"

The tall man looked over the leatherworker's shoulder and nodded. "Yes, that's perfect. Sturdy and soft with a medium buckle."

Jeremiah nodded. "I can have them for you next week. Are you getting a couple of Miss Ro's dogs?"

Edgar's lips twitched. "Yes." He nodded and added quietly as he picked up his hat and gloves, "I think that is an excellent idea." He turned to the young leather worker. "Thank you, Mr. Carter. Please, let me know when they are ready."

He stopped just outside the door of the little shop and looked at his pocket watch. Lunch time. He could return to the manse and have lunch with Charlotte and Rex or he could wander to Jocko's and see who would be about. While he considered his options, his attention was divided by two voices coming from within Duncan's supply shed.

"What about the little coolie? Redmond seems fond enough of him and I hear he's the reason the bastard is up and walking again. Seems if we take that way, we might cut the legs out from under him. Honestly, it makes me nervous as hell to see him up walking around like that."

Edgar stepped off to the side of the shed to continue listening to the conversation. He did not recognize the voices.

"Maybe. Of course, that'll probably make the reverend mad…"

"Like I care! He's just another one of Redmond's lackeys, and has been since he got into town. Alex said he married the whore from Washington."

Edgar shook his head. This would not do at all. He placed his hat on his head, drew his gloves onto his hands and then stepped into the storage shed. He made his way to the back where the two men stood, clearly surprised by his arrival.

"Gentlemen. As I am a man of the cloth and by default a man of peace first and foremost, let me give you a nickel's worth of free advice."

He very carefully looked each of them up and down. "Neither of you are large enough, strong enough or fast enough to even try and offend my manservant, let alone actually hurt him." He gestured between them. "Either alone or together. He has tricks up the sleeves of those flowing robes that you cannot begin to fathom. Should you decide a group is necessary to accomplish your goals and," he chuckled as he added, "by some small chance you should succeed, let me warn you now. Not only would you incur my wrath, which would not be insignificant, but you would also incur the wrath of the Imperial Chinese Army. If you think the Yankee Army did damage to Culpeper, let me assure you that this town would only be a distant memory and a grease spot on a map when the Chinese are through. Your ridiculous suggestions are of the kind that could spark an international incident, and given you did not fare so well in the last domestic confrontation, my best suggestion to you for a long and happy life is to stop these ruminations before they go any further."

Edgard glared at them as he lifted his jacket to show he was well armed. "And I do mean **all** of them. It would be a terrible shame if someone got hurt because they were spreading gossip like a fish wife."

~

Friday, March 22, 1867

Charlie sat in Duncan's office. On the drafting table in front of him were a number of sketches the general had drawn in his spare time. Across from him stood Duncan, Ralph Hudnut, Mr. Stevenson the coppersmith, and Mr. Butler the well digger. He had decided to try out the hot and cold running water solution in the new carriage house he was planning – the one with the proper garçonnière on the second floor. He also figured the property could use another well since they were getting more and more horses, and building a new one with a proper gravity pump from the start seemed sensible.

Charlie decided to place the new brick and glass building between the stables and the house on a slight rise so that the second floor would be accessible by a few steps, while the carriage doors would open on the stable side, making preparing the carriage for use easier. The new well would be on the stable side of the building but above the flow of water from the actual stable yard to avoid pollution from horse manure. Large sliding doors opening on the stable side provided access to the carriages, while a nice verandah with half a dozen steps up from the ground provided access to the garçonnière, which was lit with large windows all across the front.

It was difficult to tell which part of the design was more detailed. Charlie had started collecting coaches, carriages and wagons of all sorts, and the old shed was simply not sufficient to store them anymore, let alone protect them from the elements.

The garçonnière was a loving work of art, with a large room devoted to the lead soldier collection, with shelves to store and display them and tables that were pre-configured to reflect the terrain of several historical battles. His lead soldier collection had expanded; he even had Spartan, Greek and Persian soldiers to reenact the battle of Thermopylae, and small wooden and lead triremes with lead Greek and Persian sailors to represent the ensuing sea battle of Salamis. He had planned a large, tiled washroom with a large tub and hot and cold running water, a small butler's pantry to provide late night snacks and early morning coffee or tea, a study that could be used for classes, three large bedrooms, and two smaller rooms for servants.

Duncan looked at his old commander, wondering if he had lost his mind. "General Charlie, you realize this is not going to be cheap."

Hudnut nodded agreement.

Mr. Butler rocked on his heels, while Mr. Stevenson was already scribbling on a pad of paper, trying to figure out just how much copper pipe and how large a reservoir he was going to have to get to do this job and wondering where the hell he was going to get that much pipe.

"That is to be expected. I plan to use this as a model for some renovations I am considering for the main house. So take the time you need to give me a good design, and then we can get to work on it as quickly as possible."

The general was accustomed to asking the impossible from his soldiers, and they had delivered. He assumed that he could ask the same of craftsmen, and they would respond just as effectively, as long as he was willing to pay for it.

~

Thursday, March 28, 1867

It was a chilly, rainy afternoon, so Rebecca had chosen to sit with Charlie in his office, enjoying the small fire that had been lit to take the damp chill from the room. He was going through his personal mail, making comments to her as he read through it.

"Jerome has put more money into the new oil and kerosene businesses. I know they are not returning as much as some of the rail investments did during the war, but I think that oil will be the investment for the future."

"I am glad, especially since you think this will be the kind of investment that will keep the children going even after we are gone."

"Yes. Oil, timber, steel, beef. These are all things that will always be in demand. That fellow Swift in Chicago has a really clever solution with his refrigerated train cars, so they can ship dressed beef, rather than live cows. Far more economical. I really do think this is the way of the future."

Silence ruled for the next few minutes, then he opened an envelope from his old friend and commanding officer, General Sheridan. He scanned it for a moment, and then snorted a rather sardonic laugh. "Well, Phil Sheridan managed to annoy the powers that be once more. You know that he was appointed governor of the 5th Military District at the beginning of the month?"

"Yes, you mentioned it and I saw something about it in the newspaper."

"Well, he disagreed with President Johnson on several aspects of reconstruction policy, and Johnson removed him before he even had a chance to pack up and move out there. The President will have to fold to reality sooner or later. Black men will be getting the vote and full civil rights, whether he likes it or not."

"I am more concerned with the folks around here and how they will deal with this new situation. With some of these dyed in the wool southerners, who grew up treating Negros like they were subhuman, it is going to be trouble. With the likes of Bedford Forrest and the Ku Klux Klan, and the riots, burnings and killings that have already occurred in Louisiana and Tennessee, I am frightened."

Charlie took a deep breath. "You are not the only one, dear. It is part of why we have our people out at Redmond Grove. At least there, we have a chance of protecting them if things get ugly. We have all been far more careful. Hell, I have armed half the men working here, just so they can protect our horses from these malcontents."

Rebecca shook her head. "I just hope it is enough, and that calmer heads prevail."

"Me too, dear. Me too."

~

Saturday, April 6, 1867

Charlie chewed on a cigar, looking at his three queens, a ten and a single ace; he was almost positive Edgar or Richard had a full house.

"Come on, Charlie," Jocko grumbled. "The way you are trying to eat the cigar means you did not draw what you needed. Shit or get off the pot."

"Why are you so grumpy tonight?" He asked as he tossed his hand in. Jocko was generally more tolerant of everyone's tells, using them to his advantage.

"Could be any number of things," the innkeeper shot back.

"But most likely it's that my wife keeps losing all the money I win here over to that little nest of vipers your wife started in the next room."

"Oh, Good Lord." Charlie rolled his eyes. "I knew someone would get in a twist over that. I did not expect it to be you."

"I am not in a twist over it, Charlie boy. I am happy to have the women next door playing their silly little game. It's that much more money in my pocket. I just wish my wife would stop betting until she grasps the nuances a bit better. Your wife," he shook his finger at his old boss, "has apparently gotten very good at it."

Charlie grinned. He knew that was true. It had taken about a month, but Rebecca had finally caught on and now she ran at the top of the pack along with Rex in taking home an evening's winnings. He was amused by the fact that she had a small strong box in her office and she always put her takings in it. Last time he had seen inside, it was about a third full of gold and silver coins. He certainly did not consider it a silly little game, and based on the contents of that box, neither did Rex or the ladies.

"Well then, let us put your grumpy attitude to good use. I would like to ask you to give Darby some boxing lessons. I can do it, but it will not be as beneficial to him. Even with Rex's good work I am still not terribly fast."

"Aye, would be happy to." Jocko nodded. "I heard what happened. Was none too happy about it, either. Do not like the idea of my nephews getting the tar whipped out of them."

"You are in good company. I am not at all happy--"

"Charlie." Richard shook his head. "It is the way of boys."

"I know. It does not mean I have to like it, so I intend he will be able to defend himself. Any of you know anything useful we can teach the boy?" He gestured among his table mates.

Edward Cooper shook his head as he, too, tossed in his hand.

"Actually." Edgar nodded as he upped the ante. "I know someone who knows something that could be very useful in this situation."

Charlie grinned evilly. "Please tell me you mean Rex. I am not sure I could abide a solution Charlotte would suggest."

Edgar looked up and gave his friend a dopey grin when Charlotte's name was mentioned causing the General to perk up and shake his finger at his friend. "Ohhh, I know that look!"

"What look?" Edgar tried to play innocent.

"The same silly look Richard had on his face for a week after Elizabeth told him she was expecting. The same silly grin I saw on Duncan's face last week. Edgar, is Charlotte pregnant?"

The minister had the grace to try and look embarrassed but came off rather proud instead as he puffed out his chest and offered, "Yes, actually, she is, but I am not sure I was supposed to let this particular cat out of the bag."

"It was the silly grin on your face." Charlie chuckled.

Edgar continued undaunted, addressing all the men at the table, "So please, until my lovely wife actually makes the announcement among the ladies of the community, let us keep Charlie's divining abilities to ourselves, shall we?"

Sunday, April 7, 1867

Edgar had indeed meant Rex, and now Charlie, Rebecca, Darby and practically every member of the extended family was on their way to a spot between the stone barn and the hay barn that would serve as the perfect arena for what Edgar assured the entourage would be a demonstration of exceptionally honed skills and precision, well worth the wait.

The minister had asked Charlie to find half a dozen men who

would be willing to spar with Rex. Apparently, it was a very tempting offer because at least a dozen hire hands stood around the perimeter of the area watching with smirks as Rex prepared.

He removed his long green silk outer robe and handed it off to Charlotte, who folded it over her arm. He was left in black silk sandals with white socks, the long wide legged trousers that matched his outerwear and a knitted white silk shirt Charlie thought looked very familiar.

The general quirked a questioning brow in Rebecca's direction. She just smiled and shrugged as she took a seat on the back of a wagon to await the show.

Once he was disrobed, Rex began a series of stretches that further sent the prospective sparring partners into more fits of laughter.

"Oh, dear." Edgar sighed and just shook his head. When Rex nodded in his direction, he took a deep breath and said, "Ladies and gentlemen, what you are about to see is a demonstration of a truly ancient art of self-defense. It is called Shaolin Kung Fu and it has been practiced in Rex's country for more than a thousand years. I believe some of you gentlemen volunteered to help us with the demonstration. Perhaps six of you would step forward."

"Six?" Charlie's brows shot up rapidly. "At once? Without a weapon?" Even he had to laugh at the thought.

"At once." Edgar nodded. "He **is** the weapon." The minister moved again as he pointed to six of the nine men that stepped forward. "Now gentlemen, for this to work properly you must be willing to actually attack my friend here. Rex has promised not to permanently injure or maim you, but this will hurt. Dr. Walker is standing by to assist you if needed."

The farm hands and stable boys all looked at each other and laughed. They all, every one of them, stood at least six inches taller than this little bug of a man. Not to mention outweighing him by fifty to seventy five pounds each. They were not sure why General Redmond wanted them to knock the tar out of his friend, but he was the boss.

Rex was careful to watch each man. Even though Edgar had not given the actual word to start sparring, he knew the chance of someone trying a surprise attack was very high.

This was not the first time they had rolled out this particular party trick. In San Francisco, a knife hidden in the toe of a boot had left him with a small scar on his chest that had humiliated him far more than hurt. He never made that mistake again.

"So gentlemen, my companion is ready whenever you are. Please, do your best." Edgar took a seat next to Rebecca on the back of the wagon.

"A nickel on Ted!" One of the men standing at the side of the stone barn called, and that was it--the bets were on and not one of them fell in Rex's favor.

Edgar looked up and smiled raising his hand to make sure he had their attention. "I will cover all those!"

Now the men were howling with laughter. Not only was one of General Redmond's friends volunteering to get the snot kicked out of him, but another one, and the minister no less, was throwing good money away on it. Sometimes rich men just needed to learn the hard way.

The biggest man, apparently Ted, finally asked, "One at a time or all at once?"

Edgar shrugged nonchalantly. "Whatever makes you happy."

A second later, before anyone knew what happened, Ted charged forward and ended up flat on his back with a ground shaking thud. Rex pulled back his extended arm, the only part of him Charlie or anyone else had actually seen move.

Everyone was still for a moment as Ted lay on the ground groaning and rubbing his chest. Then in another flurry of movement that brought even Rebecca to her feet because she was not sure of what she was seeing, three more of the men charged forward and ended up piled on top of their leader.

Rex sniffed once and brushed a bit of dust from his trousers and eyed the last two men, who now looked wary but very determined.

It was done in less than ten minutes, and by that time, every last man that had been standing between the barns was now lying in a heap. Rex had not even broken a sweat and merely brushed a bit of dirt from his shirt and an errant piece of hay from his immaculate hair, which also had not moved while the small man laid out twelve of Charlie's biggest farm hands, leaving them in a groaning, grunting pile as he stepped over them and took his robe from Charlotte.

"Papa." Darby tugged on his father's sleeve even as he continued to stare wide eyed. "I want to learn that."

Charlie nodded, wide eyed as well. "So do I."

CHAPTER 3

Friday, April 12, 1867

Rebecca was mumbling to herself. "Food, drinks, announcements to every church and public place in town, the fellowship hall, servants lined up, Richard and his deputies to keep things in order. I know I have forgotten something. I just know it."

"Rebecca, darling, please relax." Charlie chewed a cigar as his wife paced the platform of the train station. "Robert and Mary are a normal couple, just like us."

She stopped and gave him 'the look.' He grimaced a bit and nodded. "Alright, they are just a normal married couple. They will be here for three days. We have everything planned and prepared and there is nothing for you to worry about."

"Oh, of course not." She rubbed the bridge of her nose. "It is **only** Robert E. Lee ..."

"My old friend," her husband offered quickly, trying to calm his agitated spouse. "Darling, he is coming to get me to write a check for the college, which I will happily do. In the meantime, if you could just relax, I suspect you will get to hear Mrs. Williams's head exploding when she actually sees who we are hosting this week."

That made her laugh, which made him happy. He much preferred her laughing to her aggravated. "I am sorry about all this, darling. I just want everything to be perfect."

"And it will be. I have no doubt, but even if something does goes awry, I assure you that Robert and Mary will be more than capable of rolling with the punches."

The train arrived about ten minutes late, but it did finally arrive, much to Charlie's relief. Had it been another minute delayed, he was certain his wife would have combusted.

Robert and his wife exited the train a few moments later with Lee moving immediately to Charlie and offering his hand. "It is so good to see you again. You are looking well."

"Thank you, Robert." Charlie grinned as he shook hands with his old friend. "So are you." He turned and took Mary's hand, leaning in to kiss her cheek. "Mary, you get more beautiful every time I see you."

"Charles Redmond." The woman laughed, returning the kiss to his cheek. "You are a liar, and I love you for it."

His grin widened as he gestured to Rebecca. "Robert, you remember my wife. Mary, may I present the love of my life, Rebecca Redmond. I am sure you two are going to have a wonderful time together and will become great friends."

The ladies greeted each other as Charlie directed the driver to secure the luggage for their guests and they made their way down the platform where their carriage waited. Lee stopped when he saw one man sitting atop a horse, dressed in his Confederate uniform ready to ride escort to Redmond Stables.

"Charlie..." he murmured.

"I know, but this is a young man who works for me. His name is Robert Brooks and he served under you. When he found out you were visiting, he asked to ride escort for you and I could not turn him down. I hope you do not mind. I think this may go a long way to healing some old wounds."

Robert nodded. "Then by all means. Good call, General Redmond. You know, there are times when I regret you did not join with us. The outcome might have been different. For one thing, I would have had supplies at Appomattox."

"I am not sure about that." Charlie chuckled. "I do know we have the opportunity to show the good citizens of Culpeper that there are men in the world ready to put the war well behind us. No matter what side we chose."

"Amen, Charlie. Amen." Robert nodded as the ladies joined them at the carriage.

The Redmonds and their very distinguished guests certainly did draw a crowd as they made their way through the streets of Culpeper towards Redmond Stables. It probably did not help the situation that Charlie had selected his best open carriage for the trip and had told his driver to take his time.

Robert looked at his host with a mischievous grin. "Trying to make a point?"

Charlie had the good grace to blush as he nodded. "Maybe just a little one," he agreed as he lifted his hand with his thumb and index finger spread just a bit. He then took a moment to explain about Mrs. Williams, Alex Raeburn, and the other members of the 'I Hate Charlie Redmond Club' or the IHCRC.

As they drove through town, the ladies were chatting and the gentlemen were carefully watching those watching them as they drove past. As they made their way past Mrs. Williams's house, where she sat in the front porch holding court among Alex

Raeburn and his compatriots, Lee made sure to doff his hat, making Charlie chuckle.

"Trying to make a point, Robert?"

"Maybe just a little one." The older man held his hand up, thumb and forefinger spread slightly.

The first evening at Redmond Stables was quiet and relaxed, with the Redmonds being the perfect hosts to the Lees. They watched with great amusement as Charlie and Rebecca interacted and dealt with their small herd of children.

He and Mary could only grin at each other, each of them remembering a time when their own children were so young. Robert was happy for his old friend. He, like Grant and Sheridan, thought Charlie would spend his entire life in the army. To watch him with this lovely woman and the children they had taken in and adopted as their own made him very happy for the younger man for whom he had so much respect.

The ladies had gone for a stroll after dinner, giving Rebecca a chance to show off the farm and her horses. Charlie and Robert adjourned to his office for a cigar and a friendly chat.

"So." Charlie settled back in his chair and smiled at his old friend. "Am I the first person you have hit up for a donation?"

Robert chuckled and nodded. "Yes, quiet honestly you are. I thought if I could get you on board, everyone else would be easy."

He nodded, pulling his checkbook from the drawer. "Do you have a number in mind?"

"My friend, any number you write will be most welcome. The college will most certainly benefit from your kindness and generosity."

Charlie's head bobbed as he dipped his pen in the ink. "You know education is important to me. I am happy to help you, Robert." He wrote the check. Tearing it carefully from the book, he handed it across the desk. "I hope this will help."

The older man looked briefly at the draft and did his best not to choke at the four digit number on the check. "Thank you, Charlie. This is very generous of you. The students at Washington College thank you, I am sure."

"You and the students are most welcome. Now let us discuss the reception for you in town tomorrow so my wife does not explode with worry."

While the gentlemen discussed their strategies for raising money for Washington College, Rebecca escorted Mary down to the stable yards, explaining their horse breeding program. Mary had managed the Lee's plantation, Arlington House, for many years before the war, and she still missed the daily challenges of running a successful farm.

After the stables, barns, gardens and pasturage, they strolled over to the gazebo on the pond. Rebecca explained that it had been a birthday present from Charlie, and they both loved to spend quiet evenings under the stars, in front of the brazier if it were chilly, enjoying the lovely view that stretched from the hazy purple mountains in the west to the beautiful pasture land and forests surrounding them. Mary looked around, admiring the peaceful place and the lovely view, when she saw what was obviously a newly built, or re-built, family cemetery.

"I do love that tradition of having a family cemetery on one's property. We had one at Arlington House, though what that evil man Meigs did to our beautiful property is just vile. He did it as a malicious insult, you know."

"Yes, I know." Rebecca nodded sympathetically. "I also know that Charlie does not hold him in high regard either. Far from it. I think he hates the man almost as much as you and General Lee do. And with good reason, given the quality of supplies his troops got from him."

Mary Lee considered the woman before her in a way she had never had to look at another before. Here was another southern lady like herself, but married to a former Union supporter, a man considered a war hero in some circles and a dark source of reckoning in others. A man like her husband, who had done his duty and supported the cause he truly believed in, and while those were completely opposite one another, their common reasoning in so many matters was exactly the same.

As they chatted, they strolled toward the wrought iron fenced plot with the name 'Redmond' over the entrance. "So far, there is only one marker, for my brother. He fell at Antietam, and we never recovered his body, but Charlie had this memorial built for him."

Mary read Andrew's marker, then turned to her hostess. "So you are a Randolph?"

"Oh, yes, ma'am." She nodded proudly. "My father was honored to be one of the Randolphs of Roanoke. His uncle John was a congressman and then a senator, and he was born just over in Hopewell, so we are part of an old Virginia family. You know, we are even descended from Pocahontas."

"Yes, I know. So is Robert. I believe you and Robert are cousins, though distant, through the Randolphs and the Blands. I must be sure to tell him. He can use it when dealing with the I Hate Charlie Redmond Club." Both women laughed at that.

They returned to the house, and Rebecca explained all they

had done to prepare for the reception the following afternoon - the posters and invitations, the food, the drink, the servants, the use of the Episcopalian fellowship hall as the largest meeting hall in Culpeper - all of it.

She was a bit flushed when she finished explaining the plans; her anxiety as the hostess over what was expected to be a **perfect** reception was showing.

Mary smiled graciously. "Robert, our cousin has exceeded herself, planning a lovely event for your fund-raising efforts."

"Cousin? You think Rebecca is our cousin?"

"I know she is, twice over. She is both my cousin and yours. She is one of the Randolphs. Born over in Hopewell, and great niece of John Randolph of Roanoke, one of your all-time favorite politicians."

"Ah, yes. The man who said that Henry Clay was 'a man of splendid abilities but utterly corrupt. He shines and stinks like rotten mackerel by moonlight.' I wish I could say something like that, but I have not the stomach for such an insult."

All four of them laughed.

Saturday, April 13, 1867

Charlie had again ordered the open carriage to convey them into Culpeper for the reception. Robert grinned evilly at him when the carriage pulled up in front of the house.

The gentlemen handed the ladies in, then stepped in themselves and the driver snapped the reins. They were off.

As they drove through town, they saw a number of people, dressed in their best, walking toward the fellowship hall. The yard in front of the hall was congested with coaches, carriages, traps, and even buckboards. It looked like the entire population of Culpeper and the surrounding area had turned out for this event.

The crowd, seeing who was in Charlie's carriage, made way for the guest of honor. The gentlemen dismounted in front of the hall, and handed the ladies from the carriage. Their driver immediately moved on, clearing space for other guests to arrive and disembark.

Charlie and Robert both nodded politely to Sean Cady and Max Frederick, the two deputy provosts standing on each side of the double doors leading into the hall. They were there to ensure no weapons entered. Richard was no doubt somewhere inside, watching the crowd like a hawk.

Charlie leaned over and whispered to Rebecca as they entered, "I wonder if Mrs. Williams and the IHCRC know that tongue is on the menu today."

She chuckled as she patted his arm. "It actually is. I made sure of it."

The general looked around for Mayor Frazier, while Mary and Rebecca peeled off to inspect the buffet and make sure all was in order.

"General Lee, I would like to introduce our Mayor, Horace Frazier. He has volunteered to introduce you today. He has also organized a team of reliable men to pass the hat for you."

"Mayor Frazier. It is a pleasure to meet you. I so appreciate all you and your community are doing for our little college. I assure you, it is a good cause."

"General Lee, the honor is all ours. I believe that supporting quality education for our fine Virginia youth is as important as anything else in putting our world back together after the war."

Lee retired to a small room at the back of the hall to prepare for his speech. After all these years of public speaking, he still had to gird his loins and settle his mind before stepping out in front of a crowd. Rebecca and Mary watched over the finishing touches to the buffet table preparations. As they waited, several of the other women who had helped Rebecca with the planning joined them, including Charlotte, Elizabeth, Missy Frazier, Esther Jackson, and Samantha Nailer. Introductions were conducted and the ladies engaged in the normal social small talk.

Mrs. Williams entered, escorted by Alex Raeburn and followed by the rest of the IHCRC, with one significant member missing. Brooks was standing outside of the small room General Lee was using to prepare himself. Honoring the request to not wear uniforms, he was dressed in civilian clothing, but Brooks was standing at attention outside the door, obviously a military style guard.

The room continued to fill until Richard gave Mayor Frazier a signal that there were no more people milling around outside. The room was packed. Frazier then signaled to Brooks, who knocked lightly on the door and called, "They are ready for you, General."

Mayor Frazier stepped to the front of the room. "Good afternoon, ladies and gentlemen. Thank you for coming today to offer support for Washington University and for General Lee's efforts to create another truly outstanding institution of higher education here in Virginia. We have the College of William and Mary to support our tidewater communities, Mr. Jefferson's University to support central Virginia, and now General Lee is building up Washington College to better serve our brethren in the Shenandoah Valley. Anything you can contribute, even if it only a few coins, will be appreciated, I assure you. Without further ado, let me introduce Robert Edward Lee, Chancellor of Washington College, to tell you about what he is planning for this great institution in our state."

Lee stepped forward, and a huge round of applause broke out

spontaneously. He stood quietly for a few minutes, then motioned for the crowd to settle down.

"Thank you for your warm welcome. Mary and I are so pleased to be here today as the guests of my cousin, Rebecca Redmond and my old, old friend, Charles Redmond." He gestured toward where the three of them were standing together at one side of the room and let it sink into the audience.

"I have been honored with the appointment to the Chancellorship of a small, but excellent college in Lexington that is committed to providing quality education to the youth of our state. Washington College exists to mold young men into the kind of informed, thoughtful, and knowledgeable men our state needs to lead us through the rebuilding of our country and into the next century. We at Washington College firmly believe that the education of a man is never complete until he dies, so our mission is to teach these gentlemen how to learn, and to love learning for itself and for the benefit its wise use can bring to the world."

"But learning is not the only thing that our students are being taught to love. We value honesty and courage, and seek to instill these qualities in our students. I know from personal experience you must be frank with the world. And frankness is the child of honesty and courage. So to help create the leaders of the future, we help our students shape and form this critically important quality as well."

"Quite frankly, the years of the war have done great damage to the community of Lexington and to Washington College. Now we are in a time of rebuilding; rebuilding the community, rebuilding the school, and rebuilding the lives of children and young men whose normal growth was horribly disrupted by war."

"I think it is the duty of every citizen in the present condition of the country to do all in his power to aid in the restoration of peace and harmony. It is particularly incumbent upon those charged with the instruction of the young to set them an example. The duty of all citizens, then, appears to me too plain to admit of doubt. All should unite in honest efforts to obliterate the effects of war, and to restore the blessings of peace. They should promote harmony and good feeling; qualify themselves to vote; and elect to the State and general Legislatures wise and patriotic men, who will devote their abilities to the interests of the country, and the healing of all dissensions. I have invariably recommended this course since the cessation of hostilities, and have endeavored to practice it myself. "

"It is for this reason that I ask for your help. So that we may create and mold the youth of our great state to become the wise and patriotic men we need to lead us forward. Do you have any questions that I may answer?"

Raeburn stepped forward. "General Lee, sir. How can you honestly support the northern government in the control of our state and our people?"

Lee regarded Raeburn coolly for a moment, then responded. "Sir, I am now just Mr. Lee, no longer general. Mr. Raeburn, I believe? You must recognize the truth. The questions which for years were in dispute between the state and general government, and which unhappily were not decided by the dictates of reason, but referred to the decision of war, have been decided against us. It is the part of wisdom to acquiesce in the result, and of candor to recognize the fact. And what we teach our young men is clear. Obedience to lawful authority is the foundation of a manly character. That is what I am asking you all to support with your contributions to Washington College."

The wife of one of Raeburn's companions stepped up. "Mr. Lee," she said, emphasizing the 'mister,' "How should I teach my children to love our great state and our great southern heritage without also teaching them to revile the actions of the government?"

"Madam, do not train up your children in hostility to the government of the United States. Remember we are all one country now, dismiss from your mind all sectional feeling and bring them up to be Americans. It is in this way that we will prepare them for the future."

Mrs. Williams then stepped up. "Sir, I have a battle flag, one that waved over the Second Battle of Manassas. I would like to honor it properly. What should I do with it?"

"Madam, I would advise you to fold it up and put it away. That time has passed; we must now learn to forgive our enemies. I can truly say that since the war began, there is not a day that I have not prayed for them. I suggest you do the same." He paused, then asked, "And madam, did you get your organ tuned?"

He stepped back. "Ladies and gentlemen, there are several gentlemen who will now pass among you to collect what you can contribute to the great purpose of educating our youth, and prepare them to be the leaders we will need in the coming years. I thank each of you for your contributions, no matter how great or small. I hope to be able to have a word with each of you as we partake of this lovely meal that Mrs. Redmond and her friends have provided for us."

With that, he stepped down from the dais and walked over to stand with Mary, Rebecca, Charlie and the others.

Several men carrying good sized baskets started to pass through the crowd, collecting as little as a few coins and some checks from some of the more prosperous merchants in town, including Edward Cooper, Mrs. Allen, and Jocko, as well as others. Edgar reached into his breast pocket and quietly slipped a small envelope into one of the baskets.

As the collection baskets made the rounds, people crowded around Lee, until Richard, with help from Sean and Max, organized them into a more formal receiving line that then fed over to the buffet tables. As a basket was filled, they took it to the dais, where Charlie had set a good sized strong box to hold all the contributions.

As one would expect, Mrs. Williams was one of the many people in line to shake Lee's hand and have a few words with the southern hero. Miss Simms and Miss Reynolds were, as usual, right beside her. Charlie was strolling along the receiving line, just making sure that things were going as expected, when he happened to hear Mrs. Williams comment to her acolytes. "Well, I am glad that man could bring General Lee out to meet us by using his money as a lure, but to be honest, if I were his wife, I swear I would poison his brandy."

He leaned in behind her and whispered in her ear, "Mrs. Williams, if I were your husband, I assure you I would knowingly drink it and welcome the release."

Mr. and Mrs. Lee spent the better part of the next two hours shaking hands, saying thank you and exchanging a few words with every person in the room. By the time they had shaken every hand and every mouth had been fed, Lee looked like he was ready to collapse. Charlie motioned to Max Frederick. "Would you ask Louis to bring my carriage around? It is time to take the Lees home."

"Certainly, sir."

A few minutes later, Max had not only gotten the carriage around, he had also found his fellow deputy. Together, Frederick and Cady hauled the surprisingly heavy cash box to the carriage and loaded it. Cady mounted his horse, as did Brooks, both riding escort. No one had forgotten the payroll robbery; both escorts were armed.

They arrived back at the Redmond house in quick time. Brooks and Cady hauled the cash box up to Charlie's office, and then each went on their way with both Charlie's and Lee's heartfelt appreciation. Rebecca and Mary suggested that Robert go and lie down because he looked so completely worn out, but he insisted, "I want to know how much we collected. I promise I will rest after that."

So Rebecca ordered tea for the four of them and they trooped upstairs. Charlie unlocked the cash box. There were a great many coins, ranging from pennies to a number of five and ten dollar gold pieces. There were a number of pieces of script, mostly ten dollar bills, and there were several checks, made out to Washington College, ranging from ten to fifty dollars each.

Then there was a plain white envelope. Inside was a check, made out to Washington College in the amount of twenty-five thousand dollars, drawn on the oldest and largest bank in New York, and signed by Tongzhi Xiang. A note accompanied the check. It read, "Please, establish a scholarship for promising youth with financial constraints in the name of Charles and Rebecca Redmond. Please, keep the contribution anonymous. – TX"

Edward and Mary looked stunned. Tongzhi was the family name of the current emperor of China. Rebecca and Charlie looked at one another. "Rex," they said in unison.

Charlie shook his head. "Edgar said that Rex's wealth made us look poverty stricken. He was right."

Saturday, April 20, 1867

Late in the afternoon, Alex Raeburn dropped a pile of cloths of various colors onto the back porch of Mrs. Williams's cottage. "Afternoon, Mrs. Williams," he said with his most polite manners. "I hope you do not mind, but several of the fellows will be meeting me here this evening."

"Oh, Mr. Raeburn, you know you and your friends are always welcome. And my table always has room for the six of you."

"The usual gentlemen will be here – Granville, Armistead, Rainey, Kirtley, and Brooks. And I have invited a couple of other gentlemen to join us as well; gentlemen who were as pained as you and I were on Saturday. I am heartbroken that General Lee has fallen into the clutches of that man because of his need for money for the university."

"It is certainly a sad time for all true southerners. I am sure we can find room for your other friends." Mrs. Williams was always at her most gracious with Raeburn and his cohorts. "But what is the pile of cloth for?"

"These are cloaks, like the ones my friend General Forrest and the new Ku Klux Klan wear to identify themselves to those they want to carry a message to. They mask our identities and provide another level of intimidation."

"Intimidation? So who are you planning to intimidate?"

"My boys are sick and tired of those uppity niggers in Sweetwater taking good paying jobs away from them by taking lower pay. So we are going to pay a little call on them tonight and let them know they need to stop taking jobs from their betters."

"Ahhh. That seems like a righteous thing to do, Mr. Raeburn. I wish you good fortune."

"Thank you, Mrs. Williams. We will be back around sundown."

As dusk fell, eight men rode into Mrs. Williams's backyard,

coming up the alley to minimize the number of people who saw them. One brought an extra horse behind him, with a large wooden cross strapped to the horse's back. Raeburn handed out the cloaks and hoods, and the men tied them around their necks, pulled the hoods over their heads and adjusted them so they could see out. The men all had torches with them. Raeburn and Kirtley lit theirs with a quick flair of flint and steel; the rest would light theirs when they got closer to Sweetwater.

The men rode out of Mrs. Williams's yard, going as quietly as eight men and nine horses could. The clop of hooves and the jingle of tack made a few people look out their windows as they rode by, then quickly draw the curtains. This was NOT something that most of the residents of Culpeper wanted to be involved in.

They rode down the side streets and alleys to the small settlement on the northwest of town called Sweetwater, where most of the town's more successful blacks resided, although successful was a relative statement. Here is where the Negros with marketable skills, such as smithing, carpentry, and household skills lived. Many members of Beulah's, Sarah's, and Tomas's family lived in Sweetwater.

The men rode their horses into the middle of the little community, and quickly (and rather shakily) set up the cross they had brought. Then they remounted, making sure all of them were carrying lit torches in one hand and that their side arms were clearly visible and readily accessible.

One of them reached out with his torch and touched it to the cross, which had been soaked in kerosene. It lit instantly, burning like a brilliant brand in the dark. The men rode in a large circle around the burning cross, holding their torches outward.

Raeburn, using his best battlefield voice, bellowed. "All you, niggers! Listen up! You stop taking jobs away from good white boys, you hear? Just because you can live on a few pennies less, **does not** mean you should be taking jobs that used to be reserved for white men. You keep this up and every nigger who takes a job away from a white man will either be hung from a tree or burned like this cross!"

With that, the circle of men rode in a weaving pattern among the houses in Sweetwater, whooping and yelling, threatening roofs with their burning torches and generally being as intimidating as possible.

Tomas, who was visiting his mother's younger sister, stepped cautiously out the front door. He recognized several of the men riding through the community and raising hell by their boots and their horses. As he stood just outside the door, Alex Raeburn noticed him and rode up, guiding his horse up the front step to stand with his hind feet on the ground and his front feet on the porch. Raeburn leaned down to hiss at Tomas so that others could not hear him. "You, especially, you uppity nigger. You keep your mouth shut, you hear? Or you will be the first to swing. Then it's hard tellin' what would happen to that pretty little bitch of yours."

~

Monday, April 22, 1867

Tomas knocked gently on the door to the back parlor. The Redmonds almost always had their after-dinner coffee in this room, and he hoped to find them alone.

As usual, Charlie called, "Come in."

Tomas opened the door just far enough to let him slip in. He stood, waiting, beside the door, which he had closed after himself.

The general smiled at their visitor. "Come in, come in,

Tomas. What are you doing here? I thought you were spending your time before going off to school with your family. Were you in Sweetwater when the cross was burned? Is your family all right after that?"

Tomas eased into the room and sat on the edge of the chair that Charlie indicated to him. "Good evening, Miss Rebecca, General Charlie." He clasped his hands in front of him. It was clear he was decidedly nervous. "Yes, sir. It was very frightening, but no one was hurt."

Rebecca rose and poured the young man a cup of coffee, setting it beside him. He smiled his appreciation as she said, "What can we do for you? Is there something you need for school that we have overlooked?"

"Oh, no, ma'am, I have everything I need and Lizbet is well taken care of too, thank you. No, it is just some information I have that I think you need to know." He paused again, rubbing his hands together nervously.

Rebecca spoke gently. "What is it, Tomas? Is Lizbet with child? If so, you know we will take care of your woman and your baby while you are gone."

"No, no, ma'am. I am far too smart to leave Lizbet alone with a baby while I am in Washington. But it is about a baby. One born a long time ago." He paused yet again.

Charlie and Rebecca looked confused, but interested. They waited for the young man to go on.

"As you know, I have been spending a lot of time with my family around town. Some are over in Sweetwater. Some are stuck in Slab Town. It has given me a chance to get to know a number of them and to reconnect with my parents through the friends and family who knew them. My mother died before the war, and they told me my father had been conscripted into the army at the beginning of the war and no one knows where he is or if he survived. But my mother's younger sister, Lily, is still with us, and I learned a lot from her." He stopped and took a deep breath.

They continued to look at him encouragingly.

"You see, my mother, Myrna, was apparently a beautiful young woman. From what Lily said, I suspect my maternal grandfather was white. Lily was not clear about that, since she was a number of years younger than my mother and she was not sure. They were owned by the Raeburns, and my mother was the personal servant to Mr. Alex Raeburn's mother. Lily was made one of the housemaids when she got to be old enough. My father, Luke, was their blacksmith. That is how he made enough money on the side to buy my freedom when I was born."

They nodded. They knew some of this story, but were not clear where he was going.

Tomas cleared his throat and took a sip of coffee. "Well, it seems that when my mother was younger, she had other duties than Mrs. Raeburn's maid. She was expected to attend to Mr. Raeburn when Mrs. Raeburn did not feel like servicing his," he paused briefly, but soldiered on, "masculine needs. So a few years before I was born, she had a son by Mr. Raeburn. They married her off to Luke to cover the embarrassment, but when the baby came out white, Mrs. Raeburn took him and raised it as her own. It was the only child the elder Raeburn's had, you see." He stopped again.

Rebecca looked at him knowingly. "So you have discovered that Alex Raeburn is your half-brother?"

He nodded, appreciative that he did not have to say this himself. Alex had found out that he was poking around in his family's history and had threatened him with a whole lot of hurt if he ever actually told anyone of their relationship. In fact, Tomas half suspected that the job issue was just Raeburn's excuse for burning the cross in Sweetwater. He feared the real reason was much more personal, a warning and a threat from Raeburn to Tomas.

Charlie, looking at how nervous Tomas was, surmised that Raeburn had been hard at work trying to prevent this information getting out. "Has he threatened you? Or threatened Lizbet?"

Tomas nodded, again afraid to actually voice his fears.

The general sat back in his chair, looking thoughtful. "Well, you know Miss Rebecca and I will not use this information unless it is absolutely necessary – and then only if we are sure that we can protect you, your family, and Lizbet. But I am very glad you have told us. It explains a great deal about Mr. Raeburn's behavior. Perhaps it would be a good thing if Lizbet came up to live here in the house with us while you are in Washington, and you can stay here when you come down on the weekend and for school breaks. That way, we can provide a greater degree of protection and no one will question why Miss Rebecca's personal maid lives here in the house."

Tomas looked relieved. "Thank you, General Charlie, Miss Rebecca. I am afraid that Mr. Raeburn is a very scary and violent man and I would be very grateful that you see to it that he not get his hands on Lizbet. I can take care of myself. You know Colonel Shaw made sure all of his men knew how to defend themselves. But Lizbet has no protection if I am not here, and you know he would hurt her in the worst way."

They both nodded and then smiled reassuringly. "You know we take care of our own, Tomas. Especially in situations like this." Rebecca reassured him. They spoke for a few more minutes about his preparations for going off to school and then he excused himself.

Charlie looked to his wife, shaking his head. "My God. This explains so much. The man hates who and what he is, and hates the whole world for it, scared of what will happen if it is found out. He is more dangerous than even I thought. Please, please, be careful around him, dear heart."

~

Thursday, April 25, 1867

Tarent walked into Rebecca's office early that morning. He was waiting for her when she came down from breakfast.

"Tarent! What are you doing here so early? Let me ring for some coffee. We do not usually meet until later in the day."

"I have some bad news, ma'am. Someone broke down one of the fences in the pasture on the other side of the Run. Two horses have gone missing."

Her head dropped to her chest even as she called for a coffee tray. "God, I hate horse thieves. Which horses did we lose?"

He told her, providing detailed descriptions of each horse. Both were mares, neither was in foal.

She sighed. "Well, as such things go, it could have been worse, but I will have to rework the breeding plan." She squared her shoulders. "I will send word to Colonel Polk, but to be honest, I suspect they are long gone – on their way to South Carolina or up to New York by now."

Tarent scratched his chin, which as usual was rather stubbly. "Well, ma'am, I think they probably went west – over to the valley. I do not think these fellows are smart enough nor have the funds to ship the horses out of the region."

"You could be right. Can you please tell Colonel Polk what you think and why when he gets here?"

"Yes, ma'am. In the meantime, I will see about changing the schedule for our men to ride the fences. Maybe it will help."

"And I will talk to General Redmond about getting more

help. We cannot afford to lose any more horses." She thought for a moment. "Also, Tarent, is there a way you can mark the horses shoes so that they are clearly our horses and can be easily tracked?"

"Yes, ma'am. I can mark their shoes with our initials. If that is not enough, I could tattoo something in their ears. It would not help track them, but it sure would make them identifiable. "

"Start with marking the shoes. I want us to be able to track these bastards down. Please, keep the fact that we are marking shoes to yourself. Do not let anyone know about the marks, not even Rollins or anyone helping with the forge. That way, we will keep it between you, me, Albert and the general for now. Then if we have more problems, we can start marking the horses themselves."

"Yes, ma'am."

CHAPTER 4

Monday, April 29, 1867

Charlie left the bank, his newspaper tucked under his arm, and made his way across the street to Jocko's. As far as he was concerned, it was time for lunch and maybe even a drink. A real drink. The bar was empty when he made his way through the door so he took a seat along the rail and tapped his fingers, waiting for Jocko to emerge from whatever corner he happened to be in at the moment.

He looked around wondering exactly where his old friend was. It was not normal for him to leave his bar unattended for more than a minute or two. As he stood to start looking around, Ro emerged from the kitchen.

"Sorry, Gen'l. Uncle Jocko and I were wrestling a new stove pipe into place for Esther. He'll be right out. Can I get you something to drink?"

"Coffee with a brandy shot please."

"Comin' right up." She moved behind the bar and poured the requested drink, placing it down in front of him. "Esther has some very good cold roast beef back there. She's making Uncle Jocko save it for the paying customers." She gave him an ornery wink.

"Then by all means, let me annoy Jocko by eating the good roast beef." He winked back as he measured with his hands. "A nice sandwich? About a foot thick? Coleslaw and a pickle if there is a fresh barrel."

She nodded with a smile and retreated to the kitchen. He sipped his coffee, spread his paper open on the bar and began reading, finally feeling like he was starting to relax. The past few weeks were wearing very thin on his nerves.

The door opened and he looked to see Richard for the fourth time today since he made it into town at nine in the morning. As his old friend took a seat next to him he slowly turned his head and offered, "If I did not know better, I would think you were following me. If we keep meeting like this people will talk. My reputation will be ruined."

"I am the provost. It is my job to be everywhere and your reputation is already ruined, you Yankee, carpet bagging bastard."

"I have never touched a carpet bag, thank you very much. And since I am a Southerner who supported the Union cause, I am a scallywag, not a carpetbagger. You are the carpetbagger, Richard. And everywhere just happens to be fifteen feet or five minutes behind me today?"

"Yes."

"All right then." He nodded as he perused his paper. "Have I done anything interesting?"

"Not in the least. You are the most boring human being I know. I needed three cups of coffee to stay awake."

This made Charlie smile, which is what Richard was after to begin with. He hated seeing his friend so twisted in knots. "It was not you I was following; it was your shadow."

"Indeed." Charlie casually flipped the page as he continued reading. "He is a persistent little prick."

"He is trying to make you angry."

"He is succeeding," Charlie admitted without hesitation.

"Charlie…" The Provost warned with a low growl. Before he could finish his admonishment Jocko brought out a plate with a huge sandwich, a side of coleslaw and a crisp pickle.

"Here you go, General Cocky. I hope you choke!" He practically tossed the plate to the bar from two feet away.

This made the general laugh outright as the plate settled in front of him with a bit of a spin. He knew there was no way he was going to finish this much food, and since Ro apparently did not have a dog with her he could share it with, he gave half of it to Richard.

His mood had definitely been improved by Jocko's little fit of temper, but it did not last long. The moment Alex Raeburn drew a breath from the same shared air, Charlie's head dropped. He wanted to kill him.

"Relax," Richard advised quietly as Raeburn took a seat three stools away from Charlie at the middle of bar.

"What can I get you?" Jocko asked as politely as possible to his newest patron.

"Whiskey."

Jocko nodded and poured the man a shot, reluctantly acquiescing to the silent request to leave the bottle, before beginning another round of "wipe down the already clean bar." There was no way in hell he was leaving his place unguarded with two of the biggest combatants in town sitting ten feet apart. He needed to protect his livelihood.

"So." Alex knocked the shot back and poured another. "Redmond, how's the wife these days?"

Charlie growled. Richard's face fell into his right hand as he scratched his forehead, hoping to God he would just leave it alone. Charlie nodded and took a forkful of coleslaw into his mouth, chewing a bit more forcefully than coleslaw actually required.

"Mr. Raeburn." Richard looked down the bar, past his friend, to the man who was smiling like the cat that ate the canary. "General Redmond is here for a quiet lunch. There is no need for this."

"For what, Mr. Provost?" He threw back another shot and glared at Richard. "I ain't allowed to be friendly and inquire of the great General Redmond after his wife? I have known her a hell of a lot longer than he has, you know?" He gestured in their direction. "There was a time when my family considered trying to arrange a marriage with her, but they decided that a Randolph wasn't good enough for the Raeburn name. Given that she cain't have no babies that are her own and has to take in every by-blow that comes along, guess it was the right choice."

Charlie sat up straight and looked to the revolting man. "Mr. Raeburn, I would have thought that you would have learned a very important lesson already when it comes to **my wife**." He gestured with his injured hand to the bright pink scar across the man's nose and cheek.

"For instance? She's got nice tit…"

Charlie stood and turned to face the man head on before he could complete his repulsive statement. He took a menacing step forward and snarled. "For instance, it is **bad** for **your health** to even **think** about my wife, let alone **speak of her**."

"What about the other whore who lived in your house?

Surely, I can think about her and the way she sucked my co--" Charlie took another half step towards Raeburn.

Alex took a full step back, nearly falling over a barstool. He continued with far more bravado than he actually felt, "Now that she married the minister, I wonder how the town would react if they knew…"

Suddenly there was rapid movement from Charlie and the sound of steel clearing leather. He withdrew his .36 caliber Colt revolver from a holster under his jacket and leveled it in his outstretched left arm, directly at Raeburn's nose with only a quarter inch to spare. "Keep talking, asshole." His growl was low and warning, the tip of his finger on the trigger, ready and willing to complete the pull.

Richard and Jocko only had time to think one collective thought as they watched Charlie put the gun in Alex's face. *Oh, shit!*

Raeburn's mouth dropped open.

Charlie's hand was steady as he smoothly slid back the hammer with his thumb. He said firmly, "Go ahead. Say one more **damn** thing! Let one more sound leave your foul, filthy mouth in my presence. It will be the **last** one."

As he resettled his finger on the trigger, he growled low so only Raeburn would catch it, "Most people have something to hide." His pause was purposeful. "Boy, I am tired of playing games with you." He hissed at his prey, and his silver eyes flashed and narrowed as he took perfect aim right between Raeburn's rapidly blinking eyes, "Get out. Get out **now**!"

Alex's jaw snapped shut with a click and he scurried like the rat he was through the backdoor of the bar. Charlie lowered the hammer and holstered his gun. Richard sighed with relief and Jocko crossed himself. That had been too damn close.

"I thought no one was supposed to bring weapons in here?" Richard's head whipped around at Jocko.

Jocko raised an agitated hand in Charlie's direction. "You want to search him?"

Charlie retook his seat and peacefully bit into his pickle.

~

Tuesday, April 30, 1867

Alex shook his head in disbelief as he relayed the tale to his audience. "Bastard stuck a gun right between my eyes and neither one of them did a damn thing!"

"Of course not." Eddie flicked away an imaginary piece of dirt from his pant leg as he glanced at his pocket watch. "They all were in the army together. They are still under Redmond's thumb."

"And the Irishman is not going to stick his neck out for you, Mr. Raeburn." Mrs. Williams consoled him with a cup of coffee and a piece of pie.

"Well, I will not let this insult stand. It is time that Redmond learned a lesson. A real lesson. Apparently, our gentle warnings have not been enough for him to get the message."

"What do you suggest? You are not crazy enough to try and rob that bank are you? The payroll was one thing…"

"No, he would be expecting that. We need something else." Alex drummed his fingers on the table waiting for someone else to offer a suggestion.

"Seems perfectly obvious to me," Mrs. Williams said from her spot in the corner.

"Is that so, ma'am?" Alex smiled as benignly as possible for him. "Would you care to share?"

"Seems to me that you need to strike at the heart of the

demon and his brood. There are only two things that would truly bring that man and his," she paused finding the word distasteful, "wife to their knees."

The men at her dining room table all looked at her questioningly. She savored the attention and her ability to hold it.

"Well, it is obvious, is it not? First, there are his horses. He and that woman are bound and determined to make their stables the premier horse breeders in the state."

Several of the men at the table nodded. Granville, the blacksmith, confirmed her statement. "Yes, I agree. I have spoken with Albert several times when he came in for one thing or another, and his pride in their breeding program is unmistakable."

Mrs. Williams continued. "So if you were to strike at their herd, and more effectively than you have been with your little tinkering with their fences, it will hurt. Seriously hurt them."

One of the younger members of the Kirtley family, who had served with Alex during the war, spoke up. "Well, I for one have no desire to become a horse thief. Their stock is so distinctive, if one of us showed up riding a horse from Redmond's herd, it would be noticed immediately."

The matron smiled and said sweetly, "I did not say to steal them, sir."

The men were silent at that statement. Every one of them was a horseman in one way or another and the idea of killing perfectly good horses was alien to them. Finally, Eddie spoke up. "Well, if we stole them and sold them elsewhere, say in Maryland or Pennsylvania, it would be a good source of money to fund our little activities." He had not let anyone know that he had gone back a couple of weeks ago and collected up the two horses that had run away when they tore down the fence in the back pasture, taken them over to the valley and sold them for good money.

Mrs. Williams went on. "Gentlemen, if the horses do not get the results you desire, there is always that brood of his bastards and brats they have taken on. If you really want to reduce that man and woman to their knees, go after the children. If I were you, I would start with that obnoxious little girl, Emily, the one that threw herself on that man when you hit him after church that day, Alex. Or the boy, Buddy, Redmond's bastard."

Granville, Armistead, and Brooks looked appalled. It was one thing to kill a horse, although it was distasteful to all of them. But children? They shook their heads.

"Oh, I am not suggesting that you actually kill the child, but I suspect the general would dig deep into his pockets to ransom back one of them."

~

Monday, May 6, 1867

Charlie entered Cooper's store with a list he thought was a foot long. Rebecca had assured him that everything on it was vital to the running of the house. He was not sure how four feet of blue gingham cloth was vital to the house, but he handed the list to Cooper with a smile.

"I will also settle the bill for last month while I am here." Charlie dropped his hat to the counter and pulled his wallet from his pocket.

Copper nodded and took the list. He began filling the order, being far more quiet than normal as he pulled the items from his shelves.

"Edward, is something wrong?" Charlie leaned on the counter and pulled his cigar case from his pocket, offering it to the distracted man. Cooper never turned down one of Charlie's cigars; he sighed and shook his head, declining the offered tobacco.

"Oh, now I know something is wrong." He removed a second stogie and placed it on the counter in front of his friend. "Come on, Edward, talk to me. Is it Raeburn?"

The store owner sighed and turned to the tall man. "I have no idea who it is." He reached under the counter and retrieved a piece of paper, which he handed to Charlie.

Let one more nigger in your place and it will be ashes.

The Loyal Watchmen.

"Have you shown this to Colonel Polk?"

Cooper shook his head. "Not yet. I had planned to later in the day. General Redmond, Grace does not know a thing about this and I would rather she not."

"I understand," Charlie agreed, knowing he would rather keep most of the IHCRC shenanigans from Rebecca as well.

"I am afraid I must make a request. No matter how much it pains me or how distasteful you and Miss Rebecca may find it. Please, keep your servants out of my store. I cannot risk them burning it down around my head because your wife needs a spool of thread."

Charlie nodded. "I understand, Edward, and rest assured we will keep our people out of the store for the time being."

Saturday, May 18, 1867

Raeburn and his closest allies were having a small meeting to discuss their latest piece of sabotage aimed at the Redmonds. The only men at the small table in the yard behind Mrs. Allen's inn were Alex Raeburn, Harold Kirtley, and Eddie Rainey.

"So are we agreed that something far more damaging to Redmond is needed? If we can keep this up, maybe we can run that damned bastard out of town, along with his brood of baby bastards." Alex Raeburn's hatred of Charlie had done nothing but grow as Charlie continued to hire qualified blacks and build up the little protected enclave for them at Redmond Grove.

Harold Kirtley nodded agreement. "He is even inserting himself into our traditions. My damned cousin decided he was good enough for our hunt. Since Redmond was riding, I decided not to this season. As much as I love the hunt, I refuse to socialize with that scallywag. Guess I need to find another hunt to join."

Raeburn looked at him critically. "So you have no entrée to the property?"

"Hell, no! I have never stepped foot on their place since we got back from the war. I doubt that Redmond even knows who I am."

Raeburn nodded. The Kirtleys were Presbyterians, so Redmond would not have met Harold at church either.

"So it is down to you, Eddie. I certainly cannot get on the property. Harold would set off alarms, as he is an unknown. You are the only one who has a legitimate excuse to be there and who could hang back, hide and do the deed."

Eddie looked rather like a trapped rat. "Come on, Alex. Relieving them of a few horses is one thing. This is a whole different scale."

"Yes, yes, it is. And since you are the only one who can get on the property other than Brooks, and you know I would never trust him to do something like this, you are our only choice."

Eddie shook his head. "I don' know, Alex. This could be bad."

Alex leaned into the man's face. "Any worse than being a proven horse thief? You know I could put you on the gallows for stealing his horses and selling them over in the valley. I could have you hung in a matter of days. So, boy-o, you are our man for this. Understand me?"

"Yes, Alex." Eddie was well and truly trapped between the devil he knew and the one that might be waiting for him.

~

Friday, May 24, 1867

Rebecca had not known what to expect when Charlie had told her he was building a carriage house. As she looked around the new structure, she realized she should have asked a question or six. It was huge.

A large open space that was already occupied by a dozen or so coaches, carriages and wagons and it still looked empty in the grand scheme of things dominated the structure, but Charlie was keen to show off a few of the buildings special features. Though the finishing touches still had to be made, the building was at least usable.

The first of his 'special features' made Rebecca very happy, so happy she laughed aloud. One end of the second floor was just one large room. It was a playroom for the general, his little group of troopers, and their annoying lead soldiers. The table that Charlie and Darby had plotted and planned their various military actions had grown by three times the size it had been in his office, but as long as it was out of the house, she was happy.

The next was the rest of the second floor--a series of three small apartments, complete with a small library and one of the new wash rooms with hot and cold running water he was so happily planning to put in every building on the property. He most definitely took advantage of the fact the carriage house was a new build and could be done to his specifications.

"Are you planning to move out here?" she asked as she looked around the very well-appointed apartments.

"Not unless I must." He quirked a brow. "No dear, this is to free up more space in the house. This is for Darby, John, and Freddy."

Now it was her turn to raise brows. "You think this is a good idea, why?"

"Because our eldest son is becoming a young man. It is entirely appropriate for him to have a shared space with his valet and tutor and I will not let the problems we have had interfere with their lives any more than necessary."

She shook her head, but listened as he continued.

"They have separate accommodations and then the shared common space of the library. They must still come to the main house for meals so you will still be able to lay eyes on him every day." He grinned, knowing exactly what she was thinking. He always knew what she was thinking when it came to the children. The closer they were to her the better. Letting Darby move out to the apartments would be a big step for his mother.

~

Wednesday, May 29, 1867

Charlie and Rebecca came up out of their bed at almost the same moment. As Charlie shook his head and grabbed his robe he was not sure if it was the ringing of the alarm bell, the barking of various dogs, or the shouting of people that had awakened him, but he was sure he did not care. Obviously, something was very wrong.

He moved right away to the veranda doors, like a moth drawn by a bright light he knew should not be there. "The barn is on fire!" It was the only thing he managed to say before grabbing his robe and a pair of boots, tugging them on as he ran from the room nearly going head first over Feighlí and Peri, who were on full barking alert in front of their beloved human's bedroom door.

Before he even knew how it happened, he was standing in front of his barn, which was nearly totally engulfed in flames. Men were running quickly to form a fire brigade, drawing buckets from the well, but he knew it was already too late.

He could see a few men trying to get in past the flames as the screams of frightened and dying horses filled the air. He grabbed a bucket and dumped it over his head as he made his way forward. "Douse me!" he commanded the men closest to the door. He felt more water soak his body as he dashed through the flames into the barn.

Rebecca could not keep up with him as he bolted from the house. As she managed to draw up behind him, she watched in dismay as he ran into the inferno. Her feet moved forward, even as her eyes never wavered from the flames consuming the barn. "Charlie! Oh, Charlie, come out!" she begged knowing he had been in there far too long.

She watched as one of the large cross members of the roof began to crack and give way, about to collapse. "Damn it, Charlie!"

A second before the beam broke free Jack came running out of the flames leading Tucker and three other horses that were simply turned loose and allowed to escape. There was still no sign of her husband. Her heart began beating double time as she thought he had been trapped by the falling beam.

Another timber snapped and the roof looked as if it would give way at any moment. She could only stand back and watch as men continued to try and get horses to safety. She kept looking for any sign of him.

Finally, she saw a form she instantly knew was his. He was leading another four horses from the barn by ropes hastily looped over their necks, blankets over their heads to try and stop their panic. As he managed to stumble from the barn, allowing the horses to run loose as soon as they were free from the flames, he collapsed to his knees gagging and coughing on the smoke he had inhaled.

She managed to get to him just as he struggled to his feet. It was clear he was planning on going back in. She caught him by the arm and planted herself firmly in front of him. "No! Charlie, no! Do not go back in there!"

"I have to..."

"No!" She pushed him back forcefully at the shoulders, knowing if he got past her, he would never get out a second time. "You will get killed in there!"

The words were barely out of her mouth when the roar of disintegrating timbers assaulted their ears and the heat of the inferno pushed them back physically.

The roof fell in, taking what was left of the second and third floors with it. Men scrambled to get out of the way as the flames flared up, shooting burning embers and chunks of flaming wood flying all over the barn yard. The impact was so great some of the charred stones in the walls cracked and fell, making the maelstrom that engulfed the remains of the barn even greater.

The fire settled down slowly, leaving red hot embers and sullen flames licking the remaining wood, now collapsed into a pile of burning, foul smelling rubble on what had been the floor of the barn. The stone walls were left as a charred and blacken skeleton encasing what now looked like a huge bonfire that had been built in the middle of the building. If anything had still been alive in the barn when the roof collapsed, it was dead now.

He dropped to the ground gagging again, partly from the smoke he had swallowed and partly from knowing he had a number of dead horses in that building, including several of the spring foals. They had hit them were it hurt. This could set Rebecca's breeding program back by two years.

"Shannon..." He gasped.

"Shannon is out in the west pasture."

He nodded , knowing that Jack and Tucker were also safely out. "I am sorry I could not..." He began coughing hard again, tears streaming down his blackened cheeks leaving watery white trails. Rebecca was not sure if it was the smoke or the loss of the barn and horses. "Tarent and Rollins?"

She shook her head. "I do not know. If one of the mares was foaling, they would have been in there."

"Find them, please," he gasped.

She dropped down next to him and wrapped her arms around him as she watched the last of her barn burn. "We will."

They sat there together for several minutes even as the mayhem around them played out. The entire farm was awake and it looked like the small town it actually was. Men and women were coming from every direction. Rebecca looked up when she felt a blanket settle over their shoulders to find Beulah.

"Miz 'Becca, Tess and Lizbet have the children well in hand. Sarah is setting up the kitchen. Reg has gone to town to get more people, though I 'spect the glow from the fire already has people on the way."

Charlie continued to cough and gag, wiping the soot from his face on the arm of his robe. “We need to get the gen’l inside, ma’am.” Beulah had heard men choke like that after being through a fire; she knew it was not good.

Rebecca nodded and stood up. Both women pulled Charlie to his feet and helped him into the kitchen, where Sarah and as many staff as she could gather were busy assuring that there would be coffee, tea and food for all the people who would be coming and going for the next few hours.

“Sarah,” Beulah said, making it sound almost like an order even though the woman had no right to command the cook. “Gen’l C is going to need a hot honey and mint tea right away. His throat got burnt.”

For the first time, Rebecca looked down at him, Beulah's words shaking her thoughts from the horses and barn to her cherished husband. She knelt as Sarah placed a bowl of warm water and clean clothes on the table by her hand.

“Oh, Charlie.” She gently began cleaning his face, seeing that he had a few minor burns on his cheeks and forehead. His hair was burnt in a small patch on the crown that she suspected hurt a great deal.

The water was black the first time she wrung out the cloth and it was quickly replaced by Beulah with another bowl. He began wheezing and seemed like he was having a hard time drawing a breath.

Just as Rebecca was about to go into a full blown panic, Elizabeth came through the kitchen door with Rex hot on her heals. They were carrying their respective medical kits in their hands.

“Richard and his deputies are down at the barn now,” she announced as she dropped her cases on the table. “Half of Culpeper is on its way.”

She knelt in front of Charlie right away while Rex began

extracting medical equipment and laying it out on the table. She used her reflector to get some direct light into his mouth and down his throat. “Rex, I have a chloroform inhaler in my bag; please, get it ready but I want to prepare a special mixture.”

He nodded and did as she asked. Elizabeth smiled and looked at Charlie. “Are you trying to keep us all up to date on our medical skills? There is no need to be my most difficult patient every time I see you.”

He just tried to smile as he shook his head; the motion sent him into another coughing fit.

“Easy, we will get you feeling better very shortly.” She stood and looked to Rebecca. “Are you all right, my dear? You did not go chasing into the barn did you?”

“No. I am fine.” She dropped into a chair next to Charlie and took his left hand, which caused him to flinch and she noticed a large burn on the back. She gently began cleaning his hand as Elizabeth handed her some ointment and a plaster. “You keep this up and there will not be anything left by the time you are fifty. I would rather you stop leaving bits of yourself all over Virginia.”

More coughing, this time leaving him with a mouth full of a foul tasting substance. His first inclination was to swallow it, but Elizabeth shoved a pan under his chin. “Spit. Anything you bring up, spit it out.”

A moment later, Elizabeth prepared a mixture of camphor and few other well-chosen ingredients with some boiling water into a small glass jar with a small leather mask and hose attached. Once she was happy with the way the little device was working she placed the mask over his face. “Breathe as deeply as you can.”

While Elizabeth tended Charlie, Rex moved to Rebecca, who was clearly going into a state of shock. He wrapped his arms around her and moved her to a seat across the table and knelt in front of her.

Sarah placed a cup of tea on the table and he thanked her with a nod. “Rebecca, are you sure you are all right?” He handed her the tea and she took it with trembling hands as she nodded.

~

By the time the sun came up, they had needed to turn Rebecca’s office into a small infirmary where they spent the better part of the morning treating various injuries ranging from minor burns to a broken arm.

Rebecca and Charlie had managed to get cleaned up and dressed. He was still coughing a bit and his voice was little more than a whisper, but he insisted on being up to deal with the aftermath even though both Elizabeth and Rex had recommended he go back to bed and stay there for the day.

Charlie had just stepped out on the back porch to go back down to the remnants of the barn when Richard approached. The man was covered in soot and dirt, and there were singe marks on his hat and clothes and he simply looked like hell. He looked at his friend and just shook his head, “Tarent and Rollins…” He paused. “They did not make it out. I am sorry.”

“Well, now it is murder, Richard. We need to find a way to stop this before anyone else gets killed. There has been too much damn death already.” He shook his head and went back into the house.

~

Charlie sat at his desk, his forehead resting on the knot made by his interlaced fingers. His eyes were closed and it was clear he was not at his emotional best. They had lost a good man and a mere boy in the fire.

His guilt over Tarent's death was beginning to feel a bit overwhelming. He had known the old farrier for years. They had seen each other through horrible times, bound together by their love of horses. Charlie had learned more from the older man than just about anyone else in his life.

To some extent, Tarent had been the father he had always longed for and been so cruelly denied. In his opinion, there was only one proper place to bury him. He hoped Rebecca would understand his need to lay him to rest in the family cemetery.

He would also have to find Rollins' family and somehow try to make this right by them. He was not sure if the boy had any kin or not, but he was determined to find them if they did exist.

The fire had also claimed Rebecca's entire Morgan stock, the little stud and the five mares, four of which were in foal. She had also lost two thoroughbred mares, four foals and one donkey stud. They were also sure that Madra had been killed in the fire, but her body had not been recovered yet. The barn and the storage building behind it were a total loss.

The good news was that Jack, Shannon and Tucker were indeed safe. Jack had a small burn on his rump near his tail, but he would certainly heal up with no issue. Tucker was scared witless and only settled down and came into range to be caught when Darby went out after him. Shannon had been in pasture with the majority of their herd and she was completely unharmed, but seemed distressed at Jack's anxious behavior. The horses had been collected and inspected and safely put away in the stables. Charlie had already talked to Duncan and Hudnut about starting the rebuilding, telling both men he did not care what it cost or if they had to stop other jobs to get started. He expected them to start right away.

Thursday, May 30, 1867

Rebecca awoke sensing something was amiss in her world. Reaching out and not finding Charlie, she knew what had woken her. She gathered her dressing gown and looked first in the sitting room. No Charlie there either. She, Feighlí and Peri checked his office. It was empty as well. She sighed and looked at the dogs. "He is out riding the farm again."

He had been out riding nearly every hour since the barn fire. His special saddle was destroyed, as was most of their tack and equipment. The saddle his men had given him had managed to survive only because Rebecca had put it in her office to make some adjustments since she had been using it as her primary saddle since the day Charlie had let her use it.

It was not the most comfortable thing for his leg and backside to ride without the special padding Jeremiah had created, but it did the job, especially if he spent time standing in the stirrups as he rode.

A few pieces of equipment borrowed from Richard and loaned by a couple of neighbors and they had the ability to ride their mounts and harness a buggy and a couple of wagons. It would do until they could get new equipment.

Rebecca made her way downstairs and to the kitchen. That is where she found him, sitting at the kitchen table, coffee cup cradled in his left hand, his face resting in his right, sound asleep. Very carefully, she moved behind him and rubbed his shoulders. "Please, come back to bed."

"Mmm?" He opened his very tired eyes and patted her hand. "I suppose I could stand to get a couple hours of sleep." His voice was still hoarse, in part from the fire, in part from lack of sleep.

"You could stand to get more than a couple hours. You are going to kill yourself at this rate. You cannot be awake and work twenty-four hours a day. It simply is not possible."

He nodded, knowing she was right, but not knowing how to do everything, including keeping her, the children and their farm safe from an enemy he could not predict.

~

Eddie slipped into Mrs. Allen's as soon as she opened her doors. He asked for a glass and a jar of her best, and settled into the corner to methodically work his way through the moonshine. He knew that Raeburn would be along soon to enjoy Mrs. Allen's outstanding lamb stew and her even more outstanding apple flavored 'shine. Celebrating the blow that had been dealt to that man was something Raeburn could not resist.

Eddie would have rather slinked away into a nice, quiet hole. The sound of those screaming horses had been bad enough. The damned dog chasing him from here to hell and back before he finally managed to get across Gaines Run was worse. The dog had gotten hold of his thigh, taking a piece out of his pants and leaving a pair of teeth marks just above and behind his knee. Thankfully, Kirtley had been there waiting for him with a horse.

The dog continued to chase him after he met up with Kirtley. It was only stopped when Kirtley's horse, annoyed at the snapping teeth at his heels, leveled a solid kick that landed on the damned dog's shoulder. That seriously hurt the beast, who gave up on the pursuit.

Rainey and Kirtley parted ways at a crossroad just outside of Culpeper, each to go home and get cleaned up from their hurried ride through the woods and away from the barking, snarling hellhound.

From there, Eddie finally managed to put himself together and look like a proper, hard working man going about his business. He burned the clothes he had worn in the rubbish heap behind his house. The combination of mud, the smell of smoke, and God only knew what else would have been a dead giveaway. Now he had to face Alex. And Alex's gloating smirk was the last thing he wanted to see this morning. All he really wanted to do was get something to eat and get some sleep.

A moment later, Raeburn strolled in, looking satisfied and cocky. He waved to Mrs. Allen, asking for a bowl of stew and a pint of beer, then plunked down opposite Eddie. While Mrs. Allen went to fetch the stew from the kitchen and they were alone, Alex started his gloat. "Well done. I hear they lost a number of horses. Too bad they also lost one of Redmond's carpetbagger friends and his boy. But you hit them where it hurt. Excellent job, my friend."

Eddie just shook his head. "I ain't much for celebratin' right now, Alex. I just want some food and some sleep."

"And that you shall have. My treat."

He shook his head again. Alex was just plain crazy with his hatred and desire for vengeance.

Just then, Kirtley came in and joined them. "I checked. Other than that damned dog, no one seems to have followed us."

"Good," mumbled Eddie. "Let's hope it stays that way."

CHAPTER 5

Monday, June 3, 1867

Charlie sat at his desk in the morning, as was his habit, to have his first cup of coffee and read the previous evening edition of the paper that was always brought up on the coffee tray. He was tired, having barely slept in days. Coffee was his lifeblood at the moment.

Since Tomas's leaving had left him without a valet, Reg was making sure to tend to the morning routine of the general. As he poured his coffee, he considered that he really did need another valet. He had always had a male companion to tend him, first Jocko in the army and then Tomas. Perhaps young Mr. Coleman could make a recommendation.

He flipped open the folded paper and an extraneous piece of paper dropped to the floor. He retrieved it and started to toss it in the waste can when he noticed heavy black marks. He unfolded the paper and found in bold, block printing, a warning:

WATCH YOUR CHILDREN CAREFULLY.

A FRIEND

He jumped up from his chair and ran to his room. Rebecca was still dressing; he tossed the note into her lap as he passed her, headed for his wardrobe. He yanked a set of clothes out, pulling them on as quickly as he could.

She was leaning against the bed, a look of utter shock and fear on her face. "Where are you going?"

"I am going to arrange for help. We cannot do this alone. I will explain when I get back." He plucked the note from her fingers and slid it into the inside pocket of his jacket.

He jammed his feet into his riding boots and headed out. He did not even bother to put a saddle on Jack, he just crammed the bit between the big horse's teeth, buckled the bridle on, and jumped up bareback. He and Jack took off, hell-bent for town.

He pulled up outside the telegraph office and simply dropped Jack's reins. He knew the horse would wait for him and deny any other rider.

The sound of the door being jerked open got the telegraph operator's attention. "Yes, sir, Gen'l Redmond. What can I…" The man did not get an opportunity to finish.

"Send this to General Grant, highest priority. Family threatened. Stop. Barn burned. Stop. Horses and men killed. Stop. Need help now. Stop. Respond immediately. Stop. Chas. Redmond." He dug into his pocket and pulled out a gold five dollar piece, tossing it on the counter. "I will wait for an answer."

It only took twenty minutes for a reply to arrive.

Sorry re trouble. Stop.

Appointment Pinkerton Fri Stop.

Call out troops? Stop.

USG

He sighed with relief. His shoulders relaxed and his chin

dropped to his chest. "Thank you, God. Thank you, General." He sent a quick response, confirming his arrival in Washington for the meeting and thanking General Grant. Then he went back outside, collected Jack and went to find Richard and show him the note.

Richard looked at the note carefully. It was written in plain block printing on the most common kind of note paper, in simple pencil. There was nothing to provide any clue as to the author. He shook his head. "Do you want me to send Max and Sean out to help guard your house?"

"No, I have men I trust. We will watch closely. I am going up to Washington on Thursday to meet with Alan Pinkerton and get his help. This is getting far too dangerous. In the meantime, you three need to keep looking for these bastards."

"Well, at least let Elizabeth and me come out and watch the children while you are in Washington."

"I would be grateful. I may also ask Edgar, Rex, and Charlotte, too."

"Please. The more the better."

From Richard, Charlie went to the manse. Edgar was standing on the front steps when he got there. "I heard. We will be out as soon as we can."

"How did you hear?"

"The telegraph operator sent his boy over. By now, the whole town probably knows."

Charlie drew a deep breath. "I need to get back to Rebecca. And Edgar? Thank you."

"You go back to her. I will organize your supporters here. We will be out as soon as we can, as I said."

"Could you ask Rex to come out as soon as possible? I am in severe pain."

"Of course. Now go back to your wife and children."

He pulled himself back up on Jack's bare back. They turned and Jack paced himself very carefully, trying hard to balance his rider on his back with minimal shock while still making good time.

As he rode down the road to Redmond Stables with the woods to one side of them and open fields on the other, they heard a sad, whimpering sound coming from the brush on the wooded side of the road. Charlie pulled Jack up and slid off his back to see what was making the pitiful sound.

He stepped into the brush and to his surprise and relief, found Madra lying in the high grass and weeds. They were sure she had been killed in the fire. She was battered, cut and probably badly bruised. She had several scorch marks in her fur. Her shoulder was bloodied, and there were burrs and twigs tangled and matted in her fur. It looked like one leg was twisted at an odd angle.

She looked up at Charlie with the saddest, most defeated look he had ever seen in a dog's eyes. He felt great empathy for the beast, which had spent the last four days of her life either chasing her prey or trying to get home. She had done her job admirably and deserved nothing but the kindest and gentlest treatment he could manage under the circumstances.

He looked around for anything that would help him with her, as it was obvious that she was hurt, hungry, and exhausted. Jack looked over at the situation, then nodded his head and came over beside them. He then did something the general had never seen him do before. The big horse lay down, getting himself as low to the ground as he could without rolling onto his side. The dog looked from Charlie to Jack and back. He encouraged her to get up. With more reassurance, and as much help as he could offer, she hauled herself up on three legs, limped over to Jack and very carefully stepped over him, so that his back would support her. She draped herself long ways over his back with her legs on each side and her head resting on his big rump. The General considered for just a moment that it looked like the horse was wearing a big grey rug. Jack stayed as still as he could, waiting for her to settle. He arranged the big dog securely then as he spoke calmly to her; Jack rose slowly and they walked the rest of the way to the house.

He was yelling for Reg before he reached the front steps. "Send for Miss Ro! Then come help me get Madra down and someplace comfortable. Get some blankets from the house or barn!"

Jack carefully lowered himself to the ground once again, and with Charlie's and Reg's help, Madra got off his back. The dog slowly walked on three legs up the steps, dragging her left front leg, and lay down on the front porch to wait for more help.

In the furor, Jack simply took himself off to the stables. Someone there would surely take the bridle off, give him a nice brush down and if he was really lucky, a nice bucket of oats warmed with hot water and sweetened with molasses.

Ro had already been at the house for days, running circuits with her dogs looking for any intruders and searching for Madra, so as soon as one of the footmen came running out to find her, she called in her hounds and headed to the house. Madra greeted her with a wagging tail and an effort to get up from her bed on the porch. Ro motioned for the beloved dog to stay down and dropped down beside her to start inspecting the injuries.

Someone had provided the dog with a big bowl of water and a bowl of chopped beef, both of which had been placed in snout range and which had been gratefully received by the exhausted animal.

There were burns, scrapes, and bruises, but the worst injury was a broken leg. From the injuries, it was obvious she had been kicked by a horse. Reg brought her warm water, soap, and bandages. He went to find something to make a splint for the dog's leg, and returned shortly, carefully whittling a pair of short boards into appropriately sized splints for the brave canine.

Together, they set Madra's leg, wrapped it in bandages to keep the splint in place, and then treated the other injuries the dog had experienced. Ro noticed a piece of cloth with a few sprinkles of blood on it lying beside the dog – brown twill such as many men wore as work pants. Madra, who was usually exceptionally cooperative with Ro, would not let her take it. She suspected that whoever had set the fire had also lost a piece of their pants and possibly some of their skin.

Charlotte and Rex pulled their trap up in front of the house within an hour of Charlie's and Madra's arrival. Rex grabbed his case of medicines, threw the reins to one of the footmen, and headed in to find Charlie and Rebecca.

They looked in the back parlor first, where they normally went when they needed to be together. But they were not there.

One of the footmen was on his way upstairs with a tray set for tea, augmented with a bottle of brandy. "If you are looking for the general and Miz 'Becca, they are in his office." They nodded and followed him up the stairs.

The door to the office was open. Charlie and Rebecca were sitting where they could see down the hall. Feighlí's head came up from her spot right in front of the door, until she recognized the people and knew they were friends. Then it dropped back down with a thump.

Darby, Suzanne and Em were at one of the work tables at the back of the room, with John leading them through their lessons. Their parents were watching the door to the boys' room, since

Buddy and Andy were down for their afternoon naps. Rebecca was dressed in britches and boots, and it was obvious she had something bulky in one pocket of her britches. From the shape, Charlotte guessed it was a gun. As Rex and Charlotte entered the room, both of them rose to greet them. Rex noticed that there was a shotgun propped in the corner by the door. They were taking no chances.

Charlotte spoke first. "How are you two doing?"

Rebecca was blunt, but kept her voice low and as calm as possible to keep from further upsetting the children. "Terrified! How could they threaten the children? Who would do such a terrible thing? What kind of monsters are they?"

Charlotte put her arm around Rebecca's shoulders. "They are evil men, dear. Very evil men. But your family and friends are here. And more are coming. Edgar is organizing the men in town to come and help guard you and yours as we speak. He will be out later when he is through putting together a plan of defense for you."

Rex was looking at Charlie very carefully, noting the tired eyes, the shaking hands, and the slow and careful movements he was making, as well as the odd way he was balanced in the chair. "General, you have seen what I can do as a fighter. What you have seen is just a small sample of my skills. I will stay here as long as you and yours need me, if nothing else as the last line of defense. But right now, I would say you need my skills as a healer more. Let Charlotte stay here with Rebecca, and you must come with me."

He smiled at his friend, a tired, grateful smile as he slowly hauled himself from the chair. "Yes, I do need your skills. Riding bareback was not one of my cleverer moves. And there is no one I trust more than you to protect the children after that demonstration you gave." Together, the men walked toward the door with Charlie leaning heavily on his cane, on their way to the bedroom.

As they left the room, Rebecca could hear Rex warning him that he was going to see and feel the results of that ride the next day. Time would prove him right.

Later that afternoon, a small group of men and women rode up to Redmond Stables led by Edgar and Richard. Tess had brought the boys into the library when they woke, and they were quietly playing with Peri and Feighlí on the rug in front of the fireplace. John still held the attention of the other children with games. Rex settled himself in a comfortable armchair with a book in his hand and nodded to Charlie, Rebecca, and Charlotte. He had this situation under control.

So the threesome greeted the delegation in the hall and escorted them into the back parlor, where Sarah sent up a large afternoon tea.

Missy Frazier started right in. "We have all heard of the despicable threat to the children and that you have a meeting with Mr. Pinkerton in Washington to bring guards down to protect your family and property. Until you do, the ladies and I have agreed to come and watch the children for you while the men provide protection around the house and property. We wish we could do more, but with your man Tarent and young Rollins killed and the children threatened, we have joined together to fight this evil. Enough is enough."

Edgar smiled. Missy was one of his best allies when it came to springing into action. "Yes. See here." He produced a sheet of paper. "We have set up a schedule so that we will always have people to watch and guard while you go to Washington to bring back reinforcements."

Duncan asked, "Is it true you have asked General Grant for military guards?"

Charlie smiled a little. "No, I would not impose on him like that, but I did ask him for help and he set a meeting with Pinkerton. We will be hiring him to provide guards until this problem is solved."

Richard added, "We are working diligently to identify the culprits. We all know who is probably behind these attacks, the horse thieving, and the fire…all of it. But proving it is a very different problem, and you know as well as I do if we were to arrest them without proof, this town would go up in flames."

Charlie was feeling a little better. Based on the schedule Edgar provided, it looked like almost half the town was willing to help protect the family. "Thank you. This will make it easier for us to go to Washington to get the help we need."

"You go to Washington. I am not leaving my children while they are threatened." Rebecca had her most stubborn look on her face.

Before he could respond, Missy spoke up once again. "Go with him. You will feel better if you talk with Mr. Pinkerton too. You can give him the information he needs to set up proper protections. We will take care of things here while you are gone. You both need a day or two to regroup, to be together. No harm will come to your family."

Thursday, June 6, 1867

Charlie's mind was so preoccupied with the troubles at home

he did not even notice the ember that came through the train window until it burned through his pants leg to the skin.

"Just my luck," he mumbled as he patted out the small fire trying to start in his lap. He was relieved to see that the ember had at least missed the leg of his small clothes.

Rebecca looked up from her book. She had decided to come with him, if for no other reason than to take Missy's advice and be alone with him for a day or two.

A small army of family and friends were at the house to care for the children; they would be in sight of an adult day and night. But the stress and strain at the house and in Culpeper was beginning to take its toll on them personally and they were arguing and squabbling more than normal. Everyone could see it. Rebecca's Renegades had been adamant; she should be with Charlie during this trip.

"Darling?" She looked to him as he brushed his trouser leg.

"Time for a new suit." He stuck his finger in the hole. "And a plaster for my leg."

"Oh, dear." She closed the book and leaned over to inspect his injury. "I would kiss it and make it better, but I am not sure what the conductor would say if he saw me with my head in your lap."

He chortled and patted her hand as it lay near the hole in his trousers. "It is fine dear. I suspect I will survive."

"I will properly tend you when we reach Mrs. Galloway's."

He smiled at her as he shifted across the seat to sit next to her. "I am sure you will. Rebecca, I do want to apologize for being such a bear lately."

"Sweetheart." She caressed his cheek. "The situation at home has us both under a great deal of pressure. I know it is only the only reason we have been fussing and fighting with each other. Once it resolves itself, things will get back to normal."

"I am not sure there is such a thing as normal at our house."

"There is that. All right then, as normal as we are capable."

"General Grant has arranged a luncheon meeting for us with Alan Pinkerton tomorrow."

"I wish I could say you are over reacting." She sighed, not liking the direction this was going, but knowing there was little or no choice. Alex Raeburn and his men had all but declared a new war and most of it was focused directly on her husband and farm. She feared the threat to her children was next on his twisted agenda, and she would kill him herself to protect them. Perhaps extra security would help calm everyone's rattled nerves. "What about Robert Brooks?"

Charlie nodded as he considered the farm hand. It was clear that he associated with Raeburn, but there had never been a problem with him or his work at the farm, and Tarent had liked him a great deal. The old farrier had even taken the younger man under his wing, so to speak, giving him extra responsibility with the horses. "I think Mr. Brooks is smart enough to know who is giving him the resources to feed his family. He has a wife and daughter and he seems devoted to them. We have never had an issue and until we do, my dear, there is no reason to question him or his motives."

Rebecca nodded. She could not argue with his logic. "Other than the luncheon with Mr. Pinkerton, do you have any other plans?"

"Other than buying a new suit? Not a one. I am all yours this weekend. We will have our lunch meeting tomorrow and then we will have the rest of the day and Saturday. We return home Sunday afternoon. Is there something you would like to do?"

She smiled and nodded before placing her lips next to his ear. "Spend all day Saturday in bed? I miss your touch, Charlie."

He hugged her close and kissed her forehead. "Then it shall be all yours, my darling."

~

Friday, June 7, 1867

The Oak Room at the Willard Hotel was a very nice but overly masculine location for Rebecca's tastes. The oak floor-to-ceiling paneling gave the room a dark, shadowy quality that she did not particularly care for. She knew, according to Charlie, that most of Washington's powerbrokers made their deals in this room, and given the less than ethical quality of some of those deals, she realized the atmosphere was perfect.

Mr. Pinkerton rose to greet them and smiled gently as Charlie held Rebecca's chair and she settled at the table. "I hope you do not mind that I invited my wife, Mr. Pinkerton, but she does run our farm and breeding program on a daily basis. She will be the best person to answer some of your questions."

"Of course, General Redmond, it is certainly not a problem to have such beautiful company for lunch." He smiled gently at her as she removed her hat and gloves while Charlie settled across from Pinkerton, whose Scottish accent peeked through his greeting.

The detective was a middle aged man with a crown of dark hair on his balding head and full thick beard. Like Charlie, he smelled faintly of good cigars and he had a very reassuring smile.

"So, what kind of problems are you having?"

The couple spent the first thirty minutes telling him about all of the incidents since Raeburn's return, from the first volley of punching Charlie in the churchyard to the barn fire and the threat to the children. He listened and nodded while making a few notes on the pad before him. As lunch was served, he contemplated their situation as they made small talk. Once they were onto their coffee, the pad returned to the table and he looked at them contemplatively.

"How many acres?"

"One hundred sixty, with about a hundred twenty currently in use," Rebecca said as she fixed Charlie's coffee before placing it in front of him.

"How many buildings, including your home?"

The questions continued this way for nearly an hour. He asked about the children, their ages, likes and dislikes. He asked about the number of people and animals around at any given time. He was intrigued by Ro and her dogs and asked Charlie if he could arrange an introduction when he came down.

"You will be coming personally?" Rebecca was shocked.

"Yes, Mrs. Redmond, if for no other reason than to organize my people. This is going to be a large job that will take a great deal of planning and preparation. Now, I use both male and female agents."

"Really?" Now she was amazed.

"Really, ma'am." He nodded. "One of my best people is a woman named Kate Warne. She is actually the head of my Female Detective Bureau. One of the finest agents I have ever had. Every woman who wishes to work for me must try to attain Kate's level of dedication and proficiency."

Tuesday, June 11, 1867

Charlie was delighted to catch Tomas in town as he made his way to Jocko's for lunch.

"What can I do for you, General?" The young man asked as they walked down the street.

"Well, to be honest, I need your assistance to find another valet. I am afraid that I am pitiful left to my own devices. Currently, Miss Rebecca and Reg are doing their best to make sure that my socks match and that I do not leave the house in a dirty shirt, but their desire to do so is wearing very thin." He held up his injured hand and added with a chuckle, "And what I do to myself with a razor is pathetic. Miss Rebecca is tired of blood all over the basin."

Tomas nodded and laughed. He had come to understand very quickly how much the general depended on his valet. He had been worried about leaving him so soon and had already anticipated this particular problem. "Yes, sir. I do believe I know just the man."

"Glad to hear it." Charlie stopped in front of Jocko's. "Care to join me for lunch so we can discuss the details?"

Tomas smiled but shook his head. "No, sir. It is not that I would not enjoy lunch with you, but I will not put Mr. and Mrs. Jackson in a position of having to deal with Raeburn and his crowd. "I will be happy to bring Louis by Redmond Stables next week and we can talk then."

Charlie extended his hand. "Thank you, my friend."

The black man looked around before doing so, but then he took the offered hand. He did not want to cause the general any problems, but he did not want to insult him either.

"Tomas." Charlie held onto the man's hand. "I appreciate your concern for Jocko and Esther, but you are my friend too, and I never refuse the hand of a friend."

"Thank you, Gen'l Charlie."

~

Thursday, June 13, 1867

Mr. Pinkerton had made it very clear that the arrival of his people in Culpeper would be a very public event. He told them that in his professional opinion, making it clear new security had arrived for his farm and family would not be a bad thing.

Arrive they did, about three hundred of them over a period of three days, starting the previous Tuesday. Every available room at Jocko's and Mrs. Allen's had been filled right away, as had most any other rooms in town available for rent.

Many of them had to be put up at Redmond Stables because that is where the majority of their duties would be performed. Fortunately, the new carriage house was sufficiently finished to house a number of the guards. Rebecca had not realized it at the time they had hired Mr. Pinkerton, but the arrival of his people was very reminiscent of Charlie's initial arrival. They had even had to build a few half-timbered tents to house everyone. At least this time it was summer and not the start of winter.

As the good citizens of Culpeper watched wagon after wagon of men and guns head out the Redmond Stables for three solid days, they understood that General Charles Redmond was taking no further chances with his home or family. No one blamed him for it; for all the man knew, it could be his house in flames next.

Mr. Pinkerton had also set forth a new set of rules and regulations for the safety and well-being of the Redmond household which were taking a great deal of getting used to. Anyone who entered the house for any reason had to come through the front door and be checked in by an agent whose entire purpose it seemed was to stand in the front hall. Having men just standing in the hallways and near entrances and exits was more than a little unnerving for Rebecca, but Charlie seemed to take it in stride.

Day workers were no longer allowed in the house under any

circumstances unless accompanied by an agent, and then they were to be escorted the entire time they were in the house. Mr. Pinkerton pointed out that the barn fire was probably started by someone who had held back and hidden in the barn and that if they did not want the same thing to happen to their home they would have to stop being so damn trusting.

One armed man was placed on foot to cover a two acre area. Another on horseback rode a five acre circuit, checking in with the men out on foot. Another team of three men rode the fence line. A guard house had been built at the end of the carriageway and anyone coming up the main road would be stopped well before they got to the house. Charlie was also having heavy gates and a significant length of fencing installed in the same spot, but the brick pillars that would support them would take some time to build.

Pinkerton also had some very harsh words with Charlie about his habit of riding the grounds at all hours of the day and night. "General Redmond, you must stop riding around the property. We cannot protect you when you are out there on your own. And you might be mistaken at night for an unauthorized visitor. I would hate to have you become the victim of friendly fire."

Redmond Stables was quickly becoming as secure as a military post.

~

Monday, June 17, 1867

"I am going to take you through General Charlie's morning schedule so you will have some idea of your daily tasks and responsibilities. Freddy, your routine with Master Darby will be different. I am more interested in you just getting an idea of what it will be like to work for gentlemen of Redmond's caliber."

Both young men nodded.

"The general and Miss Rebecca are usually up by about five thirty, six in the morning at the latest. You need to be well up by then, dressed, breakfast in you and ready when you hear the first bell. That will be Miss Rebecca calling for Lizbet. Once that happens, General Charlie will go to his office."

Tomas led the men into the room in question.

"You should already have the fire going if needed, and his coffee tray and morning paper on his desk. He will come down in his robe and sit here and have his first cup of coffee and read his paper. Then he will sort his schedule and commitments for the day."

"After Miss Rebecca is done with her morning ritual, it will be time to get the general started on his. The good news is he does not usually bathe in the mornings, preferring to do that in the evening. However, he will still want a shave in the morning."

Tomas turned serious eyes on Louis. "He does not have much of a beard, but it is still important to do a good, thorough job. He also has small scars just under his left ear and lower lip, and if you hit them wrong with the razor, you will cut him. Miss Rebecca does not like to see him bleeding at the breakfast table and that will be entirely your fault, so please take extreme care while shaving him."

Louis nodded his understanding.

"After his shave, it will be time to pull his clothes for the day. Normally, a valet handles all the clothes and assists with the actual dressing, but the general prefers that you lay his suit and shirt out on the bed and then allow him to get dressed on his own. He is badly scarred from the war and sensitive about it. Just step into the washroom and clean up the shaving kit. If he needs you, he will call."

"Once he is dressed, he will go back to his office and gather his notebook and any other incidentals he needs. He will leave them laying on the corner of his desk and you will fetch them and take them downstairs, where you will place them on the bench by the front door where General Charlie hangs his hat. He will be off to breakfast with Miss Rebecca and the family by then. While he is eating, you must make sure that the stable boy has whatever coach or carriage he is using up front and ready to go. He may want Jack, but he will tell you if he does."

Freddy gestured toward his surroundings. "So now we is jus' fancy slaves? House niggers?"

Tomas stood up straight and eyed the boy. "If you want better than that, you can have it here. General and Mrs. Redmond will take good care of you if you take good care of them. They do not see us as slaves. We are staff, paid servants. We are paid a fair wage and they take care of more than our basic needs. General Redmond has personally put a coin in your hand every payday, correct?"

Freddy nodded.

Tomas continued, "Boy, someone with a slave owning mentality would have left you to your bed of shit and cold baths. Now, you have to get over the mindset of being a slave. This is a good job and if you do it well, you will always have a place here. Stop thinking like a slave."

"I was born a slave…" He shot back defiantly.

"Those days are over and now we must make our own way. You can scuffle and scrabble, stealing scraps when you think no one is looking, or you can choose to do better. This is your opportunity. Do not waste it. You will never get another one like this. Master Darby is only eleven years old. Do you realize that you could have a good job with a good, kind family your entire life?"

"If I ain't a slave, why is he still Master Darby?"

Tomas sighed; he had a lot to teach this boy. "He is only Master Darby because he is a young man from a wealthy family and that is what they are called until they get old enough to be called Mister. It is only a title, like General Charlie."

Tomas moved them back to the bedroom and pulled open the doors to Charlie's wardrobe. It was perfectly neat and orderly. His suits, arranged by weight and color, hung on the left, and his special clothing, including his formal uniform, evening clothes, work clothes and hunting attire, was on the right. At the back of the wardrobe sat his boot rack with about fifteen different pairs of boots in four or five styles.

"Now, being as we work for a retired military man, he expects his boots to shine. Just dusting them off and wiping them down will not be enough. You have to learn to polish his boots properly."

He opened the top drawer of the wardrobe and gestured. "Shirt studs, cufflinks, a few of his pocket watches, the very basics of any gentleman's accessories. You will find them lying around the house on occasion. My best suggestion is pick them up and put them away because if Miss Rebecca finds them she pitches a fit about him making messes. It is just easier to clean up after him."

Rebecca placed the box labeled Charlie's Things in the center of his desk. With a sigh, she considered that from now on she was going to hold his things for ransom. Once he actually missed them, he might want them back. She was not helping his annoying little habits by returning the very things that he left lying around.

As she turned to leave his office, a very unusual laugh caught her attention, drawing her to the boys' room. Last time she had checked, they had been sleeping and should have continued to do so for another hour.

She made her way quietly to their room and peeked through the door. Buddy was standing on the edge of a chair with Feighlí standing patiently next to it while Andy held her collar, keeping her steady. Buddy gave the big dog a few gentle pats and then climbed onto her back, holding her by her scruff in one hand and her ear in the other.

The big dog did not even seem to be phased by her passenger, as Andy carefully led her around the room with Buddy perched majestically on her back. Their little game was going along nicely until Mama commanded Feighlí to sit, which she obediently did, causing Buddy to half fall, half slide from her back.

"Mama!" Both boys quickly gathered themselves and tried to look innocent. Feighlí just sat there panting, looking content and happy.

"What is this?" She gestured between them.

"She is like a pony!" Buddy bounced back and forth.

"No, my little darling, she is not a pony. She is a dog and she is not meant to be ridden."

Mama's chastising probably would have had more impact had Feighlí not moved and scooted herself under the bigger boy's splayed legs, lifting him from the ground as she stood up. Buddy squealed with delight, and Andy looked smug.

She just shook her head. She was quickly losing control over her house with the Pinkerton forces moving in, and now over both her dog and her children. Of course, keeping them locked inside the house was no doubt contributing to their desire to have some sort of fun.

~

Sunday, June 23, 1867

Alex Raeburn had invited his cohorts out to his house after church that day. In part, he simply wanted to keep his little group together and he wanted to hear what was going on out at the Redmond house.

Kirtley, Brooks, and Rainey were sitting on the porch with Raeburn drinking some of Mrs. Allen's best when Armistead and Granville rode up, both looking seriously worried.

Granville dropped off his horse and started talking before he even had tied the animal off. "What the hell have you done to us, Raeburn? There are Pinkerton men all over town. Every bed that can be rented has been, just to put them up. For the past week, men and supplies and arms have come in on the train or come down the road from up north in heavy drays. I cannot move anywhere without running into them."

Armistead had tied his horse off as well, and added to Granville's comments. "I swear, they say they are security guards, but I am not sure if they ain't federals. We know that Redmond is good friends with Unconditional Surrender Grant. What if he got a bunch of federals down here? It ain't safe. It just ain't safe. And I think at this point, it ain't safe to be friends with you, Alex. Everybody knows how much you hate Redmond and most of them believe you were behind the horses and the fire."

Brooks shook his head as the two men joined them on the porch and poured themselves glasses of 'shine. "You think the crowds in town are tough. You should be out on the farm. I can only go certain places on the property. If I try to go someplace I am not supposed to be, one of the guards is right there, not so politely asking where I am going and why. If I want to go up to the big house, I have to have written permission and one of the

Pinkertons by my side all the way. They are setting up line of site guard houses all the way around the property, and I swear, I thought I saw them bringing in a Gatling gun in one of those wagons. I doubt a mouse can come onto the property without somebody noticing."

Rainey looked up, a rather scared look on his face. "I have not been able to get on the property since the fire. I know Nailer is doing work up there – he is rebuilding the barn. But I have not been sent up there. I am sure it is because people know that I am friends with you, Alex."

Alex just smiled. "Gentlemen, they can suspect all they want, but they have to prove it. And they cannot prove anything against me. I did not take any of their horses. I did not start any fires. Well, except for a small one over in Sweetwater. Kirtley, you tore down the fences and took the horses. Rainey, you sold the horses over in the valley and started the barn fire. And you know they are focused on me, not on you, fellows. They got nothing on me, and they are not even looking at you."

Brooks could hear Eddie mumble under his breath, "Yet."

"So we let Redmond spend his money, feed a small army and worry, and we just lay low, go about our normal business, and not let it bother us."

Not convinced, Armistead and Granville just shook their heads.

CHAPTER 6

Monday, June 24, 1867

The Pinkerton forces had been in place for over a week, and the routine of guards, checkpoints, and patrols had begun to be part of their regular days. Kate Warne had settled into the household, in some ways taking the same kind of position in the family as Charlotte had when she first moved in. The exception was that Miz Kate got along with the children really well from the very start, and spent a fair amount of time with them when they were not in classes with John Foxworth. Even Darby found himself spending time with her, as she had some wonderful stories to tell of her various travels and life adventures. Had she not been an outstanding detective and body guard, she would have made a splendid travel writer.

Emily spent more time lurking around her brother when he was wheedling these tales of adventure and places far from the boredom of Redmond Stables from Miz Kate. It was the best alternative, she thought, since she could not go out and dig around the creek bed down by Gaines Run. She had not be able to get really dirty or muddy in days, and she had not been allowed to go look for fossils, rocks, or arrow heads in she did not know how long.

She had tried to talk Papa into letting her go outside, but he would not even to listen to it. In fact, he was mean about it. Papa did not usually get mean. Then she tried to beguile him and to convince him that it was important for her to be able to find new fossils and arrow heads. That just made him cross, and he warned her that if she did not stop pestering him, he would take away her butterscotch cookies.

Rebecca had asked Albert to take over Tarent's role as the barn manager. He agreed, but suggested that they would have to find a new barn manager sooner or later, since he would eventually need to focus on re-stocking their herds, and after that, on finding profitable markets for their horses. Charlie, trying to be helpful, started sitting in on Rebecca's planning meetings with Albert. He was learning a good bit about running a profitable breeding program from them.

Brooks, escorted by one of Pinkerton's men, knocked on Rebecca's office door, and then entered with his hat in his hand when she called, "Come in."

He looked around the room. Charlie was sitting to one side of her desk, looking through one of her stud books. Rebecca was making some entries in a journal. They both looked up at the man standing awkwardly in front of them.

"I hate to bother you, but I could not find Mr. Albert, and…"

"Albert went into town to see about some things for me," Rebecca responded. "You did right to come to me, Brooks."

"Well, ma'am, sir, I was looking at some of the horses hooves and several of them need to have new shoes. Mr. Tarent used to take care of them, but now…"

Rebecca frowned, looking down at her journal for a moment. "I suppose we could ask Mr. Granville to come out. Or we could take the horses in to him."

Brooks looked more uncomfortable. He dropped his head for a moment, clearly thinking hard. Charlie watched him closely. Something was going on here, and he wanted to know what it was.

Finally, Brooks spoke. "Ma'am, if I were you, I would not ask Mr. Granville to come out here. He is not a man you want on your property." Brooks started to go on, but stopped himself.

Charlie looked at him very thoughtfully. He realized right then who had sent him the warning about the children. Before Rebecca could speak, he said, very softly, "Thank you for the warnings, Brooks. We will see to finding someone who can be trusted."

"If you want, sir, I have a friend in Charlottesville who might be willing to come over for a few days and take care of them. He was, um, a unionist and one of the few men who stayed in Charlottesville throughout the war."

"Thank you, but I have a friend in Washington who runs stables and hacks up there and will be able to find me a reliable man – one who our Pinkerton guards will be able to approve."

"That sounds like a good idea, sir, ma'am. Well, I had best be getting back to work."

Rebecca smiled gently at him. "Thank you, Brooks, for everything. You are always welcome to come and let me know if anything is needed." She watched him leave with a thoughtful look on her face. She turned to Charlie and asked, "He is who warned us?"

"I would be willing to bet good money on it, dear. We just need to be careful. And watch Granville as well as Raeburn."

~

Monday, July 22, 1867

It had taken nearly a month to return Redmond Stables to something resembling normal operations. Construction on the new barn was progressing. Finally, Rebecca and Albert had time to plan for the future of the breeding program. They sat together looking over the list of animals they had lost and evaluating the disruption the fire had caused in their carefully developed plans. If they were going to have any hope of recovery, they were going to have to acquire some additional breeding stock, get them moved into Redmond Stables, and have time to evaluate their characteristics in depth.

Rebecca thought seriously about leaving this difficult and complex job to Albert, given that they were not talking about buying a few horses here and a few there, but about making a major series of purchases. "Albert, I think I need to come with you. You know I have the best eye for horse flesh in the family – even better than yours – and this is a critical buying trip."

"Who will take care of things if we are both gone?"

"Charlie has been studying and has the basic skills. With some help from people like Brooks, he should be able to handle whatever comes up."

"If you are sure, there is that major sale up in Pennsylvania Thursday and Friday, and several smaller auctions in Maryland. We could go to those, see what we can pick up, and maybe get a little ahead of things."

"Charlie, what do you think? Can you handle things for a week?"

He thought about Rebecca being gone for that long and started to panic. Between the children and the horses, being without her would be hellish. Not to mention that nighttime would be absolutely miserable. But he smiled and said, "Of course, dear heart. I used to run soldiers around on horses. I think I can handle our little band of troopers and our herd for a few days."

"Thank you, dear. Albert and I will be leaving on Wednesday."

~

Friday, July 26, 1867

Charlie wandered into the kitchen hoping for a fresh pot of coffee. Staying home and taking care of the house and children required copious amounts of coffee. When he got there, he found Sarah leaning against the butcher block, looking worn out and frazzled.

"Coffee is fresh," she mumbled as she looked over a list in front of her.

"Thank you." He retrieved his favorite cup and poured the liquid energy his body craved constantly. "Is there something wrong, Sarah?"

"Well, to be honest, Gen'l Charlie, the extra work and supplies to feed all these people is keeping me busier than a one-armed paper hanger."

He leaned against the counter, drinking his coffee and considering the situation. The arrival of the Pinkerton people had once again given the house and farm the quality of having a small army swarming the place. Keeping everyone housed and fed was a constant battle the cook and the rest of the staff fought valiantly. He looked at his pocket watch and thought carefully, based on what he knew about Sarah's schedule.

"You have already finished the stews and breads for the Pinkerton's people's supper, correct?" A soup or stew was typical of a dinner service as these were foods that could be stretched among large groups of people.

"Yes, sir. I was just getting ready to begin supper for you and the children."

"Not tonight." He shook his head. "You take the night off. Go home; see your husband and children. I will take the children to town for supper. They need to get out as well. Miss Rebecca has kept them cooped up in the house and they are about to go wild."

"Pork chop night at Mrs. Jackson's?" The cook lifted an inquiring brow. Charlie snorted coffee through his nose as the cook walked away laughing, "Thank you, Gen'l C!"

Charlie drove the small carriage into town himself. Given that it was just him, Darby, the girls, and Miss Warne, he decided to keep it as simple as possible. There were more than a few heads turned in the streets of Culpeper when General Redmond drove through it with a woman who was not Mrs. Redmond.

When they arrived in front of the tea room and Charlie smiled as he offered his hand to the pretty young brunette to assist her from the carriage, tongues began wagging. Who was this woman? Where was Rebecca? No one had seen her in days. She had not even attended services on Sunday, although this woman had. Something must be very wrong with her.

After Darby and his father helped the girls out of their transport, Charlie offered his arm to Kate and they strolled into the restaurant looking a lot like a little family to those watching from across the street.

He settled his guest and his family at a large six seat table in the middle of Esther's tearoom and was immediately greeted by her smiling face.

"Why, Charlie, what are you doing here tonight?"

"Giving my overworked staff a break and my children a treat."

"Then you will be happy to know that your favorite is on special tonight. Family style?"

He nodded with a smile. "Please."

The older woman bustled into the kitchen to prepare the dishes for her friends. Charlie got the girls settled with a little deck of cards Mr. Schwarz had sent in one of his sample boxes. It was a game called "Old Maid" and the girls loved it; it had kept them entertained and quiet for hours. Darby had a book in which his nose was firmly planted. Charlie looked into the amused eyes of his adult dinner companion.

"You are a wonderful father, General Redmond."

He smiled as he looked at his little family and ducked his head. "I do hope so. Rebecca is the real hero with them. She is an outstanding mother. I must admit I am a bit befuddled by all of it on an hour to hour basis."

"It cannot be any worse than taking care of our lost boys!" Jocko boomed as he entered from the bar side with a tray laden with three small mugs and two glasses of wine. He carefully set one mug down in front of each child.

"Uncle Jocko's root beer. Make it myself!" He smiled at each of the children, tussling hair as he moved around the table. Charlie sat back and considered it for a moment, but decided to allow this one small mug of the sweet, but slightly alcoholic beverage for each of them. Perhaps it would assist in a less painful bedtime tonight.

Jocko carefully placed the wine glass in front of Miss Warne. "I do hope you enjoy supper, ma'am. If I do say so myself," his chest puffed out proudly, "my wife is one of the best cooks in the county."

"I am sure I will, Mr. Jackson. One cannot help but have a delightful time with such charming company." She smiled at Charlie.

That did not go unnoticed by the small cluster of young ladies who suddenly had felt the need for a cup of tea after watching the general settle his family with this woman.

~

Wednesday, July 31, 1867

Charlie stood on the platform chewing a cigar nearly to oblivion and constantly glancing at his watch. The train was not even due for another fifteen minutes, but he continued to chew the cigar and look at the watch. Then the pacing began.

The general was waiting on his lady to return from the buying trip through Pennsylvania and Maryland. She had been gone a week and he was anxious to have her home. He had missed her more than he had imagined. He decided he did not like it at all when she traveled.

The rest of the house would also be very happy to have Miss Rebecca home. They had seen very quickly that the general was a mess without her. He did not cry like Em, but he most definitely moped and sulked. If he were inclined to such behavior, a puppy would have gotten kicked.

Three minutes late, the train finally pulled in and Charlie moved immediately to the passenger car, straining to try and catch a glimpse of Rebecca through the window. The conductor exited the rear of the car and placed a small stool on the ground before returning to help his passengers disembark.

Charlie resisted the urge to climb up the ladder to the little platform on the car. *Pitiful, Redmond. Absolutely pitiful.*

She was the third passenger off the train. Her husband's eyebrows nearly launched off his head when he saw her left arm in a sling. "Rebecca! Darling!"

She smiled immediately and held up her hand to stop what she could tell was about to become a frantic babble. "I am fine, Charlie."

"What happened?" He stood there, wanting to put his arms around her and kiss her senseless, but afraid he might hurt her further.

She moved closer to him and slipped her right arm around his waist, and leaned up to give him a tender kiss on the lips. "I fell. It was that simple. It was muddy; I slipped, landed wrong and broke my arm. I really am fine."

"When did this happen?"

"The second day of the trip."

"And you stayed there? Where is Albert?" He craned his neck looking for his soon to be dearly departed cousin in law.

"He stayed in Pennsylvania. He was afraid to come home. He wanted me to sort this out first." She gestured to her arm. "He was afraid you would hurt him."

She was only about half teasing. Albert had been terrified that Charlie would thump him for allowing her to fall in the first place, even though he was all the way across the sale yard. And then probably thump him again for allowing her to continue on the trip without at least sending him a wire.

Rebecca continued, "He is arranging transport for our new horses. He will be home next week."

"Do you need to see Elizabeth?" Charlie nodded absently to the porter who placed her luggage on the platform.

"No, darling. The doctor I saw in Philadelphia fixed me up. Though I will be stuck in this thing for several weeks." She could tell by the look on his face that he was flustered and upset. "I promise you I am fine. Take me home, Charlie."

"With pleasure." He raised his hand and Louis pulled the carriage closer to the platform. He jumped down from his seat and quickly and efficiently loaded Rebecca's cases onto the carriage as Charlie helped her to get settled.

He sat next to her and took her right hand, bringing it to his lips. "To think I wanted to take you home and make passionate love to you."

"It is only my arm that is broken." She laughed as she cuddled close to him. "I have been gone nearly a week, my dear. I need your attentions too." She leaned up and kissed his cheek, allowing her lips to linger as she whispered in his ear. "Time to go home and satisfy Mother. Think you can do that, old man?"

He groaned.

~

Thursday, August 1, 1867

Charlie lay very still, holding Rebecca as she slept. Her left arm was draped across his stomach, giving him a chance to touch the tips of her fingers where they protruded from the cast. He felt horrible she had hurt herself, but she seemed to be dealing with it just fine. It certainly did not seem to be slowing her down at all. He had learned very quickly to be careful of her swinging her arm about; she did not realize she had a bat on her limb. After the second solid accidental connection to his head, he made sure to keep an eye on her when she moved it about, especially in bed.

The reactions from the children had been wide and varied. Darby was sympathetic, having spent some time in a sling too, and told his mother if she needed anything, she should call on him right away. Suzanne had been worried it was permanent until Rebecca reassured her that Mama was just fine and the cast would be off in a few weeks. Of course this was not unusual with Suzanne; if Rebecca caught a sniffle, the girl was sure her mama was dying, no doubt a left over emotional scar from losing her birth parents so young.

Em had been concerned that the cast would impede Mama's ability to dig in the dirt, but when Rebecca pointed out that she had no desire to do so to begin with, the injury seemed completely forgotten by their youngest daughter. The boys were both terrified of it and cried every time Mama tried to get near them. It took several hours of her sitting in their room with them before either of them was brave enough to go near her. Finally, close to bedtime, they were calm enough for her to read them a story and tuck them in.

Rebecca's head began to move in the familiar way he knew meant she was slowly coming into wakefulness. He gently stroked her back in a fashion he knew she enjoyed and was rewarded with a closer snuggle and a happy hum.

"Good morning, Mrs. Redmond. I am so happy to have you home." Charlie hugged her tighter. "I actually slept last night for the first time in six days."

She nodded and murmured something he could not quite make out, but he was fairly certain it was, "Me too."

He continued to lie there as the sun began to come through the windows, knowing they should get up and get on with their day, but after having been separated for a week, he could not dredge up an ounce of guilt about staying where he was.

He was about to give in and go back to sleep when she drew a deep breath he knew well. She was about to stretch and then get up. He resisted the urge to whimper and ask her to stay put. Sometimes, just occasionally, he regretted that they could not just do what they wanted when they wanted to do it.

As he lay there, feeling her move away, there was some part of him that was remorseful they could not just be a carefree couple and lounge in bed until it suited them to get up. But the demands of real life had always controlled their actions. Even in the first days of their relationship, before they had really gotten to know each other, he had been wounded and needed time to recover, and before he was as healed as he would ever be, they had a complete and demanding family and a growing business.

He opened his eyes when he felt her lips against his. "Good morning, my dearest husband."

"Good morning again, my dear wife. Sleep well?"

She laughed a little and then sighed as she caressed his face. "Like a well-loved and much missed woman." She gave him another tender kiss. "Shall we go face the day?"

"If we must." He sighed as he stretched his muscles to warm them up before climbing out of bed.

"Is there anything I should know about the past week?" She asked as she slipped on her dressing gown and moved to her table to begin laying out her brush and hairpins in preparation for Lizbet to come do her hair.

"Actually." He rose and fetched his robe. Slipping into it, he took a seat on the settee next to her and leaned forward, his elbows resting on his knees. "We need to talk about the children."

"Who did what?"

He laughed and shook his head. "No dear, they were fine. They were very well behaved, for children who are locked inside the house. Darling, you have got to let them get out and play in the sunshine."

"Charlie, you know…"

"I know I have spent thousands of dollars to keep this family safe and we have a small army on this property that is perfectly capable of watching our children while they go out and play for a few hours."

"I want them to be safe."

"So do I." He took her hand gently in his. "This is why we have hired and maintained a small army. Darling, they are children who need to be out. I caught the boys riding Feighlí three times last week! They nearly got down the steps on her at one point. They are about to start trying to tunnel out through the basement, and you know, between Em's digging skills and Darby's engineering knowledge, they could do it."

She gave him a slightly guilty smile. "I will think about it."

He stood and kissed her on the forehead. "Thank you."

Rebecca settled in at her desk and looked at the stack of mail that lay waiting for her. God love him, Charlie had managed to keep both the farm running and the children alive; anything after that was a complete roll of the dice. She smiled as she placed her left arm on a small pillow on her desk and began a right handed sort of the mail.

It was typical of her personal and professional correspondence. Letters from friends like Amelia Lord or Mary Lee went into one pile. Notices of auctions and private sales that Redmond Stables might be interested in went onto another.

Private queries about which horses might be available went into a third. Advertisements from every equipment and tack dealer, wagon and coach maker, and livestock agent in six states, all of which were Charlie or Albert's fault, went into a fourth. As she sorted through the mess, she found one solitary little blue envelope looking very much out of place.

If there had been anything in Rebecca's life that resembled a normal circumstance, she would have thought it an invitation to tea from one of the ladies in town. But as usual, nothing in her life was normal, and the fact that the only script on the front said *R. Redmond* made her think right away that it was nothing close to typical.

She managed to hold the little envelope down with the back of her fingers and flick the seal with the thumb of her right hand. Pulling the little note card out, she sighed as she began reading.

Charlie made his way up from the stables. Some of the new horses had begun arriving and he had gone down to inspect them as they were brought in and inventoried. He was impressed with the quality of horseflesh his wife and her cousin had managed to acquire in just one trip. It was truly spectacular.

He stopped and poured a cup of coffee before rapping gently on her office door. "Rebecca, darling? Are you busy?"

"No. Not at all, General Redmond." She laughed as she waved him in. "I am merely wading through the flood of mail."

He chuckled and took a seat near her desk. "Anything interesting in the flotsam and jetsam?"

"Actually…" She lifted the little note between the fingers of her right hand. "Now that you mention it, you unfaithful cad! There was this little missive informing me that you have been seen keeping company, in town no less, with another woman during my…" She looked at the note to make sure she had the wording just right. "Unexpected and worrisome absence from Culpeper."

"It sounds like I have murdered you, disposed of the body, and taken in a new woman. All in less than a week. Who knew I was so talented?"

"It does indeed. You have no intention of doing so, do you? You may be keeping your new woman in a life of luxury somewhere just waiting for the chance to slip arsenic into my tea."

He gestured around him. "More luxury than this?" He shook his head. "Any woman who needs more than this is not my type." His brows came together as he lifted his cup to his lips as if he were seriously considering her first question. "No, darling. I just got you trained. I do not have the strength to take on another woman." He laughed as she swatted at him with the note before dropping it into the waste basket.

"Why do they do these things?" Charlie could only shake his head again.

"Because right now, everyone is on the 'make the Redmonds miserable' wagon. They are following Alex's lead in the only way they know how to without actually associating with him and soiling their reputations as ladies of the community. Poor, pitiful creatures." She shook her head. "Unfortunately for them, you and I have a much stronger marriage than they are prepared for."

Charlie just sipped his coffee and let it go. If Rebecca was not worried about it, it was obviously not worth being disturbed over. He did, however, remember something worth worrying about. "Darling, have you by any chance come across a small knife in here? It is about six inches long, bone handle, very sharp. I use it on the back porch, so I leave it in here, but it is not in the normal spot."

She nodded and pulled the knife in question from a cubby on her desk. “This one?”

“That would be it.” He plucked it from her fingers. “Thank you.”

“That is a very nice knife. I was pleased when I came across it. What do you use it for?”

His head wobbled a bit as he tried to explain. “Well, I am an old soldier who has spent so many years with my feet continuously stuck in boot leather that I have developed nasty calluses on each of my big toes. I use this knife to scrape them off when they become painful.”

Her eyes dropped closed as she started to say something and then her mouth snapped shut. She sat there with her eyes closed and a very odd expression on her face. It was clear she was warring with herself on what the next thing out of her mouth should be. Finally, she opened her eyes and looked at him, a slight, disbelieving smile on her face as she said, “You and your nasty knife may go now.”

He knew that look. He and the knife left. He put it on the counter as he dumped the last of his coffee down the drain and dropped the cup into the dishwater. Sarah came in and placed several lamb shanks on the counter as he snatched the blade out of her way.

“Ooo, Gen’l Charlie, does Miz’ Becca know you have her favorite apple peeling knife?”

Katherine Reynolds and Mary Simms were standing by the table at Mr. Cooper’s shop, looking through the rolls of fabric he had laid out. Well, they were pretending to look at the fabric. In reality, they were having a right proper little hen fest. When Rebecca Redmond had been seen in town yesterday wearing a sling with her left arm in a heavy plaster cast, the Culpeper grapevine had gone into a growth frenzy that would have frightened any proper vintner.

"I am sure he must have beaten her. Why, with all of the stress they have been under, horses being stolen, their barn being burned, two men dying, and I have heard that someone threatened their children. The stress must have simply just been too much for that man." Miss Reynolds was feeling entirely unsympathetic to the Redmonds' trials.

"You know, Mrs. Williams said that it would happen."

"Well, we know that Mr. Gaines beat her. I am not surprised that she finally drove that man to it as well."

Ro Jackson was looking through some blankets that Mr. Cooper had on a shelf near the fabric table. She could clearly hear these two talking about her friends. So could the nine-month-old puppy she had beside her.

The puppy was curious and stuck her head around the edge of the shelf to see the people who were talking.

"I hear she wears britches and boots to work in around the farm. Do you think he got angry at having a woman wearing men's clothing? Was she trying to wear the pants in the family? We know she can be awfully bossy." Of the two of them, Mary Simms was the one who was most occupied with being socially correct.

Ro looked down at her own garb. Today it was her usual britches and boots, a calico shirt, a twill vest with lots of pockets for dog treats and such, and a red handkerchief tied around her neck. A beat up old brown slouch hat topped her short cut hair, and she had her usual compliment of pistol and bowie knife buckled around her waist.

She could not resist the opportunity to rattle these ladies' sense of propriety.

She removed her hat as she stepped around the shelf. "Good morning, ladies. I could not help but overhear your conversation and I thought I would provide you with some insight into the situation. First, my friend General Redmond worships the ground his wife walks on. In his eyes, she can do no wrong. He will see her to sainthood himself. He would sooner drink boiling oil than bring harm to her by his own hand or deeds."

Ro's sudden appearance startled both women, especially because of the large creature standing beside her who could, they had heard from a few of the gentlemen in town, be very fierce and aggressive. Her attire did not inspire them to be particularly welcoming either.

Ro went on, not giving them an opportunity to either break in or escape. "Second, as you can see from my clothing, sometimes one simply has to dress to do one's job. Mrs. Redmond works with horses, including the muck that is part of a normal stable. I work with dogs that live in kennels and can create an abundant amount of mess. So if a woman must cope a great deal of shit in her life, dressing for it seems eminently practical to me."

While she was talking, the pup she was accompanied by slowly edged up to Miss Simms and started sniffing at her skirt. After a moment, the pup started nudging at Miss Simms's hand and making little whimpering noises, obviously begging for a pet from the pretty lady who smelled nice.

"Finally, you might not have known that Mrs. Redmond went on a buying trip to acquire new horses to replace those lost to horse thieves and the fire, and had the misfortune to slip and break her arm while she was up in Pennsylvania." Ro smiled sweetly. "Now that you have the facts, I hope you will find it in your hearts to do the Christian thing and make sure you and your friends know the truth before you begin speculating."

Miss Reynolds looked at the woman who had just admonished them so thoroughly and not with kindness in her eyes. Very coldly, she said, "Thank you for your information, Miss, um, Jackson, is it not? The tavern keeper's niece?" She turned and walked away, assuming that Mary Simms would follow her.

But Mary Simms was otherwise occupied. The pup had charmed her, and she was focused on scratching her ears and petting her curly haired head.

Ro was astonished. Normally, her dogs did not voluntarily go up to a stranger and beg for pets, even the puppies. "Miss? I am very surprised. She seems to like you on sight, something that my dogs do not normally do."

Mary Simms looked from the puppy, pointedly ignoring Katherine's frantic waving to get her away from that nasty dog woman. "My name is Mary Simms. Your dog seems to be very sweet. I am surprised that such a big dog could be so gentle."

"Ro Jackson, ma'am." She smiled as she tilted her head slightly. "A pleasure to meet you, I'm sure. I breed these dogs to be faithful companions and defenders. It seems that this pup has chosen you to be her person. If you are interested in taking her, I would love to come by and teach you how to train her. This dog was supposed to go to Dr. Walker, but they did not get along and I have promised her one from the next litter." Ro was as interested in coming by to see more of this obvious dog person as she was in placing another one of her dogs.

"Miss Jackson, I would love to have a dog of my own, especially one so sweet. Perhaps you could come by tomorrow afternoon and we could discuss the possibilities?" Something in her voice suggested that there were more possibilities than just placing another dog.

"It would be my pleasure, ma'am. The pup and I will be there around two?" Miss Simms nodded her agreement. With that, Ro took the blanket she had chosen, fished a few coins out of her pocket, dropped them on the counter, and then she and her dog strolled out of the shop. She was smiling broadly.

Katherine Reynolds came back into the shop. "What do you think you were doing? How could you possibly allow yourself to be seen with that woman?"

"Why, I was simply making arrangements to acquire a guard dog."

CHAPTER 7

Friday, August 2, 1867

Rebecca and Kate Warne were sitting in the back parlor having one more cup of coffee before each of them started their day. Rebecca was enormously grateful that the population of Pinkerton men had slowly been reduced after that huge display of power and force in June that had been part of Mr. Pinkerton's plan to intimidate the local hooligans.

Yes, there was still Pinkerton staff patrolling Redmond Stables, but while the initial staffing had been a major display of force majeure for the first month, the withdrawal had been done very quietly, a few men at a time, so that now there were only about forty people. It was still a large troop of security guards, but not as overwhelming as it had been. Kate served double duty, both as the manager of the sentries and the personal body guard for the children and Rebecca.

"Miss Rebecca, I think that the children can be let outside if we provide them with guards. If Emily is not allowed to go outside and dig in the dirt again, I think she will start climbing the walls and swinging off the chandeliers. Suzanne keeps looking out the window at the stables with the saddest look of longing, and Darby has gone through his new fishing gear every afternoon since General Charlie bought it to replace what was burned in the fire."

Rebecca looked torn. If she let them out they would be much happier, but they would also be at higher risk of something happening to them. On the other hand, they had been cooped up in the house for almost two months – and in the summer time. With the strict security, things had been very quiet. It must have been like a terrible prison sentence for them. "You have been talking with my husband."

Kate could read Rebecca's facial features. She nodded. "Yes, ma'am, I have. One of my best men is a dedicated fisherman and he would very much enjoy taking Darby out on such an excursion. I have several men who are expert horsemen for Suzanne who would be happy to let her go riding. And I will personally take Emily to dig down by the pond. These children need to go outside and get some fresh air."

Rebecca sighed. "Maybe he is planning on putting arsenic in my tea."

"What?" The detective looked startled.

She laughed and offered, "One of the local biddies sent me a note telling me that my husband had been out with another woman while I was out of town. I assume it was you the night you went to town for supper, but I asked him if he was going to poison my tea and take in another woman. His response was straight forward; he said he did not have the strength to train another wife."

Kate nodded with a laugh. "I have seen him at the end of the day after dealing with five children cooped up in this house; he is correct. He does not have the strength."

Rebecca shook her head and chuckled. She knew the detective was right, but it was still somewhat frightening to her. "Well, if you are sure. I know that I would have much happier children and husband if you arrange this."

"I would be happy to do so. If today works out well, perhaps we can get them out more often for the rest of the summer."

"One day at a time, please."

Ro put the finishing touches on the puppy, having given her a good scrub, trimmed her nails, and brushed her wiry coat until it shone.

Now it was time to put the finishing touches on herself. She bathed in tepid water, as it was simply too hot to use anything else on this bright August day. A good scrub with rosemary soap killed the dog odor that was usually part of her presence. Clean underwear was topped with her best white shirt, carefully ironed so it was neat and crisp. Her good black pants went on, and were not tucked into her boots as she usually did. Of course, it made it harder to get to the knives she usually carried in the tops of her boots, but today she was foregoing some of her usual armaments. The only knife she was carrying was the small wrist knife that buckled around her right forearm.

Her vest was one that maintained her Irish tradition, patterned with the soft blues and reds of the tartan of County Galway, her family's traditional home county. Over that, she carefully arranged her shoulder holster so that nothing was rumpled or bunched and the gun would lie under her left arm and not be obvious. She dug in the bottom of her underwear drawer in the wardrobe to find her best black silk scarf, which she carefully knotted around her neck.

She clipped a lead on the puppy's collar, a fine black leather band, and then picked up her hat, which she had brushed and picked earlier that day to make sure there were no dog hairs left in the black felt. After pulling on her coat, she was ready.

She had hitched up the buckboard before she finished brushing the puppy and herself, so she and the pup mounted the bench and they were off to town and the waiting Miss Simms.

Before she reached her final destination, she stopped at Mr. Cooper's shop. She wanted to get a ribbon for the puppy and hoped that no one would be around in the middle of the afternoon to see her.

She was wrong.

There was Uncle Jocko, standing in the middle of the store having a conversation with Mr. Cooper. *Oh, damn*, she thought. *I'm in for it.*

"Well, good afternoon, niece. What brings you out on this lovely day? And all dressed in your finest clothes." He made a show of sniffing the air. "And scrubbed up and brushed down? You goin' a courtin'?" He grinned at her, clearly planning evil harassment.

"I am going to deliver a dog to a new client and I thought I would look like a proper businesswoman rather than an escapee from the kennels." She tried to look as nonchalant as possible.

He laughed heartily. "Ro Jackson, you might look like a proper businessman, but not a businesswoman in your britches and boots. I think you have found a lady in town you want to impress. Good luck with that, girlie. The women in this town are so stuck in their sense of propriety that even letting you come on their front porch is an achievement, let alone court one."

"Well, since I am **not** courting one, but just delivering a dog, it should not matter, now should it, Uncle?" She was getting more than a little annoyed. And she still needed to get her ribbon and be at Miss Simms on time. "Now, if you would let me go about my business?"

"Certainly. And just what that might be, girlie?" He continued to grin at her as he stepped aside.

"I need a ribbon," she muttered. There were only two people in the world that could get away with this kind of harassment--her beloved Da and this jackass, his younger brother.

Mr. Cooper heard the word business and was at her elbow. "What kind of ribbon would you need, Miss Ro?"

"I need about a yard of pearl grey grosgrain, please, Mr. Cooper."

Jocko laughed again. "Making yourself a nice tie there?"

"For the dog, Uncle. For the dog." She closed her eyes and sighed as she shook her head and leaned both hands on the counter. She hoped perhaps if she could not see him, he could not see her.

"Don't remember seeing any fancy ribbons on the dogs you sent the general and Mrs. Redmond." He tormented further.

Ro shot him a dirty look that made him laugh, took her ribbon from Mr. Cooper's hand, dropped a small coin on the counter, and stalked out.

She climbed back into the buckboard and carefully tied the strip of grosgrain around the pup's neck, making a pretty bow. The pearly gray of the ribbon complimented the dog's gray and white coat nicely.

She snapped the reins and together dog and breeder headed down the street toward Miss Simms's. They turned the corner and drove past Mrs. Williams's cottage on the way to the little house that Miss Simms had once shared with her mother, who had passed during the third year of the war. Sitting on the front porch of Mrs. Williams's house, Harold Kirtley and Alex Raeburn watched Ro drive by and laughed at her as she passed. Ro pointedly ignored them.

She pulled up in front of Miss Simms's, tied her horse to the fence, and she and the pup walked up to the front door and knocked. Miss Simms opened the door immediately. "Oh, Miss Jackson. I have been waiting for you. Please, please, come in."

Ro and the pup walked in. Miss Simms had set a lovely tea for the humans and a bowl of water and one of chopped meat for the pup. "Please, sit down. How do you take your tea, Miss Jackson?"

"Ah, just a small splash of milk, if you don't mind, Miss Simms. And please, call me Ro."

"All right, Ro. And you must call me Mary."

"Mary. Hummm. You know, I grew up in Ireland, where every other woman is named Mary or some version of it. Do you have a middle name I could call you? I would like to be able to call you something different than all those other Marys I grew up with."

"Well, I am certainly not an Irish Mary. But you may call me Allison, if you want. It is my middle name."

"Then Allison it shall be. And I will be here off and on for a while to help you train the pup, if you want. Wolfhounds are very intelligent, and they learn quickly, but it will be important to teach her some rules – and to teach her to guard you and your home."

"Oh, my! You will help me train her? That is wonderful."

"It is part of the service I give all the people who buy my dogs."

At that moment, the pup finished her bowl of chopped meat and came over to Miss Simms. She rubbed her head against her knee and then gently lay down over her feet.

Ro laughed. "Well, it is clear I have no need to introduce the two of you. She has chosen you, you know. What are you going to name her?"

"Well, I suspect that "Dog" is not acceptable."

Ro chuckled. "Well, I did once have a friend who had a dog he named Deohgee."

"Deohgee?"

She nodded, a grin biting at her lips. "Say it slowly."

Miss Simms considered and finally the joke made her smile. "Very clever."

"It was, but it was the dumbest animal you had ever seen. Nearly drowned itself in a bowl of water. My dogs do not suffer from that problem. You might consider the Gaelic word for guard, since that is what she is. It is Garda."

~

Sunday, August 4, 1867

Alex chose to escort Mrs. Williams home after church that day. Having her little acolyte, Mary Simms, become friends with that Mick who was selling dogs around the town and defending that man was not something he approved of. He needed to have a discussion with Mrs. Williams about her companions.

"So, ma'am, have you noticed that your friend Miss Simms has been having that woman who sells dogs in her home a couple of times this week?"

"Yes, yes I have, and I must say I am less than happy with Miss Simms's choice in friends, but she assures me that it is just because she decided to get a dog, and that woman has been helping her to train it. You know, ever since her mother died, she has lived alone, and for a young woman to have no one to guard her safety is probably not a very comfortable way for her to live."

"Yes, well, if I were her, I would find someone more reliable than one of that man's Micks to train my dog for me."

"I would have asked either Mr. Granville or Mr. Armistead to help her with the pup, but neither of them has been around for several days. And I am afraid Mr. Rainey or Mr. Kirtley would be inappropriate, as they are both single gentlemen. And I have not seen Mr. Brooks in quite a while."

A very annoyed looked passed over Raeburn's face. His little group of followers had been defecting at a rapid rate as soon as Redmond had put on his little show of force and power. They did not have the stomach to stand up to the evils that he saw invading their world, to stand up for the traditions and the social order that had defined the best of the southern society. They lacked the spine to fight for what were their God-given rights, to keep the niggers in their place, and to keep these damned carpet baggers and scallywags from taking over his rightful place as a leader in this community. *Cowards. Cowards, every one of them,* he thought.

Monday, August 12, 1867

Kate Warne had asked for Charlie and Rebecca to make some time for her this morning. Over the course of the past two months, the Pinkerton forces had slowly and quietly reduced the number of men posted at the Redmond property, being very careful to not make the reduction in forces obvious to the residents of Culpeper. Now she wanted to review the security situation with her employers.

The three of them sat in the back parlor with cups of morning coffee. Charlie and Rebecca looked at Kate expectantly.

"General and Mrs. Redmond, I have asked to chat with you so that you clearly understand the steps we have taken to secure your property and your persons. We have set up rotating schedules so that our men are always monitoring the property perimeter. There are guard shacks within visual range all around the property line, though our men walk patrol between them unless the weather is nasty. We also have a couple of men posted at Redmond Grove around the clock to make sure your staff is guarded. You know the men and I personally watch the house, who comes in and who goes out. We escort the men working on finishing up the barn onto the property in the morning and off the property in the evening, and keep a couple of men on the building site to make sure that none of the workmen go anywhere they are not supposed to go. And of course, we escort the children whenever they leave the house. In other words, we have this property and you as carefully guarded as possible."

They nodded. Rebecca smiled at Kate and said, "You have no idea how grateful I am for it too. It absolutely terrified me when we got that note warning us that the children were at risk."

Kate looked sympathetic as she patted her hand. "I understand. Personally, I have no children, but I can imagine how terrifying it must be to have them threatened. Your children are so very sweet and well behaved. We all adore them and will make sure no harm comes to them."

She turned to look straight at Charlie. "There is, however, one thing that we must be very clear on. Mr. Pinkerton and I have asked you before, and we must now insist. General Redmond, when you ride your so-called circuit at any time of day or night, you not only put yourself at risk, but you put our men at risk. If they have to take the time to figure out of the unexpected rider in the middle of the night is you or an unauthorized intruder, you give the miscreants the time to shoot and kill our men. I must insist, once again, that you stop doing this. Someone may end up on the wrong end of a gun. It could be you, sir. If you persist with this very dangerous behavior, we will have to do the only thing we can – we will be charging you hazard pay for every day that you decide to ride out at unpredictable times of day or night."

Charlie looked at her. He floundered for a moment, declaring, "It is my property, and it is my right to ride whenever I want and wherever I want."

"And it is our job to protect you and yours. If you insist on doing dangerous and frankly stupid, risky things, we have a right to charge you for the additional problems your behavior presents. Thank you for your time." She rose and sedately left the room, with Charlie fuming behind her.

"Darling, she has a point. What if they do not recognize you at some ungodly hour in the middle of the night and think you are an intruder? Our own guards could end up killing you by mistake."

"You too, Rebecca? It is still my property and you and the children are still my first responsibility." He stomped out of the parlor and took himself off to his office to sulk.

~

Friday, September 6, 1867

Charlie lay on his stomach, looking down and waiting. He knew eventually she would come into sight. He only had to be patient. He played with the little pool of stones he had collected before taking his place up in the loft of the new barn.

Finally, he heard footfalls he knew immediately. He took up a position where he could peer over into the barn below, but no one would be able to see him if they looked up. She entered the stall that held Shannon and began giving her beloved mare a good brushing and a treat of fresh apples.

It had been a few days since the cast had come off her arm two weeks early. She had been as patient as possible, but between the itching and continually being a danger to the entire family with what amounted to a thick plaster bat on her arm, she had gone to Elizabeth and demanded she cut it off. She told her doctor friend that if she did not do it, she would go home and find a hammer to accomplish the task. Given that the hammer could result in a re-broken arm, Elizabeth agreed to remove the cast.

He was in a mood to be playful and waited patiently for her to be done, and then he took the first of his little stones and tossed it at her. She did not notice the first one at all as it landed near Shannon's front left hoof, so he tried again. This one hit Rebecca's left shoulder and bounced off.

"What the…" She brushed her shoulder and paid no further attention, continuing her ministrations to Shannon. The mare looked up into the loft and snorted. Jack nodded and stomped back and forth in his stall. He was glad he did not have to resort to such foolishness for Shannon's attentions.

Another pebble fell and then another, this one bouncing off the top of her head.

"What the Devil!" Rebecca felt the top of her head and looked up. Charlie pulled back and tried to stifle a chuckle.

As she began putting away her grooming tools, he tossed a volley of five stones down, a couple of them catching her on the arm and hand.

"All right!" She was sure she caught a glimpse of someone above her. She began climbing the ladder and when she reached the top, Charlie was right there with his finger over his lips. He crooked his finger and she joined him up in the loft. "What…"

He shook his head and placed his finger over her lips and pulled her down on top of him. Then he began kissing her and pulling her blouse from her britches. She moaned and he stopped kissing her, shaking his head again and trying not to laugh when she groaned.

She finally nodded her understanding of his cruel little game and the kissing resumed intensely, as did the quick and efficient removal of her clothes and the placement of her naked, lovely and very willing body in a nicely padded nest of hay and blankets tucked in the back corner where he would have plenty of warning of anyone coming up the ladder.

Charlie shook his head again and swatted her hands when she tried to unbutton his shirt, this time with a truly evil grin as he slid down her body, his hands making sure to caress as much of her warm, bare flesh as humanly possible while his mouth supplied soft, heartfelt kisses all the way down her torso.

Rebecca had to bite her lower lip to keep from crying out when he reached his intended destination and made it clear he was on holiday and going to stay there for quite a while. Her fingers tangled in his hair, scratching his scalp and encouraging him on. She lay back with a huge, satisfied smile on her face.

As she stretched out there, abandoning herself to his insatiable attentions, she heard the door to the barn open and the voices of two or three men filter up to the loft. She had to work hard not to panic, especially when she realized that Charlie had not stopped, but had actually increased his devotions to her. His hands, holding tight to her hips, pulled her closer to him.

Her entire body began to respond to the circumstances, but not exactly in the way she anticipated. One tiny sound, even the smallest of whimpers, could give them away. She could not believe that the thought was actually pushing her higher and higher. She was absolutely sure that the top of her head was going to come off as Charlie and his very talented lips and tongue brought her to the point of no return. Her entire body went completely rigid for what felt like an eternity as her world exploded in uncountable levels of passion and satisfaction as he took her over the edge and brought her safely back again.

Once she could breathe, she literally pulled him up by his ears, bringing his entire weight to rest on top of her. Her arms wrapped tightly around him even as his thigh came to rest where his head had recently been, asserting a bit more satisfying pressure to Rebecca's still quivering body.

"Evil!" She whispered in his ear when she could finally speak. "Simply evil." She panted as she held him close, feeling him laugh into her neck and shoulder.

~

Saturday, September 7, 1867

As it was a particularly warm evening, the respective Saturday night gaming sessions ended about an hour early and all the participants wound up on the boardwalk out in front of Jocko's having a few cool drinks and just enjoying each other's genial company.

Charlie was just about finished with his cigar and preparing to call for Louis and their carriage to take him and Rebecca home when a ruckus from the direction of Mrs. Allen's caught everyone's attention.

Alex Raeburn and a couple of his cronies stumbled down the little front porch and out into the street, where Alex caught sight of the group in front of the inn. While it was clear that he was not in any condition to do so, he immediately went into offensive mode. He straightened up to his full height and began trying to walk down the street.

Richard and Charlie just looked at each other as he continued to stagger toward them. Jocko shook his head as he watched one of Alex's friends try to warn him off, but the man continued down the street.

"Well, looky here! Standing around like he owns the damn place!" Raeburn waved his arm at the gathering. "If it ain't the great Charles Redmond and his band of merry men and their group of bar wenches! What proper man allows his wife to sit and play games for money on a Saturday night? Of course, with the company you keep, I'm surprised that you ain't opened a whore house yet. Then again I guess we should be wondering…"

Charlie, who had turned away and was standing with his back to the man in an attempt to let Richard handle it, whipped around when he heard him mumble something about "at home with the children."

Richard stepped off the porch and met the inebriated man as he approached the tavern. "Mr. Raeburn, you are drunk and I suggest that if you do not want to spend the night in my jail, you go somewhere and sleep it off."

Alex drew a deep breath and looked at Richard with slightly bleary eyes. "Why Mr. Provost, I didn't know you cared! Every time your good buddy threatens or assaults me…"

Charlie stepped down and moved in on the man with his cane raised in his left hand. Jocko was right behind him, tugging on his coat. "Charlie, don't do it, Boy-O. He is not worth it."

Edgar and Rex were in swift pursuit of Charlie and Jocko. They could tell by Charlie's body language that things were about to get very ugly.

"Mr. Raeburn, I have had enough!" The general growled as he took another menacing step forward. "If you do not want to find yourself laid out in the middle of the street, you will listen to your fellows and the provost and go home!"

"And there he goes again!" Alex gestured with a shaky hand. He looked around to see who might be witness and turned to look at a few of the men who had come out of Mrs. Allen's behind him. "You heard that? He threatened to lay me out in the street and what does the provost do? Nothing!"

"All right." Richard growled and took Alex by the arm. "You are right. I do need to do something. I need to take in the drunk who is out looking for trouble. I warned you, Mr. Raeburn."

Rebecca sat at her dressing table, readying for bed while Charlie stood on the veranda smoking a cigar and brooding.

"Are you coming to bed?" She crossed the room and turned down their covers.

"I thought I might ride a circuit first."

She shook her head as she got into bed and adjusted the pillows so she could lean against the headboard. "You know very well that Kate and Mr. Pinkerton do not like it when you do that."

He entered the bedroom and closed the veranda doors behind him. "I know, but that encounter with Raeburn has me on edge." He moved to the bed and kissed her on the forehead. "I will not be long. An hour or so."

She knew there was no sense in arguing with him. He was going to do it regardless. She hoped tonight was not the night that one of the Pinkerton men would mistake him for an intruder and shoot him. "Be careful, Charlie; it is nearly eleven. I am sure the guards are not expecting anyone to be wandering over the property this late.

~

Sunday, September 8, 1867

The pounding on the door woke the entire house, including Little Dickon. Elizabeth growled as she gathered her robe to go tend the baby. "Somebody had better be dead."

Richard jumped up and slid into his trousers, pulling his suspenders over his shoulders. He exited the bedroom and charged down the stairs for the front door before whoever was pounding on it woke the neighbors too.

Pulling the door open, he was facing Sean Cady, who was visibly shaken. "You need to come right now, Colonel Polk."

"Let me get a shirt."

"No, sir." He shook his head. "You ain't got time to get a shirt. You need to come. Now, sir."

Richard grabbed his boots, hat and jacket and followed his deputy down his walk as he jumped into the rest of his clothing. "Sean, what is going on?" He managed to shrug into his jacket by the time they reached the gate.

The young man turned to face his superior. "Alex Raeburn is dead."

"Dead! In our jail?"

"No, sir. We let him out about midnight when he woke up cussin' and spittin'. You said to keep him until he sobered up. He seemed sober enough to us."

Richard shook his head. Having heard his clock chime when he came down the steps, he knew it was now a bit after one.

"And it gets worse." The deputy shook his head.

Richard cocked his head as he moved to the buggy Sean had brought. "How so?"

"We found a pocket watch next to the body we think is General Redmond's."

The men drove quickly to the location, which just happened to be right in the middle of Main Street between the bank and Jocko's. Max Frederick was still there. Richard was thankful it was so late. At least the streets were deserted. He approached the grisly scene. Max handed him a lantern as he knelt down next to the man's body.

Alex Raeburn had indeed been shot, once in the heart and once right between the eyes. He was lying on his back in a massive pool of blood, his arms slightly out from his body and his fingers tangled in a gold watch chain with a fob engraved with the letters CHR.

"What the hell, Charlie?" Richard sighed as he looked at the fob. He absolutely recognized it. It had been a gift from Rebecca the Christmas before last and he had spent three days showing the fob, watch and the matching pocket knife to anyone who would look at it.

Elizabeth had finally gotten Dickon settled back down after the mayhem that Sean's banging on the door had created when Max Frederick appeared on the front step. This time he knocked politely rather than banged. "Dr. Elizabeth, Colonel Polk asked me to ask you to join him at the murder site."

"Murder? Who was murdered?"

"Alex Raeburn, ma'am. Someone shot him. Got him in the chest and between the eyes."

Elizabeth's head sank down until her chin was resting on her chest. "All right. Give me a few minutes to become halfway decent."

She rushed upstairs, threw on the first dress that came to hand and pulled on a pair of soft shoes. She roused their housekeeper, Ruth, and let her know that both she and Colonel Richard had been called out on an emergency, so she should listen for the baby.

With all domestic issues in hand, she joined Max in the hall. "Let us go see how bad the damage is." Max handed Elizabeth up into the trap he had brought around to collect her and together they headed up the street. They were at the murder site in a matter of minutes.

Elizabeth climbed down and carefully walked all around the body lying in the middle of the street. Alex was lying on his back, his arms slightly splayed out on either side of his body. There was a huge blood stain in the middle of his chest and a smaller one between his eyes. His face showed signs of powder burn; whoever had shot him had held the gun at point blank for what Elizabeth was sure was the second shot because of the angle of the exit wound. Most of the top rear of Raeburn's skull was blown off and there were bits of bone and brain as well as blood and scalp scattered in a halo above his head. She carefully searched in the dirt above his head, retrieving a single deformed slug from the sand.

She handed it to Richard, who looked at it, and mumbled, "44 caliber. There are more Colt 44s around than there are men in this town."

Very carefully, she knelt beside the body, checking the condition of his skin, his eyelids, and the muscles in his neck. The immediate pallor of death had passed, which meant to her that he had been dead for at least a half hour, but rigor mortis had yet to begin setting into even the smallest muscles, meaning he had not been dead for more than an hour and a half.

Based strictly on the condition of the body, death had occurred sometime in the past hour. The cause of death was obvious. The first shot had been to his heart, and he had been standing when it hit him. Given that he had grabbed the shooter's watch chain, it was close, but not so close as to leave extensive powder burns on his shirt. The second shot had been delivered when the man was lying in the street, aimed straight down at point blank range in between his eyes. It looked as if the first shot had not fully penetrated his heart, and she suspected he was still alive when the second shot was fired.

She looked up at Richard, who nodded at the watch. She carefully removed it from the dead man's hand, recognizing it at once.

Under her breath, she mumbled, "Oh, my God, Charlie. What have you done?"

CHAPTER 8

Sunday, September 8, 1867

Richard, Sean, and Max went out to carefully search the street as soon as there was enough light to be able to see clearly. They wanted to get out and get a good look at the murder site before people started trooping into town on their way to one of the several churches. They roped off both ends of the block first thing that morning.

As the sun rose high enough to light the area, the three men walked slowly down the street. Richard was in the middle; Sean and Max each took one side. They were looking for anything that would help them reconstruct the events of the previous night.

As they moved down the street, they noticed several hoof prints with the distinctive mark of Redmond Stables. Some were clear, others partially obscured by wheel tracks. There were many other hoof prints and a number of different shoe prints crisscrossing the street, tracking over one another. Near where they had found the body was no different – multiple tracks from horses, wagons and carriages, shoes. But there was nothing significant. No bullet casings, no cards, nothing that could specifically be linked to any individual. They also tried to find the slug that had gone through Raeburn's chest, but had no luck there either. It could be anywhere.

~

Edgar was keenly aware that something was very, very wrong in Culpeper on this particular Sunday morning. Even as he, Rex, and Charlotte prepared for services, the lack of traffic to the church was startling.

Once it was time for the actual service to begin, there was panic on Charlotte's face when the Redmond pew remained empty for the first time she could ever remember. Edgar and Rex surveyed the crowd, noting that Richard, Elizabeth, Raeburn and several of his compatriots were missing as well. All three of them had the feeling things had just gone from bad to worse in Culpeper.

Rex did not stay for the sermon; he immediately returned to the manse and gave the order to the stable boy to get the carriage ready. He knew as soon as they could, the trio would be on their way to Redmond Stables.

~

Richard stood on the portico looking at the front door. Behind him, Max and Sean sat atop their horses and waited patiently for him to perform his lawful duty. They knew exactly how hard this had to be for the normally gentle man.

The provost looked at his watch as he heard the carriage

pulling around to the front of the house. He groaned; of course the entire family would be on their way to Church. Could his life get any more miserable?

The door opened and he was face to face with Rebecca, who was surrounded by the three oldest children. Miserable was going to be a deep, dank pit this morning.

"Richard? What are you doing here so early?"

"I need to speak with Charlie." His tone was formal and a bit strained.

"Of course, he will be right out. What is wrong?"

"Perhaps it would be best if the children…" He gently nodded.

She could tell something was very wrong, so without hesitation she sent the children off with Tess to the schoolroom to wait. "All right, what has happened?"

He shook his head. "I really need to speak with Charlie."

"Well then, come in." As Richard stepped inside, Charlie entered the hall from the rear parlor.

"Richard? Good morning! What…"

He interrupted, "Charlie, we have a problem. A big problem."

"Which is?"

"Alex Raeburn is dead."

"I thought you said there was a problem." His brow quirked. "Was it lead poisoning?"

Richard groaned. "Charlie, just stop talking."

Kate slipped into the hall, listening very intently. She, better than anyone else in the house, knew what the look on Richard's face implied.

Charlie chuckled, very confused by his friend's reaction to the joke. "What? Richard, what is going on?"

"Charlie, please, you have to understand. There are a lot of people out there who are really, really angry. I am doing this as much to protect you as I am to be doing my job." With a huge sigh, the provost removed a pair wrist shackles from his pocket. "I am taking you into custody."

The general looked stunned. "What? Richard, have you lost your mind?"

"No, Charlie. I found your pocket watch near the body."

"Not possible."

"The gold one Rebecca gave you for Christmas. It was on the ground next to Raeburn's body. I have to take you in, Charlie. We need to go. Now."

Richard's eye flashed a silent warning Charlie knew well. "Can you give me a minute to say goodbye?"

"A minute is about all I can give you. I am scared that if we do not move quickly, you may find yourself looking in the face of a lynch mob."

Charlie took a deep breath and then turned to Rebecca, taking her in his arms. "Telegram Jerome and tell him what happened. He will find us the help we need." He kissed her. Then he extended his wrists to Richard.

She sobbed. "Richard, keep him safe. Please, keep him safe!"

Richard drove the buggy with Charlie shackled beside him. Max and Sean rode on either side. The provost had been right. As they drew near the edge of Culpeper, there was a large group of men, some riding, others walking, all headed toward Redmond Stables.

As they drew near, Richard pulled the buggy to a halt and stood up. Sean and Max both drew their shotguns from their saddle holsters. Richard had been afraid they would have to confront something like this and told them to come well-armed.

In his best field commander voice, he addressed the mob. "Gentlemen, what is the reason for this? As you can see, I have already placed Charles Redmond in custody. We will conduct this according to the law. And I WILL NOT TOLLERATE A LYNCH MOB IN THIS TOWN. GO HOME. HAVE FAITH IN THE LAW. JUSTICE WILL BE DONE, I ASSURE YOU. NOW GO HOME!" Richard's last words were stated so forcefully they echoed off the surrounding buildings.

The four of them sat there, watching as the mob started to break up. Yes, there was some grumbling, but facing two men with double barrel shot guns and breaking the law when it was clear the provost was doing what he was supposed to do was not something most of them had the courage to do.

When the crowd had dispersed enough for the buggy and horses to get through, Richard moved on to the county jail. "Charlie, you saw them. If you are to have a hope in hell of surviving this, I have to go by the book, chapter and verse. Otherwise, that mob will be back, baying for your blood."

Rebecca was in Charlie's office, frantically going through his address book and business card file. She had to get telegrams to Jerome Lord and General Grant immediately. She would need their help and support. She had already ordered a trap brought around and it was waiting for her in front of the house. As she collected the things she would need, Kate Warne entered Charlie's office.

"I am ready to go into town with you whenever you are ready, Rebecca."

She looked up from the desk a slightly confused look on her face. "What?"

"There is absolutely no way that you will be going into town alone, but I understand why you must do so. My men and I are ready to escort you when you are ready to go. We will be waiting out front for you."

Rebecca nodded absent mindedly as the detective turned to leave. A few minutes later, she had Charlie's notebook and several of his Washington contacts. She decided to start with Jerome and Generals Grant and Sheridan. If there were three men in the world who could help Charlie, it was them.

Thirty minutes later, Rebecca was pounding on the door of the telegraph operator's home. As it was Sunday, the office was closed, but she was determined that she would get the needed telegrams out today.

George Randall was surprised to not only see Rebecca but another woman and a half dozen well-armed men, looking prepared and serious. "Yes, Mrs. Redmond?"

"I am very sorry to disturb you on a Sunday morning, but I must send some telegrams to Washington immediately. It is an emergency."

"Well, yes, ma'am. Let me get my keys." There was no way the rattled man was going to refuse the panicked woman, especially since her friends were so well armed.

Ten minutes later Rebecca handed him a message that made him flinch.

Urgent. Stop.

Charlie arrested for murder. Stop

Require immediate assistance. Stop.

Rebecca Redmond.

After receiving the confirmation from Jerome that he would be on his way to Culpeper as soon as possible, she then tried to make her way to the jail. She was horrified to see the building surrounded, ten deep. People were everywhere--men, women and even some children. Some of them held firearms, some of then carried ropes and they were all shouting for one thing, Charlie's blood.

Cady and Frederick stood outside, both armed with shotguns as they protected the entrance to the jail. People continued to push forward, and even though they were vastly outnumbered, they stood their ground heroically.

Kate put her hand on Rebecca's arm. "There is absolutely no way we are going to try and get through that mob. We will all be killed."

She gestured to her men and before Rebecca knew what was happening, she and her escorts were headed back to the farm and away from Charlie.

"I need to see him!" She demanded even as Kate drove the buggy away from the jail.

"And you will. Just not at this very moment. Mrs. Redmond, that is a hanging party back there. If we try to get through it, we risk them trying to hang us as well. When we get back to the farm I will send a couple of men to get a report from Colonel Polk. Right now the safest place for you is the farm, and that is where I am taking you."

Monday, September 9, 1867

The afternoon before, Edgar, Charlotte, and Rex had circumvented the mob that was gathering around the jail and had taken back streets and roads to get to the farm. Even though it was unusual for a woman in the late stages of pregnancy to go on social calls, they knew that Rebecca was going to need all of the support she could get and Charlotte was determined to be by her side for the duration. This was going to be a trial, not just for Charlie, but for the entire Redmond family.

They were surprised when they got there, and Rebecca, along with Kate and a small contingent of armed guards were not. Rebecca, never being one to dally, especially in an emergency, had taken the firsts steps she needed to make sure Charlie had the defense he would need to survive the accusations that were being leveled against him. She kept George Randall and the telegraph wires very busy that day. So they were waiting for her when she arrived home later that day.

Seeing them, she collapsed into their arms, sobbing and shaking her head, still unable to absorb all that had happened in those few dreadful moments after Richard had told them Alex Raeburn was dead.

Uncle Edgar took on the unenviable task of explaining to the children why their father had gone away so very suddenly. For the time being, he told them that Papa had to help Uncle Richard and would be gone for a few days. After that, they would figure out what was next. Dinner that night was a very somber affair, much like Thanksgiving and their visit from Aunt Victoria. As Darby contemplated the situation, he once again knew something was not right, but it was clear that he needed to play along. For the sake of his brothers and sisters, he did so.

Kate put the security guards on high alert and scheduled a meeting with all of the Pinkerton staff for first thing the following morning.

As dawn was breaking, Kate walked into the large room in the carriage house that housed Charlie's collection of carriages and coaches. All of her staff were gathered, some just coming off their shift, others just getting ready to go on duty.

"General Redmond has been taken into custody for the murder of a local man named Alex Raeburn. We have all gotten to know him in these past months. I truly do not believe he did it, but there are too many people in this town who would love to see him lynched as a scallywag on general principle. We have a duty and a responsibility to protect his family while they go through what I am sure will be a terrible time. We also have an obligation to do what we can to provide the law enforcement officers with the most complete information we can. So I am asking you to go through your notes for Saturday night and Sunday morning, making sure you have noted absolutely everything you remember – times, places – everything. And yes, I know General Charlie made one of his damned circuit rides that night; if you saw him, note it, note the exact time if you can, note the place – everything!"

"There is a mob in town who wants to do without a trial and just lynch him. If you want to keep an eye on the jail during your off hours, feel free to do so. If you want to add to the defenses here at the house, that will also be welcome. His wife and children are scared senseless as you can well imagine, so any extra attentions you can give the children to keep them occupied will be most welcome."

The men in the room looked around at one another, then as one they stood, and saluted. "Whatever is needed." "I know he could not do it." "We will take care of this family." And other similar statements were chorused.

Kate looked at them and smiled. "Thank you, gentlemen. Let us do the best we can."

Richard was in his office by seven that morning. He carefully prepared several telegrams. The first was to Major General John M. Schofield, commander of Military District Number One, and to Governor Francis H. Pierpont, who was nominally in charge of the civilian government in Virginia. His carefully crafted messages conveyed the problem and requested the assignment of a special prosecutor as quickly as possible. The second was a more detailed message to Generals Grant and Sheridan, whose help Charlie was surely going to require.

He was waiting at the door of the telegraph office when the operator arrived and did not leave until he had watched his missives being transmitted. As he walked the block back to the jail, Horace Frazier caught up with him.

"Jesus Christ, Richard. What are we going to do? These people are angry and if we do not do something quickly, they will riot."

"I have already asked Richmond for a special prosecutor to be assigned as quickly as possible. I could suggest that you convene an inquest, so people see the legal process is already at work. You only need to call me, Sean, Max and Elizabeth to declare Raeburn's death a murder. And there is nothing in an inquest that even begins to suggest who did it."

"All right," he agreed. "I can do that. As Justice of the Peace as well as Mayor, I can hold a civilian inquest, but a response from your people in Richmond will be crucial."

Richard nodded. "I agree. By the way, can you find a few more men who are reliable and are not biased against General Redmond to help guard the jail? We are going to need them. I am afraid that some of the good citizens are set on a premature lynching. "

"I will see what I can do."

The two men parted, each with their work cut out for them.

Richard made his way through the small crowd of people milling around the court house square, and around the corner to the jail.

"Good morning, Charlie."

Max looked at his chief, and at the prisoner, then scooted out of the jail, mumbling something about getting breakfast.

Charlie was perched on the edge of the narrow cot in the cell, staring at his clenched hands. Ironically, it was the same cell that Raeburn had been in to sleep off his drunk on Saturday night. It was hard to tell if he was praying or if he was trying to keep himself from hitting on something.

He looked up, slightly wild eyed. "What the hell is good about it? I am sitting in a jail cell, suspected of the murder of a man everyone in town knows I hated, and, damn it to hell, I did not kill him! Oh, yes, I wanted to a couple of times. I readily admit that. Like when he assaulted my wife. And we both know he stole my people's payroll and sent it to Devil Forrest. I am pretty sure he burned down my barn or at least had it done, and murdered Tarent and Rollins, but can I prove it? No! And yet here I sit, in jail for something **I did not do**!"

He stopped, panting, a look of mixed anger, pain, and overwhelming bewilderment on his face. "What am I supposed to do, Richard? What are **you** supposed to do?"

"Well, for starters, I am going to keep that crowd from turning into a mob and keep them from lynching you on the spot. Then I am going to do my best to figure out who the hell actually killed Raeburn. But I have to tell you, Charlie, he was found with your watch in his hand – the one Rebecca gave you for Christmas with your initials on it. With that and the number of times you threatened him, it is going to be tough. And Charlie? I cannot show you **any** preference. You will get exactly the same treatment any other prisoner would get. I am sorry, but that is how it has to be. For both of us."

"I understand. I really do. Anything seen as preferential treatment and we are both done for."

"Exactly." Richard nodded. "I have to go as soon as Max gets back with your breakfast, such as it is. Expect the inquest to be as soon as possible. Horace has to do something to keep these malcontents under control."

Charlie's hand popped through the bars to his old friend, who took it without thinking twice. "Thank you, Richard."

~

Tuesday, September 10, 1867

Horace Frazier had pulled together a coroner's jury made up from local men he believed he could trust to be neutral. He acted as quickly as possible so the citizens of Culpeper could see that law enforcement and the government, both local and federal, were taking Alex Raeburn's death seriously and taking whatever steps were necessary to see that justice was done promptly.

So, at ten in the morning, Horace, as justice of the peace, convened and sat the jury of twelve local white men. It had been a bit of a task to find men that were truly neutral on the issue. Most of the men he talked to either worked for Charlie on the farm or knew him through the bank, or they had served with Raeburn during the war. He was not surprised that his search had actually reached into the outlying areas where folks had less knowledge of the Redmond-Raeburn Culpeper Conflict of 1867.

He had talked with Richard that morning and was very grateful to find he had received a prompt response from General Schofield informing him that an investigation team and a prosecutor was being assigned from the Judge Advocate General's office and would be arriving in Culpeper within the next few days.

Frazier intended that this hearing be as short and to the point as possible, so he asked that only four people testify – Max

Frederick and Sean Cady as the men who had found the body, Elizabeth Walker as the physician who had examined the body in situ, and Richard Polk as Provost of Culpeper County.

Charlie, his hands shackled in front of him, was escorted into the only court room in the county courthouse. The selected witnesses were present. So was a group of eight off-duty Pinkerton guards, who had volunteered to make sure no one threatened Charlie or his guards as he was taken from the jail to the courtroom.

Horace Frazier took his seat as the supervising official. "This is an inquest into the matter of the death of Alexander Fancher Raeburn, late of Culpeper County, Virginia; Captain of Company C in Forrest's Cavalry Corps of the Army of Tennessee. On or about the evening of Saturday, September 7, 1867 or the early morning of Sunday, September 8, 1867, Alexander Raeburn did meet his death in an untimely manner. The purpose of this inquest is to determine the nature of this death."

Horace turned to the coroner's jury, who he had seated in the hour before he opened the inquest. "I will remind you that the purpose of this inquest is only to determine the cause of death of Mr. Raeburn. Under no circumstances is this hearing to either identify possible suspects or to bring charges if this coroner's jury finds that the cause of death was anything other than a natural death. Any effort to do so will result in an immediate charge of contempt of court and will result in an immediate sentence of five days in jail. Am I understood, gentlemen?"

The twelve men on the Coroner's Jury all nodded assent to the terms laid down by the Mayor, saying, "Aye."

"Then without further discussion, let us call the first witness. Recorder, are you ready?"

The court reporter nodded.

"Will Max Frederick please take the stand?"

Max walked forward and laid his right hand on the bible being held by the bailiff.

"Name, rank and posting?"

"Sergeant Maximilian Frederick, Provost Command, 1st Military District."

"Do you swear to tell the truth, the whole truth, and nothing but the truth so help you God?"

"I do."

"Please be seated."

Mayor Frazier started by asking him to describe the events of the early morning of September $8^{th,}$ 1867.

"I was walking my normal rounds. I had been on the north side of town, and walked down East Street to Mason Street. I crossed over to Main Street, as I usually check in on Mrs. Allen to make sure everything is all right. I turned to walk back north on Main Street when I saw a body lying in the street, halfway between Mason Street and Asher Street. I suspected it was someone who had had too much to drink at Mrs. Allen's and was sleeping it off in the street, but when I got to the body and shown my lantern on the face, I realized it was Alex Raeburn, and that he was much more than just dead drunk." Max took a deep breath. "He was just dead. I blew my whistle for Sean – Master Sergeant Cady – and checked my watch. It was twelve forty-two in the morning. Sean came up a couple of minutes later. We looked at the body and realized there were two wounds; one in the middle of his forehead, one in his chest. I stayed with the body while Sean went for Colonel Polk."

"Did you see anyone else on the street at that time?"

"No, sir. It was quiet. Mrs. Allen usually closes down around midnight, and Mr. Jackson had actually closed a little early. It was hot and sultry for a September night, and a lot of people just wanted to get somewhere cool."

"So what happened then, Sergeant Frederick?"

"I waited for Sergeant Cady and Colonel Polk. Sergeant Cady had gotten the buggy we keep handy at night for emergencies to get Colonel Polk, and I took it back to get Dr. Walker. I had to wait a few minutes for her to get dressed, and then I took her back. She inspected the body. When she was done, Sean and I loaded the body into the back of the buggy and took it to the cold room over by the undertaker's."

"Thank you, Sergeant Frederick. Do you have anything to add?"

"No, sir. To the best of my recollections, that was how it happened."

"Thank you, Sergeant. You are dismissed for the time being, but be aware you may be recalled."

"Yes, sir." Max stood up and returned to the table where he, Sean Cady and Charlie all sat. Mayor Frazier called Cady next.

"State your name, rank and posting, please."

"Master Sergeant Sean Cady, Provost Command, 1st Military District." He was then sworn in.

"I will ask you the same question, Sergeant Cady. Please state the events of the evening of September 7th and the early morning of September 8th, 1867."

"I was walking down West Street on normal rounds, making sure the town was buttoned up for the night when I heard Sergeant Frederick's whistle. I ran over to Main Street and down about four blocks till I found him standing beside the body. I looked at the man's face and immediately identified Alex Raeburn. I had taken him off to the jail to spend a couple of hours sobering up earlier in the evening. He had had a couple too many slugs of moonshine at Mrs. Allen's that night and tried to pick a fight with General Redmond. Colonel Polk asked me to take him over to the jail to sober up a bit, and then send him home to sleep it off. I picked him up at Mr. Jackson's at about nine forty-five. I let him out of jail and sent him home at about ten minutes before midnight. Yet here he was, about an hour later, with a hole in his head. So I sent Sergeant Frederick to fetch Colonel Polk."

"Did you do or see anything while you were waiting for Colonel Polk to arrive?"

"I looked over the body. I noticed that there was a bullet hole between his eyes and a large exit wound from the top back of his head. I also noted that there was a bullet wound in the middle of his chest and a lot of blood. In his left hand, there was a watch chain. Otherwise, he was dressed exactly the same way as he had been when I let him out of jail and sent him home."

Sean shook his head. "He should have done what I told him and gone home. Anyway, Max came back with Colonel Polk and then went to get Dr. Walker. Dr. Walker came up just a few minutes later and inspected the body. Then Max and I took the body over to the cold room."

"Thank you, Sergeant Cady." Sean stepped down as Mayor Frazier called Richard to the stand.

After swearing him in, Mayor Frazier asked the same question again.

"I was awakened by Sergeant Max Frederick pounding on my door at a few minutes before one in the morning. My mantle clock struck one as I was pulling on my boots to go with him. I arrived at the scene at approximately five minutes after one, and confirmed that the body was of Alex Raeburn, and that he had been shot. I found a gold watch chain gripped in his left hand. I immediately sent Sergeant Frederick for Dr. Walker. We assisted Dr. Walker in her examination. I had the body removed to the cold room over by the undertaker's. The watch had been under Raeburn's side, so I took it when we moved him, wrapped it in a clean handkerchief and placed it in the safe at the jail, as I felt it was probably important evidence."

"Thank you, Colonel Polk. Do you have anything to add?"

"Not as testimony, but I would like a moment after the inquest to inform you and the good people in this room of the status of this investigation."

"Thank you, Colonel."

"Dr. Walker? Are you ready to present your testimony?"

"Yes, sir."

She was sworn in and asked to present her information.

"I was summoned by Colonel Polk. He sent Sergeant Frederick and a buggy for me. I left my son Dickon with his nurse, as the whole household had been awakened when Sergeant Frederick first arrived to get Colonel Polk and things were in a bit of an uproar. I dressed quickly and was escorted to the scene by Sergeant Frederick."

Elizabeth stopped and took a sip from the glass of water that was sitting on a small table beside the witness chair. "When I arrived at the scene, I found Alex Raeburn lying on his back, his hands slightly splayed from his body. I examined the body and found two gunshot wounds."

"The first was a shot directly to the center of his sternum. While there was a good bit of blood under the body from this wound, I do not believe it was a killing shot. The killing shot was delivered at point blank range between the victim's eyebrows. There were powder burns around the entry wound. The exit wound was through the rear crown of his head, indicating that the shot was delivered at an angle. There was a halo of blood, brain matter and bone fragments around the top of the victim's head."

"I had the men lift the body and found the exit wound from the shot to the chest. It was slightly off center to the right of his spine, a through and through injury that supported my evaluation that it was not a killing shot. It may have nicked the heart, and I think it nicked the descending aorta, so there was a good bit of blood, but not enough to suggest it was a killing shot."

"In my years as a field surgeon during the war, I had seen a number of wounds like this chest wound, and knew it to have been survivable. The first shot was probably delivered from as few as one to three feet away, and no more than five feet away, as there was a scattering of fine powder burns over a fairly wide area on the victim's shirt. The entry wound was approximately a quarter inch hole; the exit wound on his back approximately an inch around. The impact of the shot was sufficient to knock the victim off his feet."

"The second shot was the killing wound. It was clear that the barrel of the gun had been set against the victim's forehead, directly between his eyebrows. There were powder burns all over the face and a ring of burned skin around the entry wound. As I said, the shot was delivered at an angle, so the bullet emerged from the back edge of the crown of the victim's head – right around the cowlick. The exit wound caused a great deal of damage, with blood, flesh, bone fragments and brain matter haloed around the top of his head. From the angle of the shot, and the pattern of burns from the gun, it was obvious that the second shot had been delivered when the victim was lying on the ground."

"When my examination of the body was complete, I had the two sergeants remove the body for a later, more detailed examination. I also searched the ground and found one spent lead slug. It was rather deformed and was in the dirt at the bottom of a small trench that stretched from the exit point of the head wound to about six inches beyond where the top of the head had been. It was from a .44 caliber gun."

"When I examined the body the next morning, I confirmed that the first shot to the chest was indeed a non-fatal through and through wound, shot from a short distance from the victim so that the impact knocked him off his feet but did not kill him. The fatal wound was indeed the shot to the head, and from the amount of blood loss, the victim was still alive when the second shot was delivered."

"Dr. Walker, could you estimate the time of death, based on the condition of the body?"

"While I cannot provide a specific time of death, I can provide a range of time within which the death occurred. I arrived at the site at one twenty in the morning. At that time, the first indicator after death, pallor mortis, which occurs immediately after death and lasts for approximately twenty-five to thirty minutes, had already passed. The body had not yet started to cool noticeably, an event that normally happens within one and a half to two hours after death in weather such as we had on Saturday night and Sunday morning. I carefully examined the body for any sign of rigor mortis, which normally begins within two hours of death. There were no signs of rigor at all. Nor were there any signs of livor mortis – the pooling of blood in the lower parts of the body, which also normally begins within two hours of death. Therefore I would say that Alex Raeburn died no more than an hour and a half before I arrived, and no less than an hour before I arrived, or between midnight and twelve-thirty, based on the condition of the body."

"Thank you, Dr. Walker. Do you have anything else to add?"

"No. I think that the cause of death is very obvious in this case, and the time of death from my examination is within a reasonable range."

"Dr. Walker, based on the nature of the injuries, is there any way that these gun shots could be accidental or self-inflicted?"

"No, sir. The angles of the shots were such that they had to be delivered by another person. And there was no weapon discovered at the site, a condition I would consider fairly important to a finding of accidental or self-inflicted death."

"Thank you, Dr. Walker."

Mayor Frazier turned to the jury. "Gentlemen, you have heard the evidence of death. I ask you to consider the information and return a finding of one of the following. Was this a natural death, an accidental death, a self-inflicted death or a murder? You may retire to consider your finding."

The men of the jury looked at one another, then their leader stood. "We do not need to retire. We find the death of Alexander Fancher Raeburn to have been murder. Committed by one or more persons."

Mayor Frazier, still focused on maintaining the form of the inquest, looked at each man in turn, asking each, "Do you concur?" They all did.

"Then it is the finding of this coroner's jury in the inquest into the death of Alexander Fancher Raeburn that the cause of death is murder, which this inquest finds to have occurred between the hours of midnight and twelve-thirty on the morning of September 8th, 1867. Gentlemen, your services are greatly appreciated. You are now excused."

Richard stood. "Excuse me, sir."

Mayor Frazier looked a little confused. Then he remembered that he had promised Richard a few minutes at the end of the hearing. "Yes, Colonel Polk. Please, make whatever announcement you need to make."

"Thank you, Mayor Frazier." He turned to the jury members. "I have a telegram from Brigadier General John Schofield, commander of the First Military District." Richard cleared his throat. "This is the message:

"To Colonel Richard Polk, Provost, Culpeper County, First Military District.

"Be advised that this is a capital offense and falls under military jurisdiction. Given your position within the community, I will be sending a team of independent investigators and a prosecutor from the Judge Advocate General's office. Will arrive in Culpeper no later than Thursday, September 12th. Please, provide all support and compliance. Will formulate a tribunal when the prosecutor declares the case ready for trial. Please, assure community that an impartial trial will be held.

By John Schofield, Commander

First Military District"

"As the message says, this case will be investigated by independent investigators, prosecuted by an independent military prosecutor, and resolved as quickly as possible when all of the evidence has been gathered and evaluated. Justice will be served."

With that, Richard signaled Max and Sean to escort Charlie out. The four of them left the little court room, with the Pinkerton men following quietly behind. As they emerged onto the courthouse steps, the crowd that had been waiting broke into yells of "Murderer!" and "Hang him now!" The Pinkerton men moved closer, surrounding Charlie and his escort.

Before Richard could say or do anything, Harold Kirtley stepped in front of them and raised his hands and his voice. "Calm down. They are doing the right things – the legal things. Do NOT take the law into your own hands, like Alex's murderer did. We are better than that! Alex was my best friend – we played together as boys, we fought together as men, and together we were doing what we could to rebuild after the war. If Colonel Polk was trying to protect his friend, I would know and tell you. Let the law work the way it is supposed to."

There was grumbling, and some outright cursing, but the crowd backed off and gave Richard and his deputies the room to take Charlie back to jail. Richard nodded to Kirtley as he passed by, acknowledging his contribution to keeping things as calm as possible.

CHAPTER 9

Tuesday, September 10, 1867

Charlie was reclining against the wall on his cot, tossing cards at his upturned hat. This had become his favorite game. When it was all he had to do for twenty four hours a day because sleeping was not an option, he was getting very good at it too. He and Richard had settled into an uneasy silence, with the provost trying to pretend he did not have his best friend in a cell.

The crowds outside, baying for his blood, had finally started to disperse when word had been spread that an outside investigator was being brought in from Richmond. Even though Richard was taking great pains to go by the book, to make sure it was clear Charlie was getting no special privileges, treatment or benefits, there was a loud vocal crowd that made it clear they did not think Colonel Polk, former second in command to General Charles Redmond, could or would perform an impartial investigation. Generals Grant and Sheridan were doing everything in their power to make sure that an impartial investigator and judge would be dispatched to Culpeper from the Judge Advocate General's office to ease the anxiety of the citizens.

The feud between Redmond and Raeburn was well known and it was really not a surprise to anyone that one of them had ended up dead. The shock to some folks was which one it actually was. They had thought Raeburn would kill Charlie at his first chance. Not the other way round.

Charlie knew through notes sent in by Rebecca that Jerome had been notified and was gathering a team of attorneys and they should be arriving any day. He looked at his pocket watch. It was getting close to supper time, and even though the food provided to the jail was disgusting, at this point he was hungry enough to eat it. He just hoped the bread would not try to crawl across his tray tonight; he did not have the energy to chase it down. This food was as bad or worse than some of the rations he had been expected to serve his men.

He did not bother to look up when he heard the door to the cell open. He just stayed on his cot, knowing Richard or one of the deputies would open the door and put the so called food on the table right inside. He did not want anyone to have a heart attack with fear that he might try an escape.

"Good evening," Rebecca said softly when he did not look up.

He was on his feet immediately, taking her into his arms. "Oh my God! Rebecca!"

He held her tenderly, his hands traveling gently over her slender frame to confirm her actual presence in his nightmare. His lips pressed to her forehead as he murmured her name over and over.

"Charlie." She tried to pat his arm, but her encumbered hands made it nearly impossible. "Darling, please, let me put these things down."

He had not even noticed the basket and satchel she carried. He took them both and set them on the floor at their feet and took her back into his arms drawing her tightly to his chest, running his hands over her back. "What are you doing here?"

"We made a deal." She tilted her head back to Richard, who had relocked the door and sat back down at his desk. "I get to have supper and some private time with you and I stop calling him nasty names in public. Sarah sent a number of your favorites, including a lovely chicken pirleau."

"I do not care about the food. I am just so happy to see you."

"And I am happy to see you, but you are going to eat. Every bite." She began unpacking the basket, placing several dishes that carried the aroma of home to Charlie's nostrils. She made him sit as she began serving the meal to his plate. "Every bite, Charles Redmond. Custer gave his annoying life for this pirleau."

"Yes, dear. Please sit with me. Please?" His voice was nearly begging as his hand caught her wrist.

She settled on the other little stool at the small table, their knees touching as they ate in absolute silence. Rebecca had been told by a couple of the farm hands who had spent some time in Provost Polk's Bed and Breakfast what kind of meals Charlie would be getting, and she was desperate to get some good food into him, but the hostile crowds around the building had forced Richard to order everyone except his staff to remain away from the jail for the first few days.

Even though she had begged him to take the food in, he had refused, stating that he could not be seen giving Charlie any special treatment. It was only when Elizabeth stepped in as his physician and ordered better food for him at least once a day that Richard agreed to let Jocko provide Charlie's meals at

Rebecca's expense. He reasoned the jail should not have to foot the bill for or the extra time expenditures for special food. It was not lost on Charlie that it meant he got to spend a few minutes with Jocko every day and got a bit of the gossip going around town.

"How are the children?" He suspected he already knew the answer.

"Frightened and upset. I am making Darby remain on the farm. There is no need for him to go to school right now. Jeremiah has been wonderful, coming out every day to make sure he is doing all right."

"I agree about school and that is what best friends do; they look out for each other." They both heard Richard shuffle the papers on his desk just a little more than necessary. "Even when it does not seem like it."

"Mr. Pinkerton's people and Ro are making sure the house and the farm are very secure; please do not worry about that."

"I cannot help but worry."

"Jerome and several of his associates will be arriving Thursday."

"Do you know who he is bringing?"

She nodded and removed a telegram from the satchel at her feet. "He is bringing Mr. Blair, Mr. Lincoln, Mr. Waite, and a Mr. Holmes."

"Montgomery Blair?"

"It does not say. Just they are coming and will be here tomorrow."

She removed a small metal jug and poured two cups of hot coffee. He did not even bother to put sugar in it before he picked it up and gulped it down. "Oh, that is so good. All I get from the little place across the way that provides meals is some very weak tea with breakfast and lunch and a warm, flat beer with supper."

"Well, now that things have settled down, Jocko and I will make sure you get at least one good meal every day."

The last treat for Charlie was an enormous piece of Sarah's lemon cake. It was his favorite. As he sat gleefully eating the sweet, the barboy from the pub brought in the meal that he would have been eating. "You can give that to the provost." He grinned as he popped the last piece of cake into his mouth.

"I brought you some things since we have no way of knowing how long you will be here." Rebecca reached once again into the satchel at her feet. "Socks."

She handed him three pairs of heavy wool socks. The boys had also told her how damp and cold the jail could get. She needed to keep him warm and dry; if he got sick there would be no one to care for him and his breathing had never been quite right since the barn fire. She was concerned a simple cold would turn into something far worse.

"A muffler and a sweater. Slippers and your robe. There are also three shirts, two trousers and three sets of your underclothes. A small box of cigars, half your regular brand and half of Rex's special blend. We could not send any Lucifers with them. You will have to ask for a light." She smiled, pulling a small brown bag from the satchel. "And a bag of butterscotch cookies, saved up by Em and Suzanne this week from their lunch and supper."

She looked around at the barren, exposed space with a single cot containing a rough wool blanket and a small, dirty pillow. There was the small table they both sat at and a chamber pot. There was not even a pitcher and basin for washing up. She wanted to cry at the way he was expected to live. "Oh, Charlie, how do you manage?"

"Carefully," he said quietly.

Rebecca shook her head, feeling very helpless. She retrieved two books for him. "Your bible and a selection from Darby."

Charlie looked at the book and smiled. "How appropriate. *The Count of Monte Cristo*."

"He thought you would approve."

"I do," he said with a smile. He took her hand, tenderly kissing her fingers, "I wish, my dear, that we had a more private space."

"Oh, I thought of that too." From the very bottom of the satchel she pulled a heavily folded sheet. She snapped it open and looked at the bars. "Help me, Charlie; you can reach higher than I can."

He stood and took the corner of the sheet preparing to tie it to the top of the bars on one side. Richard stood up and shook his finger. "Now just a minute! I must insist!"

"You said we could have private time, Richard," Rebecca shot back. "Even though you are a dear friend, with you sitting fifteen feet away, it is hardly private. At least this will protect your modesty and we promise to be quiet. Or at least **I** promise to be quiet." She gestured to Charlie. "He really cannot. He has a **very** particular grunt when he is," she paused and smiled broadly, "engaged, that I am sure you will find," she paused again, this time licking her lips, "stimulating. I certainly do."

Charlie nearly choked trying not to laugh. He was feeling much better with Rebecca's company and some good hearty food from Sarah in his stomach.

"Rebecca, I must insist!" The provost protested and took a step forward.

"All right then! Have it your way!" She dropped her end of the sheet and turned to Charlie with an evil grin. She backed him up. Pressing him hard against the wall as she kissed him quite soundly caused him to moan loudly as his hands settled on her hips while their tongues battled back and forth.

"Shhhh...," she teased as she pulled back, her fingertips

caressing the lips she had missed so much. "We have to be quiet or Richard will hear," she practically panted as she began working the buttons on his vest.

Richard stood there, rooted to the spot as he watched Rebecca push Charlie's vest off his shoulders with his suspenders quickly following. He could not believe that she was going to seduce her husband right there in front of him or that he was going to let her do it.

He blinked and shook his head when he saw her pull Charlie's shirt out of his trousers and start working the buttons on the britches with frantic fingers. When the flap was undone to her satisfaction she stuck her hand down the front, using a trick Charlotte had assured her would clear the room if she had the courage to do it. No proper gentleman would stand by to watch. Courage was not something Rebecca Redmond was short on at the moment.

Charlie looked completely poleaxed. He could not believe it was happening either. She groaned sensually as her hand pushed down his trousers. "Hello, Little General, I have missed you."

Richard's disbelief began to diminish when she dropped to her knees in front of Charlie and purred, "Let me get you out of there and at attention so I can say hello properly." That was when Richard decided to make a hasty retreat, slamming the door behind him. If he had been in possession of a white flag, he would have been waving it.

Charlie and Rebecca dissolved into full-fledged laughter as they heard the door lock as well. Quickly securing the sheet to the bars, they took full advantage of their time alone, making the best of a bad situation on the rickety cot. It was not nearly sufficient for either one of them, but at least they were alone for a few minutes and could hold each other. The separation of the last few days had been hell for them both.

Once he had his arms wrapped securely around her and he was equally safe in hers, Charlie immediately fell asleep. Rebecca just lay there holding him close as he slumbered for the first time, she was sure, in days. She knew she was going to have to get a real bed in there, if for no other reason than to make him more comfortable.

When Richard returned two hours later, he carefully pulled the sheet back and found them both sound asleep in each other's arms, having to lie together so tightly that Rebecca's skirts served as a cover for Charlie's legs too. They both looked so tired and worn he could not bring himself to wake them to make her leave. He might pay for it later, but it was a small thing in this grand mess. Quietly, Richard backed out of the room and locked the door securely. He sat down in a chair next to the door and watched the night pass by the window in front of him.

~

Thursday, September 12, 1867

Jerome felt no compunction about spending Charlie's money under the circumstances. He booked a private express train for Thursday morning and he and the group of outstanding attorneys he had assembled to help Charlie left the station promptly at seven in the morning. They arrived in Culpeper shortly before nine and the five counselors went directly to the jail.

Richard, Sean, and Max were having their morning meeting before Sean and Max headed home to catch a little sleep, something they had not had a lot of in the past five days. The arrival of the five attorneys made things in the little jail decidedly crowded.

Jerome started with introductions, both for the benefit of Charlie, who was seeing his defense team for the first time, and for the provosts, who to be honest, he wanted to intimidate into cooperative submission.

"Gentlemen." Jerome nodded to Richard. "Let me introduce General Redmond's attorneys. First of all, I am Jerome Lord, the family's personal attorney. This is Mr. Montgomery Blair, a member of the Virginia, Maryland and Supreme Court bars. He is assisted by Mr. Morrison Waite, a member of the Ohio, Virginia, Maryland and Supreme Court bars. They are accompanied by their clerks, Mr. Robert Todd Lincoln and Mr. Oliver Wendell Holmes. They will be conducting their own investigation, and I ask that you provide them with all of the information you acquire and provide them with access to all individuals associated with this case, including unlimited access to their client."

Jerome turned to the attorneys. "Gentlemen, these are Colonel Richard Polk, provost of this county under the 1st Military District authority, and his assistants."

Richard looked stunned. Standing in front of him were two of the most famous attorneys in the country; men who regularly pled cases before the Supreme Court. And of course he knew Montgomery Blair--he had been one of a group of men who had been trying to negotiate a settlement to the southern insurrection before the final days of battle.

Blair looked around the barren little room, a look of disgust on his face. He turned to the provost and inquired bruskly, "Has General Redmond been charged with any crime?"

"No, sir."

"Has a warrant for his arrest been issued?"

"No, sir."

"Has an arraignment been conducted?"

"No, sir. We have had an inquest and found Alex Raeburn to be the victim of murder, but no further action has been taken. We are waiting for the arrival of the prosecutor and independent investigators from the Judge Advocate General's office."

"Then why, sir, is General Redmond a prisoner? Habeas Corpus was reinstated in Virginia in February so that it applies in all cases where any person may be restrained of his or her liberty in violation of the constitution, or any treaty or law of the United States. General Redmond has no charges against him, but you have restrained him. That is a clear violation of the law, Provost Polk. Please, release General Redmond. Now! I assure you, he is not a flight risk."

Richard gulped and then motioned for the frozen with fear Sean to unlock Charlie's cell.

Charlie tugged on his boots, grabbed his jacket and his personal things, which he threw into the satchel they had come in. As he emerged from the cell, Blair extended his hand. "General Redmond. My team and I look forward to providing you with the best legal advice and support possible. I believe your wife is waiting for you at home. Shall we go?"

The six men stepped outside, where Louis was waiting with the large carriage. "Ah, Louis, good to see you. Did you pick up the gentlemen's bags from the train station?"

The young black man nodded as he smiled. Only General Redmond would be concerned about the treatment of his guests thirty seconds after being released from jail. "Yes, sir, Gen'l Redmond. Good to see you too, sir."

"Then let us go home."

The men climbed into the carriage and Louis snapped the horses into motion.

Richard, Sean, and Max followed them out, watching them drive down the street. Then Richard headed for Mayor Frazier's office. They needed to figure out their next actions.

The attorneys sat quietly in the carriage on the ride back to Redmond Stables, giving Charlie a chance to pull himself together before their arrival at the house. It was clear he had not expected to be released from jail and he was trying to wrap his mind around how quickly it had happened.

The carriage had barely stopped before he was up and jumping out to grab Rebecca into his arms as she came down the steps. He hugged her tight, lifting her from the ground, kissing her cheek and ear as she cried tears of relief into his neck and shoulder, her arms wrapped snuggly around his neck.

Jerome gestured his colleagues onto the porch where Reg and several footmen were ready to collect luggage and show the men to the rooms that had already been prepared for them. "Let us go get settled and give the general and Mrs. Redmond some time. We will have plenty of time to speak with him after he sees his wife and children."

Charlie nodded his appreciation to Jerome as he continued to hold Rebecca close to him. As they turned to go into the house themselves the door burst open again. Darby, Suzanne, and Emily charged onto the porch, all of them grabbing for a spot around Charlie's waist and nearly knocking him over.

He hugged each child and assured them he was well and home for a few days at least. When they all looked panicked, he promised them that it would be all right, even if he had to go away again. Right now, there was something that he and Uncle Richard had to work out. The excuse worked for the girls, who only knew what they were told, but Darby shook his head. He knew exactly what was going on and was not nearly as sure as his papa that everything would be all right.

Jeremiah had told him what was being said around town. He

knew why Charlie had been taken away and that there were a lot of people who wanted his papa dead. He nodded when Charlie palmed his cheek and asked, "Are you all right, son?" He would not worry about all that now. All that mattered was Papa was home. He fell into the tall man and hugged him tight.

Once the children were sure their papa was home and not going anywhere for a while at least, they were content to do as their mother said and join Mr. John in the schoolroom for their lessons. Rebecca turned worried eyes on Charlie. "I love you, darling, but you need a bath. You are a bit ripe." She reached for the pull and rang for Reg.

"I am sure of it." He sighed as he turned for the stairs. "A hot bath is a very good start on a long list of things I need."

Charlie sighed with great delight, his eyes falling closed as Rebecca gently cradled his neck and washed his hair. She knelt next to the big tub, having decided against joining him to allow him a chance to get clean and relax. She smiled when he groaned as she scratched his scalp with her nails causing the soap to gather a nice, rich lather. "I cannot believe that the jail does not even have the basic necessities for keeping clean." She rinsed his hair and pushed the soap from it.

"My dear, it is a jail meant for keeping drunks overnight. Not for long term occupants."

"And if they had kept a damned drunk overnight we would not be having these problems." She slushed another cup of water through his hair.

"Please, do not be so hard on Richard and the boys. They are only doing their jobs. They had no way of knowing someone would kill Alex that night. Hell, the person that killed him may not have known he was going to do it. Raeburn had that effect on people."

Her hands stilled and she moved around to look in his eyes. "Did you do it?"

He maintained eye contact, his head bobbing a bit, understanding why she had to ask the question, and then he shook his head. "No. I promise you. I promise you on the lives of our children I did not kill Alex Raeburn."

~

Thursday, September 12, 1867

Richard strode onto the train platform to meet the 1:15 from Richmond. He had received a telegram an hour before informing him that the prosecutor and investigators were due today. He had made arrangements to house them at Jocko's, since that was the only facility with enough room to provide rooms for all of them in the slowly rebuilding town.

At least they would be well-fed and properly tended to. Esther saw to it that the beds were clean, comfortable, and free of bugs. Jocko was not terribly happy about housing the men he knew were going to go after Charlie, but there were no real alternatives, so he reluctantly agreed.

As the train pulled in, four men jumped down to the platform before it had come to a full stop. Three of them wore the crossed rifles of the Infantry; one had the crossed cannons of Artillery. One wore the eagle of a full colonel, one the silver oak leaf of a lieutenant colonel, and two the silver bars of captains. None of them were faces that were familiar to Richard.

The colonel walked up to Richard. "Colonel Polk?" Richard nodded, and saluted, and when it was returned, he extended his hand. "I am Everett Salton, your prosecutor. My companions are

Trevor Veriton." The lieutenant colonel saluted. "And Jason Bailton and Randall Lightborne." The two captains also saluted.

Richard snapped them a clean salute. "Welcome to Culpeper, gentlemen. I wish it were under better circumstances. Shall we go to your lodgings and get you settled?"

Salton shook his head. "I would rather we get right to it. Lodgings can wait."

"Then get your bags. My office is just a couple of blocks away." Richard led the way. The men walked in silence, waiting until they were in a more private space to talk.

Arriving at the jail, they looked around the small space and Salton immediately decided this would not do. "Is there a space in the courthouse we could use? This is not going to be sufficient to support our needs."

"Certainly, sir. Follow me." Richard took them around the corner to the side entrance to the courthouse, and up one flight of stairs. "This is the room that is normally used for town meetings. I am sure Mayor Frazier will be happy to let you use it for your office for now."

"Thank you, Colonel Polk. May we talk to the men who found the body first? I understand you have had an inquest and determined this was indeed a murder. May I also have the transcripts of that event?"

"Yes, sir, I have them here for you." He pulled a folded pile of pages from his inner coat pocket. "My men will be available later this afternoon. They patrol the town in the evening, and so tend to sleep in the day."

"As soon as possible, I would also like to talk with the examining physician."

"Yes, sir. I will go and get her for you."

"Her?" Salton asked quizzically. "Your physician is a woman?"

"Yes, sir. During the war, she was assigned to General Sheridan as a field surgeon."

"Oh, yes. You must be talking about Elizabeth Walker. Her reputation precedes her."

"Yes, sir. I am proud to say she is now my wife."

"You are indeed a brave man, Colonel Polk."

Richard left them reading the inquest transcript while he went to fetch Elizabeth.

"So, husband, who are they? She asked as she settled into the buggy next to him.

"Officers I have never met – artillery and infantry men, brusque, to the point, and I think wanting to get it done and over with."

"Will they be fair?"

"I think so. I would certainly hope so. They are all out of the Judge Advocate General's office and are professionals."

"We shall see."

Elizabeth entered the room carrying her notes from her examination of Raeburn's body. All four men stood and saluted her.

Salton stepped forward to offer her a chair at the table. "Dr. Polk."

"Sir, my name is Dr. Walker. While I am married to Colonel Polk, in my career, I was and still am Dr. Elizabeth Walker."

Salton looked a little startled, but carried it off with as much grace as he could. "Of course, Dr. Walker, excuse me. Will you please sit and join us? We have questions, as I am sure you expected."

With the grace of a battleship sailing on the high seas, or as much as Elizabeth's slight frame would accommodate, she settled herself at the head of the work table. "Gentlemen, what would you like to know?"

"Could you give us the details in the cause of death, and your basis for estimating the time of death on the issue concerning one Alexander Fancher Raeburn?"

"Certainly." She cleared her throat, and opened her notes. "I arrived at the scene at approximately one twenty in the morning. The victim was lying on his back, his hands slightly splayed away from his sides. There were two obvious wounds--one to his chest, the other to his head. There were two pools of blood--one under his torso, the other above his head. I examined the body for signs of pallor mortis, but enough time had passed so it had dispersed. Therefore, the victim had been dead for more than thirty minutes. I examined the body for any sign of rigor mortis, especially around the face and neck, but rigor had not begun to set in at all; therefore, given the temperature at the time, the man had been dead for less than two hours. I estimated the time of death to be between midnight and 12:30 in the morning."

"Upon closer examination later in the morning, I confirmed the following findings. The first shot was delivered from a short distance, because there was a dispersed pattern of powder burns, none of which was intense, across the surface of his shirt. The shot to his chest entered the body dead center in the middle of his sternum, travelled a level path through the body and emerged from his back approximately one inch to the right of his spine, at an angle of approximately 10 degrees off direct shot from center to right. I measured this by inserting a straw through the entry wound to the exit point and measuring the angle of the shot. While the shot nicked the descending aorta, it was a messy but not a killing shot, made while the man was standing upright. The angle of the shot would indicate that the shooter was right handed."

"The second shot was delivered directly to the center of the forehead between the eyebrows. The shot was point blank; there was a burn around the entry wound that corresponded to the muzzle of a .44 caliber pistol. There were extensive powder burns over the face. The shot was administered while the victim was lying on his back on the ground, based on the amount of blood under the torso from the chest wound. The shot was fired at an angle of approximately twenty degrees off of directly down, as the exit wound was from the rear crown of the victims head, at approximately the point of the victim's cowlick. The exit wound was extremely destructive, blowing brain matter, blood and bone into a halo around the top of his head in a roughly three inch area. I recovered the bullet from this wound buried in a trench from the center of the exit wound into the dirt above his head about six inches from the top of the skull. It was a lead bullet, somewhat deformed by the impacts of the shot, from a .44 caliber pistol. This second shot was obviously the killing shot. Based on my experience of chest wounds of similar impact from the war, I would suggest that the victim was knocked down from the first bullet impact, but was still conscious when the killing shot was delivered."

"Dr. Walker, did you find anything else at the site of the murder that would provide insight into the possible perpetrator?"

"The victim was clutching a gold watch chain with a fob in his right hand. The watch itself was under the victim's side. Colonel Polk removed the watch as evidence when I gave permission to move the body."

"Did you recognize the watch?"

"It resembled a watch that General Charles Redmond received from his wife last Christmas; part of a set that included a matching fob and pen knife."

"Did you find the fob or the pen knife?"

"The fob was attached to the watch chain; the pen knife was

not found or available to be entered into evidence when I went through the victim's pockets."

"Did you find anything else in the victim's pockets?"

"A few small coins, such as a man would have after an evening at the local tavern."

"Had the victim been drinking?"

"Yes, and based on the aroma, rather heavily."

"Thank you, Dr. Walker. Your analysis was very concise and thorough."

The men stood. Elizabeth understood she was being excused. "If you have any further questions, I would be glad to answer them." With that, she sailed out of the room, her head high. Showing a presence of confidence and professionalism was critical if Charlie was to have a hope of surviving this.

The men returned to the table and invited Richard to tell them everything he could remember of the night Alex Raeburn died.

He did. At length. In detail. Repeating his story several times as the investigators took abundant notes on who, what, when, and where. Then they verified them. And did so again.

By 5:00, Richard was exhausted. When the deputy provosts came on duty at 4:00, he asked Max and Sean to come in at 8:00 the next morning so they could go through the same interrogation process.

"Gentlemen, may I walk you to your lodgings? My wife usually serves dinner at six and she is less than happy if I am late without a good reason."

"Certainly, Colonel. I am sorry we are moving so quickly, but General Schofield asked that we handle this situation as quickly and efficiently as possible." They gathered their personal items, locking their notes in a case they had brought with them, and exited the room. "Can we also lock the door?"

Richard dug into his pocket and handed them a key. "Yes,

gentlemen. The only other person who can get in is our mayor, Horace Frazier. I will introduce him in the morning."

"Thank you. Shall we go?"

The provost escorted them over to Jocko's. The tavern owner was conspicuously absent; Esther met them, took them up to their rooms, and saw to it that their supper was served.

Salton looked at his investigators. "So tomorrow we figure out who wanted Alex Raeburn dead."

The other three men nodded. "Based on what Colonel Polk said, there are a number of people who disliked the man. But the watch – that is our key piece of evidence."

CHAPTER 10

Friday, September 13, 1867

That morning, Morrison Waite, Robert Todd Lincoln, and Oliver Wendell Holmes were standing in the rain, waiting at the door of the courthouse for the military investigators to appear.

"Good morning, gentlemen. We are General Redmond's attorneys and as is our right, we wish to accompany you as you conduct your interviews with potential witnesses."

Colonel Salton looked at the three men standing before him. "Come in, gentlemen. Let us get out of the rain first." He led the way into the courthouse, up the stairs, and unlocked the door to the room they were using. Introductions were made around and the men all pulled chairs up to the large work table in the middle of the room.

"So," said Salton. "Shall we establish some ground rules?"

"By all means, Colonel." Waite was being cordial and professional, at least to start with. "I would suggest that my two clerks accompany your captains while I work with Colonel Veriton to capture all of the evidence reviews and depositions you conduct. That way, we will both have the same information and we will be able to ask our questions during the depositions, saving both of us time."

Salton looked thoughtful. "I see no reason to object. Shall we begin by reviewing the inquest results and the initial interviews with Dr. Walker and Colonel Polk?"

"As good a place to start as any. I asked Mr. Jackson to send over some coffee, tea, and biscuits to sustain us during our efforts." Waite smiled collegially. Establishing good will was important during this phase of the investigation. Confrontation would come later, during the trial.

While Waite and the clerks were off with the military investigators, Blair and Jerome were sitting with Charlie in his office at Redmond Stables.

Montgomery Blair sat at Charlie's desk, with Lord and Charlie sitting opposite him. He had a set of papers covered with his initial notes in front of him. "So, General Redmond, it is clear that a good number of people in Culpeper believe you killed this man. Would you care to explain to me why they think this?"

He sighed, a deep, heartfelt sigh. "I would say it started as soon as Alex Raeburn returned from the war. He showed up at church a year ago January, and popped me in the face. I had never met the man, but he felt that as a Union officer, I deserved to be flattened."

Blair asked, "That would be January of '66?"

"Yes, sir. He said he owed it to me ever since Vicksburg."

"You were at Vicksburg?"

"Yes, sir. I came east with Sheridan and Grant after that, and my troops served in the eastern front during the last year of the war."

Blair nodded. "Do you know who Raeburn served with?"

"I believe he was with Nathan Forrest, but I am not positive."

"So cavalry against cavalry?"

"Yes, sir."

Blair rubbed his chin. Devil Forrest's troops were not known for being particularly forgiving or conciliatory after the war, especially after Forrest put together this group called the Ku Klux Klan and started recruiting vigilantes. "So what happened between you and Raeburn next?"

"Over the next few months, Raeburn would follow me around town, just watching me. It was disconcerting, to say the least. Periodically, he would make snide remarks about how unwelcome scallywags were in Culpeper."

"A not uncommon feeling among returning Confederate veterans, I am afraid."

"Yes, well, Raeburn seemed to have carried it to extremes. Then in August..." he hesitated and flexed his hands trying not to ball them into fists at the thought. "He laid hands on my wife, on Rebecca. I caught him backing her into a pile of lumber, his hands on her breasts. It looked like he was trying to force her..." He choked on the memory. "I laid hands on him, beat the hell out of him for that. Duncan Nailer and his men pulled me off." Charlie decided not to add before he managed killed Alex that day.

"Why were there no charges brought?"

"They decided against it. He put his hands on my wife, said crude things about my cousin, who is now married to our minster by the way, and I beat the hell out of him for it. I guess they figured it was even; that was enough."

"So not only did you have reason to dislike Raeburn, but so did the minister and his wife? Your cousin?"

"Yes, I suppose. But I cannot imagine either Charlotte or Edgar shooting the man in cold blood."

"No, but I can see that there are others in town who might want Raeburn out of the picture. That may be important to your defense."

Charlie shook his head, but said nothing.

"All right, General. Let us go on. What happened next?"

"Other than the by now normal snide cuts and annoyances when we encountered one another in town, nothing happened until December. I had two men who would bring our farm payroll funds from the bank in a lockbox. They were robbed and beaten on their way out with the payroll in mid-December of '66. Richard looked for the culprits, but got nowhere."

"Could your delivery men not recognize their attackers?"

"They were hooded, and if they could identify them from their horses or their clothing, I suspect they were too frightened to do so. Raeburn could be very threatening."

"So what makes you think it was Raeburn?"

"Oh, that is simple. I got the strong box back in February. Delivered right to the front door of my bank. Inside there was a note from Nathan Bedford Forrest, thanking me for my contribution to his new Ku Klux Klan organization. An ordinary robber would have taken that much money and run; it was nearly five hundred dollars. Ten years' salary, plus some, for the average man. And Raeburn is the only one in town with the ties to Devil Forrest."

Blair shook his head. "I am beginning to think that we might have a case of justifiable homicide starting to come together here."

Charlie looked disgusted. "You might. **If** I killed him. I did not."

The general continued, "Then in March, two boys, sons of Raeburn's crowd of cronies, beat the snot out of my son. In April, there was an incident in Sweetwater, a Negro section of town. Several men in hoods came in, burned a cross, and threatened several members of my staff and their families. Within three days of that, two of our horses were stolen. We had been having problems with fences being torn down; this time they actually took horses. I suspect it was Raeburn and his gang, but cannot prove it. I think he was trying to threaten us, showing us that we were not secure on our own property."

He stopped for a moment, taking a long draw on his coffee cup. "Then I did something I am not proud of. Raeburn came into Jocko's tavern one afternoon while I was having lunch. He started baiting me, saying rude and disgusting things about my wife. I had enough of his attitude and his crude language. I drew my gun, pointed it at his head and told him to shut up and get out or else."

"When was this little failure in your manners, General?"

"That would have been the end of April. It had been a rough month, between Darby being beaten, my staff being threatened in their homes, horse rustling, and his appalling insults to my sweet Rebecca…" He shook his head.

"I am surprised you did not horse whip him. Myself, I admire your restraint, General. How many people witnessed this particular event?"

"Oh, hell." He shook his head and began raising fingers to count off. "Jocko Jackson, the tavern keeper, his niece, Ro Jackson, Colonel Richard Polk, probably Jocko's wife Esther, and whoever else was in the bar or the attached tearoom."

"Hmmmm." Blair nodded, chewing his lip. "So in April you

threaten to blow his brains out and last week someone did? Not a particularly good thing, that. I suspect that has a lot to do with why folks around here think you killed him."

"Oh, it gets worse. Just a week after I threatened Raeburn, the local dry goods purveyor, Mr. Cooper, got threatened. They said if he continued to sell to blacks from the front of his shop they would burn him out. Then on the twenty-ninth of May, someone burned down my barn. I lost two of my best men--my farrier, Tarent, who had been with me for years, all through the war, and a young man, no more than a boy really, who was apprenticed to him. We also lost several horses, including several breeding mares, a few studs, and a couple of newborn foals. I started riding patrols around the property then. Five days later, I received a note warning me to guard my children. The threats kept getting more and more serious. So I brought Pinkerton guards down here to help protect my family and my property."

"Under the circumstances, a perfectly reasonable response. What was the provost doing to find the party or parties responsible for the robberies, the arson, and murder?"

"I think Richard was doing his best with limited resources, but no one in this town would say a word. Raeburn had most likely threatened them and they were scared to talk, to be honest."

"So did anything else happen between the fire and the evening of September seventh?"

Charlie looked at his attorney. "Is that not enough? Please notice, Mr. Blair. Not once did I start any of the conflicts with Raeburn. In each case, the man goaded me into responding to his attacks on me and mine, either verbally or physically."

"I see that, General Redmond. Raeburn obviously was taunting you, and his attacks kept getting more and more violent.

But he is still dead, and the townspeople still think you did it. So let us talk about the evening of September seventh."

Charlie sighed. "On Saturday nights, a small group of local residents, myself and my wife included, gather at Jocko's for an evening of gaming. The gentlemen play poker in the bar. The ladies play mah jong in the tearoom."

"Who was there that night?"

"In addition to me, Richard Polk, Jocko Jackson, Edgar Vile, Duncan Nailer, and Edward Cooper were there playing poker. The ladies in the next room were my wife Rebecca, Elizabeth Walker, Missy Frazier, Esther Jackson, and Grace Cooper. Edgar's man Rex plays mah jong with the ladies. Normally, my cousin Charlotte, Edgar's wife, joins the ladies as well, but given her delicate condition, she was not there that night."

"Who is Rex?"

"Rex is Reverend Vile's manservant and major domo. He is a Chinaman who taught the ladies their game." Charlie grinned. "In the name of honest and full openness between us, Rex is also many things, including a skilled physician who helped me get back on my feet. He has helped me recover from the wounds I suffered at Appomattox. Because of him, I have regained perhaps seventy percent of my mobility. Obviously, there was nothing he could do about the missing bits," he said raising his right hand, "but he has helped me use the muscles I have left as well as can be done. Not to mention that he is also a member of the Chinese royal family and has more money than the rest of us put together. He has been Edgar's traveling companion for many years."

"So what happened that night?"

"The games broke up around nine or nine thirty, which was a little early, but it was hot and several of us were tired. We wandered out onto Jocko's front porch and were having a final drink before we headed home, when Raeburn, with a couple of his chums, came staggering out of Mrs. Allen's just up the street. He saw me standing in front, so he came over to insult me some more. One of his companions, I think it was Granville, tried to warn him off, but that was not on Raeburn's agenda. So Richard Polk told him to go home and sleep it off. When he would not leave, I stepped forward. I told him I would lay him out in the street if he would not leave. Rex, Reverend Vile and Jocko all held me back. Then Colonel Polk had one of his deputies take Raeburn off to the jail to sleep it off."

He shrugged. "Everyone else went their own way and Rebecca and I packed up and came home. We were home before ten thirty. I was feeling a bit twitchy, so I decided to go ride a circuit around the property before I went to bed. I left around eleven, and was back in the house by twelve thirty. The next thing I knew, Richard was at my door just after breakfast and taking me to jail. On the way, we encountered a mob that I suspect, if he had not been taking me in, would have come out to Redmond Stables to lynch me."

Blair looked thoughtful for a few minutes. Then he asked, "So, General Redmond, how did it come to happen that Raeburn was holding your watch in his hand as he died?"

"I have no idea, sir. My watch and its matching pen knife went missing sometime last spring. I have a number of watches, but wanted that one and the knife for a trip I had to make to Washington. I am terrible about leaving things lying around the house – it makes my wife somewhat crazy, actually. She promised to look for them, but then the children came down with the measles, and I came home with a terrible cold, and it just slipped through the cracks."

"Were there any people in the house who could have taken it? And was anything else taken?"

"We have done a great deal of renovation around the house

and property in the past year, with a number of workmen in and out of the house. Any one of them could have seen it lying around and taken it. And no, I do not remember anything else specific going missing, but as I tend to leave pocket money lying around, it could have."

Blair nodded and raised his eyebrows. Not many men would be willing to misplace a gold watch without looking for it. He decided to turn to another issue, that of creating an alibi for the evening of the seventh.

"So, General Redmond, let us go over the evening of the seventh in detail." He looked at his notes. "You went out onto the porch and were having a final drink. Alex Raeburn came up and insulted you. Polk had his deputies take Raeburn into custody at nine forty-five. What happened then?"

"We went back inside and finished our drinks while we waited for my carriage to come around. We left about 10:15 and were home by 10:30. We came in the front door and said hello to Simon, the Pinkerton guard in the front hall. Rebecca and I went upstairs and she got ready for bed. We talked as she did her evening routine – you know, brushing her hair, getting into a night gown – and I decided to go for a circuit ride. As I left the room, I heard the clock strike eleven. I went out the back door and down to the barn to get my horse. The moon was about half full so I did not need additional light. I saw one of Pinkerton's men at the barn as I led Jack out. I mounted up and rode over to the fence line, where I saw another of Pinkerton's men on patrol. I rode down to the apple orchard, dismounted, smoked a couple of cigars while I sat and thought for a bit, trying to shake off the anger I felt at Raeburn, ate a few of the early ripe apples, gathered up a few more to drop off at the house in the hope that Sarah or Rebecca would make me a pie, and rode back to the barn. I put Jack away, then walked up to the house and put the apples on the kitchen table. I saw the hall guard as I was headed up to my bed. I heard the hall clock ring the half hour as I was getting dressed for bed. Rebecca was already asleep. I was asleep before one, as I do not remember hearing the clock chime the hour."

Blair sat staring at his client for a few minutes. "All right, General Redmond. We will do what we can to validate your timeline with the Pinkerton people. But you realize you have virtually no alibi for the time between eleven thirty and twelve thirty. Raeburn was shot sometime between twelve and twelve thirty, and he was holding your watch, the one you say was lost, but for which you have no external corroboration. It does not look good."

Charlie looked bleakly at his attorney. "I swear to you, Mr. Blair, I did not kill Alex Raeburn, much as I was tempted to on occasion."

"Somehow I believe you, General. But will a tribunal?"

Friday, September 13, 1867

Salton looked around the table. They had spent the morning going over the information they had, including examining Charlie's watch, looking through the inquest transcript, and going over the notes from their interviews with Elizabeth and Richard.

"Well, gentlemen, from what we have here, I would say we have a viable motivation for General Redmond to have killed this Raeburn fellow. As for a .44 caliber pistol – well, there are more of those running around than I care to count. So that gives us means and motive. Shall we start looking at opportunity? And then there is the critical question. How did General Redmond's watch end up in the dead man's hand?"

Waite looked at Salton. "Colonel, I would also ask you to consider the possibility that General Redmond's watch had been stolen and placed in Raeburn's hand specifically to mislead the authorities and turn suspicion from the real culprit. I would also ask you to consider Dr. Walker's contention that the shot to Mr. Raeburn's chest was made by a right-handed gunman. General Redmond's right hand is badly crippled from war wounds; he is incapable of handling a heavy pistol like a .44 with his right hand."

Lt. Colonel Veriton spoke up. "Mr. Waite, we will be as thorough as possible, but I will remind you that the angle of the shot does not necessarily indicate a right-handed shooter. The gunman could have been left-handed and standing to one side of Mr. Raeburn when he pulled the trigger the first time. As for the watch, well, we shall see, shall we not? Our first goal will be to discover if General Redmond had the opportunity and the motive to do this deed, and if not, to find the person who did."

Salton stepped in to interrupt what he considered a premature discussion of possible guilt. "Before we get to making charges, I suggest we assemble a witness list so we can begin our process of conducting interviews. We will need to talk to anyone and everyone who was a witness to the activities of that night. Shall we split up? Bailton, you take the folks who were at," he paused and looked at his notes, then continued, "Mrs. Allen's that evening. Lightborne, can you take the people who were present when Mrs. Redmond was allegedly assaulted by Mr. Raeburn and General Redmond beat him for his presumption? Colonel Veriton, can you take the people who were at Jocko Jackson's tavern that evening? I believe that they are also the witnesses to General

Redmond threatening to shoot Mr. Raeburn between the eyes back in the spring. I need to begin the process of assembling a tribunal and defining the procedural processes basis for trial, which I will be happy to review with you, Mr. Waite, when I am done."

Waite nodded. "That seems reasonable." He turned to his clerks. "Robert, will you accompany Captain Bailton? Holmes, you are with Captain Lightborne. I will accompany Colonel Veriton." All six men rose, gathering their coats, hats, and note pads. "Colonel Salton, until later. When shall I tell General Redmond you will be out to question him and his staff?"

"I expect we will be out to Redmond's place on Monday. Until then, be sure he stays put, please. The mood here in town is decidedly unpleasant."

~

Saturday, September 14, 1867

As soon as breakfast was over, Jerome and Blair met with Kate Warne. She brought all of the logs her men had submitted for the night of September 7th. This was the best source of information to attempt to build an alibi for Charlie. And he really needed a solid alibi.

Kate sat down the log books from her men, with the one on top being the one kept by the front hall guards. "Gentlemen, this is the best we can provide. They are the logs from our men who guard the house and grounds. I have marked all of the entries for the night of September 7th and the morning of the 8th. Shall we go through them?"

"Please, Miss Warne. You and your men's testimony will be critical."

"Right. Let us see what we can do." She opened the front hall guard's book. "According to the guard, the Redmonds returned to the house at 10:32 in the evening. They went directly upstairs to their room." She continued to scan. "At 11:04, General Redmond came down and headed to the back stairs, stating he was going to ride a circuit of the property." She switched books to the one kept by the man who rode the southern border of the property. "At 11:25, one of our men saw the general at the southern edge of the property by the run. He turned up the run and rode toward the bridge to the east fields." She opened yet another journal. "At 11:35 our guard at the vineyard saw the general riding into the apple orchard, across the run from where he was posted."

"No one saw the general for approximately thirty-five minutes. However, at 12:15, our guard at the barn reports that the general was there, grooming his horse, and that he then went up to the house, carrying apples in his hat. Our hall guard corroborates that, as he reports that General Charlie came up the back stairs and headed up to his bedroom at 12:25. I have taken the liberty of drawing a map that notes where and when on the property General Charlie was spotted by my men."

Blair looked thoughtful. "Did your man happen to note what kind of condition the horse was in? Had he been ridden hard or was he just out for an evening stroll?"

"No, sir, but we can certainly ask him."

"Please do. That may be important. And thank you for the map and timeline."

Kate left to find the guard who had been on barn duty that evening.

Blair looked at Jerome. "Damn, damn, damn. He was on the north east side of the property from 11:35 until 12:15 with no witnesses. It is not that far into town – a brisk ride from that corner of the property of perhaps ten minutes at the most. We need to nail down that time of death more accurately. In the meantime, we need to determine how quickly he could get back to town on his horse, and more importantly, get back here. We know where he was at 12:15. And we also need to see if there is anything that would support him being in the apple grove for a while – cigar butts, apple cores, anything. And do it soon, before time and weather kill any hope of circumstantial evidence being left."

"Mr. Blair, does it strike you that someone should have heard two shots from a .44 at that hour? There are several people who live within half a block of where Raeburn was killed. Would that help with the time issue?"

"Yes, yes, it would. Let us hope Waite and his boys find something."

Kate came in at that moment, followed by a large, robust man who was looking rather tired. "I managed to catch Simpson before he headed for bed, as he has been on the night shift." She turned to her man. "Can you tell me if General Redmond's horse was heavily lathered last Saturday night or if he looked as if he had been on a casual ride?"

"When I saw General Charlie that night, he had just gotten the saddle off Jack. The saddle pad was not even damp, so General Charlie just gave him a quick brush down, fed him an apple out of the bunch he had in his hat, and headed into the house."

"Thank you, Simpson. You may be asked to testify to this in the future."

"Yes, ma'am. Now, if you do not mind, I would like to go get some sleep."

"Go, man. You have helped, I think," she offered with a pat to his arm.

"One thing before you go, sir, if you do not mind." Blair raised his hand. "Did General Redmond seem in any way…" He searched for the right words. "Harried, distressed, or upset?"

"No, sir." The man shook his head. "He seemed maybe a little tired, but it was nearly 12:30. He was not in a hurry and did not seem pressed in anyway."

Jerome jumped on board. "Did you notice if he was armed?"

Simpson shook his head, "I do not think so. However, it is possible, as I had no reason at the time to notice if perhaps he had a gun on under his suit coat."

"Thank you, Simpson. Get some sleep." Blair nodded his dismissal of the man.

Jerome looked at Blair. "Timing is everything, but if Charlie did not ride Jack hard and did not seem distressed, that is in our favor."

Rebecca led Jerome and Kate down the well-worn path to the apple orchard. Shannon tossed her head happily, knowing it meant her favorite treat. Rebecca smoothly dismounted and opened the gate to let them through. As she led Shannon through, she pointed to the left. "It is over there. Charlie's favorite spot."

Jerome and Kate quickly dismounted and made their way under the little grove of trees to a small clearing holding a stump, the top of which was about three feet off the ground. Very carefully, they looked at the ground as they approached. Jerome smiled as he pulled a small bag from his pocket. "Look what we have here." He plucked three cigar butts from the ground, depositing them in the bag, and then began looking for the apple cores. "Charlie said he was eating apples."

"Yes, but some animal could have come along and made off with the cores," Kate offered quietly.

"True." The lawyer agreed.

"At least we know he was here that night." Rebecca nodded.

"Just like he said he was."

"Yes, but for how long?" Jerome shrugged. "Did he have enough time to sit here, smoke three cigars, make his way into town and kill Raeburn before coming back to the house?"

Kate interjected. "Or did he kill Raeburn and come back here and smoke the cigars before going back to the house?"

"We can prove Charlie was here. Just not exactly when." Jerome shook his head. "It is not hurting us, but it may not actually help us either."

The military investigators, followed by their shadows from Charlie's team of lawyers, reassembled at the courthouse late that afternoon.

Veriton dropped into his chair. "Well, I did not find out a single damned new piece of information. Everyone says exactly the same thing Polk did. And what has me bewildered is that there were people around town at midnight – people within a half block of the shooting, but no one heard a thing. You would think someone would have heard a .44 go off – not once, but twice. But nothing!"

Lightborne stood at the end of the table. "I found nothing new on the attack of Miss Rebecca either. It was exactly as Richard Polk said. Even the black porters who saw it said the same things."

Bailton shook his head. "Mrs. Allen said that Raeburn had been drinking with his friends, fairly heavily. He left a little after nine thirty with James Granville and Eddie Rainey. They heard shouting in the street and went out to see Raeburn haranguing Redmond. Then Colonel Polk blew his whistle and one of the deputy provosts came and took him off to jail to sleep it off.

According to Mrs. Allen, Granville and Rainey came back in and had a couple more drinks with their friends Armistead, Brooks, and Kirtley. They left a little after eleven and she closed up her shop by 11:30. She lives above her little tavern, but heard nothing."

"We found Brooks, Armistead, and Granville. They confirmed Mrs. Allen's story and their wives all attested to them being home before 11:30 that night. We talked to Kirtley as well. He also confirmed Mrs. Allen's story, and says he rode home, and arrived by 11:30, but there was no one who could corroborate his story. We have not yet spoken to one Christopher Edward Rainey, a known compatriot of Raeburn's known around town as Eddie, but if he follows true to form, he will say the same thing."

"Thank you, gentlemen. And again, no one heard any gunshots? Damn."

Later that evening, the military investigators sat at the dinner table with Salton drilling them on what they had found. They were all exhausted, so shortly after 9:00, they retired to their rooms upstairs to get a decent night's sleep. All four were sound asleep when an ungodly racket awoke them. It was a train whistle. One long blast, two short ones, as the Saturday night freight train came roaring through Culpeper. Salton looked at his watch. It was exactly midnight.

He looked up at the ceiling. If this was a regular occurrence, he had his answer as to why no one had heard anything. He also had the exact time of death.

Sunday, September 15, 1867

Charlie was sitting out in the gazebo with a little fire in the brazier, strumming his guitar as he watched the children play near the pond. It was a little chilly, but the sun was shining and they were having a wonderful time. All five of them were running around, chasing each other and generally acting like normal children as squeals of delight rang through the morning air.

He stopped playing long enough to make a note on a pad of paper he had with him. He would never admit it, but he had started writing music after he had discovered he truly enjoyed playing the guitar, and not just for the therapeutic benefits to his hand. There was something that touched his soul.

As he began strumming the strings again, Rebecca appeared on the steps with a footman behind her hauling a large tea tray. "Private party?" She asked with a slight smile.

"You, madam, are always welcome at my parties, private and otherwise." He smiled, standing to greet her and give her a kiss on the cheek as the young man placed the tray.

"Thank you." Rebecca smiled as the servant ducked his head and retreated to the house. She fixed two large mugs of tea and settled down in her chair, next to her husband's. "Beautiful morning."

"Indeed." He nodded and took his seat next to her, taking her hand in his. "I am sorry we could not go to church this morning."

She shook her head dismissively. "Do not be. I am sure we were better off here based on what is being said in town these days. I am sure Edgar will come out and tend to the spiritual needs of the family."

He nodded, still feeling guilty that his family was being forced to suffer the consequences of the current situation. "Still, I wish things were different."

"It will all be over soon enough. I cannot believe for one moment that military men from the Judge Advocate's General office will find you guilty of anything."

"They will follow the evidence. If the evidence says I am guilty, they will find me guilty. Do not be complacent just because this is a military tribunal."

Before their conversation could go any further, it was interrupted by the sounds of buggies and carriages pulling up the drive. They both stood and peered back toward the house to see a large contingent of their friends making their way toward the gazebo.

Edgar had a huge smile on his face as he escorted Charlotte and her very pregnant belly, followed by Rex and the Coopers, the Nailers, the Fraziers, and the Jacksons. Rebecca was a little startled to see Ro, Mary Simms, and Robert Brooks along with his wife and daughter among the group as well.

Edgar offered as he helped Charlotte settle onto the well-padded seat Charlie had vacated immediately upon her arrival. "We decided that if you cannot come to Church, Church will come to you. Richard and Elizabeth would have come, but under the circumstances, they decided it would be better not to at the moment."

All the families assembled in the gazebo, taking seats on the benches. Charlie could only shake his head as he looked at his friends. "What about regular services?"

"Oh." Edgar waved dismissively. "I did a sermon at the Church this morning."

Charlotte laughed outright. "If you can consider 'Judge not, lest ye be judged. See you next Sunday,' a sermon."

Edgar grinned. "I have a better basis for a sermon for you and yours, my dear friend." He raised his voice so everyone could hear him.

"My message for the day is taken from Genesis, Chapter 22. We who have assembled to support our dear friend, Charlie Redmond, must always remember that no matter what, we are leaving a legacy, one that can overcome all of the perfidy of our world today. Charlie and Rebecca have led the way in establishing this legacy; we are following their lead. For as the bible says:

That in blessing I will bless thee, and in multiplying I will multiply thy seed as the stars of the heaven, and as the sand which is upon the sea shore; and thy seed shall possess the gate of his enemies;

And in thy seed shall all the nations of the earth be blessed; because thou hast obeyed my voice."

"Charlie and Rebecca, you have been given a great gift by the Lord, our God; you have been given five beautiful children who know how to speak the truth, how to be men and women of honor and faith, with kind and stalwart hearts to lead us into the next century. Regardless of what happens in the coming days, you have been given a great gift, and as a result, you have given our community a great gift. Look to your children; they will speak truth to the enemies in your gate; and from them will come the peace and blessing of the Lord."

By mid-morning, Mr. Blair and his colleagues were ready to start working with Charlie again. Knowing that the men from the JAG office would arrive in the morning, they were ready to spend all day with Charlie to make sure his statements remained consistent. When he looked for Charlie both in his office and the parlor to no avail he was becoming a bit irritated at his client's apparent lack of concern about how serious the situation was.

Then he managed to track the Redmonds to the gazebo, where he found them surrounded by family and friends. Edgar had indeed delivered a wonderful sermon to his little congregation and, as they sat afterward waiting for Sarah to throw together a lunch for the unexpected guests, Mr. Blair considered that it was a good thing General Redmond had such noble friends. He was going to need them.

Monday, September 16, 1867

An hour after breakfast, Reg escorted the prosecution contingent up to Charlie's office, where he and his defense team were already ensconced, once again going over every move he had made between Saturday night and Sunday morning. Charlie was fairly certain that at any moment they would be asking him about outhouse visits.

They sat together for about forty-five minutes going over, for what he felt like was the millionth time, his routine for the Saturday before and Sunday of Raeburn's death. Finally, they all decided there was only one thing left to do at the farm, as far as the investigation part of the process was concerned.

It was time to test Jack and his ability to make time to Culpeper and back with an experienced rider. All gathered agreed that there was no way to let Charlie make the ride. Even if he were capable, if anyone saw him riding hell bent for leather he would most certainly get shot. It was also agreed that Darby was too young to make the ride that would be required on the big horse, so Albert was pressed into the cause.

After pocket watches were all synchronized, one man from each team of attorneys and investigators were paired off. Two were sent into town to stand and wait at the murder scene. Two more were placed about half way along the route to be able to help time Albert's ride. Finally, Charlie, Jerome, Mr. Blair, and Colonel Salton walked down to the apple grove with Albert leading Jack from the rear.

"This is the spot." Charlie gestured to a stump that had about three feet sticking out of the ground. "This is my favorite place down here."

"Very well." Mr. Blair motioned Albert forward and issued the instructions. "Mr. Randolph, it is crucial that you do this ride as quickly as possible. You know where your destination is?"

"Yes, sir."

"When you arrive, Captain Lightborne will be there with a loaded revolver. Please dismount, take the revolver, fire two shots, and return as quickly as you can."

"Yes, sir." Albert mounted Jack as Charlie held the bridle. "Just let Jack do the work, Albert. Give him his head and let him go."

"All right, Charlie." Albert hated this task. He knew it was important to Charlie's defense, but he also knew how fast Jack could get to town and back and he was not sure this test was a good idea.

The general rubbed the big horse's nose and laid his forehead against his broad face. "Tear it up, old friend. My life may depend on it."

Albert settled into the saddle and as soon as Mr. Blair gave the word, he and Jack tore out of the apple grove at a speed that made Blair and the other men blink, several times.

As Albert made the half way point, the two men waiting for him noted the time and Jack's condition. They were also surprised at the speed the big horse went ripping by, a large cloud of dust in his wake that left them choking.

As he made his way into town, several people stopped to

watch the big black horse charging through the streets as if his life depended on it. As Albert brought him to a bouncing halt in front of the two men waiting for him, he jumped from the saddle, took the gun from the captain, fired two shots into two bags of flour, one hanging at the height of a man's chest, the other on the ground, and was back on Jack returning to the farm in less than thirty seconds.

By the time Albert got Jack back to the barn, the big horse was exhausted, heavily lathered and snorting hard. Charlie immediately took control of his animal as the men compared and made notes.

Charlie led Jack to his stall and quickly began removing his tack. "Good job, Jack." He soothed the horse as he poured fresh water into his trough and grabbed his grooming tools from the shelf. He immersed himself in grooming and taking care of his faithful mount while the gentlemen in control of his fate sat on bales of hay and discussed the outcome of their test when the other members of the teams returned to give their information.

After twenty minutes or so, Mr. Blair and Jerome joined Charlie at the stall, leaning on the gate as the other men left the barn.

"Well." Jerome sighed. "We have good news and bad news."

"Of course you do," Charlie barked with a humorless laugh, continuing to brush Jack.

"The good news is you have an incredibly fast horse," Jerome offered with a bit of a chuckle.

Charlie stopped brushing and turned to the men. "Let me guess. The bad news is I have an incredibly fast horse?"

"Pretty much." Jerome nodded.

"However," Mr. Blair offered as he glanced at his notes and back to Jack. "Sunday morning, when you brought Jack back to the barn, we have a witness that says he was not in the state he was in today. It is clear Jack can make the run, but if he had, you both would have shown the signs of it."

"There is also the fact that Charlie cannot ride like that." Jerome gestured to his friend, referring to his war injuries.

"Actually." Charlie's head dropped. "I made a ride very much like that. One way at least, the morning I got the warning about the children. I rode him hard into town, bareback."

Mr. Blair groaned as he closed his eyes and shook his head.

"However, I had to ask Rex out to give me a physical therapy treatment afterward. I was in excruciating pain. I could barely walk for two days after. And I did not ride him back hard. As a matter of fact, it was as leisurely as I could manage bareback and we actually stopped when I found one of our guard dogs injured in the weeds."

Both Jerome and Blair shook their heads. "What?" Jerome managed to get out.

Charlie sighed and dropped his grooming tools back on the shelf as he joined the men at the gate. "Madra, one of our guard dogs, the one who guarded the barn. She chased the person who burned it. It took four days for her to get home because she had been so badly injured. We think she was kicked by a horse. When I was riding home, I found her in the weeds at the edge of the property and brought her to the house. She's been back with Ro Jackson since then. Ro thinks that Madra can identify the culprit and she has been taking her into town and around various places since she recovered from her injuries, but so far she has not identified anyone."

Mr. Blair's brows rose as he considered it. "Is there anyone in town that would take the testimony of a dog?"

"Well, so far she has not been able to offer any, so it is a moot point." Charlie left the stall and closed the gate with a click. "Shall we go back to the house and have some lunch?"

CHAPTER 11

Tuesday, September 17, 1867

Charlie and Rebecca stood on the porch waiting for the coach to be brought around that would convey them all to town. In less than one hour they would know for sure if Charlie was going to be charged with the murder of Alex Raeburn.

The ride to town was a quiet one. Rebecca clutched her husband's arm in one hand and held a handkerchief in the other. There was not a gentleman in the coach who would add to her distress by discussing what might happen.

As they approached the courthouse, they saw a large crowd assembled outside. Both of Richard's deputies, as well as several Pinkerton men, stood outside keeping an eye on the assemblage. Richard had been ordered to find more men and deputize them in order to effectively control the crowd, but so far he was having little luck. He was going to be reduced to men who were 'less' hostile at Charlie before it was over with.

Louis pulled the coach around to the back as he had been instructed by Mr. Blair. A large group of armed Pinkerton guards were ready to escort them into the courtroom. The actual proceeding had been closed to the public, for no other reason than to protect all those involved in the decision making process. If Charlie was charged, the crowd would want to lynch him. If he was not, there was a very real fear they would want to lynch the panel instead.

Once inside, Rebecca was settled into the seats in the gallery behind Charlie and his attorneys, who were at a table in the front of the room. The JAG officers entered and took their seats at the table opposite Charlie and his team. Polite greeting and handshakes were exchanged by all the men. Even Charlie shook each man's hand and thanked them for being there as they awaited the arrival of the tribunal panel.

Charlie spent his time waiting, turned to Rebecca, holding her hand and smiling at her, doing his best to reassure her with a false bravado. He was not sure at all. There was something in the pit of his stomach that told him things were not going to go well, but she had convinced herself that a military tribunal would not find one of their own guilty. Ironically, so did most of the people outside the courthouse hoping and praying for a lynching of the scallywag.

The three senior officers who had been selected to sit as the military tribunal had arrived the night before. They had gone immediately to the rooms that Mayor Frazier had prepared for them at his home, offering them further isolation from the citizens of the town. The head of the tribunal was Brigadier General Alfonse Mayberry, US Army Artillery. He was accompanied by Colonel Constantine Douglas and Colonel George Allenby, both infantry men. All three were assigned to the Judge Advocate General's office. Neither Charlie nor Richard knew any of them.

Once the men of the tribunal were seated and the proceeding brought to order, the prosecution made their case and in less than twenty minutes the panel retired to consider their decision. The defense team could only wait and hope. If charges were brought, then it would be their time to shine.

Rebecca proceeded to try and shred her handkerchief as they waited. Charlie really wanted one of Rex's special blend cigars and the attorneys looked bored. After forty-five minutes, the panel returned and reconvened the tribunal.

"It is the conclusion of this tribunal that one Mr. Alexander Fancher Raeburn of Culpeper Virginia was the victim of murder on or about midnight, Sunday, September 8, 1867. It is also the conclusion of this tribunal that one Charles Huger Redmond of Culpeper, Virginia not only had the opportunity, but the motive and the means to commit the crime of murder against Mr. Raeburn. Therefore, it is the recommendation of this tribunal that Charles Huger Redmond be taken into custody and charged with the murder of Alexander Fancher Raeburn."

Mr. Blair was on his feet immediately. "The defense requests bail until such a time as the trial can be scheduled."

"Mr. Blair, it is quite clear to us that not only could Mr. Redmond make bail but that he would be a flight risk as he has the means to leave not only the state, but the country. Bail request denied. The suspect will be taken into custody immediately."

"Sirs," Blair tried again. "While I appreciate the logic of your decisions, General Redmond is a man with particular physical needs as a result of the injuries sustained during the final days of the war. I would ask that you allow General Redmond to be held on house arrest at his home, until such time as the local detention facility can be refurnished to provide the level of care and comfort he requires. The jail is seriously lacking in even rudimentary facilities. General Redmond was required to go without basic needs, like being able to wash, when he was held once before, against the recently reinstated Habeas Corpus, I might remind this tribunal."

The men of the panel looked to each other and then, after bringing their heads together for a few moments, the lead jurist nodded to Mr. Blair. "We understand the special physical and medical needs of General Redmond and we are agreeable to the stipulation that he be held for no more than seventy-two hours at his home under guard. This should give you time to find the furnishings you require to make the general's incarceration less taxing on his person."

Friday, September 20, 1867

When Charlie arrived at the jail for the second time it looked very different from his first stay. Another small stove had been installed nearer his cell so he would be warm. Fall had arrived and the season in Virginia tended to be wet and chilly. The cell had been cold and damp the first time and it had worried Rebecca to no end. Mayor Frazier was kind enough to allow the installation of the stove at Redmond's cost. It was money Rebecca was happy to spend.

Duncan and Eddie had removed the horrible little cot with the paper thin mattress and assembled a custom made bed with a thick down mattress and heavy quilts, and two beautiful down pillows made with silk covers, embroidered with their initials. Rebecca had made sure to use hers for a few nights before he left and he was grateful because now there was something of her there with him.

A table had been added that held a pitcher and basin along with a mirror and Charlie's shaving kit. It was clear Louis had come in and set the table. A small dresser held his clothes, and had a stack of clean soft clothes and soap, along with his toothbrush and brushing powder on the top. Now he would be able to wash and keep clean in the dingy confines.

Then came the privacy screen donated by Rex. It was a beautiful thing, nearly eight feet wide broken into four sections with embroidered scenes of snow covered mountains and ornate dragons flying through the air. He would be able to block most of the bars when he felt the need for a bit of privacy from the constantly prying eyes of guards, investigators, and citizens who happened to 'need' something from the provost or his growing roster of deputies.

And with the final additional touches of a well-padded wingback chair, a small side table, and his guitar, she felt like Charlie had the absolute basics to be comfortable.

Charlie flipped the lid of his cigar box open and plucked two of his best from it. He stood and leaned against the bars, extending his left arm, holding the cigar out to Richard. "Trade for a light?"

Richard shook his head and stood up. He crossed the room, pulled a box of Lucifers from his pocket and handed them to Charlie. "Keep them."

The prisoner raised a brow. "Are you sure? I may set your jail on fire."

"I think your sense of self-preservation will keep you from immolating yourself in your cell. I let you have your razor and you have not cut your own throat yet, so I am fairly certain I can trust you with a box of matches."

Charlie waved the cigar at his friend. "Come on. Join me. You know I hate to smoke or drink alone. It is late and we are the only ones here. No one will see you having a cigar with your old friend. I promise it is all right. I really do understand. You are doing exactly what I would want, hope, and expect you to do."

Richard took the cigar, and with a laugh had to borrow a light from Charlie. He then settled on the corner of the desk nearest his friend. They just stood there together in silence for a minute, and then Charlie finally asked as he let a stream of smoke loose slowly. "You think I did it? I know it looks like I killed him. "

Richard sighed and shook his head as he took the cigar from his mouth. "I do not know what to think, Charlie. I know you two hated each other with a fiery passion. I know you would do anything to protect Rebecca and the children and that Raeburn had pushed you to the edge several times. I know I saw you threaten him a couple of times. Perhaps he just finally exceeded the limits of your patience and good judgment."

Charlie nodded, understanding why his friend could be of a divided mind on the subject. He hoped that what he was about to say next would put the issue to rest between them. "Richard?"

The provost looked up into the very serious eyes of one of his oldest and dearest friends. "Yes, Charlie?"

"I swear to you on the life of every man we lost I did not kill Alex Raeburn."

~

Saturday, September 21, 1867

Jerome entered the jail with his briefcase and notebook. The guard was quick to unlock the cell and let him in. He put his case and notebook down, removed his suit coat and rolled up the sleeves of his shirt.

"All right, Charlie. One more time."

"One more time what?"

"We are going to go over that Saturday night, Sunday morning."

Charlie sighed, a disgusted moan. "Jerome I have already gone over it with Mr. Blair and his three colleagues separately and together. I have gone over it with the investigators. I have gone over it. Over and over again."

"And you are going to go over it again, with me. We are going to go through it as many times as necessary. Unless you are content to swing at the end of a rope. All we have is today and tomorrow to get it exactly right."

Charlie shook his head and immediately acquiesced. "I am sorry." He nodded and took a seat on his bed. "You are right." He waited for his friend to get settled.

Once Jerome had his pencil and notepad open in his lap, he made a few quick notes and then looked to Charlie. "All right. Saturday. Tell me about Saturday. Everything. From the moment you woke up to the time you finally went to bed."

"Everything?"

"Every last detail. I do not care how personal you think it is."

"I knew eventually we would get to outhouse visits."

"And let me tell you, old friend, if I can prove that you were in the outhouse at midnight, I can and will use that information to clear you of murder." He smacked his hand against the pad. "Tell me everything!"

Charlie nodded. "Rebecca and I woke up at our normal time, around five thirty. We got up about six fifteen."

"Why the delay?"

"Do I really need to answer that? It was morning and I was obviously in bed with my wife."

"Yes, you need to answer it."

"We made love. Do you want the details, you old reprobate?"

Jerome's brow went up as he made a note. "For forty-five minutes? Damn, Charlie." He chuckled his admiration as he looked up at his friend. "You know if you had stayed home and done that again Saturday night…" He gestured aimlessly and Charlie nodded as he added. "Go on."

"Once we were up, I went to my office for coffee and to read my paper while Lizbet tended to Rebecca's morning routine. When she was done, Louis and I adjourned to the bedroom. He shaved me and then I got dressed and went down to breakfast. It was about eight by then. I had breakfast with the family. Then I went and spent about an hour in the barn."

"What time were you done in the barn?"

"Ten, ten thirty in the morning."

"After that?"

"I had a meeting with Kate Warne for about thirty minutes in my office at the house. She yelled at me again for riding my property."

"Well, I suspect you are going to hear a lot of that in the next few weeks. It is that little problem that is giving us the greatest issues with your defense. We cannot account for you during the time Raeburn was murdered."

"I was in the apple orchard."

"Doing what?"

"The same thing I have said a dozen times already, smoking, thinking. Eating apples."

Jerome sat up in his chair and eyed Charlie seriously. "How many cigars?"

"I do not know, two or three."

"Exactly how many?"

Charlie stared at the ceiling, looking for divine inspiration. Finally he said, "One of Rex's special blend Perfectos, two of my regular Marevas."

Jerome nodded. This agreed with the butts he and Kate Warne had found around the stump in the grove. He liked it when things added up, no matter how small.

"How many apples?"

He shook his head and stood up from the bed, throwing his hands in the air. "One or two, maybe. I do not know for sure. I ate a couple and took a few back to the house. I left them on the kitchen table for Sarah or Rebecca. I was hinting for a pie."

Jerome made a note and nodded. "Where were you specifically within the orchard? Do you remember?"

"Yes, it was a little grove right by the gate. To the left, there is a stump that is a good height for me to sit on. I like to go down there and think sometimes."

Jerome smiled. That added up too. It was exactly the spot Rebecca had indicated and where they had found the stubs of the stogies. "All right. After the apple orchard, what did you do?"

"I took Jack back to the barn, brushed him out, dropped the apples in the kitchen, and then went up to bed."

"What time was that?"

"Mmmm, I do not know for sure, maybe twelve or twelve thirty. The Pinkerton guard on the front door should be able to say for sure. He saw me come in and we spoke briefly before I went up to bed. As I told Mr. Blair, I do not remember hearing the 1:00 chime, so I was asleep by then."

The lawyer nodded and made yet another note. "And you went directly to bed?"

"Yes."

"Can Rebecca confirm it?"

"I have no idea. She was asleep, but when I got into bed, she moved next to me like she always does. She likes to sleep with her head on my shoulder. I have no way of knowing if she was awake enough to know what was happening. Even if she could, she would have no way of knowing what time it was. For all she would know it could be three in the morning."

"Oh, yes, Charlie, **please,** continue to make it that much harder for us to do our jobs. You have got to stop saying things like that. Richard told me what you said in the hall the morning Alex was murdered. How do you think that is going to look to the inquest panel? Let me give you the most important piece of advice I can. Do not say any more than is required for your answer. Do not offer ideas, concepts, or opinions. If you do, your wife is going to be a widow twice over. Stop talking, Charlie."

The general nodded as he twisted his hands. "Yes, Jerome. I will do whatever I need to do. I just want this to be over and I want to go home to my family."

"I know you do, my friend, and trust me when I say we are doing everything we can to make sure that is exactly what happens."

~

Monday, September 23, 1867

General Mayberry convened the military tribunal promptly at eight in the morning. The prosecution team filed in behind Colonel Salton and took their seats at the table to the right of the room. Montgomery Blair led Charlie's defense team in and took their seats to the left. Richard and Sean escorted Charlie into the room, though not in manacles.

Behind the two groups of attorneys came the many people who had been summoned to testify. Robert E. Lee escorted

Elizabeth to her seat behind the prosecutor's table and took a seat behind Charlie. He was joined by Rebecca, who was escorted in by Ulysses S. Grant and Philip Sheridan. Behind Elizabeth, looking absolutely miserable, came Jocko, Duncan, Edgar, and Edward Cooper. Rex took a seat behind Rebecca and was joined by Frank Halliburton and Eloise Langley.

The next row was occupied by Kate Warne and several of the Pinkerton guards. Tomas Coleman came in and sat in the last row behind Rebecca, where he was joined by his aunt Sarah. Mrs. Allen was escorted in by James Granville and followed by Henry Armistead, Robert Brooks, Harold Kirtley, and Eddie Rainey. George Randall, the station master and telegraph operator, came in last.

When the witnesses were all assembled, the three members of the tribunal entered the room. All stood as they entered and took their seats at the front table. Mayberry gaveled the session to order and everyone sat down. He consulted with the court reporter, who nodded his readiness, and the Sergeant at Arms, who was serving as his bailiff. In a very formal voice, he intoned, "In the matter of the First District, United States Army versus Charles Huger Redmond, Brigadier General, US Army, Retired for the murder of Alexander Fancher Raeburn, this tribunal is now in session. The prosecution will now state their case."

"Colonel Everett Salton, US Army, First District, for the prosecution, sirs. The prosecution will demonstrate that General Charles Huger Redmond, on the 8th of September at exactly midnight, did shoot and kill Alexander Fancher Raeburn. We will demonstrate that General Redmond had the motive, the means and the opportunity to do so, after multiple incidents between the defendant and the deceased. We will also show that the defendant did threaten the deceased that very evening, that on at least one other occasion had assaulted the deceased with the intent to kill him, and on at least one other, separate occasion the defendant had threatened the deceased with a gun, which he pointed at exactly the same place on the deceased's anatomy that was the location of the killing shot."

Rebecca gasped; her eyes dropped closed for a quick prayer. This was going to be more difficult than she had expected.

Mayberry nodded. Salton sat down and Blair took his place. "Gentlemen of the court, Montgomery Blair for the defense. The defense will show that while General Redmond had been severely provoked on multiple occasions over a two year period by the deceased, he had not been driven to the point of murder. We will further show that the defendant was not a man who would or could commit cold blooded murder. Finally, we will demonstrate that in a purely circumstantial case, General Redmond's ability to commit this murder was highly improbable, based on the physical limitations imposed on his physique by the injuries suffered in his heroic actions at the Battle of Appomattox Station, which contributed significantly to General Lee's surrender of the Army of Northern Virginia to General Grant at Appomattox Courthouse."

Mayberry nodded. "Thank you, Mr. Blair. Colonel Salton, please call your first witness."

Salton called Max Frederick first. He described finding Raeburn's body, sending for Colonel Polk, and seeing the gold chain in Raeburn's hand. Then Sean Cady described his part in the investigation that night after having taken Alex to jail earlier to sleep off his drunk and then releasing him and sending him home at ten minutes to midnight. Richard was then called, and he added to the picture of the events of the evening. Finally Elizabeth gave her testimony as to the cause of death and her opinion that the shooter was right handed because of the angle and trajectory of the shot to his chest. Salton pressed her on that question, forcing her to admit that the shooter could have been standing to one side of the victim and shot at an angle, giving the impression of being right handed. The rest of the opening testimony went as all expected, establishing the presence and ownership of the watch, fob and chain found in Raeburn's hand.

Salton next called on the people who had been at Mrs. Allen's that night. Mrs. Allen told the tribunal of how Alex Raeburn and his friends Harold Kirtley, Eddie Rainey, James Granville, Robert Brooks, and Henry Armistead had all been in her establishment, and that Raeburn had been drinking heavily. "At a little after nine thirty," Mrs. Allen said, "Alex left my establishment, and his friends followed him outside. He was angry and yelling, so I followed them into the street, and watched as he went up towards Mr. Jackson's tavern, yelling and cursing at Charlie Redmond, who was standing on the porch smoking a cigar. Granville attempted to warn him off, but Raeburn kept going toward General Redmond, cursing and threatening him. General Redmond eventually responded, walked toward Alex and threatened to lay him out in the street if he did not move on. At that point, Provost Polk stepped in, whistling for one of the deputies, who took Alex into custody. Provost Polk told Deputy Cady to put him in the jail to sleep it off. The other boys came back into my place for another round. They left shortly after eleven."

Salton looked thoughtful. "Mrs. Allen, you live above your shop, correct?

"Yes, sir."

"And Mr. Raeburn was shot approximately a block and a half up the street from you?"

"Yes, sir."

"Yet you did not hear any gunshots?"

"No, sir. I didn't hear anything until that deputy started

blowing his whistle and making a ruckus when he found the body."

"Mrs. Allen, are you sure you did not hear any noises at all?"

She thought for a minute. "No, sir. At least not unless you count the freight train that comes through every Saturday night. That whistle could raise the dead."

"Thank you, Mrs. Allen."

Salton briefly called each of the men who had been with Alex that night. They each confirmed Mrs. Allen's story.

The next witness was George Randall, the Culpeper train station master. He testified that a freight train comes through Culpeper every Wednesday and Saturday night at midnight, and gives three blasts of the steam whistle – one long and two short – as a warning at the crossing. The train was on time that night."

Duncan was the next witness that Salton called. He was asked to describe the beating that Charlie had given Alex beside his storage shed.

Charlie smiled a reassuring smile at Duncan, who rubbed his hands together before beginning. He more than anyone knew Duncan's stutter would be pronounced as it always was when the man was nervous or stressed. "W-well, sir, it seems t-that Mr. R-raeburn h-had laid his h-hands on G-general R-redmond's wife, and not in a h-helpful or w-welcome way. General R-redmond p-p-pulled him off her and b-beat the s-snot out of h-him with his c-c-cane before the b-boys and I c-could p-p-pull him off."

"Mr. Nailer, is it your opinion that General Redmond's intent at the time was to beat Mr. Raeburn to death?"

Duncan gave a huge sigh and nodded, not wanting to make the admission. "I t-think so, sir, if w-we had not p-pulled him off and c-calmed him down."

Richard was next on the stand, this time to address the issue of motive. “So, Colonel Polk, how long has this antipathy existed between General Redmond and Mr. Raeburn?”

“Well, gentlemen, I believe it started when Mr. Raeburn laid General Redmond out cold in the churchyard in January of last year. Raeburn hit the general in the face, telling him he deserved it for the battles he had fought in Tennessee during the war. Raeburn would follow General Redmond around town, lurking and threatening him on multiple occasions. Then in August, Mr. Raeburn laid his hands on Mrs. Redmond; the general caught him and beat the tar out of him, as Mr. Nailer said.”

“Excuse me, Colonel Polk, but why were no charges brought then against either man?”

“Well, Mrs. Redmond did not want to deal with the social stigma, scandal and stress of a sexual assault charge, so they basically called a truce – no charge of attempted rape for no charge of assault, although I suspect most juries would have found General Redmond’s actions that day to be completely justifiable.”

“Thank you, Colonel Polk. Were there other instances of conflict between General Redmond and Mr. Raeburn?”

“There were.” He nodded. “In December of last year, General Redmond’s payroll was robbed. In February, the strong box that had held the payroll was returned with a thank you note from Nathan Bedford Forrest in it. While we did not have sufficient evidence to prove that Mr. Raeburn had stolen the payroll, it was fairly obvious, since Raeburn had served under Forrest in the Army of Tennessee and the thank you note was for the contribution to the creation of General Forrest’s organization, the Ku Klux Klan. Shortly after that, we had an incident here in Culpeper that was very much like the Klan’s actions, where a cross was burned in the local colored town and a number of Negroes were threatened. General Redmond’s son Darby was beaten rather severely by the sons of two of Raeburn's close associates in March. He and his wife had several horses stolen as well."

"Was there not an incident between General Redmond and Mr. Raeburn that you were witness to in April?"

"I am afraid so. General Redmond was having lunch with me in Jocko Jackson's tavern when Raeburn came in and said some appallingly insulting things about General Redmond's wife and cousin. General Redmond pulled a pistol, aimed it at Raeburn, and told him to shut up."

"In your opinion, do you think that General Redmond would have pulled the trigger if Raeburn had continued to insult his wife and family?"

"To be honest, I do not think so. I have known General Redmond for a number of years; in fact, I was his second in command when he took over the 13th Pennsylvania Cavalry shortly before the Battle of the Wilderness. Charlie Redmond is many things, but a cold-blooded murderer he is not."

"Were there any repercussions from that confrontation in April?"

"Well, in May, General Redmond's barn was burned in an obvious case of arson, and two men and a number of horses died in the fire. I could not prove it, but am fairly certain it was Raeburn or one of his associates. He also received an anonymous note warning him to guard his children closely. At that point, General Redmond hired the Pinkertons to come in and provide protection for his family and property."

"So you are telling me that it is your belief that General Redmond would not seek to end Alex Raeburn's life after his wife was assaulted, and his wife and cousin were insulted multiple times. His son was beaten, his horses were stolen, his money was stolen, his barn was burned, two of his men were murdered, his horses destroyed, and his children threatened? Supposedly all by this man? The deceased, Alex Raeburn?"

Richard Polk blinked and stared at Salton. No one had ever put it to him like quite like that.

Then he responded. "Sir, as I said, I have known Charlie Redmond for a long time. I have seen this man order our troops to collect up **all** wounded after a battle, regardless of which side they fought for, and expend our medical supplies to care for the enemy as well as for our men. I have seen him take every step possible to preserve men's lives, even when it put him at risk. I have seen him rip an eager young officer to shreds when the man's stupidity and eagerness to partake in the so called glory of battle cost needless lives. He came here after the war and since he has been in Culpeper, he has taken innumerable steps to rebuild this town. No stranger was ever turned from his door; no refugee went without because of Charlie Redmond. He and his wife have adopted five war orphans and are raising them as their own. No, I do not think that Charles Redmond would commit cold-blooded murder."

"Sir, even the most saintly of men have their limits. Thank you, Colonel Polk."

"Will John Xavier Jackson please take the stand?" Jocko went up and was sworn in.

"Tell me, Mr. Jackson, how well do you know General Redmond?"

"I probably know Charles Redmond as well or better than any man on the face of the earth. We met during the Mexican conflict, when we were both still wet behind the ears recruits. Cannon fodder, you know. Shortly before the Battle of San Jacinto, he and I were sent to ride reconnaissance. We were ambushed by a troop of Mexican soldiers in a box canyon outside of town and I was badly wounded. There was no way out, so Charlie Redmond bandaged me up as best as he could, strapped me to his back, and climbed the wall of the canyon to get us out of there. Two hundred feet straight up, under fire; hand over hand with no ropes or straps. I survived thanks to him. So after the war, when they sent him off to The Point to become an officer, I went with him to be his batman. Been his batman from then until he retired after Appomattox. Now I run a tavern here in town and Charlie and I are still friends. He is **my best** friend."

"So, Mr. Jackson, you were present the day General Redmond drew a gun on Mr. Raeburn and threatened to shoot him."

"Yes, sir."

"And would you say that General Redmond was very angry when he did so?"

"Yes, sir."

"Angry enough so that if Mr. Raeburn had pushed him too far, he would have pulled the trigger?"

"Well, sir, that is truly hard to say. Mr. Raeburn was being a right proper asshole, what with calling both Mrs. Redmond and Miss Redmond, excuse me, Mrs. Vile now, you know the minister's wife, whores and sluts, and their children bastards and by-blows. Why, I was hot under the collar at Raeburn for what he was saying, and they ain't my women or children. I think that the fact that General Redmond did not pull the trigger on that .36 caliber Colt of his right then speaks more to his self-control and sense of ethics than anything else. So, no sir, I do not think he would have pulled the trigger. He just wanted to put the fear of God into Raeburn, I'd say."

"So General Redmond thinks he speaks for God?"

Blair stood up. "Objection, gentlemen."

"Objection sustained. Colonel Salton, please refrain from sarcasm in your questioning."

"Let us turn to the night of the murder. Was General Redmond at your tavern that night?"

"Yes, sir, as were several others. There is a friendly game of cards played on Saturday evenings by a group of men in the community, while the ladies go over to my wife's tearoom and play mah jong."

"And who was at this friendly game of cards that evening?"

"Well, there was General Redmond, Colonel Polk, Reverend Vile, Mr. Nailer, and Mr. Cooper."

"And are these the usual players?"

"Well, General Redmond, Colonel Polk, Mr. Cooper, Reverend Vile and myself are the regulars at the table. The others sit in from time to time, as Duncan did that night, yes, sir. "

"So what happened?"

"Well, the cards weren't falling good for anyone, and it was hot and sultry for a September evening, so the game broke up a bit early; around 9:30. Several of the men got fresh drinks and stepped out on the porch to smoke a cigar and catch whatever little bit of breeze they could find. We waited for Rex and the ladies to join us when they finished their last round. A few minutes later, Alex Raeburn came staggering up the street, drunk as a skunk, and shouting crude curses at General Redmond, talking about the ladies." Jocko stopped and took a drink of water. "General Redmond turned his back on Raeburn at first because he could tell Colonel Polk had it under control. He was talking to me and the other men, trying his best to ignore Raeburn. Then Raeburn said something about Charlie's children."

"And what did General Redmond do then?"

"He stepped down into the street, told Alex to shut up and leave him alone, go home and sleep it off, or he would lay him out then and there."

"And do you think General Redmond meant he would kill him where he stood?"

"No, sir. He was not armed that night. I think General Redmond was thinking of taking his cane to the man again, but then Colonel Polk stepped in and sent Raeburn off to jail to sleep it off."

Salton nodded. It was not exactly the answer he had wanted, but he felt he had enough so that with the hole in Redmond's timeline that night, he could make his case.

At that point, General Mayberry interrupted, saying, "It seems to be a good point at which to break for lunch. Court is adjourned. We will reconvene at 2:00." With a bang of his gavel, the tribunal stood and filed out. Richard and Sean escorted Charlie back to jail, along with Rebecca and his lawyers; Jocko ran to collect the lunch he knew Esther had waiting for them.

Charlie sat on his bed with Rebecca beside him, their fingers threaded tightly together. Blair flopped into Charlie's armchair while the others stood ranged around the small cell.

Charlie cleared his throat, then asked, "So, how do you think it is going?"

Waite looked at Blair, then spoke up. "I think they have done a good job of establishing motive. The man has dogged your steps for months and has definitely upped the ante each time. But their work to establish that you plotted his murder outright was less successful."

"What do you think they will do next?"

"Call Kate Warne to the stand to establish your timeline. The train whistles pretty much established the time of death as midnight exactly."

"And I have no alibi for midnight. So the question is, given that I did not know when Richard or Sean was going to let him out of jail, how could I know to go back to meet him? And given my physical condition, how could I get from home to Culpeper in that amount of time, not to mention the fact that I cannot hold a .44 in my right hand, let along shoot one?"

"Well, we know that you could make it to Culpeper on Jack in ten minutes, so that part is arguable."

"And bring him home covered in sweat and lather."

"Yes, well…all we can do is keep going. We will get our turn soon."

As Waite had predicted, Kate Warne was indeed the next witness called. She came to the stand carrying all of the log books from her staff for that night.

Her testimony established a clear record of where Charlie had been seen by the Pinkerton guards that night, and the notebooks were entered as evidence. Charlie had returned home at 10:32 that night and had gone upstairs. Charlie had been in the front hall, heading downstairs at 11:04. He was seen at the southern border of the property near the creek at 11:25, riding to the north toward the apple grove. At 11:35, he was seen riding into the apple grove. He then was seen at the barn at 12:15, and went up to bed at 12:25. Kate was required to state that Charlie's whereabouts could not be determined for forty minutes; between 11:35 and 12:15, and that he certainly had plenty of time to ride into Culpeper at a walking pace and be there by midnight.

Salton then called Captain Lightborne to the stand. Lightborne testified that they had conducted a test to determine how quickly General Redmond's horse Jack could travel from town to the barn with a man of similar size and riding skills as General Redmond. He described the test in detail and noted that all observers had timed Jack's run from town to the barn at eight and one half minutes. Therefore, it was possible for General Redmond to have been in Culpeper at midnight and be seen grooming Jack in the barn at 12:15.

Salton rested his case.

The members of the tribunal consulted with one another and then decided to adjourn for the day. The defense was to begin presentation of their case first thing in the morning.

CHAPTER 12

Tuesday, September 24, 1867

Blair opened his defense promptly at 8:00 that morning. His opening statement was concise and to the point. "Gentlemen, I will show that General Charles Redmond at no time ever initiated the conflict between himself and Mr. Raeburn, but only responded in the moment to the insults, assaults and threats offered by the victim. I will provide evidence to the effect that General Redmond is not the kind of man to plot and execute a cold-blooded murder. I will demonstrate that the permanent injuries General Redmond sustained during the Battle of Appomattox Station were such that it would have been very difficult for him to perform the acts necessary to kill Mr. Raeburn."

After a moment, he continued. "I will provide physical evidence to show that General Redmond was in his apple grove at the time that Mr. Raeburn was shot. And I will demonstrate that the watch that was found on Mr. Raeburn's body had been missing from his home for many months. In fact, gentlemen, I will demonstrate that General Redmond would not, could not, and did not commit the cold-blooded murder of Alexander Fancher Raeburn."

Blaire stopped and took a sip of water. He wanted that pause to let that last line sink into the tribunal members' minds.

"I would like to recall Mr. Duncan Nailer."

Mayberry spoke to Duncan. "Mr. Nailer, let me remind you that you are still under oath."

"Yes, s-s-sir." Duncan settled into the witness chair.

Blair smiled at the young man. "Mr. Nailer, you have known General Redmond for several years, have you not?"

"Yes, s-s-ir. For about five years now, I guess."

"And how did you come to know him?"

"He was m-m-made c-c-commander of t-the 13th, s-sir."

"And as a commander, how was he in dealing with the men?"

"He, he t-t-tried to t-take g-g-good care of us, s-sir."

"And when there was a problem?"

"B-b-by the b-b-book, s-sir. Even when th-th-there was a r-r-rape, and he had t-to order a h-h-hanging, he he was b-b-by the b-b-book."

"So, Mr. Nailer, were you witness to any of the confrontations between Mr. Raeburn and General Redmond?"

"Yes, s-s-sir. The f-f-first time I ever s-s-saw Mr. Raeburn w-was after ch-church. M-m-must have b-b-been almost two years ago – in winter. General Charlie, um, R-redmond, came out of ch-ch-church; R-raeburn walked up to him, and hit him s-s-square in the f-f-face. S-s-second t-t-time was l-l-last summer. Raeburn was b-b-b-being w-w-way too f-f-friendly with Miss R-rebecca, Mrs. Redmond. Heck, I d-d-do not get that f-f-friendly with my w-w-wife unless I know we are alone. Miss R-r-rebecca was s-s-struggling. General Charlie s-saw it, m-m-moved like l-l-lightening, p-p-pulled Raeburn off his w-w-wife and then b-b-beat the s-s-snot out of h-him. M-my boys and I p-p-pulled him off and t-took him inside. B-b-by the t-time I came back out, Colonel P-polk had s-s-sent R-raeburn off to Dr. Elizabeth."

"Did you ever see Mr. Raeburn and General Redmond together after that?"

"Yes, sir. After the c-card game the night R-r-raeburn w-w-was s-shot."

"And what happened?"

"It w-w-was like Jocko said yesterday. R-r-raeburn was d-drunk and n-nasty. He s-said all s-s-sorts of things about General C-charlie's w-wife and children. General Charlie ignored h-him for a while, then t-turned around, t-told him to s-shut up or he'd lay him out in the s-street. General C-charlie raised his c-c-cane and shook it at Raeburn. Then Colonel Polk had him hauled off to j-jail to sleep off his d-drunk."

"In your opinion, given how well you know General Redmond, would he have come back to shoot Mr. Raeburn?"

"N-n-no, sir." Duncan shook his head emphatically. "T-that was n-not G-general C-charlie's way. He m-might have b-beat the hell out of h-him again if he insulted the w-women or c-children, but he w-would not have c-come b-back to shoot him."

Duncan was excused. Blair then called Richard back to the stand.

"Tell me, Colonel Polk. Have you been present at every confrontation between General Redmond and Mr. Raeburn?"

"Yes, sir."

"Why was that, Colonel Polk?"

"Well, Mr. Raeburn seemed to have a particular, focused hatred for General Redmond. And we have evidence that Mr. Raeburn was involved in some way with General Forrest's new organization the Ku Klux Klan, and had been involved in one incident involving a cross burning and threatening of some of the black folks over in Sweetwater. So my men and I tended to keep a close eye on Mr. Raeburn's activities. We also had reason to believe that he was involved in the theft of General Redmond's payroll, and of several of his horses. Though we have no evidence, I suspect Mr. Raeburn was also involved in some way in the arson that burned down General Redmond's barn and killed two of his men and several of his horses. Bluntly, Raeburn was a trouble maker, and I was trying to keep the trouble to a minimum."

"Colonel Polk, at any time did you see General Redmond instigate a confrontation between himself and Mr. Raeburn?"

"No, sir. In fact, several times, I saw General Redmond go out of his way to avoid a confrontation. In every case when there was a confrontation, it was started by Mr. Raeburn."

"And on the night that Mr. Raeburn was shot?"

"Mr. Raeburn was definitely drunk. He started by insulting the ladies in Mrs. Jackson's tearoom. General Redmond turned his back on the man, pointedly ignoring him. Mr. Kirtley tried to warn Raeburn off and hold him back. General Redmond continued to ignore Raeburn until he insinuated a threat towards the general's children. Then and only then did General Redmond turn around and threaten to beat Mr. Raeburn – to lay him out in the street."

"And what did you do?"

"I summoned my deputy and sent Mr. Raeburn, still yelling insults, to jail to sober up."

"In your opinion, and from your knowledge of and your friendship with General Redmond, do you think that he would plan to return to town to kill Alex Raeburn?"

"No, I do not. General Redmond had a temper, like all men.

When he is pressed too far, for example when his children or his wife are threatened and insulted, he is liable to snap. But to commit cold-blooded murder? I have known him for a number of years, and I do not think Charlie Redmond is capable of doing so."

"I have to ask you, Colonel Polk, how did General Redmond react to your inability to find the culprits who stole his money and his horses, and who set fire to his barn, killing two men and a number of horses?"

"His response was very straightforward. He told me that he trusted the law to take care of the miscreants eventually. In the mean time, he hired personal guards from the Pinkerton organization to protect his property and his family. He also purchased several trained guard dogs to further help protect his family and property. To him, that was the only reasonable approach."

"So he never said anything to you about wanting Raeburn to be removed from the community?"

"No, sir. He said he suspected Raeburn and his associates. To be honest, I suspected them as well. But General Redmond left it to me and my men to find proof, if proof could be found."

"Thank you, Colonel Polk."

Elizabeth was next on the stand. She was asked to describe in detail the injuries that General Redmond had sustained at Appomattox Station and the degree of permanent limitations those injuries had left him. She described his injuries in depth, noting that he had only limited use of his right hand, with the last two fingers missing entirely, and very limited use of the middle finger. She also described the damage to his right buttock and leg, limiting his ability to ride any distance without the use of a special saddle without experiencing extreme pain and ending his ability to jump a horse at all without immediate and paralyzing agony.

"Does General Redmond have such a special saddle?"

"He had one, but it was destroyed in the barn fire and, as his saddles must be specially crafted, it had not yet been replaced."

"From what you have described, Dr. Walker, I am surprised General Redmond can ride at all, let alone walk without the use of a cane."

"There are times when he still needs a cane to walk, but he has received some expert therapy from a man trained in oriental medicine that has improved his mobility."

"And who might that be?'

"His name is Dr. Tongzhi Xiang. We call him Rex. He is a traveling companion to Reverend and Mrs. Vile. I have learned much from him in the treatment of serious injuries."

"Thank you, Dr. Walker. You are excused. I now call Tongzhi Xiang to the stand."

Rex rose and stepped forward, glancing at Elizabeth with a smile as they traded places. This was not the coolie that so many people thought him to be. This was a man in a custom made western suit, not clad in his normal oriental silk robes. This was the Oxford educated member of the Chinese royal family. He took his position and was sworn in.

Mayberry interrupted before Blair's questioning could begin. "Excuse me, Dr. Xiang? Is it proper for you to swear your oath on a Christian bible?"

Rex looked at the general and smiled, slowly. "Excuse me, General Mayberry. My family name is Tongzhi. Xiang is my given name. And yes, it is. I am baptized into the Church of England and am a deacon within that organization." The upper class British accent was striking in this room full of southerners and gruff military officers.

"Can you please tell the court what kind of medical training you have received, Dr. Tongzhi?"

"Certainly. I studied eastern medicine at the Shaolin monastery in Henan Province in China. The monastery has been teaching medical techniques since 477 AD and is the leading school for physicians in China. I studied western style medicine at Oxford University in England and am licensed to practice western medicine in England and all her Majesty's territorial holdings."

"So with that background, can you tell me what you have done to assist General Redmond in regaining his physical capabilities and what permanent limitations you believe he still has? We are especially interested in his ability to handle a gun and ride a horse."

"General Redmond has progressed as far as either Eastern or Western medicine can manage. His right hand is very limited in what he can do with it. He can hold a pen, a pocket or table knife or a fork, possibly his razor, but not much more. This is because not only does he lack the last two fingers of his right hand, but the tendons and muscular structures of the remaining two fingers are damaged. He certainly cannot hold the weight of a .44 caliber pistol in his right hand, let alone fire it. As for riding a horse… Well, about half of the muscle of his right buttock is gone, as is a fair bit of the musculature of his right thigh. In particular, it limits his ability to bear weight on his extended right leg. With physical therapy and exercise, he is able to walk without his cane on a good day, but some days he is not able to walk without the cane, as he does not have the muscle strength to maintain his balance effectively. He can ride with a specially designed saddle, but he does not have the leg strength to jump his horse over anything but the smallest of obstacles."

After a pause, Rex added, "General Redmond suffers from

chronic low-level pain in both his hand and his right side and leg. Western medicine would typically prescribe laudanum for such chronic pain, but with the other injuries that General Redmond sustained, the opium in laudanum presented multiple unfortunate side effects. Therefore, I prepare customized cigars for his use to provide sustained, low level and non-addictive pain control. I use a combination of high-grade Turkish tobacco and cannabis. While this solution cannot address extreme pain, such as he would experience from a hard ride, it does control the daily, constant, nagging chronic pain without introducing any unfortunate side effects."

"Is there anything that distinguishes your cigars from others, so they would be uniquely recognizable?"

"Yes, there is. They are small cigars, both short and slender. They are wrapped using an unusual tobacco leaf that has been smoked over tea leaves. It is a very dark color; almost black, in fact. They are only obtainable from my contacts in Washington, therefore it is extremely unlikely that there would be another cigar in the area that would look like it and I only make them for General Redmond."

"So is it your opinion that General Redmond could not have made the ride to Culpeper, shot Mr. Raeburn at midnight and returned to be grooming his horse at 12:15?"

"Theoretically, he could have made that ride; however, he would be in debilitating pain and unable to walk, even with his cane, on the following day. When General Redmond's children were threatened, he rode into Culpeper to summon help at the same rate of speed he would have needed to ride at to return to the barn by 12:15 on the night in question. I was summoned to treat him that particular afternoon, as he was in so much pain, and there was much bruising because of his lack of muscle in the right buttock and leg, that he was unable to walk without my assistance. A number of people saw him the next day after the Raeburn incident, myself included, and he was walking without his cane and showing no signs of being in pain. Therefore, it is my professional opinion as a licensed physician that General Redmond could not have fired the .44 caliber pistol with his right hand, nor could he have made the ride in the timeframe allowed without showing signs of extreme pain on the following day, which he did not."

"Thank you, Dr. Tongzhi."

At that point, General Mayberry called a recess for lunch. Blair would continue the defense that afternoon.

After lunch, the defense then called Ralph Simpson, the Pinkerton man who had seen Charlie grooming Jack that night.

"Mr. Simpson, I understand you saw General Redmond grooming his horse at the stables at 12:15 in the morning. Can you confirm that and describe the condition of both the horse and of General Redmond when you saw him?"

"Yes, sir. When I saw him, it was exactly 12:15. General Charlie had just pulled the saddle off of Jack; the saddle pad was still on. The horse was playing with General Charlie's hair as he was brushing him down. It only took a couple of minutes; Jack wasn't even sweaty under the pad. General Charlie gave him an apple out of a bunch he was carrying in his hat and then headed toward the house."

"Was General Redmond showing any signs of distress?"

"No, sir. He was laughing at the horse's antics, telling him there was no one awake in the house to get the hay off his back the horse has just put down his collar. And that he, Jack the horse, should be ashamed of himself." The guard chuckled. "He talked to that horse like it was a person."

"So you are sure that the horse showed no signs of having been ridden hard, nor did General Redmond show signs of having ridden hard."

"No, sir. No sweat on the horse or the man, and no dust on either of them."

Kate Warne was up next for the defense. She pulled the bag with the three distinctive cigar butts in it, and explained when and how they were found. She pointed out that there had been a fairly heavy rain on the night of Friday the 5th, which would have destroyed any butts put in the grove before Saturday, and how she and Mr. Lord had found the butts on the ground, damaged by dew and curious animals, but as there had been no rain between the 7th and the 14th when they found them, it was reasonable to assume they were from Charlie on that night. This was reinforced by the fact that no one in town smoked the same brand or style of cigars, and those that Rex had made for Charlie were absolutely unique.

Blair briefly recalled Rex to identify one of the butts they had discovered in the grove, which he did.

After the brief recall of Rex, the defense called Sarah Coleman to the stand, which created a bit of a stir in the room, but the tribunal accepted her as a witness. She simply testified to the fact that when she arrived the morning of the 8th to prepare breakfast and entered the kitchen at 4:00 in the morning, she found a bowl of apples that had not been there the night before.

Next up was Tomas Coleman, who had arrived the day before on the train from Washington.

Tomas was sworn in. His voice was clear and his accent immediately labeled him as a well-educated man of color. He cleared his throat as Blair asked him to state his military history, his employment history with General Redmond, and his current activities.

"Gentlemen, I was born to slave parents here in Culpeper, but my father purchased my freedom when I was an infant and sent me north to be raised and educated as a free man of color. I was raised by a Quaker family in Pennsylvania and educated with the objective of becoming a physician serving the colored community. I am a survivor of Colonel Robert Gould Shaw's 54th Massachusetts Infantry Regiment's South Carolina campaign, and saw action at the July 18th assault on Fort Wagner, where I served as a medic for our regiment. I remained with the regiment after Colonel Shaw's death until the final battle we fought at Boykin's Mill. After the war, I returned to Culpeper to re-establish connections with my remaining family. I took a position with General Redmond as his valet, where I served him for several months before General Redmond and Dr. Walker made arrangements to allow me to continue my education as a physician, so I am currently a member of the first class of medical students at Howard University in Washington, D.C."

Blair showed Tomas the gold pocket watch. "Mr. Coleman, do you recognize this watch?"

"Yes, sir." The young man nodded. "It was a gift to General Redmond from Mrs. Redmond two Christmases ago. There is a matching pen knife that bears both their initials. A 'CR' on one side and 'RR' on the other. I believe if you open the watch you will see the cover has a matching engraving that reads, 'To CR From RR Christmas '65'."

"And do you remember this watch going missing?"

"Yes, sir. General Redmond was going to Washington to meet with a number of people to finalize the plans for his banking proposal and he wanted to take this watch and its matching pen knife with him, but he could not find them. He mentioned it to

Mrs. Redmond before departing and she told us to keep an eye out for them. Mrs. Redmond's lady's maid, Lizbet, and I looked for them but could not find them at the time. General Redmond has a terrible habit of leaving things lying around the house – pocket change, watches, pen knives, sometimes his money clip, and whatever else he may have in his pockets. There are always a number of people gathering his things up and placing them in his office--myself, Reg and Miss Rebecca included, so we assumed that the watch and knife would show up eventually."

Blair looked thoughtful. "So did you continue to search for the watch and pen knife?"

"Unfortunately, no. The children came down with the measles at that same time, and General Redmond returned from his trip with a terrible cold, and, well, it rather slipped my mind, to be honest. General Redmond has several watches and pocket knives, so it was not as urgent an issue as caring for five sick children and the gentleman of the house."

"Can you remember anything else that went missing?"

"No, sir. However, given General Redmond's habit of leaving things lying around, including money, it is not possible to say if other small items were pilfered without anyone noticing."

"As General Redmond's valet, I assume you know what weapons he has and if he carries weapons on a regular basis?"

"Yes, sir. General Redmond owns a number of weapons. His cane is weighted at the handle, and he carries it regularly, whether he needs it to walk or not. General Redmond has a pair of military issued side arms – Colt Army .44's which he keeps in a sealed display case along with a set of his insignia, a uniform sash, and his medals. Miss Rebecca had it all done up for his birthday as a very striking center piece for his office. He started going armed sometimes after the cross burning in Sweetwater in April of this year. He carries a Colt .36 caliber pistol in a shoulder holster under his right arm. Then he has a collection of assorted rifles and shot guns for various purposes."

"So he does own a .44 caliber Colt?"

"As I said before, sir, he owns two of them. They are sealed in the display case in his office, which would have to be broken open to get to them."

"And to your knowledge, has the display case been opened?"

"When I arrived at the house yesterday, it was still on its place on the mantle. The case is still sealed, sir."

"Thank you, Mr. Coleman."

Blair took a moment to check with Waite. "Do we have all of the means and opportunity issues covered?"

"As well as we can. I think we are down to character witnesses."

"Lee first or Grant?"

"Lee, I think."

Blair leaned over to the two generals sitting behind Rebecca. "Gentlemen, would you mind giving your testimony tomorrow? It is getting late and I would like to be able to put all of the character witnesses on the stand together."

"Certainly, Mr. Blair," Lee spoke first, with Grant concurring.

Blair then addressed the tribunal. "Gentlemen, it is getting on past 4:00. Would you consider adjourning for the evening and resuming defense testimony in the morning?"

Mayberry did not even bother consulting the other members of the panel. "An excellent idea, Mr. Blair. Court is adjourned until 8:00 tomorrow morning." With a bang of his gavel, everyone in the room rose as the tribunal filed out of the room.

Wednesday, September 25, 1867

As promised, Blair continued the defense with Charlie's character witnesses.

"General Lee, will you please take the stand?"

Lee was sworn in and Blair began his questioning. "General Lee, how long have you known Charles Redmond?"

"Charlie and I met during the Mexican war. I was a captain then, fresh out of West Point, and he was enlisted. We met during several reconnaissance missions and I helped him out when he was given a field promotion. I also was one of the officers who recommended he be sent to West Point. It was obvious even then that he was officer material. When I chose to place my allegiance with my state at the beginning of the war, I asked him to join me. He declined, and served with Generals Sheridan and Grant. I very much wish he had joined me; I would probably have received supplies at Appomattox, which would have, I believe, changed the outcome of the war."

Lee looked at Charlie. "Since then, Charlie has demonstrated his support and commitment to effective reconstruction in several ways. My wife and I have visited him and his wife here in Culpeper and have seen the work he has done to support the rebuilding of this community. He has also supported the fund raising efforts I have pursued for Washington College."

"General Lee, you have known Charles Redmond for a very long time, and have, apparently been close friends even after the conflict that separated you. In your opinion, is Charles Huger Redmond capable of planning and committing cold-blooded murder?"

"Charles Redmond is one of the most honorable men I have ever known. Yes, he is a soldier; yes, he is capable of killing other men in the heat of battle. I suspect he is capable of killing another man in a moment of extreme anger if confronted with a threat to his wife or children, but I do not believe Charles Redmond is capable of coldly plotting murder."

Lee saluted the tribunal and then resumed his seat behind Rebecca, patting her shoulder as he went by. Grant rose, expecting to be called next. And he was. After being sworn in, Blair asked him to describe his relationship with General Redmond.

"Charles Redmond served with me during the Mexican War, and like General Lee, I recommended him for education at West Point. General Lee and I both served in Mexico under General Winfield Scott, but if we met, I do not recall it. Then when the rebellion broke out, Redmond served under me during the Tennessee campaign and came east when President Lincoln assigned me to the Army of the Potomac. I gave him the 13th Pennsylvania Cavalry, which had lost its regimental commander, and he led that force from the Wilderness battle to the end of the war. Since then, I have called on General Redmond to provide advice and support for the reorganization of the army in my role as General of the Army under President Johnson. If I could, I would bring him back to active service, as he is one of the most level-headed, thoughtful gentlemen I know. On June 3rd of this year, I received a telegram from General Redmond." Grant pulled it out of his jacket and read it. "'Family threatened. Stop. Barn burned. Stop. Horses and men killed. Stop. Need help now. Stop. Respond Immediately. Stop. Chas. Redmond.' I immediately set up a meeting for General Redmond with Alan Pinkerton."

Blair nodded. "So, General Redmond's response was not to take the law into his own hands, but to retain professionals to guard and protect his family and property."

"Exactly, sir."

"In your opinion, do you think that Charles Redmond could have committed the murder with which he has been charged?"

"No, sir. Redmond might kill if his wife or children were directly and immediately threatened in the moment, but he would not plot and commit a cold-blooded murder, especially since he would have had to be a mind-reader to do so. If I understand correctly, Mr. Raeburn had been incarcerated under the order of Colonel Polk for the evening as he was drunk and belligerent in public."

"Thank you, General Grant."

Blair then recalled Mrs. Allen. When she resumed the stand, Blair asked, "Mrs. Allen, to your knowledge, has General Redmond assisted any of the people in Culpeper to rebuild their economic base and their lives without regard to the individual's allegiance during the recent rebellion?"

"Yes, yes, he has. He helped me get my payment for boarding Union soldiers during the war. He opened the bank, and they have made loans to a number of the local farmers and merchants, many of whom were in the Armies of Virginia and Tennessee. I am sure if you asked any of the folks around here, they would tell you the same thing."

"Thank you, Mrs. Allen."

Blair asked for an adjournment for lunch at this point. He wanted to have the character witnesses' testimony to be considered, and he wanted a few minutes to coach Charlie in preparation for his testimony.

As they went back into the courtroom after lunch, Blair stopped Charlie at the door, holding him by both arms and looking straight into his eyes. "Charlie, whatever you do, answer only the question asked. Salton is going to try and get you hot under the collar. Mayberry may as well, as he is allowed to ask questions. So whatever you do, keep your temper and only answer the questions as asked. Do NOT offer any additional information."

"Yes, Montgomery. You and Jerome have drilled that into me. I am ready – or as ready as I will ever get."

Charlie was sworn in and went to sit in the hard wooden chair that was placed for the witnesses. He tried to get comfortable in it but it was not possible. Blair chose to request a brief interlude to allow the bailiff to obtain the cushion that Charlie had been sitting on at the defense table for the witness chair.

Once that was settled, Blair began by asking Charlie very basic questions. "How long have you resided in Culpeper, General Redmond?"

"Well, I guess that depends. Do you want to know when I arrived? October of 1864, and I have not really left since, except when my duty to the Union during the war or my business commitments after the war required it."

Blair nodded, pleased that Charlie seemed to have finally gotten the message about not giving more information than needed.

"In October 1864, you arrived as part of Union forces under the command of Generals Sheridan and Grant?"

"Yes, sir."

"Your orders were to find suitable lands for winter quarters?"

"Yes, sir."

"And you did so? You made arrangements to billet your men on the lands belonging to Rebecca Gaines?"

"Yes, sir."

"Why?"

"As Mrs. Gaines' land had previously been a horse farm, it was exceptionally well suited to winter a cavalry unit."

Blair carefully walked Charlie through his short and intense relationship with Rebecca. It had been a necessary evil, since it had been suggested that she had been forced or coerced into her marriage. Then through the final months of the war and his return to Culpeper and then his long months of recovery with Rebecca's dedication and loving care.

Blair knew what he was doing--it was critical that everyone, most importantly the panel, see Charlie as a man who had overcome the complications of his injuries with the care and support of his family and friends. He needed to drive home the fact that this was a man with a loving woman at his side who did not doubt his innocence, and five children to care for.

After that, a few moments were spent recounting Charlie's efforts to help the town of Culpeper and its people get their lives back together. This led quickly to recounting his encounters with Raeburn over the past two years.

Charlie drew a deep breath. "I first met Alexander Raeburn on the last Sunday in January of last year. He had just returned to Culpeper after the war and this was the first time he attended church since his return. We met him in the churchyard after the service as people were filing out. My wife introduced him, and rather than shake my hand, he told me he had sworn to hit me in the face after Vicksburg if he ever had the chance. He then did so, knocking me to the ground in front of my wife and children. My three year old daughter, Emily, threw herself over me to, as she said, protect me from the bad man."

"And what response did you and the others in the churchyard have to that?"

"Colonel Polk and several other men restrained Mr. Raeburn, as he looked as if he were prepared to deliver another blow. I told him that if one blow was all the retribution I had been promised, I was a lucky fellow. Mr. Raeburn stepped back from the restraining men, excused himself, and left."

"And when did you next encounter Mr. Raeburn?"

"Over the next several months, I noticed Mr. Raeburn following me around town on occasion, but there was no confrontation. In fact, on the 4th of July, a number of the local ex-soldiers, Mr. Raeburn and me included, found the fireworks to be discomforting. We all retired to Mr. Jackson's tavern until they were over. We were all fine that night. Things remained quiet until August 8th. My wife and I had gone to town to run some errands. She had stopped by to call on Dr. Walker while I attended to business. Dr. Walker had been called away, so Mrs. Redmond started walking toward the bank, hoping to catch me in time for lunch. On the way, she encountered Mr. Raeburn by Mr. Nailer's lumber stores. He cornered her. I was coming into Mr. Nailer's at the same time to check on a small project I had asked him to handle, and happened to see Mr. Raeburn pinning her to a pile of lumber, fondling her breast and trying to kiss her. I went to my wife's defense. I beat him with my cane until Mr. Nailer and his men stopped me. I confess I told him that if he touched my wife again, I would kill him. I suspect there is not a man in this room who would not have done the same."

Blair raised his eyebrows at Charlie, signaling *too much information.*

"General Redmond, why were no charges brought against Mr. Raeburn for sexual assault or attempted rape?"

"My wife did not wish to face the public scandal that such a charge would bring and believed that the beating I had given Mr. Raeburn was enough to warn him from repeating the assault."

"When did you next have a confrontation with Mr. Raeburn?"

"I think it was the second Saturday in December during our weekly card game at Mr. Jackson's tavern. His niece, Roselle Jackson, who breeds and trains Irish wolfhounds as guard dogs, came in to get dinner. Mr. Raeburn and his friends were there and made fun of Miss Jackson for her clothing and her dog. Miss Jackson commanded her dog to guard me. One of Mr. Raeburn's friends, Mr. Rainey I think, approached my table, and the dog immediately went into a defensive stance. Miss Jackson called the dog back to her, but Mr. Raeburn decided to insult me about bringing in foreigners to take jobs from local men. He insulted my habit of hiring qualified negroes, carpetbaggers and Irishmen, which he called 'Micks,' a term that did not endear him to either Mr. Jackson or his niece. I pointed out to him that I had hired a number of local white men who had returned from the war. I asked him what he had done to create new jobs in Culpeper. Reverend Vile and Dr. Tongzhi tried to interrupt the confrontation, but Mr. Raeburn accused me of forcing my wife, turning the town upside down, bringing in carpetbaggers and foreigners, and taking away his 'southern heritage' and his rights. Miss Jackson's dog did not like Mr. Raeburn's tone and again took a defensive position. Mr. Raeburn and his friends left a few minutes later."

"So, even though the initial object of Mr. Raeburn's derision was Miss Jackson, he managed to turn his insults toward you?"

"Yes. I judged it was one of those situations where staying put was the wisest option."

"What was the next event that put you and Mr. Raeburn at odds?"

"Well, on December 13th, I had two men bringing the funds for me to meet my payroll on the following day. The men were attacked, badly beaten, and the strongbox containing the payroll money was stolen. While we could not prove it, Colonel Polk was fairly certain the robbery was the work of Mr. Raeburn and his companions."

"I take it that Colonel Polk was unable to prove that Mr. Raeburn was involved with the theft?"

"Yes, sir."

"And when did you next meet Mr. Raeburn?"

"It was in early April at a fundraiser that Mrs. Redmond and I hosted for General Lee to raise funds for Washington College. We saw one another, but did not speak. Then I saw Mr. Raeburn in Jocko's tavern on April 29th. He came into the bar while I was eating lunch after having followed me around town all morning. He started drinking and then he asked after my wife. I did not respond, and Colonel Polk warned him off. Mr. Raeburn then outright insulted my wife and my children."

After a pause, he went on. "My wife and I had recently had two more horses stolen, and again Colonel Polk suspected but could not prove it was Mr. Raeburn and his associates. Since the attack on the colored community in Sweetwater, I had begun carrying my Colt .36 when I was out and about. In the previous six months, my men had been attacked and my payroll stolen and the strong box had eventually been returned with a thank you note from Bedford Forrest. On two separate occasions, I had had horses stolen from our farm. My son had been beaten up by the sons of two of Mr. Raeburn's associates. I have to be honest; I was feeling a bit touchy."

Charlie sighed. "I know I should not have done it, but Mr. Raeburn and events associated with him had pushed me pretty hard. The insults to my wife and children were a little too much, particularly as he was commenting on my wife's breasts. He then referred to my cousin, who is now married to the Episcopalian minister, as a whore. I pulled my pistol, aimed it at Mr. Raeburn's forehead and told him to shut up and leave. He did. I felt very embarrassed about it afterward, as I do not normally let my temper get the best of me."

During this entire recitation, both the members of the tribunal and the prosecution attorneys had been busy scribbling notes. Waite took notice of this, and feared Charlie was in for a rugged cross examination.

"So what, if anything, happened after that?"

"I do not remember seeing Alex Raeburn for quite a while. However, just ten days later, someone committed arson. They burned my barn down, killing two of my best men in the fire, and burning a number of horses to death. After the barn burning, I took to riding the boundaries of my property at night to protect me and mine. Four days after that, I received a written warning in my morning paper to guard my children. I was feeling besieged, and very threatened, so I contacted General Grant, who put me in touch with Mr. Pinkerton, and hired his guards to protect my family and property. That afternoon, one of my dogs, the one who guarded the barn and who we thought had been killed in the fire, came home, badly injured, and carrying a piece of brown gabardine, such as most of the men around here wear as work pants. Miss Jackson believes that the dog will be able to identify the person who set the fire."

"Did you see Mr. Raeburn again at any time before the day he was killed?"

"I may have seen him around town, but made no note of it. The next time I remember seeing him was the evening before he was killed."

"Can you please describe exactly what happened that evening, from the time you saw Mr. Raeburn from the porch of Mr. Jackson's tavern until you retired to bed that night?"

"As you have heard, the poker game broke up early, around 9:30. The ladies were still playing mah jong so the fellows and I walked out on the porch to have a last drink and a smoke while they finished up. Mr. Raeburn and a couple of his friends came staggering up the street from the direction of Mrs. Allen's. He saw me on the porch and started insulting my wife and cousin, again calling them whores. I turned my back on him, ignoring him until he started in on my children. I turned around and stared at him. Colonel Polk intervened and suggested to Mr. Raeburn that he go home and sleep it off. I stepped forward and raised my cane. Mr. Jackson tried to stop me. I told Mr. Raeburn that I had had enough, and if he did not want to find himself laid out in the middle of the street, he would listen to his friends and the provost, and go home. Then Colonel Polk arrested him and sent him off to jail, I think with Deputy Cady, to sleep it off."

"My buggy came around a minute or two later, and my wife and I went home. We got there around 11:00. Mrs. Redmond and I went up to our room. She went to bed, but I decided to go ride the property. I told her I would be back in about an hour or so. I went to the stable, saddled Jack, rode south, then east to the creek, crossed the creek and went to the apple grove on the northeast edge of the property. I saw several of our Pinkerton guards as I went. There is a stump in the middle of the apple grove, so I dismounted, sat on my stump, smoked a couple of regular cigars and my before-bed special cigar, collected up some early ripe apples, and went back to the stable. I saw one of the Pinkerton guards at the stable. I brushed Jack down and dropped the apples off in a bowl in the kitchen on my way up to bed. I was in bed by about twelve thirty."

"Did anyone see you between the stable and the bedroom?"

I saw one of the Pinkerton guards as I was brushing Jack down, and another when I came up the stairs from the kitchen."

"When did you discover Alex Raeburn had been killed?"

"The next morning, when Colonel Polk and two of his

deputies came to the house, took me into custody, and took me to the jail. That was the first I heard of it."

"General Redmond, did you kill Alexander Raeburn?"

"No, sir. As far as I knew, Mr. Raeburn was in jail, sleeping off a drunken evening. I never left my property after getting home from the poker game."

"Thank you, General Redmond." Blair turned to General Mayberry. "The defense rests."

General Mayberry looked at Colonel Salton. "You may cross-examine the witness, sir."

Colonel Salton sat at the prosecution table for a full two or three minutes before he even bothered to look at Charlie. Then with a sniff, he plucked the pocket watch from the table and moved to the witness stand.

"Do you recognize this watch, General Redmond?"

"Yes."

"Please." Salton leaned on the banister nearest the chair that Charlie sat in and gestured, causing the watch to swing near the defendant's face. "Tell us more."

"It was a gift from my wife. Christmas time, two years ago. It came up missing last spring and I have not seen it or the matching pen knife since."

"And you are so thoughtless of your wife's gifts that you did not look for it?"

"Sir, I found it to be missing as I was preparing to go to Washington for a week of meetings. I asked my wife and household staff to keep an eye out for it, as I have an unfortunate tendency to leave things lying around the house. When I returned, all five of my children had the measles, I had a miserable cold, the household was in turmoil, and it slipped my mind."

"So, how did it get in Alex Raeburn's hand the night he was murdered in the street?"

"I have no earthly idea." Charlie shook his head.

"Alex Raeburn did not yank it from your vest when you pulled the gun and shot him in the chest? Before he fell back and you delivered the killing blow between the eyes?"

"No."

Mr. Blair was in his feet instantly. "Objection, leading the witness!"

"Objection sustained. Colonel Salton, please remember yourself."

The man nodded and returned to the table, where he dropped the watch with a clunk. Then he turned to Charlie again and drew a deep breath before asking, "You hated Alex Raeburn?"

Charlie nodded.

Salton put his hand to his ear and leaned in toward the witness box. "Speak up, General Redmond. I am afraid we will need a verbal response."

"Yes."

"Yes. You hated Alex Raeburn. You had threatened Alex Raeburn's life on more than one occasion?"

Charlie's head dropped and then he lifted it and answered. "Yes."

"Alex Raeburn had humiliated you in front of your wife, your children, your friends and members of your church? Specifically the Sunday morning in January of 1866 when he hit you unexpectedly and knocked you to the ground?"

Charlie nodded. "The morning of my wedding anniversary. I celebrated with a black eye and a swollen jaw."

"But you did celebrate?"

"Yes. Quietly with my wife, that evening."

"Are you aware that last week would have been Mr. Raeburn's birthday? Too bad he did not have an opportunity to celebrate."

"Objection!" Blair raised his hand again. "Badgering the witness!"

"Sustained. Colonel Salton, I really do not want to have to warn you a third time."

"Yes, sir. My apologies to the panel." He drew a deep satisfied breath; it was going to be easy to get Charlie Redmond to slip the noose over his own neck.

"You said that you and Colonel Polk believed that your payroll theft in December was committed by Mr. Raeburn and his friends, though you could not prove it. I submit to you, General Redmond, that anything that happened to you that was untoward was something you would attribute to Mr. Raeburn, given your antipathy toward him. What have you to say to that?"

"Sir, my wife had been assaulted. Mr. Raeburn had specifically announced his desire to revenge himself on me for the outcome of the war. And my strong box was returned with a thank you note from Bedford Forrest for a contribution to support 'his boys,' which I assume meant the Ku Klux Klan. Mr. Raeburn served under General Forrest. The implications are clear; Mr. Raeburn was clearly suspect under the circumstances. Then my barn was burned by an arsonist, and two men, one of whom was still a boy, and a number of horses were killed. No one else in the community was the object of such attacks! Finally, my children were threatened! I believe I had every reason to suspect Mr. Raeburn and his associates, and to protect my family and property from future attacks." By the time Charlie was finished, his face had reddened, his voice had risen, and you could see the veins standing in his temples.

Blair, Jeremy, and the other members of the defense team simply shook their heads. Charlie had lost his grip, possibly disastrously. The summations were going to be critical.

General Mayberry looked at Blair. "Mr. Blair, do you have any more witnesses?"

"No, sir. The defense rests."

Mayberry looked out at the crowd, which was getting restless, whether over the possibility that Charlie would go free or just the length of the testimony he could not tell. But he decided to hold summations until the following day.

"Gentlemen, ladies. Thank you for your support. Colonel Salton, Mr. Blair, you may present your summations tomorrow. Court is adjourned."

CHAPTER 13

Thursday, September 26, 1867

Once the court was settled that morning, Mayberry got things underway quickly. He turned to Salton. "Colonel Salton, you may begin your summation."

"Thank you, General Mayberry. Colonel Douglas, Colonel Allenby." Salton bowed slightly to the tribunal. "Gentlemen, we have demonstrated a history of escalating antagonism between General Redmond and Mr. Raeburn, to the point where General Redmond believed, without proof, that Mr. Raeburn was responsible for some serious crimes – even heinous crimes – against his family and property. As far as General Redmond is concerned, as you have just seen, Alexander Raeburn was a serious threat, for whom the mere mention of his name could put General Redmond in a state of extreme rage. I suggest to you that General Redmond had more than sufficient motivation to want Alexander Raeburn dead. That extreme antagonism had been fired up yet another level when Mr. Raeburn insulted General Redmond's children, his wife and his extended family that night, a confrontation that ended with General Redmond threatening to lay Mr. Raeburn out in the street."

Salton took a sip of water. "So I think we have demonstrated that General Redmond had ample motivation for removing Alexander Raeburn from the face of the planet."

"As to means, I submit that there are more Colt .44's in this town than there are men. According to General Redmond's valet, he owns a set of them. Whether he used the ones in the display in his office or he picked up another one, from say Mr. Jackson's tavern, which I noticed he keeps on the back shelf in his tavern, in plain view of anyone, is moot. Gaining access to a loaded .44 in this town is a simple thing. Dr. Walker has suggested that the shooter was right-handed because of the angle of the bullet trajectories through Mr. Raeburn's body. I will concede that General Redmond's injuries prohibit him from firing a .44 with his right hand, but if General Redmond had been standing slightly to the right of the victim, rather than directly in front of him, the same angle would have been the result. And General Redmond had threatened to lay Mr. Raeburn out in the street, which the shooter certainly did, and had threatened to shoot Mr. Raeburn between the eyes on a previous occasion. The prosecution therefore contends that General Redmond had the means to shoot Mr. Raeburn in cold blood that night."

Another sip of water gave the tribunal time to absorb his words. "So we come to the issue of opportunity. Let me summarize the timeline of the evening. Shortly after 9:30 that evening, Mr. Raeburn and several of his friends emerged from Mrs. Allen's establishment, and walked up the street toward Mr. Jackson's Tavern. They saw General Redmond standing on the front porch of Mr. Jackson's and Mr. Raeburn started taunting

General Redmond. Several people warned Mr. Raeburn off, but he did not stop his haranguing. General Redmond threatened Mr. Raeburn with his cane, and Colonel Polk intervened, taking Mr. Raeburn into custody to sleep off his over-indulgence. Shortly after that, Mrs. Redmond was ready to depart for home."

"General Redmond and Mrs. Redmond arrived at home at 10:32, according to the logs of the Pinkerton guards at the Redmond home. At 11:04, General Redmond emerges and tells the hall guard he is going to ride around the property. By 11:25, another Pinkerton guard logged the General at the south east border of the property near the creek. At 11:35, another Pinkerton guard reported that he saw the General riding into the apple grove on the north east corner of the property. No one saw General Redmond again until 12:15, putting his horse away in the stables."

"At the same time, Deputy Provost Cady released Alexander Raeburn from jail at 11:50. Evidently, Mr. Raeburn walked south. Because no one in the community heard the two gunshots, and because of Dr. Walker's detailed estimation of the time of death, we believe Alexander Raeburn was shot at exactly midnight, as the Saturday night freight train came through the town and made a great deal of noise with its steam whistle as it did so, masking the sound of the gun shots. The shooter could have mounted his horse and been back at Redmond Stables in less than ten minutes riding briskly."

"Gentlemen, I believe t hat we have adequately demonstrated that General Redmond had the means, the motivation, and the opportunity to waylay Mr. Raeburn, shoot him dead in the streets of Culpeper, and return to his home riding a fast horse, which his normal mount is, within the time frame for which no one can account for General Redmond's location. We ask the tribunal to find General Redmond guilty of the pre-meditated murder of Alexander Fancher Raeburn and to sentence him accordingly."

Rebecca sobbed quietly. Charlie looked stunned. Blair, Waite, and Jerome looked at one another grimly. Blair's summation had to be fantastic.

Blair stood, bowed to the tribunal and looked back at Charlie.

"Gentlemen. Before you is a man who has repeatedly demonstrated his restraint in the face of profoundly disturbing, repeated assaults on his family and his property – assaults that have resulted in physical attacks on his wife and son, repeated public insults, loss of property, and finally the murder by arson of two of his valued employees, one of whom was just a boy. His wife and children were threatened, not just with insults, but as the attacks on his family and property escalated, it was reasonable to assume that those threats were for more damaging than just a beating such as his son received after school one day. Yet what was General Redmond's response to all of this provocation?"

"He turned to the local representatives of the law, and when that was not sufficient, he hired professional guards to protect his family and fields and **PREVENT** these miscreants who have been harassing him past tolerance from having an opportunity to do more harm. Men who seek personal vengeance do not hire guards; they go out and address the issue personally. If General Redmond was going to confront Alexander Raeburn, why did he not do so after the burning of his barn and the murder by arson of his men, Mr. Tarent and Mr. Rawlins? But no."

"The worst that General Redmond ever actually did was to beat Mr. Raeburn rather soundly after he caught Mr. Raeburn in the act of **ASSAULTING** his wife. Yes, he threatened Mr. Raeburn on two occasions, once with his pistol and once with his cane, but I point out to you that threats are not the same as actions. All General Redmond has ever done when he threatened Mr. Raeburn was attempting to protect his wife and family. He had multiple opportunities with greater provocation to attack Mr. Raeburn, but restrained himself."

"Gentlemen, I ask that you consider what you yourselves would have done if confronted with as much threat and provocation as General Redmond has faced, and if you would have been able to restrain yourselves and turn to the law and professional protection as he did, rather than take matters into your own hands?"

"Colonel Salton has suggested to you that Mr. Raeburn's repeated public insults to General Redmond, his wife and his family, coupled with the illegal acts for which General Redmond and Provost Colonel Polk had good reason to suspect were at the instigation of Mr. Raeburn, was sufficient motivation for General Redmond to ambush and kill Mr. Raeburn."

"I point out to you that General Redmond had an established pattern of deferring to the legal representatives of the government whenever possible; and in this case Colonel Polk placed Mr. Raeburn under constraint for public drunkenness. With far greater provocation in the past, why would General Redmond change his pattern?"

"In addition, we have heard from multiple individuals from General Redmond's past and from this community about the contributions he has made to rebuilding the community of Culpeper, and that those contributions in no way showed preference to unionists over rebels. His interest was in returning the community – the WHOLE community – to peacetime prosperity."

"There are those who might say that with the threats and damage done to him and his, General Redmond might indeed be justified in taking the law into his own hands. The representatives of the law had been unable to prove the most damaging of the assaults the Redmond family and staff sustained, though they were making every effort to do so. There are some communities that would judge horse thievery as justification for homicide. General Redmond and his family and staff suffered far worse than just horse theft at the hands of this man, yet General Redmond continued to defer to the representatives of the law to handle the matter."

"So in reference to the issue of motivation, I ask you, why would General Redmond, who has demonstrated repeatedly that he would leave the issue of Mr. Raeburn's outrageous and even heinous threats and outright assaults to the representatives of the law all of a sudden choose to ambush and murder this man whose post-war vindictiveness seemly knew no bounds?"

Blair took a deep breath, walked back to his table and seemed to refer to his notes. He then looked up and considered the panel. "As to means, gentlemen, there are two issues to address. First, could General Redmond have handled a Colt .44 effectively with his right hand, or accurately with his left hand?"

"Second, could General Redmond have made the ride back from downtown Culpeper to be seen in his barn, grooming his horse at 12:15 when the murder was committed at exactly 12:00 so as to mask the gunshots with the sound of the train passing through without having a serious impact on his physical condition that others would have observed on the following day?"

"We have heard from multiple witnesses that the loss of the last two fingers on his right hand, coupled with the damage to the muscles and tendons to the rest of his hand made holding a .44 caliber pistol in his right hand impossible for General Redmond. Indeed, General Redmond had retired his own military issue side arms to a display rack in his office and chose to carry a smaller, lighter Colt .36 caliber pistol in a shoulder holster accessed by his left hand. As Army officers yourselves, would any officer give up his valued side arms for a smaller pistol if he did not have to?"

"Dr. Walker has suggested that the shooter was right handed, based on the angle of the shots. Colonel Salton suggests that this interpretation is subject to the stance or position of the shooter. I point out to you that the pattern of powder burns would be different if the shooter was standing where Colonel Salton suggested, and that since it is obvious that General Redmond could not use his right hand to manage a gun, he is not the shooter."

"As to the ability to ride his horse to and from Redmond Stables, there are several issues that suggest this did not happen. First, while General Redmond's horse Jack is capable of making the ride from Culpeper to his stable in approximately eight minutes, that time requires the horse and rider to be going at an all-out gallop. Dr. Tongzhi has testified that the only other time General Redmond has made such a ride, he was debilitated to the point of being unable to walk without great pain and with the use of his cane on the following day – and that after extensive treatment for the ensuing injuries by Dr. Tongzhi. Multiple people saw General Redmond the morning following the murder moving quite easily and without the use of his cane, and he did not summon Dr. Tongzhi to treat pain or injuries."

"In addition, Pinkerton guard Simpson saw General Redmond a mere fifteen minutes after the murder grooming his horse. For Jack to have made the run from Culpeper to his stable in roughly eight to ten minutes the horse would have been sweaty and very dusty; General Redmond would have been wind-blown, dusty and disheveled. Neither animal nor man showed the inevitable results of such a ride."

"Based on the evidence, General Redmond did not have the means that Colonel Salton suggests to ride to town and kill Mr. Raeburn without showing extensive physical pain afterwards, which he did not do. Nor could he handle a Colt .44 with his right hand and using his left and shooting from an angle would have left a somewhat different pattern of powder burns."

"Finally, General Redmond was seen entering his apple grove at 11:35. He testified that he smoked three cigars while he sat and thought, and gathered newly ripened apples until returning to the stables and then his house. You have heard testimony that the butts of three cigars were found in the apple grove, two of General Redmond's usual brand and one of the special cigars that Dr. Tongzhi provides him for controlling chronic pain. These are very distinctive cigars. I point out that it had rained on Thursday night prior to the murder, and has not rained again until after the cigar butts were found. If it had rained, the water would have destroyed the butts, therefore the only way those butts could have gotten to the grove was if General Redmond smoked them that night as he said he had. I also remind you that Pinkerton guard Simpson saw General Redmond with a hat full of apples and the Redmond's cook Sarah Coleman found a bowl of fresh apples on her kitchen table the following morning. It is not reasonable to believe that General Redmond entered the grove at 11:35, smoked three cigars, rode to Culpeper to arrive by 12:00, and returned by 12:15 after gathering a hat full of the first ripe apples of the season."

"As to the watch, General Redmond and several others have testified that the watch had been missing for several months prior to the murder. There had been a number of workmen in and out of the house, and General Redmond had the unfortunate habit of leaving things like watches, pocket knives, and coins around the house. Anyone could have taken the watch, and had it grabbed by Mr. Raeburn from the thief."

"Finally is the question of prescience. General Redmond knew that Mr. Raeburn had been arrested to sleep off his alcohol consumption at the local jail. He had no way of knowing that Deputy Cady would let Mr. Raeburn out of the jail that night, nor that Mr. Raeburn would be in a place where he could be shot at exactly midnight when the train came through town. How could he? Deputy Cady did not know he was going to release Mr. Raeburn until he made the decision to send him home that night."

"I contend that there are far too many coincidences that would have to occur to provide a scenario where General Redmond would have reasonably had the opportunity to murder Alexander Raeburn."

"Gentlemen, I submit to you that General Charles Huger Redmond is an honorable man doing his best to raise and protect his family, contributing significantly to the reconstruction of the town and community of Culpeper, and while extremely provoked, did nothing more egregious than defend his wife and family. He is not the murderer you seek, and I ask you to find him not guilty. Thank you."

Blair bowed again and returned to the defense table.

General Mayberry stood, followed immediately by Colonels Allenby and Douglas. "Gentlemen of the Prosecution and Defense, thank you for your presentations. To all witnesses, this court expresses it appreciation. We will now retire to consider our decision." They filed out of the room. Charlie turned to the people now standing behind him. "Thank you all for your support." Then he was escorted back to his cell by Richard, Cady, and Frederick, with Rebecca surrounded by his lawyers and specifically supported by Jerome, following closely. Summations were finished in time for lunch.

~

Mayberry sat looking at the other two panelists. All three had been McClellan's men, and all three were agreed; cavalry men were arrogant show offs who thought they could get away with anything. "So, what do you think?"

Douglas spoke first. "I have no idea if he did it or not, but if we do not do something, that mob out there is going to lynch someone – either him or us or…" He trailed off, knowing full well that if they did not find Redmond guilty, the odds were good that Culpeper would become a firestorm of angry people. They did not need problems like they had in Louisiana and Tennessee.

"Well," said Allenby, "if this was a civilian trial, I would say that Blair raised enough reasonable doubt to get him off."

Mayberry nodded. "Fortunately for us, this is a military trial and we do not have the same standards. Our rules are based on reasonable suspicion, not reasonable doubt. So let us look at this rationally. Personally, if I were Redmond, I would have called Raeburn out and shot him long ago. But that would have brought a dueling charge, which would be just as messy as this is. Motivation is **not** a question. Raeburn was an obnoxious, vindictive bastard who taunted Redmond for nearly two years, but he was also a southern war hero – and there are too many damned rebels around here who want Redmond to hang."

Douglas looked thoughtful. "What about the watch? If my wife had given me a gold watch with my initials on it and it had been misplaced, I would have torn the house up looking for it, and if I could not find it, would have reported it as stolen to the provost."

"Yes, but Redmond is an extremely wealthy man. I suspect they do not notice the same things a typical, common man would find problematic and since the provost is also an old friend, he knows about General Redmond being a messy gentleman who leaves things lying out where anyone can pick them up – or where they can easily be knocked behind a piece of furniture, behind a mantle – anywhere." Allenby was good at being a devil's advocate.

Mayberry tapped his fingers on the table. "On the other hand, maybe he did not lose it; maybe he just did not tell anyone he had found it. And if someone did steal it, having the initials engraved on the cover would be something of a giveaway, I think."

"Unless the thief had the same initials as the general. Then who would ask?"

"I will give you that one, Allenby. But who has the same initials?"

Both Allenby and Douglas shook their heads.

Mayberry went on. "What about the horse? I grant that that the general's regular horse was not ridden hard. We cannot get around Simpson's testimony on that. But what if he had another horse waiting in the grove and simply turned it out after the ride, and switched back to his usual mount? The Redmonds breed thoroughbreds, and at least some of them must be bred for speed."

"If he were fit, I would agree with you, sir, but he showed no signs of the effects of such a ride."

"And both physicians are his friends. Dr. Walker was with him all through the war, and Dr. Tongzhi lived at his house while they were waiting for the old minister to die and now manservant to Redmond's cousin? Their testimony is at best questionable."

"As for the apples and the cigar butts, who knows when they

were put there? He may have had the butts in his pockets, left over from the card game, and just dumped them, for all we know."

The three panelists went on, examining each piece of evidence, questioning each piece of alibi for the rest of the afternoon and into the evening.

~

Friday, September 27, 1867

The attorneys sat around the table looking uncomfortable and unsure. Charlie paced frantically, easily covering the length of the room in four strides. Rebecca sat in a chair near the window tearing a handkerchief to ribbons as she watched the crowd swarming around the courthouse.

These people wanted Charlie to pay for a crime he did not commit. She was terrified he was about to do just that. She had seen the looks on the faces of those men when they had adjourned to deliberate. They were not friendly looking enough for her comfort.

Blair and Waite had both expected the decision to come back the afternoon before. The delay was not a good thing in their mind. And they knew both Mayberry and Salton. Neither of them was known for their love of cavalrymen.

Finally, there was a knock and a clerk stuck his head in, "The panel is back."

"Oh, God!" Rebecca came out of her chair in a near panic. "It cannot be good that they took so long!"

Mr. Blair shook his head as they all stood and prepared to go back to the courtroom. "I am afraid, Mrs. Redmond, it generally is not a good sign at all."

Once everyone was back the panel returned and the men took

their seats. Rebecca's heart sank and she began to feel very sick to her stomach.

"The defendant will stand," General Mayberry ordered. Charlie and Mr. Blair both stood. "In the matter of the State of Virginia verses Charles Huger Redmond, on the charge of pre-meditated murder, we find the defendant guilty." And with a loud crack of a gavel that made Charlie jump, it was over.

A disbelieving gasp ran through the room. Charlie's head dropped as he tried to catch his breath. Rebecca heard someone outside yell to the crowd outside, "Guilty!" and the responding roar of approval from those gathered around the courthouse. She noticed Margaret Williams standing on the steps looking very satisfied.

Everything was a blur for Charlie as he tried to wrap his mind around what had just happened. It was only when he heard Mayberry call his name that he raised his eyes back to the table. He had not heard one word the man had said until the very end. "Hung by the neck until dead."

Mayberry continued. "Provost, please have the gallows prepared as quickly as possible. I would like to be able to perform my role as official witness on Monday and then get home."

Charlie stared at Mayberry in disbelief, but found his voice to ask, "General Mayberry, sir? Monday is my son's twelfth birthday. With your permission, sir, I would prefer he not remember that his father was hung on his birthday for the rest of his life. Please, may I have that one day?" Tears fell freely from Charlie's eyes as his guts seized at the thought of being hung on Darby's birthday.

"I understand, General Redmond. Provost, arrange for the punishment to be executed on Tuesday."

Charlie stood there, immobilized by the realization that he

was about to die, not because of any crime he had done, but because he had not followed Pinkerton's orders and had taken a late night ride around the property. It was unbelievable. He blinked, not sure how long it was before he realized that he was being shackled again. He suddenly felt panicked when he recognized he had lost track of everything including his wife. "Rebecca!"

He tried to look around but two guards had him by the arms leading him from the room. The room was a flurry of action and movement. He could hear people yelling, some laughing. Someone was crying, and over near the window where Rebecca had been sitting, he saw her being tended by Elizabeth and Rex after clearly having fainted. That was the last vision Charlie had as they forcefully hauled him through the door and back to the jail.

Given the atmosphere in town and around the courthouse after the verdict, Rebecca was immediately placed in a closed coach and whisked back to the farm by Jerome, Kate, Edgar and a contingent of Pinkerton guards on horseback. Edgar held Rebecca tight against his chest as she sobbed. No one said a word. The only sounds the entire trip were the clopping of horses hooves and Rebecca crying.

When the coach pulled up to the house, she suddenly sat up and looked to Edgar with panic in her eyes. "The children! Oh, my God, Edgar, I have to tell them he is never coming home! How am I supposed to do that?"

Jerome and Kate shared uncomfortable looks before shifting their gaze to Edgar, who looked truly miserable. He tightened his hold on the distraught woman and said quietly, "You know you have my help and support, Rebecca. We will tell them together."

By the time the foursome were collected enough to leave the coach, Reg and Beulah were on the front porch. They could tell the news was not good and the second they saw Rebecca, Beulah broke into tears. "Oh, Lord, they are gonna hang him!"

Jerome could only nod to answer her as he and Edgar helped Rebecca inside and took her to the rear parlor. Before Kate could join them, she turned to the sound of another carriage coming up the drive. She was relieved to see Elizabeth; she knew very well that Rebecca would need her doctor. Before Elizabeth was out of her buggy, Kate requested a tea tray be brought to the parlor, then she met the doctor and walked in the house with her as Reg took care of making sure a stable boy took her horse and buggy to the barn.

Elizabeth sat her bag down, stripped off her coat and hat and looked to Rebecca. She was sitting in a chair near the fire, her arms wrapped around her middle, and she was nearly doubled over. Jerome looked on from his spot at the mantle; it was clear his was at a loss for what to do. Edgar was slowly and carefully rubbing circles on the distraught woman's back as he knelt near her, speaking softly. He raised his eyes to Elizabeth and nodded as he rose and stepped back.

She moved to the patient and knelt in front of her. "Rebecca, look at me."

Slowly, she raised her face and began sobbing again. "They are going to kill him, Elizabeth! They are going to hang Charlie!"

"I know," the doctor soothed as best she could. Reaching for her bag, she removed a small envelope and poured a powder into a glass of water sitting on the table next to Rebecca. "Drink this."

"I do not want it." She shook her head.

"I know, but you need it. It will help you calm down. It is only a mild sedative."

"Rebecca." Edgar took the glass and handed it to her. "Please, drink it."

Elizabeth was careful to keep an eye on the glass as Rebecca took it with very shaky hands. After she consumed the entire contents, the glass was deftly plucked from her fingers.

Kate met Beulah at the door and helped her bring the tea tray in. "Is there anything that we can do for Miss Rebecca?"

"Could you please bring a pitcher and basin?"

"Right away."

Twenty minutes later, the sedative was working and Rebecca allowed Elizabeth and Kate to help her freshen up before it was time to talk to the children. She managed a cup of tea and a bit of toast as well. She sat there with her cup clutched between her hands staring into the fire. "What am I supposed to tell them?"

"I think we must tell them the truth," Edgar offered softly as he rubbed her shoulder. "They are old enough to pick up talk around town; anything less will be a disservice to them."

She nodded and took his hand. "Thank you for being with me."

"Of course. Shall I go get them?"

She nodded again and closed her eyes, her mind quickly trying to find the words for the most difficult conversation she would ever have. Within minutes the door opened and Edgar escorted the three oldest to the sofa in front of the fireplace. They each took their seats, hands dutifully folded into their laps as they waited for whatever it was that the adults needed to tell them.

Rebecca took several deep breaths before managing to say, "I have some bad news."

“It is Papa?” Darby nodded. He really did not have to ask. He knew.

“I am afraid so.”

“Is Papa sick?” Emily was on her feet right away.

Edgar could see the panic rising in her little face and he immediately swooped in. He gathered her up into his lap and smoothed her hair back. “Emily, your Papa is not sick. However, there is another problem.”

“What problem?” Suzanne was up now and at Rebecca’s side, her hand on her mother’s arm. “When is Papa coming home?”

“He is not.” Darby stood and glared at all the adults. “They are going to hang him.” His tone was flat. His face showed his anger.

“What!” Emily sat straight up in Edgar’s lap, turning disbelieving eyes on her brother.

“Right?” Darby looked to Kate, then Jerome before turning tear filled eyes on his mother. “They have found him guilty of murdering that man and they are going to hang him!”

“Darby, please do not be so harsh around your sisters.” Rebecca stood and started toward him but he backed away from her.

“Why not? They need to know the truth! They need to know that they are going to hang Papa and he is never coming home!”

As both girls latched onto what their brother had said, they both dissolved into tears, Emily falling into Edgar and Elizabeth picking Suzanne up from the floor near the hearth. Rebecca was trying to follow Darby, who had bolted from the room, but Kate stopped her. “I will tend to Darby. You see to your daughters.”

She watched from her place in the crowd. It could not possibly be real. She could hear the sounds of the people around her. She could feel Charlotte's arms wrapped tightly around her shoulders. She could smell the rain in the air that had fallen that morning.

But seeing Charlie standing on those gallows could not possibly be real. It could not be true that they were binding his arms and legs to keep them from thrashing when the trap door dropped out from under him.

It could not be genuine that Edgar was standing next to him, giving him last rites and absolution. She watched in complete horror as Richard placed the dark hood over Charlie's head and then reached for the noose.

She thought she would be sick, her knees threatening to buckle when the rope was placed around his neck and tightened behind his left ear. She could see him shaking and she knew deep in her soul he was terrified and there was no way to comfort or save him.

Richard stepped back and raised his hand. Without a word, he dropped it and the trapdoor Charlie was standing on fell open.

Rebecca screamed and came up out of her nightmare. She immediately began searching for him and collapsed into frightened, agonized tears when she remembered he was gone. The dreams just kept getting worse.

CHAPTER 14

Friday, September 27, 1867

Charlie sat on the edge of his bed with his head in his hands. He had already vomited twice and he was certain there was nothing left in his stomach. His whole body was shaking and he was not so sure he was not about to pass out.

He was going to be executed in four days. Hung for a crime he did not commit.

He was going to be hung for killing Alex Raeburn and he had not even had the satisfaction of doing the deed. That really pissed him off. He was going to have to put his affairs in order for Rebecca and the children immediately.

"Guard!" He was on his feet at the bars yelling as loud as he could. He at least had found one last purpose and he would carry it through. "Guard!"

"What!" The annoyed young man, one of the temporary

guards Richard had been forced to deputize opened the door. "What do you want?"

"My attorney, Mr. Lord."

"What you want him for? They didn't do you no good."

"Just get him."

"When I have time." The man shut the door. Charlie flipped his table in frustration.

Two hours later, Jerome and Rebecca came through the door with the irritating little deputy. He gestured for Charlie to sit on his bed before he would unlock the door. He sat down with his hands clearly lying on his knees, shooting the guard a dirty look. Once they entered the cell the door was relocked and the guard mumbled, "Not nearly so high and mighty now, is you?"

Once the despicable little man was gone, Charlie stood and wrapped Rebecca up in his arms. "I am so sorry." His tears started now as he was faced with the reality of everything he was losing. "Jerome, I think it will be best for Rebecca and the children to leave Culpeper. Will you make sure…?" He felt her tremble in his arms.

"Of course, Charlie, if that is what Rebecca wants. I will do anything she needs."

Charlie tilted her head to look at him. It was clear there were simply no more tears for her at the moment. Her eyes were red and her face thoroughly tear stained. "I think it will be best. Perhaps you could find some land near Richmond. Close to Hopewell. I am sure you still have people there, family, who will welcome you and the children. You have plenty of money; I did not spend it all." He tried to tease, hoping to stop his own tears.

She hugged him tighter trying to believe she could stop this nightmare by holding onto him. "I do not want to live anywhere without you." She cried, her fingers digging into his shirt, "You are my husband – my only husband. Yes, I was married before, but he was never my husband. You are. You always will be."

"Rebecca, listen to me. You have to think of yourself and the children. You have to be able to make a life for them and yourself as well. I just do not think you will be able to do that here now. I am so sorry. Your life with me is costing you everything. I never meant for this to happen. If I had known, I would never have come back here. I never would have…"

"Shhh," she soothed, holding him tight. She did not want to hear him apologize for something that was not his fault. "Just hold me. Just keep me safe."

Charlie's willpower completely collapsed with those words. He held her like a drowning man grips a lifeline. His body heaved hard as he tried to choke back the sobs that wanted to erupt from his chest. He wanted to howl with anger and frustration but he knew it would do no good and only serve to upset Rebecca even more. He moved them toward the bed and sat down with her, continuing to just hold her tightly in his arms.

Jerome took a seat in Charlie's chair and leaned forward, his arms resting on his knees. "I cannot believe this is happening. I am so sorry. I just do not even know what to say."

Charlie sighed. "You did everything you could. I suspect the Good Lord Himself could have testified for me and the outcome would have been the same. They needed to hang someone and I am someone."

"It is murder," Rebecca mumbled from her spot on his chest. "Just like Alex was murdered, they are murdering Charlie too! State sanctioned murder!"

"Darling," he tried to soothe her, but he knew there was little he could say or do.

Their attention was brought back to the outer door, where they could hear raised voices. "You will let me in!"

"Is that so?"

"Yes! You are murdering my father. That makes me the man of our house now and I have a right to see him!"

"You're a cocky little shi…"

"Guard!" Jerome was on his feet yelling to make good and sure that the people on the other side of that door knew he was listening.

The door opened and Darby burst into the room even as the deputy made a grab for him. He was standing at the bars reaching through. "Papa!"

Charlie was on his feet taking the boy's hands. "Son, you should not have come here."

"I needed to see you. We cannot let them do this! You are innocent!" Darby gripped his papa's hand so tightly it actually hurt the tall man.

"Darby, there is nothing we can do. But you are right about one very important thing. You are the man of the house now and you will need to be very strong for your mama and your brothers and sisters. Yes?"

The boy nodded as tears spilled down his cheeks. The jailer entered the room and started to try once again to remove him. He grabbed him by the scruff and was trying to drag him out when Richard entered the room.

"Leave the boy alone," the provost demanded as he entered the office. "And unlock that damn door and let him in!"

"It is against regulations," the deputy challenged.

"To hell with regulations!" Richard charged across the room and snatched the keys from the man. "I am still provost in this God forsaken town and I can change the damn regulations!" He unlocked the door and sighed. "Go on in, Darby, it is all right. Stay as long as you like."

"Thank you, Uncle Richard." He gave him a quick hug

before dashing to his father and wrapping himself tightly around his waist.

Richard stood in the door of the cell for a moment and finally said, "You all have every right to hate me. I promise you I did my duty to try and ensure that Charlie would get a fair trial without anyone trying to say…" He faltered as tears pooled in his eyes. "I never expected this. I thought if we made sure everything was correct, it would be all right. I was wrong and I am truly sorry. There is nothing I can do to ever make it right by you or your family." He shook his head and backed away. "I am so sorry."

~

Monday, September 30, 1867

Richard had relieved all the guards and deputies except for himself, Cady, and Frederick. The office door was locked and they all sat at a table in the hall playing cards. Inside, Charlie and Rebecca were actually using one of the desks as a makeshift supper table. It was much better than the tiny table in his cell. The desk was covered in food, more food than the two of them together could eat in a week, but it was their last night and their last meal together, and Rex and Sarah had made sure to provide a bit of everything.

"Richard is willing to let me stay the night if you like," Rebecca said quietly as she sipped her brandy.

He smiled. "I would like that very much, but…"

"No buts." She covered his hand with hers. "I want to be here."

He nodded knowing exactly what she meant. He wanted her there too, but the thought of their last night together being spent in a jail cell made him sick in the pit of his stomach. "Have you decided what you and the children will do?"

Rebecca just shook her head. There was no way she could even consider going on without him while he was still sitting in front of her. "I cannot, Charlie. Not right now, please do not ask me to." Tears welled in her eyes.

"All right, love." He nodded, not wanting to push her limits any further than necessary.

In the three days they had to wait for the gallows to be built, they had cried until there were absolutely no more tears from either of them. They had talked about a bit of everything, neatly avoiding the obvious. They were both quite numb with shock and disbelief.

Now the obvious was creeping up on them. At 10:00 in the morning, Charlie would be taken from the jail and made to walk the gallows steps.

"I do not want you there," he finally said as he sipped his brandy.

"Of course I am going to be there. I want them to have to look at me. I want them all to see what they have done."

"Rebecca..."

"No! Damn it, Charlie! Our marriage vows said until death do us part and I intend to be there with you. To the very end." She reached out and took his hand. "I also intend that we are going to go over there and make love tonight."

She tugged him to his feet and led him to what would be their last bed. With painful slowness she undressed him, touching every spot on his body with such intensity he realized she was trying to memorize it. He began the same excruciatingly slow process with her.

~

Tuesday, October 1, 1867

When Charlie heard the outer door open, he quickly checked to make sure not only was Rebecca's still nude form covered completely by the quilts, but that the privacy screen was well in place between the bars and the bed.

"Breakfast, Charlie boy!" Jocko called.

He quickly grabbed his robe and slid out from behind the screen. His old friend put a large tray down on the desk and stepped over to his old boss. He took him by the arms and just shook his head. "Charlie, I…"

"Promise me you will look after Rebecca. I am terrified she is going to try and remain here. Please, Jocko?"

"I promise. I will not let any harm come to Rebecca or the children."

"Thank you." He looked to the food and shook his head. "I hope you understand if I am not terribly hungry this morning."

"Of course. I was using it as an excuse to get to see you for a few minutes. To say…well…"

"Good bye?" Charlie felt a few more tears emerge as he looked at his oldest friend.

Jocko shook his head. "I cannot do that, Charlie boy. How about until next time? Hmm?"

He nodded as he pursed his lips and took Jocko's hand. "Until next time, my friend."

Jocko pulled him into a hug and gave him several pats on the back. "You be good; don't you be going and giving the devil a hard time. Save some for me."

Charlie laughed as they stepped away from each other. "You know I will. Thank you for being my friend. You made my life," he had to clear his throat, "not only easier, but," he paused needing the exact right word, "acceptable. You helped make me the man I am today. You know, I did not kill…"

"I know." The Irishman nodded. "You could never…" He drew a deep breath and offered, "It has been my honor and privilege to call you friend. I will never have one better." He nodded again, knowing he had to get out of there before his own reserve was completely gone. With one last pat to Charlie's arm, he turned and left the office.

Just before 9:00, Lizbet and Tomas arrived with Rebecca's and Charlie's clothes. Tomas had provided the basics for Charlie--short boots, dark trousers, a white shirt, and a dark vest. Lizbet had brought a black walking skirt for Rebecca and also a white shirt and a dark vest. The Redmonds were identically dressed for what would be their last public appearance together. After taking a few minutes to speak with Charlie, they left their employers to get ready on their own.

They were sitting together holding hands, Charlie gently caressing Rebecca's face when Richard and several deputies entered. He leaned in and gave her one last tender kiss on the lips. When he tried to pull away she caught his face in her hands and kissed him again, so deeply and passionately the guards looked away, embarrassed. He straightened, smiled, and removed his West Point ring, curling it into her fist. "Maybe, some day, one of the boys will want this."

He stood and faced Richard extending his wrists for the shackles.

Richard stepped up and put them around his wrists. Rebecca rose from the chair she had been in and looked at the provost with flashing eyes. "You make sure, Richard Polk, that you are the one who puts the noose around his neck!"

His eyes widened as Rebecca took a step forward and poked him in the chest. "You did this! This is your fault, Brutus, so you make sure you complete the job properly!" She was nearly screaming at him as she continued to poke him.

"Rebecca…" Charlie tried to console her, but it fell on deaf ears as she continued to rage at Richard.

"I want you to feel the agony I feel! I want you to be right next to him when he drops through that door! I want you to hear him struggling to breathe when you put the rope around his neck and allow it to choke the life from **your best friend**! I want you to hear the snap of his neck. When you leave our children without a father! When you leave…me and them…alone."

She was practically pounding his chest before she collapsed into him gasping and sobbing as she clutched his vest. Half sobbing, half whispering, she finished. "You are the only one **I trust** to get the knot right. Please, Richard, do not let him suffer."

Richard closed his eyes tight to stop his own tears and nodded. He sucked in a deep breath, unable to say a word, but grateful when Edgar appeared and he could hand Rebecca off to him.

Charlie was transported to the gallows site in the back of a buckboard with Edgar and Rebecca following behind in his buggy. The entire town of Culpeper was going to be in attendance for the hanging of Charlie Redmond and there was one common thought among everyone, no matter what side of the issue they were on. They could not believe he was actually going to be executed.

His supporters were clearly in disbelief and his detractors were gleeful. There was an obvious split in the crowd gathered at the site. Edgar escorted Rebecca through the crowd to a spot near the front and left her with Darby, Elizabeth, Rex, and Charlotte. He went off to tend to Charlie.

Charlie sat in the back of the wagon taking several deep breaths. He felt like he might be sick again.

He needed to be strong.

He needed to be defiant.

He needed a miracle.

He looked up into the gray sky, realizing that the weather was perfect for the way he was feeling. He remembered it had been the same way when they hung Montgomery. It seemed appropriate there was no sunshine.

The general was pulled from the wagon and after everything was in place, he was led to the steps. The crowd became deathly silent. Where there had been conversations and murmuring while they waited for him to be brought out, it all stopped as he took his last dozen steps.

He felt his heart beat a bit harder with each step and by the time he was at the top, it was pounding so loudly in his ears no other sound could get through. He felt dizzy and disoriented as they led him to the trap door. Looking out into the crowd, he found Rebecca right away. He tried to smile at her, but could not as he shook his head to clear the tears.

Charlie was startled to see Darby standing beside his mother, holding her arm. Darby looked into his eyes, tears falling, but still looking proud. Darby mouthed, "A Redmond never runs. Love you, Papa."

He could feel his chest rising and falling rapidly as he tried not to hyperventilate. He felt a tremor work its way through his entire body. Then the slight shaking after that, like the times he had a fever and Rebecca had so gently tended him. He closed his eyes and remembered the first time she had seen him through a cold when he wintered on her property.

He barely heard Edgar as his friend and minister stood next to him offering last rites and absolution for sins never committed.

His opened his eyes and scanned the crowd. He could see their friends supporting Rebecca and making sure she was safe.

Ro stood by with Madra and Feighlí on leashes. Jocko and Duncan were clearly watching the crowd. Charlie did manage a smile, knowing they would always do their best to keep her safe. Even though he had personally failed in his promise to her, they would bring his hopes for his family to fruition.

He made eye contact with her again and mouthed, "I love you," as the tears spilled down his cheeks and the guards securely tied ropes around his arms and legs to keep them from flailing during the final drop.

He drew a deep breath and let it out slowly and faced into the crowd as he felt Richard step up next to him. He tried not to flinch when he heard the rope being pulled into place over the beam. He did not want Rebecca to think him a coward now. He had to be brave for her and for Darby, who himself was being so very brave.

He had to squint a bit when the sun suddenly broke through the clouds, shining a bright light down on the crowd, catching painfully in the clouds of the unshed tears in his eyes. Charlie shook his head as a flash of gold caught him squarely in the face. He focused in on it and managed to choke out just as they began to slip a black hood over his head in preparation for the noose. "Edgar!"

He began to struggle against the noose going over his head as he yelled for Edgar again. To the casual observer in the crowd it looked like the great general was panicking just before justice was served. They expected to see him wrestled into position so the noose could be placed securely around his neck.

The minister quickly stepped up and looked to Charlie, who was pointing with his shackled hands into the crowd. He had to push the rope away and remove the hood from his head to fully hear what he was trying to say.

"Edgar! Eddie has my knife! The mate to my missing watch!"

"Stop!" The minister commanded Richard and the deputies by holding up both his hands, as he turned to look where Charlie was pointing. Eddie stood at the front of the crowd. He had been absentmindedly picking his nails with the gold inlaid penknife while waiting for Charlie to be hung. Edgar saw the yellow flashing and pointed, "Stop that man!"

Eddie realized they were talking about him and tried to make a break for it. The crowd parted and it looked as if he was going to get away until his path was blocked from two sides by snapping jaws with large teeth and gnashing fangs attached to two massive gray dogs.

Madra and Feighlí held him between them, growling and snapping. Every time he tried to move, they blocked him and sent him backward with a lunge and the click of their ferocious jaws and piercing teeth.

Edgar helped Charlie sit in a chair that had been provided while Richard and his men moved into the crowd. There was no use in them trying to get to Eddie with the dogs so near him. Richard shouted to Ro, "Call them off!"

Rebecca approached and stared at the terrified man. "You killed Alex Raeburn! You stole my husband's watch and then you killed Alex. You dropped the watch to pin the blame on General Redmond."

Eddie stood there, his head whipping back and forth between the two animals. "Yes!" he shrieked. "Yes, I killed him. I didn't mean to drop the watch, but it does not matter now! CALL THEM OFF!"

"I should let the dogs tear you limb from limb," Rebecca

threatened before allowing Ro to control the animals as she turned to run to the platform. Darby was right beside her.

Before he could fall out of the chair from relief, Rebecca was at Charlie's side. "Get these off him!" She growled indicating the shackles. She reached out and untied the ropes that had bound his arms, while their son worked on those that tied his father's legs.

Darby moved to the side, helping to brace his father in the chair, as he was truly afraid he was going fall out of it. Then Rebecca knelt in front of him and took his face in her hands and then ran them down and around his neck to ensure the rope had not had time to make a mark. "Are you all right?"

He was pale and shaken, but he nodded as the deputy took the shackles off. Their foreheads came together even as they sat there with their eyes closed as the miracle of the last second exoneration washed over them.

Darby, Edgar, and Rebecca had to help him get down the steps. His legs were still so shaky they did not trust him to get safely down on his own. At the bottom, they met Richard, who was dragging a now shackled Eddie to the wagon that had been used to transport Charlie. General Mayberry was standing to one side, looking dumbstruck.

"I am taking him home," Rebecca stated flatly to both men. "You can come out later and sort out anything that is left."

Richard only nodded and watched them walk away. Mayberry hurried into the courthouse to begin the proceedings against Eddie Rainey. The crowd parted without a word as Rebecca directed Charlie to the carriage that Tomas had brought as close as he could. He jumped down and made sure to help Charlie and Rebecca in. Darby jumped up onto the box beside Tomas. He knew when to leave his mother and father to themselves. Lizbet immediately gave Rebecca a blanket which went over a trembling Charlie's shoulders. She had brought it to cover his dead body; using it to warm his live one was much better. She then joined Darby and Tomas on the box.

"Darling, are you all right?" Rebecca wrapped her arms around him, kissing his brow. She could still feel the perspiration against her lips.

He nodded, not quite sure he could speak at the moment. He just needed a few minutes to gather his wits.

Tomas got the carriage on the move as the crowd began to disperse; leaving the good citizens of Culpeper denied their mornings entertainment.

Tomas took his time getting them home. The general needed the time to find his composure, and by the time they turned up the carriage way, he was looking and sounding much better. Charlie drew a deep lungful of the midday air. He was very grateful he could do so.

He and Rebecca held onto each other as if their lives depended on it. Even Darby could tell they would be hard pressed to be separated from each other for a long time to come.

When the carriage stopped in front of the house, the front door opened immediately. Reg, Beulah and the rest of house staff were there, dressed in dark attire, prepared to see Rebecca home and deal with what they had thought would be Charlie's body. Shock and then wonderment clearly registered on every face when the general stood and opened the carriage door, jumping down before handing Rebecca down.

Darby jumped down from the driver's box on the carriage and scurried into the house, intent on finding his sisters and letting them know that Papa was home and everything was going to be all right.

"Gen'l Charlie!" Beulah flew across the porch, down the steps and right into his chest. "Oh, Lord, it is so good to see you safe!"

Reg and the rest of the staff came down to shake his hand and welcome him home. He tried to say hello to each one, but their excitement was a bit overwhelming given his current emotional state. Rebecca carefully and gently extracted him and walked him up the steps. He paused as he looked at the black wreath on the door. It felt a bit unusual to come home to your own funeral.

"Reg." He looked back at their faithful major domo. "I would very much like for you to collect up every last item that appears to have announced my imminent but fortuitously delayed demise and put it in a large pile out at the side of the house, please. And have someone bring me a can of kerosene from the shed."

Reg grinned and removed the wreath from the door. "Yes, sir, Gen'l Charlie, me and the boys will get it done right quick! It will be a true pleasure, sir!"

Charlie looked to Rebecca and lifted a knowing brow. "It is in the formal parlor?"

She nodded.

"Was it really expensive?"

"Of course!" She laughed. "I got something slightly better than a pine box."

"Good. I have never enjoyed losing money more. Reg." Charlie gestured to the door of the front parlor. "The casket too."

He moved to the stairs and Rebecca knew immediately where he was going and she did not even try to stop him. She watched rather indulgently as he took the stairs as quickly as he could. She did, however, follow closely behind because she did not want to miss this.

He stopped at the top of the stairs and put his fists on his hips as he yelled, "Where are my little troopers?"

A door was flung open and three children bolted into the hall. They stopped when they saw him, not sure he could even be real, even though Darby had told them he was back. Mama had said he would never come home again. The girls finally shook themselves and ran to him. He scooped them both up, kissing them each several times on their little faces.

When he looked over to his oldest son, he put the girls down and moved to the boy, who immediately buried his face in his father's shoulder and started sobbing. Charlie hugged him close and said, "Let it go, son. You have been so strong, and so brave and so grown up. You can go back to just being a boy again. I am here and we will all be all right eventually."

Darby pulled back and grinned through his tears at his father. "So what will happen now?"

"I will be happy to tell you the whole story as soon as I know it. You know as much as I do right now. Now let me go. I have a few things I need to do."

"Yes, Papa." Darby tightened his arms around Charlie's neck for a moment, then let him go. "I am so glad you are home!"

Tess stood in the doorway to the nursery with the boys. Their papa scooped them up, giving them kisses that made them giggle. He looked at all of them dressed in their dark clothes. "Please, Tess, get them out of these morbid things and make sure they get to the pile Reg is building."

"Right away, Gen'l Charlie," she complied with a smile.

Once the children were sent off with Tess, Charlie guided Rebecca to their room and closed the door, locking it securely.

"Get out of those." He gestured to her attire as he began stripping off the clothes he was wearing. She watched him move determinedly around the room, kicking his boots into a corner and immediately stripping off the socks and vest, dropping them in a pile on the boots. He turned and started toward her, but stopped in his tracks when he saw it, laid out on the bed, waiting for her to return with his body but not with him.

Picking up the black mourning dress, he moved to the

veranda doors and flung them open before chucking the dress over the side of the house. "Reg! Make sure that damn thing is right on top!"

The men building Charlie's little pyre seemed a bit startled when the black dress caught the air and floated to the ground like a giant bat. He returned to the bedroom and closed the doors, eyeing Rebecca who was still quietly watching him as she sat and removed her boots. He said, "Why are you still dressed?"

"Why am I getting undressed?" She unbuttoned her vest, standing and moving slowly toward him.

"Well, in the first place, I intend to burn everything associated with today, including the clothes we are wearing. In the second place, I intend to take you to **our** bed and make **very passionate** love to you for the next two hours or so, but you must be naked in order for that to happen. You, Mrs. Redmond, are mucking up the works." He stripped off his shirt and trousers, throwing them in the pile and then he gestured to his small clothes. "All right, I am not burning everything. I refuse to give these up."

She smiled, finally understanding his need. He had survived another life-threatening battle, and like the times before when he would have turned to someone like Lizzie, now he was turning to her. She would not deny him, no matter what his needs were tonight.

"Will you give them up if I come over there and take them off of you?" She asked as she dropped her walking skirt and pantaloons in one swift motion. Then she began working the buttons on her blouse letting it slip to the floor, before quickly unhooking and dropping the corset and lifting her chemise over her head.

He nodded dumbly as all the blood in his body rushed south at the sight of her fully exposed flesh. "Un-huh."

It was just turning to dusk when Charlie, now thoroughly scrubbed in his lovely big bathtub by a very attentive and loving wife and dressed as he normally did for working around the farm, picked up the five-gallon can and began dumping it on the pile. He was careful to make sure to soak the base, where each end of his casket was sticking out from under the pile of fabrics collected from around the house. Even the servants had contributed their funereal clothes and returned to their normal garb.

Not only was he burning every stitch of mourning clothing but all the bunting and covers that that been draped over mirrors and across windows and doorways. If an item even pretended to be part of his not so illustrious death, it was in the pile.

Rebecca and the children watched from the bedroom veranda as Charlie stood back, tossed the now empty can into the mess and pulled one of Rex's special blends out of his shirt pocket.

He stuck the cigar in his mouth, struck a Lucifer against his thumb, lit the cigar and then tossed the match to the pile. It caught instantly and with a roar and a rush, sent a plume of dark smoke into the early night sky.

Stepping back, quite satisfied with his not so little bonfire, he turned and grinned up at his wife. Placing the two fingers of his right hand to his lips, he kissed them then lifted them in her direction. She laughed as she leaned her elbow on the rail and looked down at him. "You are a crazy man."

He nodded. "Maybe just a little bit tonight, yes."

Wednesday, October 2, 1867

Rebecca awoke the next morning quite surprised at the apparent time. The sun was fully up and streaming in the windows. She glanced at the clock on her bedside table. It was nearly eight in the morning.

She rolled over, planning on waking a still slumbering Charlie, until she looked at his face. Even in a deep sleep he looked exhausted. There were dark shadows under his eyes and heavy, thick lines etched in his forehead and around his mouth from the stress and worry of the last few weeks. To her, it looked as if he had aged ten years. She decided to let him sleep until he woke up on his own.

By lunch time she was actually beginning to worry when he had not emerged. She took a tea tray up and carefully entered the room. He was still sound asleep. She shook her head, hating to do it, but knowing if she did not, he would be up walking the halls in the middle of the night.

After placing the tray on the table, she moved to the bed and gently began running her fingers through his hair. "Come on, sleepy head. It is time to wake up."

He nodded and gave a little growl as his head burrowed deeper into the pillow.

"That does not look like waking up." She traced the edge of his ear with her finger.

He smiled, still not opening his eyes. "That will not get me up."

"No?" She smiled at him, moving from his ear down his jaw to trace his lips.

"No." His arm crept out from under the covers and wrapped around her waist. "Come back to bed."

"I thought you were getting up. I did not realize I would be coming back."

He drew a deep, happy breath and let it out slowly. "I intend to spend a week sleeping, eating, playing with the children and making love to you. Not necessarily in that order."

"Is that so?" She chuckled when she felt him trying to work a button on her blouse.

"Yes."

She nodded slowly and smiled when she felt the first button give way. "I think that is a plan I can support."

~

Monday, October 14, 1867

Rebecca was in absolute heaven. Her body thrummed and pulsed. She was alive with Charlie's most adoring, intimate touch. She had discovered quite by accident, but much to her delight, that his right hand was just the right shape and size to offer her the most intimate of connections with her beloved husband. Moans were torn from her as they moved together, Charlie groaning and grunting low in her ear, the way he knew drove her higher.

They were in rare form on this particular afternoon, even for them. Their lovemaking was always passionate in the sense that they always desired each other to the point of distraction, but on those very rare occasions, their couplings bordered on the truly transcendent.

This was one of those occasions. After weeks of separation while Charlie was in jail, their desire to make love every moment of the day had not abated in the two weeks since he had come home and today it had started all over again when Rebecca had come into the bedroom to find him sound asleep on top of the bed in his knitted shirt and shorts.

She did so love seeing him in those. She was delighted to discover her gift had served many, many important purposes. She had not expected this particular benefit, but she enjoyed it. A great deal.

She undressed quickly and quietly, leaving her own underclothes on, then she joined him on the bed, straddling his hips, looking down at him as she rubbed his arms. She smiled the second he did.

"You were faking," she whispered as she leaned forward and kissed him soundly.

"No." His voice was rough with sleep. "Not until I heard you curse that last button." He smiled as his hands ran over her back, sliding under her chemise to caress warm skin.

"I think it is under the sofa," she offered before giving a gentle bite to his neck.

She pulled back and smiled down at him; his hands were as always warm and tender. He had never done anything to hurt or frighten her when they were like this. He had always treated her mind and body as if they were treasures to be protected at any cost.

He had also never allowed himself to request or explore more than the gentlest of relations. It was as if he was afraid he would scare or hurt her. Her tales of Gaines had made Charlie an extremely careful lover. Almost too careful, Rebecca considered silently.

It was these moments when she realized that she loved and trusted him with everything, that she truly felt comfortable giving in to some of her own more carnal desires. He was always eager and willing to go wherever she led them because it seemed to allow him some fulfillment of his own held back needs and desires. They played together for more than an hour, with excruciating slowness, taking their time to undress and touch each other, whispering words of love and encouragement.

Rebecca was still straddled across his hips, but they were

both upright holding each other as closely as possible. Her head fell back as the rush of fire tore through her body with his most intimate touch. She felt his lips on her neck, the tips of his fingers of his left hand on her back as she arched into the familiar and cherished touch of his right hand.

"'Becca…" He breathed heavily into the warm, slick, salty skin of her throat. "My darling, my heart, my soul." The sounds coming from her only served to make him more determined to satisfy her in any way she required. "Tell me. Tell me what you need."

"Only you," she moaned, nails dug deep into his back as she leaned forward and bit his neck with a tad more force than usual causing him to growl and increase his attentions.

"Oh, yes!" she ground out, nodding her approval as she felt him shifting. Helping make the change so the connection would not be lost between them, she hummed with sheer pleasure as the weight of him came to rest over her. With him, this was paradise, a dream to be captured and memorized with every lick of fire that tore through her.

Their pace was frantic and given to true abandon as their bodies moved together. Arms and legs entwining and caressing, in constant erotic motion, their bodies becoming more heated. They were both so close to the precipice and they would go over together, in each other's loving arms. It was, no doubt, the entire reason they had not heard the door to their room click open.

"Mama?"

Charlie nearly fell off the bed trying to find something to cover up with. Rebecca groaned with a level of frustration never heard before as she too managed to find a rumpled sheet to pull around her body before turning eyes on Buddy.

"Yes?" There was a pause that made Charlie wonder if she was reconsidering her relationship with the toddler. "Son?"

The tot, completely unaware of his unfortunate disruption, giggled madly and flung himself with abandon at the big bed, forcing his papa to make a grab for him to keep him from falling when he tried to jump onto it. "Easy, son." Charlie laughed as he tightened the quilt around his shoulders. "Let me get my robe and I will return him to Tess. I suspect he is supposed to be napping. They always seem to escape at nap time."

"No." Rebecca rose and fetched her robe from the back of a chair. She smiled sweetly at her husband. "You get back in bed. I will take him. Then I will be back. I am not quite done with you yet."

He chuckled outright as he sat down on the bed when she scooped Buddy into her arms. "You are very lucky I love you." She tickled her son's tummy as she left the room with him, pulling the door closed.

Charlie just lay back on the bed and grinned.

CHAPTER 15

Sunday, October 27, 1867

In the three and a half weeks since Charlie had been saved from the gallows in the last seconds before the trap was to have fallen, they had not been to church at all or even into town. He refused to be separated from Rebecca and the children for even a moment and she expressed no desire to go into town for anything. The only person they had seen was Edgar, who had been out several times to pray and give thanks for Charlie's last-minute reprieve, holding private services for the family.

Finally, and with Edgar's encouragement, Charlie faced the reality that if he and the family did not return to town, people would begin saying they were hiding something. So that Sunday morning they had all dressed in their best and were prepared to face the people of Culpeper.

As they drove into the churchyard, there was a great deal of whispering and pointing by the people filing into the church, but nothing offensive was heard. Several people came up to greet them, including Duncan and Samantha, with Jeremiah in tow; Missy and Horace Frazier, who shook Charlie's hands vigorously and hugged Rebecca; and the Coopers, who took their arms and escorted them into the church. Richard and Elizabeth stood to one side, smiling broadly. They would have time to greet them later. Charlie grinned back at both of them, Rebecca pointedly ignoring Richard as she nodded to Elizabeth.

They settled into the Redmond pew with Charlie on the aisle end and Tess and Ginnie holding the boys at the other. They faced forward and bowed their heads to read their bibles as they waited for the service to start.

Edgar emerged from the back of the church, where he had been in the bell tower as was his wont, and strode up the center aisle, speaking the opening lines of the liturgy in a ringing voice. By now, the congregation was used to their minister's unusual way of starting the service.

Today's sermon began with a reading from Daniel, Chapter 9, Verses 7 through 10.

"O Lord, righteousness belongeth unto thee, but unto us confusion of faces, as at this day; to the men of Judah, and to the inhabitants of Jerusalem, and unto all Israel, that are near, and that are far off, through all the countries whither thou hast driven them, because of their trespass that they have trespassed against thee."

"O Lord, to us belongeth confusion of face, to our kings, to our princes, and to our fathers, because we have sinned against thee."

"To the Lord our God belong mercies and forgivenesses, though we have rebelled against him;"

"Neither have we obeyed the voice of the LORD our God, to

walk in his laws, which he set before us by his servants the prophets."

Edgar's sermon went on to explain how failure to find forgiveness in your heart was indeed failure to follow God's law and will. He focused on the forgiveness that was necessary to reunite the country, but also spoke of forgiving the smallest injustice to the most horrendous atrocities. For the damage, he pointed out, was not to the one who you would not forgive, but to yourself, to the kindness and love and wholeness of your own spirit. Failure to forgive eats away at the fabric of your soul and brings you to the confusion that comes from loss of faith and awareness of God's love.

He went on to talk of God's justice, of the miracle that was God's truth and the wonder that was God's forgiveness. Looking straight at Charlie, he pointed out that while man's justice had nearly made a terrible mistake, God's loving justice and forgiveness had intervened at the last minute to shine a bright light in an otherwise dreary day onto the one piece of evidence that would allow the truth to be known, the innocent to be absolved, and the true trespasser to be identified. He finished with a ringing cry. "God's justice, and God's forgiveness is the light that must guide us all."

The closing hymn that day was "Forgive Them, Oh, My Father." It was perfect to hammer his message home. Unusually, Rex had been the organist for the service, rather than Charlotte. As the final chords of the stirring hymn finished, Charlotte cried out. "Oh, my God. My water broke!"

The women in the congregation all grouped around Charlotte. It was common knowledge that she was carrying twins, and this was exciting. But Charlotte called out for only one person. "Rebecca! I need you, Rebecca."

At the sound of Charlotte's cry, Rebecca looked very startled, but she went to her side. "Come on, cousin. We need to get you home and into bed."

"Stay with me, please, Rebecca."

She patted her hand. "Of course, dear. Now let us get out of here." She slipped her arm around Charlotte's back. Elizabeth moved to her other side, offering the same support. Between them, they walked her out of the church and over to the manse.

Edgar hurriedly finished his obligations to the congregation, with many of them laughing and sending him on his way. Rex quietly slipped from behind the organ and was actually waiting for Charlotte and the other ladies when they arrived, gently helping Charlotte walk, which Elizabeth knew was the best thing she could be doing right now.

As Rebecca and Elizabeth settled Charlotte into a comfortable chair in her bedroom, she grabbed Rebecca's hand. "Please, stay with me. You are the closest thing I have ever had to a real family, a real sister. I am scared. So many women do not make it through labor. And having twins – well, I am very, very scared."

"It is all right, Charlotte. Elizabeth is here. Esther will be along soon. And I suspect Rex knows a thing or two about getting a woman through a successful childbirth too. And of course I will stay with you. Let me just go and send Charlie and the children home. I will be right back."

She scooted out of the manse and back to the church, where she found things were in a bit of a furor. There was a circle of women gathered beside a bench under one of the large old trees in the churchyard. Samantha was at the center of the circle, with Esther White on one side of her, and Duncan, looking exceptionally nervous, on the other.

Rebecca spoke up. "Samantha, are you all right?"

"Oh, yes, Rebecca. I am fine." She paused and a look of

extreme pain washed over her face as she gripped Duncan's hand so tightly he flinched. "The baby is on the way."

"Oh." Her response was dead flat. She was trying desperately to process this information. *Two deliveries at the same time? Oh, hell, what is Charlotte going to do?*

Esther patted her hand. "Let us get you home, child." She looked at Duncan. "Get her home. I will be with you in a few minutes. I just need to stop and get my bag from the house."

She looked up at Rebecca. "I am sure Charlotte will be fine with you and Elizabeth. I can look after Samantha." With that, Esther bustled off, with Jocko doing a quick march to keep up with her.

Rebecca looked around for Charlie. He was trying to herd the children into the carriage. They were trying to see what all the excitement in the churchyard was about. Suzanne and Emily were particularly concerned with Aunt Charlotte's condition.

Rebecca hurried over and explained to the family what was going on, and that Charlotte particularly wanted her to stay with her as the babies were born. She suggested that Charlie take the children home, but he had different ideas. "Darling, do you remember how stressed Richard was when Dickon was on the way? Someone is going to have to look after Edgar and Duncan, and I suspect that Rex will be occupied with supporting the birth of twins. So I need to take care of the gentlemen."

Rebecca smiled and shook her head. "All right." She turned to Tess. "Can you take care of the children until we can get home?"

"Of course I can, Miz 'Becca." She looked at the children. "And you will be happy to be good children while your mama and papa help Miss Charlotte and Miss Samantha have their babies, because you are good children."

In chorus, the girls answered, "Oh yes, Mama. We will be

good." Darby just grinned and climbed up on the driver's box beside Louis. Ginnie had already settled the boys in the carriage.

Rebecca turned to Charlie. "I will send word when she delivers. I assume you will be a Jocko's?"

"Where else, love? Give Charlotte my best wishes."

Rebecca headed back to the manse. Charlie went to gather up Edgar and Duncan.

It was a long afternoon and evening. By mid-evening, Samantha had delivered a fine baby boy, big and healthy, and Duncan had headed home grinning from ear to ear. A little after midnight, Charlotte had two small, dark haired babies cuddled, one in each arm--a little girl, who was first to arrive, and a little boy. Rebecca was exhausted, Rex and Elizabeth were both a bit the worse for wear, Edgar was so nervous and happy that he was almost climbing the walls, and Charlie was ready for some peace, quiet, and sleep. Louis had waited patiently for them, and drove them home through a beautiful night with a half moon illuminating the road and two very tired passengers.

~

Sunday, November 3, 1867

A smiling Edgar had delivered a loving sermon that day, speaking of the birth of Sarah's child Isaac, and the joy that children brought to a family. He based his sermon on Genesis, Chapter 21.

"And the LORD visited Sarah as he had said, and the LORD did unto Sarah as he had spoken. For Sarah conceived, and bare Abraham a son in his old age, at the set time of which God had spoken to him. And Abraham called the name of his son that was born unto him, whom Sarah bare to him, Isaac. And Abraham circumcised his son Isaac being eight days old, as God had

commanded him. And Abraham was an hundred years old, when his son Isaac was born unto him. And Sarah said, God hath made me to laugh, so that all that hear will laugh with me. And she said, Who would have said unto Abraham, that Sarah should have given children suck? for I have born him a son in his old age. And the child grew, and was weaned: and Abraham made a great feast the same day that Isaac was weaned."

Not only had Charlotte given birth to twins, a girl and a boy, but Samantha had also given birth to a son that had Duncan grinning like an idiot all week.

The congregation was smiling and the ladies were remembering when their children were born as they gathered their possessions and worked their way through greetings, Edgar's blessing, and a few words with friends as they milled out the door. The Redmonds, because their pew was at the front of the church, were some of the last to leave.

Charlie hung back to have a word with Edgar. He had discovered that Rebecca had turned down a request to support some community project at the church and he wanted to make it right. As they stood in the entrance area below the bell tower talking, Rebecca and the children stepped out into the churchyard.

Margaret Williams's back was to the church. She was speaking in a loud voice to several of the other members of the biddy brigade. Rebecca could not help but hear what she was saying. "…do not care if he was not the one who killed poor Alex. He should have hung for all of the other things he has done…"

She got no farther. Rebecca flew down the steps to stand behind her. She grabbed the older woman by the shoulder and spun her around. Her face was flushed a deep red, and the veins were throbbing through the normally pale skin of her forehead and neck. Her blonde eyebrows practically glowed standing out in harsh relief against the red of her face.

"Margaret Williams, you miserable, vindictive, vicious old bitch! You should be ashamed to show your face in a House of God! Let us talk about the things my husband has done, shall we? The hundreds of hours he put into opening a bank for the community? The loans he gave personally before it was open to help people start or rebuild businesses? The jobs he has created in this town by making sure everyone had a fair chance to restart? The hay we sold at a loss or outright gave away so local farmers could feed their horses and cattle this past winter? And you! You hateful old hag!"

Rebecca shook her finger in Margaret's face resisting the urge to claw out her eyes. "You have an income for one reason and one reason only! Not because the citizens of this town came together to raise the money for your worthless old hide when your husband died, but because my husband – or as you call him, "That Man" – takes your stipend out of his army pension every month so you have food in your larder, wood to heat your hearth, and a roof over your miserable, evil head! Do you know why he does it that way? Because I refused to let him fund you from our house or farm accounts! He takes it from his own pocket! And you used it to feed and give succor to the same men who stole the money from our employee's pockets. The very men who burned my barn. Killed Tarent and Rollins and my horses. Those men who burned crosses on the lawns of our black folk, and who threatened the wellbeing of our children– is this what my man should hang for? If he had hung, you would be out on your old ass with no means of support! You ungrateful, vengeful sow! If I never ever see your face again, it will be much too soon!"

Charlie and Edgar had emerged onto the steps of the church just as Rebecca was telling Mrs. Williams the litany of Charlie's good deeds and generosity for the town of Culpeper. They both started to move forward to restrain the angry woman, but Elizabeth stopped them by placing an arm across their chests as they started down the steps.

"Let her go. She needs to do this. And to be honest, I think there are many people here in Culpeper who need to hear what she has to say. Rebecca has to get this off her chest. The good citizens need to realize what petty little asses some of them have been. To be honest, I am surprised Rebecca lasted this long without exploding. Perhaps it will help her get past some other issues as well."

Rebecca stood there, panting.

Margaret Williams had flushed a bright, angry red, but as she looked around at the faces of people who had heard this tirade and were nodding agreement with Rebecca, the blood drained from her face. She looked for someone, anyone, who would ally with her and come to her defense, but no one in the crowd would meet her eyes. Misses Simms and Reynolds, who had for so long been her acolytes, turned away when she looked in their direction.

Missy Frazier stepped up to the older woman. "Margaret, it is time for you to go." She escorted her down to the pathway that led down the street toward her cottage.

Grace Cooper stepped to Rebecca's side. "Well said, Rebecca. Well said." A number of other women, many of them previous members of the biddy brigade, clustered around Rebecca, expressing their admiration for her courage and her forthright speech. Surprisingly, Mrs. Allen, the local vendor of outstanding moonshine, was one of the first in line to address Rebecca. "Mrs. Redmond, I apologize. I sold them friends of Raeburn's 'shine and happily took their money, but if I'd a knowd what they were planning, you can be sure I would have told Colonel Polk and Gen'l Redmond right away."

Rebecca looked a little embarrassed at her own outburst, but as the women clustered around her, congratulating her on her courage and her outspokenness, a small smile crossed her lips, and a look of relief and then, yes, satisfaction came over her. She looked up, watching Margaret Williams walking slowly down the path toward the house that Charlie had made possible for her to live in, her shoulders slumped, her step slow and halting. Her place in Culpeper society had been destroyed forever.

~

Monday, November 11, 1867

It had been six weeks to the day since Charlie had been released from jail. He was still struggling to get his life back on a normal routine, and for the most part was having some success. Today, he was upstairs in his office, sitting at his desk, reading the financial news prior to going through the pile of bank paperwork that Frank Halliburton had sent out early that morning for his review.

In his opinion, Frank had been doing an outstanding job of taking care of the bank while he had been incarcerated, having made several judicious loans to local farmers and merchants, and adjusted some of the bank's short term investments to improve their cash position.

As he was just finishing reading the newspaper, his office door slammed shut. He looked up, startled, as he had not heard anyone enter, though it was easier for someone to slip in now that he no longer shut the doors when he entered a room if he was alone.

Elizabeth stood there, looking angry and frustrated. He rose hurriedly to go to her, and she waved him off. "I need a whiskey. Now!"

She walked over to one of the chairs in front of the empty fireplace. Charlie poured her a whiskey, adding a splash of water. He went to put the bottle back in its place, but Elizabeth forestalled him. "Bring it over here. I will need more. Soon."

He handed her the whiskey and sat down across from her. "Elizabeth, what is the problem? I do not think I have ever seen you quite so upset."

"My husband and your wife. We have to do something about them. Or I am going to lose my mind."

Charlie sighed. He was perfectly aware of just how angry Rebecca still was with Richard, even though the man had only done his duty, knowing full well that if he had shown any special consideration at all for Charlie it would have made things far worse for both of them.

"If Rebecca does not stop cutting him in public and we cannot find a way for you two to visit and talk about what happened, he is going to fade away, or I am going to kill him. I have stayed out of trying to come between those two, but this has simply got to stop." Elizabeth reached for the whiskey bottle and poured herself another healthy glass full.

Charlie nodded and sighed. "I have also tried to keep from getting between them, but you are right. This has gone on too long. I thought she understood that Richard was only doing his duty, as distasteful as it was to him. And if he had shown me any special consideration, that mob that wanted to lynch me and get it over with would have had their way. But this stubbornness that Rebecca is showing is ridiculous. My God – Richard is my best friend!"

Elizabeth had knocked back her second glass of whiskey while Charlie talked. She poured herself a third and continued.

"Ever since that day when he had to come out and arrest you, Richard has done nothing but mope around the house, sit at his desk and brood. He goes to work when he is supposed to, he comes home, he pushes food around on his plate, he goes into his office, and eventually comes to bed, where he tosses and turns all night." She poured yet another whiskey. "Every time he sees Rebecca, he gets this sad, hopeful look on his face. When she cuts him, he looks like a child who just had to watch his father kill his pet dog for no good reason."

Charlie quietly reached over and moved the whiskey bottle a little further away from her. "Easy there, lady."

"Easy my ass, Charlie Redmond! I am so frustrated and angry I could drink that whole bottle and still perform surgery."

Not on me, thought he to himself. He pointedly moved the bottle back to within her reach.

"He is ignoring our boy, your godson! Little Dickon crawls up and tugs on his pant leg, trying to get this father's attention, and Richard just ignores him. I cannot go on this way, Charlie. We have to do something!"

She poured herself yet another whiskey. She was knocking back the whiskey faster than most soldiers after a tough battle, and he was afraid she was going to poison herself at this rate.

"He and I have not made love since the day he arrested you. I tell you, Charlie, I cannot do this any longer. You have to do something. You know it is a sin when a man will not touch his wife!" More whiskey went into her glass, then into her throat. Tears started sliding down her cheeks. "A sin I tell you." She shook her head. Then she raised a drunken, questioning eye. "I bet you have bedded Rebecca… "

He shot up from the chair as if someone had just set fire to his trousers and dashed out into the hall. Standing at the top of the stairs, he looked around for Rebecca, then bellowed in that voice that could be heard over the din of actual battle, "**Rebecca Anne Randolph Redmond! I need you in my office! RIGHT NOW!**"

Reg stuck his head out of the front parlor door and called up the steps. "I think she is in her office. I will go get her, sir."

His voice had carried throughout the whole house. Rebecca was already on her way up the back stairs when Reg found her. He flattened himself against the wall to let her pass. She continued to hurry up stairs and arrived outside of Charlie's office slightly breathless from running full tilt up two flights.

"What is it, darling? What is wrong?"

He pointed into his office. Rebecca peeked in and saw Elizabeth sitting there with her back to the door. "**That** is what is wrong! **You** have created it; now **you** need to fix it." He shook his head forcefully. "I cannot help her with her current problem."

Rebecca looked at him, startled and still a little confused. But he offered no further explanation; he simply turned and stalked down the stairs.

She went into his office and gently touched the doctor's shoulder. "What is wrong, Elizabeth?" Rebecca pulled out her handkerchief and offered it to her friend, then she moved over to the chair that Charlie had so recently occupied, sat down and just looked intently at her friend, who was quietly sobbing in the chair opposite her.

Elizabeth used the handkerchief to sop up the worst of the tears, then looked at Rebecca accusingly. "What is wrong, you ask? What is wrong? You are! Ever since Richard had to arrest Charlie, you have been an evil, nasty, vindictive woman. And it was all aimed at my husband. He was only doing his duty, but you had to blame him for everything. I swear you have been as bad as Margaret Williams and not even on her worst day."

Rebecca looked shocked for a moment, then came back at

Elizabeth. "But Elizabeth, how could he do that to Charlie? Charlie was his best friend, and yet he put him in shackles and in that horrible little hole of a jail. He could have found a way to prove Charlie was innocent, but he did not. I almost think he thought Charlie did it. He almost destroyed my family. And never even paused in doing what he called 'his duty.'"

Elizabeth poured herself another shot of whiskey. "If he had not done his duty, that lynch mob would have killed Charlie on the spot and you and the children might have been hurt as well. You think any of this was easy for Richard? He came home the night he arrested Charlie and cried his eyes out. He has not eaten or slept properly for weeks. He ignores Dickon when the baby asks for his papa's attention. And I have not had sex since the day all of this happened. I am sure you have had Charlie happily between your thighs many times since he came home! I can tell from the look on your face, but me? Me? I have had nothing other than an occasional perfunctory kiss on the forehead for weeks."

Elizabeth knocked back another drink. By now her language was starting to slur and her hands were shaking so that she sloshed a little whiskey onto her lap as she steered the glass to her lips. "And that isss not the worssse of it. Sssince Charlie was releassshhed, you have been nothin' but a bitcchhh to him. All you do is be a bitch to him or ignore him. And whether you like it or not, Richard is sssstill Charlie'ssss bestest frien'." She paused and licked the spittle from her lips. "You need to do somethin'." She dissolved into tears again.

Rebecca stood and rang for Beulah. Then she went over and put her arms around her friend, kneeling in front of her. "It will be all right, Elizabeth. These things just take time."

The doctor looked up at her with reddened eyes. "Itsss been time. And itsss not better." She hiccupped. "Make it better,

'Becca. Pleash?" Elizabeth hiccupped again, then suddenly her stomach lurched and Rebecca had a lap full of the whiskey that Elizabeth's stomach had finally rejected, along with the remains of her last meal. The aroma was impressive.

Just then Beulah bustled in. She had been waiting for the summons, having heard General Charlie's bellow and knowing that when something went wrong in the household, sooner or later, her skills would be needed.

The scene that greeted her made even the imperturbable Beulah pause for a moment. There was Dr. Elizabeth, one of the steadiest women the housekeeper had ever known, sitting with her head lolling on Miz Rebecca's shoulder, sobbing. Both women were covered in vomit, as was the very expensive Turkish rug that Miz Rebecca was kneeling on. The room reeked of whiskey and puke. Beulah went to the bell pulls, and urgently rang for Sarah, Lizbet, and Reg. Together, they might make a decent start on cleaning up this mess.

Rebecca cast a pleading look at the housekeeper. She stepped carefully behind the chair Elizabeth was in, avoiding the puddles, and saying, "There, there, Dr. Elizabeth. You come with Beulah and we will get you cleaned up an' feelin' more yo'self."

She took the sobbing woman's shoulders and guided her up to a standing position, something Elizabeth was no longer capable of doing without assistance. The big woman got her arm around the smaller woman's waist and literally lifted her over the puddles of puke, then set her on her feet, still holding her up. Reg and Lizbet arrived at the door. As Beulah steered Elizabeth toward the wash room, she asked Lizbet to get a robe for the doctor, as her dress was a disaster.

Rebecca continued to kneel where she was, looking at the mess and realizing to some extent, this was a message from somewhere in the universe.

Lizbet ran to get a robe and drop it in the washroom, then returned to General Charlie's office. The lady of the house was still kneeling where she had been, staring into space now and looking totally stunned. "Come on, Miz Rebecca. We need to get you cleaned up." She helped her mistress gather her skirts so she would not drip the vomit onto the floor as they also headed to the wash room.

Sarah had been warned by General Charlie as to what was probably coming, so she had grabbed as many men as she could lay her hands on quickly to haul as much hot water up to the wash room as possible. She had a tray of tea and dry biscuits in her hands, and was followed by four well-muscled men, each carrying large buckets. She took a quick survey of the hall, then concluded the action had moved from Charlie's office to the wash room. Without knocking, she opened the door to make sure everyone was still as decent as possible, then ordered the men in to pour four of the buckets into the tub, leaving the other four for whatever use was needed. Sarah went into the washroom, set the tea down, and waded in to help Beulah with the by now nearly limp Dr. Elizabeth. The first thing she did was grab an empty bucket. There was more stuff in Dr. Elizabeth's stomach that was trying to escape.

Reg stepped into the hall and called all four men to him after the buckets were deposited. He made sure that General Charlie's papers were weighted down so they would not be blown all over the office. The men opened the windows to try to air out the room and then moved the unsullied furniture from the rug. One chair and the table beside it were decorated with puke and the rug was a disaster. Carefully, the men rolled up the rug and carried all of the vomit encrusted items down the back stairs and out into the yard for a thorough cleaning. One of the men trudged back upstairs with rags, a bucket of hot water with pine scented soap and a mop to clean up the floor under the rug. Reg went looking for any small puddles that may have fallen on the way to the washroom, and together they cleaned up several spots in the hall.

Meanwhile, Sarah, Lizbet and Beulah had their hands full. Lizbet helped Rebecca strip out of her clothing and get cleaned up, then went to prepare a bedroom for Dr. Elizabeth. The two of them looked at the dress and together decided it was a lost cause. Sarah and Beulah had a harder time stripping Dr. Elizabeth down, as she had all of the coordination of a partially filled sack of flour and kept needing the bucket, though there was little left in her stomach by now. Beulah lifted the now naked doctor bodily into the tub of hot water, poured another bucket over her, and proceeded to wash her from head to foot, as nothing had escaped her amazing imitation of a geyser.

Once Elizabeth had been thoroughly soaped down, Sarah grabbed the buckets and together the two women rinsed her down. By now, both Sarah and Beulah were also soaked, but Elizabeth's head was starting to clear and she was being a bit more helpful and a lot apologetic as they dried her off and wrapped her in a warm robe. Sarah poured her a half cup of tea and helped her ease it down her very sore throat, followed by a dry biscuit to help settle her still roiling stomach.

The women walked Elizabeth down the hall to the room Lizbet had hastily prepared and settled her into bed. Unfortunately for Rebecca, Elizabeth was now wide awake, still drunk as a skunk, and needed to talk. So Rebecca sat with her, letting her expound at length and very repetitively on how terribly the whole thing with Charlie's accusation had affected Richard and their family, and how hurtful Rebecca's refusal to forgive him for just doing his duty was to him. Rebecca sat with her for what seemed like an eternity, although it was in reality only a couple of hours, feeling guiltier and guiltier, but still not quite ready to welcome Richard back into the arms of her family.

Charlie had sent word into town to let Richard know where his wife was and that she would be staying the night. He did not tell him just how upset Elizabeth was, nor did he explain that she had managed to drink herself into a stupor. That would be for them to discuss the next day.

Since his office was uninhabitable, Charlie went in to grab his papers, then retreated to the back parlor to await his wife's appearance. Dinner came and went, and still no Rebecca. The children were put to bed, with Charlie doing good night duties, and still no appearance of the Redmond matriarch.

He had his after dinner coffee and one of Rex's special blend cigars, and still no Rebecca. Finally, he headed up to bed. He found her slumped in the love seat in front of the fireplace in their private sitting room, sound asleep, still in the dressing gown Lizbet had provided when she was stripped out of her dress that morning. Rather than try to wake her, he rearranged her into a more comfortable position, covered her with an afghan and went to get a decent night's sleep himself.

The next morning was interesting. Rebecca appeared for breakfast looking like she had been kicked in the gut and was feeling guilty because somehow she deserved it. Elizabeth, dressed in a day dress of Rebecca's that was a bit too large for her small frame, looked like a text book description of a hangover.

Sarah personally served Elizabeth her breakfast, which started with a very large glass of The Cure, followed by a second very large glass of water, a small serving of softly scrambled eggs and a pile of dry toast. The children looked around and had the good sense to eat their breakfast very quietly and then went about their business as quickly as they could.

Shortly after breakfast, Richard knocked on the front door. Charlie came out to greet him and explain a bit about yesterday's happenings. Richard declined to come past the entry hall while he waited for Elizabeth to collect herself and make her escape. Meanwhile, Reg sent down to the stables and had Elizabeth's little cart brought around. Richard tied his horse to the back of the cart, loaded his still miserable wife in, and set off for home.

Charlie, after seeing them off, went in to find his wife. She was waiting for him in the morning room. Her expression was unreadable.

He looked at her silently for a moment, his face also expressionless, and to be honest, rather cold.

She looked at him. "Do you want to discuss this now or would you rather wait?"

He stood there, very carefully considering what he was about to say. He had never done anything like this in the entire time they had known each other. Rebecca steeled herself for one of their rare fights. She was perfectly aware that he was not happy with her.

He finally spoke. "No, my dear. I do not believe a mutual discussion about this matter will be required. Unlike all the other times when I have valued your input and perspective on an issue, on this particular one I must put my foot down and be master of this house. Richard Polk is my best friend. I will tolerate no further hostility towards him. He will be welcomed back into our home. He will be treated with courtesy and even fondness when we see him in public. You will smile, you will be gracious, and you will be welcoming. Richard and Elizabeth are responsible for the two of us being together in the first place, and together they have saved my life on more than one occasion. Your behavior is hurting Richard, and by extension, Elizabeth and our godson Dickon. And it is hurting me to see two of my closest and oldest friends distressed. I do not care if you ever forgive Richard…"

Rebecca tried to interrupt him. "But--"

He raised his finger, cutting her off with a stern "No." He drew a deep breath. "Rebecca, I love you and I always will no matter what transpires between us, but your behavior toward Richard is entirely unacceptable. It is petty and vindictive. I will not have you treat my best friend in this manner. There will be no more discussion. You will remember your place and do as I have commanded on this issue, Mrs. Redmond." With that, he turned on his heel and stalked out of the room.

She sat there, stunned. He had never spoken to her in this manner. He had never ordered her to do anything, let alone something she did not want to do.

Rebecca thought long and hard. Finally, she rang for Reg and asked him if he would send a note to Edgar. While Reg went to get someone to serve as her messenger, she sat down and wrote a note card.

Please, Edgar, I fear I have made a serious mess of things and I need your help. Could you come see me as soon as it is convenient for you? – Rebecca R.

CHAPTER 16

Monday, November 11, 1867

Edgar was sitting in his office writing his Sunday sermon when Rebecca's note was delivered. He had been expecting it, so he quickly set his pen aside, closed the ink well, and stepped into the hall. He called, "Charlotte! Rex! I am headed to Redmond Stables. Rebecca has caught a glimpse of the light and needs help."

Rex ran to the little barn behind the house, though running was not something he normally did, to saddle Edgar's horse while the minister pulled on his boots.

As Edgar entered the parlor and gathered his things, dropping them in his saddlebag, Charlotte had only one thing to say as she traced her finger across the tiny cheek of her son nursing at her breast. "About damned time."

He smiled, kissing her on the top of her head before he

touched his son's little ear. "Absolutely. We have a Christening soon and we need the godparents to be of sound mind."

Twenty minutes later, he pulled his horse up at the Redmonds' front steps. He dropped off the lightly lathered horse's back, threw the reins to Reg and tersely asked, "Back parlor?"

The butler just nodded as Edgar strode in. He did not bother to knock, but just walked in to find Rebecca sitting alone, looking lost.

"Good morning, dear lady. What is the problem?" As he spoke, he stripped his hat, gloves and coat off, dropped them on the table, and poured himself a cup of tepid coffee, then sat down opposite her prepared to listen.

She looked at him with vacant eyes. "Oh, Edgar, I have made such a mess of things. Charlie is furious at me and has ordered me to let Richard back into our home. Elizabeth is a mess. She was here yesterday and drank and cried herself into a stupor. I have never seen her behave in such a way. And no one seems to understand me!" She ended with a wail.

Edgard had been expecting this. Rebecca's inability to see any point of view except her own was a serious problem. Reality needed to intrude on her grudge. He thought for a moment, then started in on what was about to be a very stern lecture.

"So, you feel like Richard should be punished for doing what he did?

"Of course! How can I let him into our home when he arrested Charlie and almost hung him for something he did not do? He almost destroyed our family."

Edgar blinked. There was the opening he needed. "Almost, but not quite. Do you remember the mob that was outside of the jail?"

She nodded. Of course she remembered that mob. Some of

them had literally arrived at the jail with ropes in their hands. It had taken about three days before Richard and the deputies had made it safe enough for anyone to see Charlie.

Edgar continued. "They wanted to hang him right then and there. If Richard had not come out and arrested him, and put him in jail where he could be properly **protected**, that mob would have been out here, and would certainly have hung Charlie right then, probably from that big oak tree right outside your bedroom window. Charlie's secret might have been discovered too, and then you both would have been hung on the spot. They would have at least hurt you and possibly the children, and might have even tried to burn down your home. So, Richard doing his duty actually saved Charlie's, and quite possibly your life and the lives of your children. And probably also saved a lot of people from getting hurt. The Pinkerton guards would have tried to deal with the mob and that would have been a horrible mess. I would not have been surprised if people would have gotten shot, possibly even killed in the mayhem. "

She looked stunned. "I never thought of it that way."

He went on. "It was not Richard who found Charlie guilty. It was the military tribunal--a panel of old-school soldiers who just wanted to get the trial over and have somebody pay for Raeburn's death so the town would not go up in flames. If Richard had not followed the rules, Charlie would never have been able to see Eddie with his knife and he would have hung that day. Once again, Richard doing his duty saved Charlie and eventually caught the real culprit. My dear, you need to let go of your anger and be grateful to Richard, not resentful."

He drew a deep breath. "And because Richard followed the rules, all of the rules, Eddie Rainey confessed – to Alex's death, to burning your barn and killing Tarent and Rollins, to stealing the money, the horses, and the watch and penknife. Eddie killed

Raeburn because he threatened to turn him in to Richard that night. He waited for Alex to be released from jail and took advantage of the train coming through to cover the sound of his shots. You have not been in town, but you should know that Richard hung Eddie less than ten days after Charlie was to be hung – and on the same gallows – **because Richard followed the rules**."

She looked down at her feet. He was making it clear that he understood her, and equally clear that she was just downright wrong. She did not like being wrong.

"Furthermore, dear, because you will not let this go, and will not forgive Richard for doing things he had to do to protect you and to protect his friend of over fifteen years, doing the best he could in a terrible situation, your actions are hurting many people to the point where they are no longer acting themselves. Charlie is angry with you and for the first time in your life together ordering you to do something instead of treating you as a partner and equal. Elizabeth is so distraught that she felt the need to get drunk yesterday. Rebecca, what if someone had needed a doctor last night? Your actions would have hurt yet another person. Richard is so depressed and saddened at the results of this whole mess that he is damaging his family and simply going through the motions. Where is he going to find the energy to deal with any problems that arise in town? How many more people do you want to hurt? And your children, who love their uncle Richard and aunt Elizabeth, are seeing you being petty and vindictive, as well as having been cut off from two people who are key parts of their young lives. You are teaching them that it is acceptable to be vindictive, to hold a grudge and to be unforgiving. Until you let go, forgive Richard, and more importantly, forgive yourself, no one's life can return to normal. It is up to you, dear."

She just sat there, looking at him with disbelieving eyes. *How could he... I love these people. I love my children. Am I really being this big an ass?* Her mind ranged all over the place, desperately seeking a way to justify herself, but everywhere she turned, all she could find was more examples of her own stubborn resentment.

Edgar sat quietly, letting her think. He resisted the temptation to reach out to comfort her. She needed to find the answers for herself.

Finally she looked up at Edgar. "Is there something in your rituals that will give me absolution for being a nasty idiot?"

He thought for a moment, then said, "Yes. It is called the Reconciliation of a Penitent. You must confess to me and I can provide you absolution. You start by saying, "Bless me, for I have sinned." Then you must confess your sins, express your sorrow at having committed them, and pray to God to have mercy on your soul. I will coach you through the rite. Let me get my book and stole."

He stepped out into the hall, asking Reg for his saddle bag. Reg, clever man that he was, had it to hand, sitting on one of the benches in the hall. Edgar quickly pulled out his stole, wrapped it around his neck, flipped through the Book of Common Prayer for the ritual of absolution and went back into the back parlor. He looked at Rebecca and quietly commanded, "Kneel."

She did so, and he placed the book in front of her open to the page with the ritual.

"Bless me, for I have sinned," Rebecca began.

Edgar intoned, "The Lord be in your heart and upon your lips that you may truly and humbly confess your sins: In the Name of the Father, and of the Son, and of the Holy Spirit. Amen."

She read the opening words of the next section. "I confess to Almighty God, to his Church, and to you, that I have sinned by my own fault in thought, word, and deed, in things done and left undone." She halted, took a deep breath, and started to enumerate her sins of anger, resentment, and vindictiveness. Before she was done, she had managed to cover her acts of the past few weeks toward nearly every citizen of Culpeper, starting with Richard and her family, and extending out as she thought about all the times she had been rude, nasty, thoughtless, or just plain mean. By the time she got to the end of the confession, she was exhausted. She finished with, "For these and all other sins which I cannot now remember, I am truly sorry. I pray God to have mercy on me. I firmly intend amendment of life, and I humbly beg forgiveness of God and his Church, and ask you for counsel, direction, and absolution."

Edgar smiled at her. "Be kind, Rebecca. Be forgiving of yourself and others. And be willing to look at things from more than just one point of view."

She smiled wanly. "Yes, Edgar. Thank you. Dear Lord, I was even mean to Margaret Williams."

The minister looked rueful. "God will most likely give you that one." It did not seem to be the time or place, if it ever were, to tell her that three days after Rebecca's diatribe in the churchyard, Margaret Williams had confessed to identifying the children as Charlie's weakest point and had then left town – for good.

He cleared his throat, then completed the ritual. "Our Lord Jesus Christ, who has left power to his Church to absolve all sinners who truly repent and believe in him, of his great mercy forgive you all your offenses; and by his authority committed to me, I absolve you from all your sins: In the Name of the Father, and of the Son, and of the Holy Spirit. Amen."

Rebecca responded softly. "Amen."

She stood up and walked to the little writing desk. "Could

you wait a few moments while I write a note to Richard and take it to him?"

"Certainly. May I ring Sarah for some fresh coffee?"

She smiled and nodded.

Edgar rang, and Sarah appeared a few minutes later, bearing a fresh pot of coffee, having anticipated the minister's needs. "Bless you, Sarah. You are a wise woman."

Meanwhile, Rebecca wrote the following letter.

Dearest Richard,

I am deeply ashamed and mortified that I have allowed my fear, anger and frustration get in the way of our family relationship, as I recognize that you are more than just Charlie's best friend. You are his true brother and did the best you could to protect him and by extension me and mine in a terrible situation.

I would appreciate it if you and Elizabeth could come to dine with us at your earliest convenience for a quiet family supper. Please feel free to bring Dickon.

Love,
Rebecca

She gave the letter to Edgar without folding it, so he could read it before delivering it.

He smiled and said gently, "It is a start. I think a very good start." With that, he picked up his gloves and book, taking off his stole and folding it. "I will see you Sunday. And I expect a good dinner, with Richard and Elizabeth in attendance, Sunday afternoon."

Edgar rapped on the door of Elizabeth and Richard's house. Ruth smiled as she opened the door and showed him in. "Colonel Polk is in his office, Reverend Vile. Doctor Elizabeth is not feeling well today and is lying down in her room. I can fetch her if need be."

"Oh, no." He shook his head and dropped his hat on the stand in the hallway. "Leave Dr. Elizabeth right where she is. I am aware of why she is feeling under the weather. My business is with Colonel Polk. I will show myself in."

Ruth nodded and closed the door. Edgar turned the corner and rapped gently on Richard's office door. Once given permission, he entered and closed the door quietly behind him.

"Edgar, what can I do for you?" Richard rose to greet him, but he looked terrible. It was clear this was not a man who was taking care of himself in anyway.

"I think it is not so much what you can do for me, but I can do for you." He handed him Rebecca's note.

Polk unfolded the note and read it carefully before looking to Edgar. The minister offered, "I was with her for more than an hour. She really does feel horrible. This invitation is made with honesty, love and a bit of trepidation on her part. She realizes you have every right to be upset as well, but I will tell you like I told her. You must forgive her and more importantly yourself before any of us will be able to go forward. Rebecca has made her confession of sins and received absolution. The rest is up to you, Richard. You may choose one of two options--accept Rebecca's apology and move forward or dig in your heels and allow the rift to continue and grow."

Wednesday, November 13, 1867

With a little prodding from Edgar and support from Charlie, a small, friendly dinner party had been organized for that Wednesday evening. Rebecca asked Richard if he could come out to the house a little early. Ro volunteered to watch the tavern with Esther's head cook so Jocko and Esther could join in. Charlotte and Rex carefully packed up the twins for their first foray into the big wide world and Elizabeth was riding out with them. Duncan and Samantha did the same with their new little boy. All three babies were scheduled for baptism the following Sunday, so one of the things on the evening's agenda was finalizing names for each of them.

Rebecca was waiting in the hall when Richard arrived. She smiled a little hesitantly at him as he entered and surrendered his hat, coat and gloves to Reg, and then invited him to join her in the back parlor.

"Thank you, Richard, for taking the time to speak with me privately before everyone else arrives. I owe you an enormous apology, one that I am not sure you will ever fully accept as being genuine, but I assure you, it is." As she spoke, she went to the tantalus and poured him and herself a glass of brandy, then handed it to him, gesturing for him to sit opposite her in front of the fire. As they settled themselves, she went on.

"I became so absorbed in what we almost lost, I never realized that if it were not for you and what you did, we would have surely lost Charlie and possibly so much more. It was your courage and your determination to do what you had to do that in the end made it possible for what did happen." Rebecca cleared her throat. "What you did must have been horribly difficult. What I have been doing has done nothing but make it worse for you and everyone else. I was wrong, and I am terribly sorry."

Tears were running down Rebecca's cheeks, but she continued to look straight into Richard's eyes. "I was wrong. I know that you and Charlie are as close as brothers, and what you did must have been terribly hard, when I suspect you just wanted to help him get away. It was enormously brave of you to do what you did. Can you forgive me? Oh, can you ever forgive me?"

Richard was more than a little moist around the eyes as well as he took Rebecca's hands and pulled her into a gentle embrace. "Of course I can. You wanted to protect him as much or more than I did. I just thank God that Eddie Rainey had the bad sense to use Charlie's penknife when he did. It was indeed a miracle."

Richard fished his handkerchief out of his pocket and offered it to Rebecca. The two of them sat together quietly for a few minutes, savoring the restored companionability and peace between them. Then they heard someone arriving in the hall, and the bustle of people being divested of their wraps. Rebecca rose. "We had best go greet the rest of the party!"

Samantha and Duncan had arrived and were just handing their buggy off to Reg and his associates just as Edgar, Rex, Charlotte and Elizabeth were pulling into the driveway. Within moments, the entry hall was flooded with adults pulling off overcoats and babies swaddled in layers of soft woolen blankets and hand-knitted wrappings. Tess and Ginnie, along with the housemaid who helped them when needed, were there to take charge of the little ones, having set the nursery up to accommodate the newborns as well as the two boys, who would be three in February and would soon be moving into a real bedroom and out of their cribs, which could no longer contain them when they chose to escape.

But before the babies could be whisked off to the nursery, the ladies had to hand them around, oohhing and aaahhhhing over them. The soft black fuzz on Charlotte's twins' heads was ruffled by everyone, as was the reddish-blond top knot that graced Duncan and Samantha's boy. All three babies still had blue eyes, but time would tell if they stayed blue. As they passed the babies around, the ladies moved slowly to the back parlor. Reg had set out glasses and some very dry amontillado sherry as an aperitif, knowing full well that with babies as part of the guest list, the women would congregate in this, the warmest room in the house.

While the ladies loitered with their attack of baby-lust, Charlie led the gentlemen into the smoking room for a drink before dinner. There was scotch, Kentucky whiskey, and brandy in the open tantalus, along with glasses and branch water. Once everyone had a glass in hand, the gentlemen broke into several clusters, chatting about this and that. Jocko buttonholed Charlie and pushed him into a corner.

"All right, Charlie-boy. You have had your time to be a hermit and avoid coming to town, avoid your friends, avoid your business associates. It is time for this bullshit to be over, and for you to come back and take your place in the community. And damn it, I want the poker game to start back up. I need the business. Not to mention feeding you lunch most days. So I expect you to come back to life – your whole life – by Monday at the latest, or I will be out here to get you."

Charlie blinked, startled at Jocko's words. He was always blunt, but this was harsh, even for him. "But…"

"No buts, boy-o. Just get your ass back in town and back to your life." With that, Jocko turned around and stomped over to talk with Edward Cooper.

Charlie stood there, gawking at his oldest friend. Fortunately, Reg stuck his head in the door just then and announced dinner.

Dinner that evening was a major event, as it not only brought Richard and Rebecca back together, it was really the first time since the trial that Charlie and Rebecca had hosted a dinner party. It was also the first time the three new residents of Culpeper were being brought out into the great wide world. Sarah had gone out of her way to make a meal that catered to Richard's tastes, while attempting to prepare something special for each guest. It was quite an impressive spread.

She started dinner with a rich cream of wild mushroom soup flavored with a touch of sherry, one of Jocko's favorites. Richard got his beloved mustard and pecan crusted rack of lamb, with the crispy, spicy green beans that she had learned from Rex for Charlotte, and a delicately sautéed spinach with garlic for Elizabeth.

Her biscuits were favorites with everyone, while New Orleans style dirty rice was served for Duncan and Samantha. Dessert was especially made for Edgar and Rex--a beautiful trifle with a mix of Sarah's own special preserved strawberries and raspberries, lady fingers soaked in framboise liqueur, a classic egg custard and plenty of fresh whipped cream.

The Coopers' taste in wine and their love of Charlie's special vintages was acknowledged as well, with Charlie choosing several bottles of his precious Jaboulet La Chapelle red Hermitage Bordeaux to compliment the rich and spicy lamb. Reg had opened it right after lunch to allow this magnificent, rare and very expensive wine to breathe. He had also pulled out several bottles of Charlie's best vintage Armagnac, 20 year old brandy from Armagnac-Ténarèze that had aged in oak to a rich honey brown and a beautiful fruity taste.

At Duncan and Samantha's request, seconded soundly by Richard, Darby had been invited to join the adults for dinner that night. What none of the other guests knew was that Duncan and Samantha had a surprise question for Darby. They had decided to ask the young man who had shown so much maturity and bravery if he would honor them by being their son's godfather. Each child needed three godparents, two of their own gender, and one of the other sex. Rex, Charlie and Rebecca and Elizabeth were slated as the twin's godparents, but Samantha and Duncan had not shared their thoughts on the subject with anyone until they could talk to Darby.

Once food was served and the guests had complimented Sarah on the lovely dinner, conversation around the table turned to the names for the babies. Charlotte and Edgar looked proud as they announced that they intended to name the twins Rebecca Elizabeth and Edgar Charles. Charlotte had considered calling little Rebecca Elizabeth "Reb" but decided that was probably not the wisest course of action in this still painfully divided community. So the little girl would be "Becky."

Little Edgar Charles was another issue. Since he did not share the same middle name as his father, he was not a "second" or a "junior," but having two Edgars in one household, especially as the son grew older, could be confusing. So they decided to call the little boy "Chas," using the common abbreviation for Charles. The attendant guests all smiled and nodded or voiced their agreement with this selection of names and nicknames. Rex and Rebecca, as godparents to both babies, were entirely pleased, not only with the names, but that they were easy to remember for the christening ceremony the following Sunday.

Once Edgar and Charlotte's decision had been discussed and approved, the assembly turned to Samantha and Duncan. They were both smiling. While everyone had known the role Rebecca and Rex would play in the twins' lives, Duncan and Samantha had been very closed mouthed about their choices, both for names and for god parents.

Samantha looked at Darby, who had been very quiet, savoring his inclusion with the adults at dinner and trying very hard to not draw attention lest he be excused. "So, Darby. Duncan and I have been talking, specifically about you. We think you are a very mature, courageous young man. You have certainly shown yourself to be so in the past weeks, with all the trouble with your father and the town. We think we would like you to be a role model for our son, Samuel Duncan. Would you be willing to be our son's godfather?"

Darby turned an amazing shade of red as all eyes at the table turned to him. They were all smiling encouragingly and nodding agreement with Samantha's assessment of this young man.

"I… I do not know what to say!" His blush deepened, turning almost purple. "I am honored, but what do I have to do?"

Rex put his hand on the shoulder of the young man sitting beside him. "You have to hold the baby while Edgar baptizes him after you tell little Sam's names. You have to see him every so often and give him gifts at Christmas, Easter, and on his birthday. Other than that, not much unless something happens to Duncan and Samantha. Then you get to finish raising him."

Darby took another deep breath and looked around the table, a slight panic setting in.

Edgar grinned. "I doubt you will have to finish raising him. We plan to keep Duncan and Samantha around for a good long while."

The young man grinned back at Uncle Edgar and then smiled at Samantha and Duncan. "Then I would be honored to be one of Sam's godfathers. Who are the other godparents?"

Duncan spoke up. "General Charlie, would you?"

Charlie smiled and nodded.

Samantha smiled and added. "I have asked Mary Simms if she would also stand up for little Sam. Since she escaped the clutches of Mrs. Williams and has been spending time with Ro Jackson, she has turned into an exceptionally nice young woman. I have found her to be a very pleasant friend in the past few months. I wanted to bring her with us this evening, but she decided to have dinner at the tea room, since Ro is tending bar this evening."

Rex chuckled. "Yes. That is turning into a rather interesting relationship, is it not? On the surface, one would not think the two women had anything in common, but it seems their love of animals has formed an unusual alliance."

Charlotte bit her lower lip. "I doubt it is just their love of animals, dear man."

Darby escaped to his room to consider the honor he had been given by Duncan and Samantha. What he realized was that the adults in his life were treating him less as a child and more as a young man. He was very pleased with the idea that they could see he was growing up. Perhaps soon he would find a way to remind his mother of that fact, as Rebecca had a tendency to try and keep her children rather close to her side. He would have to consider the possibilities that this acknowledgement that he was growing up might open for him.

After Darby retired from the table, the adults continued to enjoy the after dinner coffee and brandy. As their celebrations deepened, the gentlemen got into a story telling contest. As the brandy continued to flow, the stories became more and more off-color.

"But I did change my ways! I started at the bottom of the page!" Edgar slapped the table as everyone else caught the punch line of his joke.

Richard hid his face behind his napkin as the rest of the table roared with laughter. He shook his head as he looked at Edgar. "I cannot believe you told that joke with the ladies present!"

"Then in the future do not stake such a dare with the ladies present, Richard!" Edgar laughed outright as everyone else tried to compose themselves.

Charlie dropped a ten dollar gold piece on the table in front of Edgar. "You win. That is by far the dirtiest joke I have ever heard and I have heard more than a few." He looked sheepishly to all the ladies, who were still appropriately laughing behind their napkins.

This was exactly what they needed. The small group that were more family than friends, allowed to absolutely cut loose and relieve some of the stress and anxiety of the last few months. They were eating too much, drinking too much and laughing so loudly, occasionally a servant would check to make sure they were all right when someone choked or lost their breath.

Charlie was comforted to find that the tension between Richard and Rebecca had dissipated after they had spent over an hour alone in the rear parlor talking and working out whatever was left between them. When they emerged, they were arm in arm with sincere smiles on both their faces.

Elizabeth and Charlie could not be happier. It had taken several weeks, even more than the original trauma, but they all seemed to be occupied to get past it. Judging by the laughter at their supper table, it was working.

"By the way." Charlie lifted his hand to get everyone's attention. "Just so you all know, this year's New Year's ball will be masked costume. We wanted to tell you know, so you would all have time to find costumes."

Wednesday evenings at Jocko's tended to be fairly quiet after the gentlemen had stopped in for a quick one after work and on their way home. The two salesmen staying upstairs had already finished their dinners and retired early, as they were scheduled to catch the train to Richmond early the next morning. The bar had emptied out, so Ro and Allison Simms were sitting at the table by the door to the tap room having just finished having a quiet dinner together.

At least it had been quiet until Harold Kirtley swaggered in. He kicked a bar stool to one side and planted himself at the bar. "Keep – get me whiskey and keep it coming."

Ro calmly wiped her mouth, laid her napkin down beside her plate and strolled into the bar. She pulled a glass and a bottle of Kentucky whiskey from the back shelf and poured a neat shot, placing the glass in front of Kirtley.

"Leave the bottle," he growled, dropping a five dollar gold piece on the bar.

"Anything else, sir?" Ro asked politely.

Kirtley looked around the empty room, and then through the door to Miss Simms sitting quietly at the table in the other room. He thought for a minute, then leered at Miss Simms. "Nothing unless you're willing to share your little bit of ass, you unnatural Mick."

Ro drew herself up to her full height, which was not insignificant. She was over six feet tall. She drew in a deep breath and just managed to keep herself from coming over the bar at him. "Mr. Kirtley, you will apologize to Miss Simms for that incredible insult and then leave this establishment immediately."

"Who is going to make me, bitch? I don't see one of those dogs you used to corner poor Eddie Rainey here tonight."

Taking very measured steps, Ro came out from behind the bar. "I do not need a dog to kick a wretched cur out the door,

Kirtley." She stopped beside him and neatly pulled him off of his bar stool. "Now. Apologize to the lady."

"What lady? I don't see no lady. I see a bit of misguided southern fluff and an unnatural Mick, but no ladies."

Ro's movements were lightning fast. One fist went into Kirtley's gut. As he started forward from having the wind knocked out of him, the other fist met the edge of his jaw, snapping his head back on his neck. As he staggered, she caught his arm and pulled him forward. She moved him a step forward and twisted his arm behind his back until she heard a neat popping sound. "I said APOLOGIZE!"

Kirtley just grunted.

Ro released his arm. He spun around and stepped back, glaring at her. But he did not have time to do anything else before her foot caught him between the legs. He crumpled, clutching at his groin as he dropped to his knees.

"Want more, cur? Or are you ready to apologize to the lady?"

Kirtley looked up at the woman standing over him and saw nothing but carefully controlled rage in her eyes. He thought he could take this bitch, but from where he was right now, he realized that was not the case. Sullenly, and with very little conviction, whether it was because of resentment or lack of air in his lungs from the injuries he had received in a matter of seconds from the Amazon in front of him, he mumbled, "Sorry, ladies."

"Much better, MISTER Kirtley." She pulled him to his feet by his collar and duck marched him to the door. "Now, get out and **stay** out! You are no longer welcome at this establishment. I will make sure my uncle knows about this, as well as Colonel Polk." With that, she unceremoniously heaved him out the door. He staggered across the porch, slipped and sprawled in the dirty street. Ro did not see what happened next; she turned and went to tend to Allison.

"Ro," Allison was a little breathless as she spoke. "Are you all right? Did he hurt you?"

"My dear lady, he never laid a finger on me. He was so occupied with the idea that he was the man and no woman could ever possibly consider trying to hurt him, let alone succeed at it, that he was completely unprepared. But how are you? What he said was appalling!"

"Yes, yes, it was. But then, Mr. Kirtley is appalling. Was he not part of the group of men who supported Alex Raeburn and Eddie Rainey? I believe he is one of the men who burned the cross out in Sweetwater and threatened our colored people. He is an embarrassment to the very concept of a southern gentleman." She looked into Ro's eyes, admiration shining from her own. "And how did you ever manage to keep your temper and stay in such control? I was amazed!"

"I learned when I was very young that letting your temper get the better of you is a great way to give your opponent an advantage, and possibly a lethal one. The conflict between the English Protestants and the Irish Catholics in my home country is vicious and dangerous; it is no better in New York, where gangs run the streets in the poorer sections of town. So I learned early to control my anger and maybe be able to take advantage of someone else's anger and arrogance."

"Well, you certainly did with Mr. Kirtley. Thank you, Ro. I have not had anyone who would stand up for me for a long while. It is… rather nice, I have to admit."

"Having a real friend in a new town is also very nice, Allison. We seem to be doing well together. You love the dogs and they love you. You have done wonders helping me get started here as a dog breeder, you know. Introducing me to people, showing them that my dogs are true purebreds, not mutts. I was wondering…"

Allison looked at her companion intently, waiting for her to finish. "You were wondering?"

Ro cleared her throat. "I was wondering if…" She gulped. "If you would be interested in, well…" She stumbled again, then finished in a rush, "If you would like to move in with me and help run the dog breeding business." She went on, her tongue falling over itself in her rush to get the whole idea on the table. "I know you do not like living alone, with no one there to help if you feel unwell or if something were to happen, and you and I are doing so well working together, I thought…" She ran out of words at this point.

Allison could not help but smile at her friend's nervousness. "It is very much a part of southern tradition that when two women rub along together as well as we do, that they may become what we call companions. To be honest, dear, I enjoy your company, far more than I have ever enjoyed anyone else's. Yes, there are a number of single men in town, with the soldiers having returned, but to be honest, there is not one of them that I would care to spend my life with, and I think you are right – we do get along together very well. I would be honored to become your companion and your business partner."

Ro flushed a bright pink. "I am so pleased. Perhaps you can come out tomorrow and we can talk about how we are going to make this work so that we are both comfortable? And then perhaps I will have Mr. Nailer come out to make whatever changes you want made?"

"That sounds like a lovely idea. I have grown very tired of living alone. And while there are some lovely pieces at my house we may want to bring out, I rather like the idea of ridding myself of leftovers from my mother's tastes and making a new start – something we can have together."

The guests at Charlie and Rebecca's first celebratory dinner party had departed after a long evening of laughing, joking, and several serious talks. Rebecca was tired, but feeling more relaxed than she had in a long while, and Charlie was doing his best to further improve her sense of relaxation and comfort. He sat on one end of the sofa by the fire and she was stretched out across it with her feet in his lap.

Her head fell back as she moaned with great delight, "Ohhh yessss…"

Charlie chuckled as his thumb hit a particularly sensitive spot on the sole of her foot.

"Any man who will rub my feet like that has my heart." She groaned as he continued to rub, his thumbs finding **the** spot through the middle of each foot.

"Are you telling me, wife, you can be bought for a foot rub?"

"Yes. I am afraid so. If you plan to stop anytime in the next fifty years, I will replace you, I swear to God I will."

He laughed heartily as he continued to offer the most dedicated of ministrations to his loving wife. "So, my place in your world is assured as long as I rub your feet?"

"Yes."

His entire body shook as he continued to laugh and tend his wife. "I am very glad to hear it."

She took a deep breath and looked at him seriously. "Are you happy with the situation now?"

"Between you and Richard?"

"MmmHmm." She nodded, closing her eyes again against his expert touch.

"Yes, dear." He leaned over and kissed her cheek. "Thank you."

"My pleasure," she hummed as he began working the other foot. They continued along in amicable silence, Charlie rubbing and Rebecca luxuriating.

"I want to take a trip," he said out of the blue, causing green eyes to open and stare at him.

"Why do you want to go away?" Rebecca sat up abruptly, staring at him. *Where the hell did that come from?*

"Not just me, darling. Us. I want us to take a trip. Let us take the children and go somewhere for a month or so."

She nodded. Since Charlie had avoided the noose, he had been nothing but a devoted father and loving husband, but he also seemed a bit preoccupied with something, and on occasion Rebecca could see a wistful look on his face. She knew he needed something, but had no idea what it was. Perhaps this would give her some insight.

"All right, where?"

"I do not know. I just need to be away from here for a while, but I cannot bear the thought of being separated from you and the children. While I was sitting in jail, I realized that I have spent my whole life as a soldier travelling from place to place, seeing new things, meeting new people. Sitting in jail brought it home to me that I could no longer do that – at least not while I was locked up. I felt like I understood what it was to be a slave, to not have control over your own life."

Charlie was obviously having trouble expressing himself. Each word emerged as if it were being forced from his throat unwillingly, as if he were groping in the dark for words that did not exist. His hands that had been so gentle on Rebecca's feet were now clenched so tightly that his knuckles were turning white. "My God, Rebecca. In the past two and a half years, I have nearly died three times, and never because of something I had chosen. I need to get away from here for a while and I think Culpeper needs me to get away for a while."

Rebecca took his hands in hers and rubbed them until they relaxed. Looking deeply into his eyes, she smiled. "I understand entirely. Would you be willing to wait until spring? I do not think winter is the best season to try and travel with five children."

"Agreed." Charlie nodded. "Thank you, darling."

"Of course, but there is something I expect from you in return."

"Yes?"

"I want to hear a few of those jokes you know."

Charlie laughed, sipped his tea, and then resumed his foot rubbing duties. "Are you going to tell them at the mah jong game?" He took another sip of tea.

"Oh, no." Rebecca grinned evilly as she flexed her feet in Charlie's lap. "We talk about sex at the game."

He blushed and choked, but managed to hold his tea in his mouth. Maybe it was a good thing they had not gone back into town for those games after all.

CHAPTER 17

Sunday, November 17, 1867

After weeks of staying away from the Sunday service, the entire Redmond family trooped in that morning and took their position in the pew at the front of the church. Charlie was surprised at the number of new people who smiled and nodded, greeted him, and reached out to shake his hand. When they had come to church last month, Charlie's friends had welcomed him with open arms. Today, it was people who up until now would not give him the time of day. Evidently, the community was appalled at finding out what Eddie Rainey, Alex Raeburn, and the men who had supported them had actually done. The ladies of the biddy brigade had been amazingly cordial to him and to Rebecca, especially since Mrs. Williams had been run out of town for her role in the plots against the Redmonds.

Edgar delivered a short sermon that day, given that he had

three christenings to do after church. Christenings and weddings were always Edgar's favorite services; two of them today also gave him great personal joy. So he chose one of Solomon's songs, Psalm 127, for his text that day.

"Except the LORD build the house, they labour in vain that build it: except the LORD keep the city, the watchman waketh but in vain. It is vain for you to rise up early, to sit up late, to eat the bread of sorrows: for so he giveth his beloved sleep.

Lo, children are an heritage of the LORD: and the fruit of the womb is his reward.

As arrows are in the hand of a mighty man; so are children of the youth.

Happy is the man that hath his quiver full of them: they shall not be ashamed, but they shall speak with the enemies in the gate."

"Our community has been faced with many challenges in the past months. We have faced the enemies at our gates of crime, murder, false accusation, malicious gossip, resentment, unforgiving intolerance, and a host of other vanities and sins. Yet our community has emerged stronger, more unified, and strengthened in our faith and souls. Now, God has seen proper, in his vast and unquestionable wisdom, to reward our community with the greatest gift that He can grant a human, with the birth of not one but three new souls, come into the world to bring the happiness that only children can give."

"We have seen the faith, the strength, and the nobility that a man can manifest in the face of terrible stress for the sake of his children." Edgar nodded at Charlie, smiling broadly. "We have seen the punishment that the Lord and his people will mete out to those who threaten those children." The reference to Mrs. Williams was unmistakable.

Edgar went on to talk about the joy of new life, whether it was new life as represented by children or new life as experienced from a rebirth – a rebirth of the nation, a rebirth of the community, a rebirth of a man's soul through the grace and forgiveness of God. It was one of his best sermons to date.

As he did every Sunday, Edgar stood at the door of the church, smiling, chatting, blessing people as they filed out. The Redmonds remained in the church, as did Duncan, Samantha, Jeremiah and little Samuel Duncan. Mary Simms stood at the back of the room with Ro standing beside her. Finally, the only people left were the participants in the christenings.

Darby went over to Miss Simms. "Good morning, Miss Simms. Um, I am a little nervous, so could you, um, guide me through this?"

Mary Allison laughed. "It is not that difficult, Darby. We hold the baby, we answer the questions that Reverend Vile asks, he sprinkles holy water on the baby, and we hand him back to his parents. Think you can do that?"

"Yes, ma'am. I can do that." The young man grinned, then extended his arm to her, the proper gentleman offering to escort her to the altar, join his father and begin the service.

As they reached the steps up to the altar, Edgar approached from one side, and Duncan and Samantha carrying the baby from the other. Samantha carefully transferred Samuel Duncan to Darby's arms, while Miss Simms reached in to sooth the confused and now whimpering child. Charlie stood behind them, smiling benignly.

Edgar cleared his throat and began the service.

"Dearly beloved, ye have brought this child here to be baptized; ye have prayed that our Lord Jesus Christ would vouchsafe to receive him, to release him of his sins, to sanctify him with the Holy Ghost, to give him the kingdom of heaven and everlasting life. Ye have heard also that our Lord Jesus Christ hath promised in his Gospel, to grant all these things that ye have prayed for: which promise he, for his part, will most surely keep and perform. Wherefore, after this promise made by Christ, this infant must also faithfully, for his part, promise by you that are his sureties, (until he come of age to take it upon himself,) that he will renounce the devil and all his works, and constantly believe God's holy Word, and obediently keep his commandments."

"Dost thou, in the name of this Child, renounce the devil and all his works, the vain pomp and glory of the world, with all covetous desires of the same, and the carnal desires of the flesh, so that thou wilt not follow nor be led by them?"

Together, Darby, Miss Simms and Charlie said, "I renounce them all."

"Dost thou believe in God the Father Almighty, Maker of heaven and earth? And in Jesus Christ his only-begotten Son our Lord? And that he was conceived by the Holy Ghost, born of the Virgin Mary; that he suffered under Pontius Pilate, was crucified, dead, and buried; that he went down into hell, and also did rise again the third day; that he ascended into heaven, and sitteth at the right hand of God the Father Almighty; and from thence shall come again at the end of the world, to judge the quick and the dead? And dost thou believe in the Holy Ghost; the holy catholic church; the Communion of Saints; the Remission of sins; the Resurrection of the flesh; and everlasting life after death?"

"All this I steadfastly believe," they each answered.

Edgar continued with the service, which was not terribly

long. At the appropriate point, Miss Simms and Charlie helped Darby strip off as much of the clothing and wrappings as possible. Edgar took the little boy into his hands and asked the godparents to name the child. Miss Simms and Charlie both urged Darby to state the name.

In a clear voice, Darby said, "This is Samuel Duncan Nailer."

Edgar smiled at him, then dipped the little boy in the holy water in the baptismal font. As he did so, he said, "Samuel Duncan Nailer, I baptize thee in the Name of the Father, and of the Son, and of the Holy Ghost. Amen."

Even though Rex and Charlotte had seen to it that the water was warmed before the service, the sudden dunking startled little Sam, who immediately started wailing. That set the twins off as well. It took a few minutes for calm to return to the little group of participants so that Edgar could finish up the service.

"We receive this Child into the Congregation of Christ's flock, and do sign him with the sign of the Cross, in token that hereafter he shall not be ashamed to confess the faith of Christ crucified, and manfully to fight under his banner against sin, the world, and the devil, and to continue Christ's faithful soldier and servant unto his life's end. Amen." Edgar made the sign of the cross on Samuel's forehead. He handed the baby back to Darby, then continued with the service. "Seeing now, dearly beloved brethren, that this child is regenerate and grafted into the body of Christ's Church, let us give thanks unto Almighty God for these benefits, and with one accord make our prayers unto him, that this Child may lead the rest of his life according to this beginning." He finished with the Lord's Prayer, which everyone recited.

As Darby gave the baby back to Samantha, Edgar grinned at the group, and said, "One down, two to go!"

Rex stepped up holding Edgar Charles in his arms. Rex was dressed in an elegant day suit of western style, rather than his usual subdued black silk pajamas. He was looking very proud as he stood there with Charlie and Rebecca through the service. He handed Chas to Charlotte, then took Becky while Elizabeth exchanged places with Charlie.

When all three babies were done, settled from the shock of being dipped in the baptismal font and re-wrapped in warm robes, Rex looked at the assembly. "I have prepared a special lunch for you all. It is waiting at the manse, so please join us."

The rest of the Redmond tribe joined them, escorted by Tess and Ginnie with the boys, and they all walked over to the manse. A meal by Rex was always a special treat.

Monday, November 18, 1867

Charlie was about to go down the stairs when he saw Rebecca exit the parlor, headed for the kitchen and then probably to her office. "Darling, could you come up to my office, please?"

She stopped and turned to look up at him. "There are not any drunken doctors up there, are there?"

"No." He chuckled, shaking his head and gestured for her to join him. "I promise. But I do have a surprise for you."

She began climbing the stairs, carefully lifting her skirts to do so. "I have been upstairs with you before; I doubt it will be much of a surprise."

"Cheeky." He just shook his head and took her hand, leading her toward his office. She just gave him a wide, unrepentant grin as she followed him dutifully down the hall.

It was clear right away what he wanted to show her. Gone

was his old oak desk and now in its place was a large mahogany partner's desk with two matching chairs opposite each other.

"Charlie, it is beautiful."

"I am glad you like it. I thought maybe…" He moved to her chair and pulled it out for her. "Maybe we should promote Brooks to barn manager and give him the office in the basement. You could move up here with me."

She sat in her chair and ran her hands over the smooth, cool wood. "I think that is an excellent idea. We need to get Albert back on the road and I certainly think Mr. Brooks has proven his loyalty and honor."

"I agree." He kissed her on the top of her head and took his seat. "You know you will have to learn to live with Sheridan? He was here first."

"I am certain that after all this time we have managed to make our peace." She did look around for her feline competitor.

"You think that. Wait until he wants to lie on the ledger or books you are trying to work on. My personal financial ledgers have little inky paw prints all over them. Jerome curses a blue streak every time he sees them."

"Of course he will have to learn to live with Peri and Feighlí too, because you know we will not be able to keep them out of here."

He knew it was true as he looked to the fireplace where his pup, Peri, was curled up near the fire. Feighlí had been turned out about an hour ago to go have a run and probably a pee. He knew she would be taking up floor space sooner than later. "Peri is not an issue. They have a truce. Feighlí on the other hand…"

"Will simply eat your cat if he annoys her," Rebecca said bluntly as she opened the drawers on her side of the desk and gave it a proper inspection.

Thursday, November 21, 1867

"Well, this is interesting."

Rebecca raised her eyes from her breed books and lifted a brow at Charlie, who simply handed her a letter.

She scanned it and grinned. "So it is. Are you going to buy it?" She handed the letter back.

He leaned back in his chair, dropped the paper on his desk, and smiled. "Oh, I think so. It never hurts to own more property and it looks like Miss Simms has," he bit his lip to stop the grin, "investment plans for the proceeds."

"And who are we to stand in the way of true love?" His wife shrugged as she flipped a page in her ledger.

"Indeed." He grinned as he sat forward and started composing the letter to Miss Simms agreeing to her offer to buy her little home in town and setting her an appointment with him at the bank for next week to finalize details. "I think they make a very cute couple."

Rebecca laughed and nodded. It was very clear that Ro Jackson and Mary Simms had found more in common than just the pup that Ro had sold her. In the months since the pup had been very well trained, they seemed to be inseparable. To the point that Mary was spending her days at Ro's kennels, only coming home in the evening to keep gossip to a minimum, but now it looked as if that was no longer a concern either. *Good for them.* Rebecca grinned, knowing if they could manage the storm, it would be worth it. She had to find a way to make sure they would know that she and Charlie would always be there if they needed it.

"We should start offering them an invitation to Sunday supper," Charlie said as he signed the letter and used his blotter to keep his signature from smearing. "I am sure they would enjoy it since Jocko and Esther are here as well."

"Grand idea. I hate to say this but it will offer them a certain 'status' that they are going to need as they get settled."

"As in, if the Redmonds do not see it as an issue, why should anyone else?"

"Yes."

Charlie just shook his head, still finding it hard to believe or even grasp that his family was still setting the standards in the community. After his ordeal, when he started going back into town for a few hours, a couple days a week, he discovered that the residents on the whole were much friendlier. Whatever hostility Alex Raeburn had managed to cultivate had died on the vine.

Business at the bank was up as people who had refused to do business with the scallywag Union general were more than happy to do business with the honorable southern gentleman many of them had discovered him to be after hearing and reading some of the testimony at his trial. Though it had been a horrible experience, he was coming out of it all right.

Rebecca had noticed several things since he came home. First and most noticeable was the fact there were no longer little piles of his things left around the house. She had not found even one since the day he came home. This made her very happy, though the reason behind it haunted her every day.

Second was that he no longer closed doors if he was alone in a room. He had not taken his incarceration well at all. There were most definitely some emotional scars left over. She could only hope that in time she could help them fade as she had the physical ones.

Third, he never seemed to spend more than an hour or two out of the house and away from her and the children. While

Charlie was going into town every day after Jocko had pigeonholed him, he did not stay long. They had not even started going to the Saturday evening gaming sessions again. This bothered her. She knew those evenings with the gentlemen were as important to him as any of his other social obligations, probably more so. Some part of her wondered if he was a bit afraid to go to the game.

~

Saturday, November 23, 1867

Charlie looked down the hall when he heard his bedroom door open and close. At this time in the morning that was unusual. He waited for a few minutes realizing that whoever had gone in had not come out. Though he hated to do it, he had to make sure that whoever was in that room was supposed to be. This particular left over from the Raeburn incident still stung quite a bit.

He made his way to the bedroom and knocked before entering. Then he slipped in to find Rebecca near the fireplace putting a kettle on the hob. "Darling?"

She looked at him with a clearly pained expression, but tried to wave him off. "I am fine, Charlie."

That was clearly not true and he made his way to her side in two strides. "What is it?"

"Nothing that every woman in the world does not deal with regularly."

Charlie's brows crept up his head as his mouth formed a tiny, "Oh." Yes, while that problem was not one that had plagued him for years now, he did have rather miserable memories of being young. He gestured to the kettle. "Hot water bottle?"

"Yes." She nodded, looking a bit more miserable.

He sat down in front of her and pulled off her boots. "I am going to get you a night gown and I want you to change and get into bed."

"I just need to spend a few minutes with the heat of…"

"No, my dear, you are miserable. That is clear. Rest. Come on."

A few minutes later she was tucked into bed with a pile of pillows behind her and a nice hot water bottle tucked between the covers and her very crampy stomach. She smiled when he pulled a comfortable chair next to the bed and brought over their book of poetry.

"You are going to spoil me."

"Probably." He nodded. "I already called for lunch to be brought up here as well." He settled in the chair and found his place in the book. This volume was the one Rebecca had given him when they first met and he must have already read it to her cover to cover a dozen times, but she never asked for any other. He did not even actually have to read the words anymore, the pages were as much a part of him now as her smile, voice or touch. Just as he was about to begin, he noticed a flash of pain cross her face. "This one is particularly hard?"

She just nodded, pressing the hot water bottle closer.

He fished one of Rex's small dark cigars from his shirt pocket and lit it. Once it was properly smoking he tried to hand it to her. "Here. Draw the smoke in very slowly and gently. If you try too hard, you will choke. Badly. Hold it for a few seconds then let it out."

She looked at the little cigar like it might bite her. In her entire life she had never done anything quite like that. He gestured gently, offering it to her again. "Trust me. It will make you feel much better."

Gingerly, she took it as he looked on with a smile and coaxed her through taking a draw. She did manage to do it without outright choking herself, though as expected for anyone who had never smoked before there was a bit of a cough when she exhaled. He guided her through two or three more and a few minutes later she was lying back relaxed, with a silly smile on her face.

"Oh, you were right."

"Yes, I know." He nodded with a grin as he looked at the slightly ridiculous look on her face. "They are very good for this sort of thing."

"You do realize you will have to share from now on?"

"Yes, dear."

~

Thursday, November 28, 1867. Thanksgiving

Thanksgiving for the Redmond family was a very private affair this year. Charlie and Rebecca did something that would have shocked and appalled their more traditional southern neighbors if they knew about it.

They sat down to Thanksgiving dinner in the formal dining room with all of their house staff joining them. Sarah had extended herself, preparing a meal that she, her staff, and Reg's staff could bring up and set on the sideboard so they would not have to run up and down the stairs.

It had been important to Charlie to do something special for their staff after all the loyalty they had shown his family during the trial. Things had been so chaotic, they had not been paid properly while it was all going on, but every last one of them stayed and came to work every day. They made sure the house did not fall apart and he wanted them to understand he was grateful.

After the meal was completed, Charlie proceeded to hand out cash bonuses to every one of them. He also told them that when Christmas time came around he would be providing each household with a goose for their Christmas celebrations with their families.

It was a quiet, peaceful, and very pleasant day spent in good company.

~

Saturday, November 30, 1867

Darby sat at the breakfast table trying to decide which parent to spring this on first. He turned to Papa. "Sir?"

"Yes, son?" Charlie asked absent mindedly as he piled eggs on his toast.

"I would very much like to move to the carriage house."

"Absolutely not." The answer came from Mama.

Charlie groaned. His eggs were going to get cold. He put down his fork and looked to his wife first. A lovely little storm cloud was forming over her head. He looked to his son and sighed. "You could not wait until I managed to get down a little toast and coffee?"

"I am sorry, Papa."

"And would you two," Rebecca gestured between them, "please stop talking as if I am not sitting right here?" The way she tapped her finger showed her irritation. "You can both just be the damn powder monkey. Oh, yes." She nodded at their startled expressions. "I know all about your little game." She eyed her husband. "When boys are being boys, women always know what is going on."

Charlie mumbled to Darby, "I think your chances just went way down."

"Charles Huger Redmond…" She was pinching the bridge of her nose.

The girls loved this. They sat at their places watching the happenings at the table as if a hot rock were being passed back and forth. Suzanne had no idea why Papa and the boys always seemed to try Mama's nerves but they were very good at it. Apparently, it was just easier to be a girl. Mama did not get nearly as upset at her and Em. Unless Em went digging in the dirt like a boy, then she got mad. Yes, Suzanne decided it was just easier to be a girl.

"Darby, sweetheart. Why do you want to move out there?" Mama looked to her eldest with concerned eyes.

"Because I have four brothers and sisters who are all much younger than I am and no matter how hard Mr. John and I try to have a quiet place to study, someone is always interrupting. It is becoming harder and harder to get any lessons done. Papa has that beautiful space just waiting for us and collecting dust. Please?"

Darby shot Suzanne a baleful look when she stuck her tongue out at him.

Charlie warned his oldest daughter, barely giving his head a shake. "Do not tease your brother, Sue."

Rebecca sighed and poured another cup of coffee.

Charlie thought he would go ahead and wade in, though it meant he might be moving out to the carriage house before it was over with. "He will still have to come to the house for meals, dear. We could do it on a trial basis. Let them go for say two weeks and see how that works?"

She wanted to be disagreeable about it, but how could she? They would be less than three hundred feet from the house. In one of the newest buildings with all of Charlie's modern improvements. Of course he wanted to go live out there. Now that she considered it, she probably did, too. "All right."

Darby jumped up, knocking his chair over as he ran to hug his mother around the neck. "Thank you! I promise there will be no problems and you will always know where I am."

"Go! Before I change my mind." She gestured to somewhere behind her with her left hand. "See if Reg has a couple of men available to help you move your things."

Darby started to run from the room but stopped and turned to Charlie, remembering his manners, "May I be excused, sir?"

Charlie nodded and Darby was gone like a shot. He looked to Rebecca and smiled as he picked up his toast, which was still warm. "Well done, dear."

"Eat your eggs before they get cold," she chided from behind her coffee cup.

Darby burst into the schoolroom on the first floor next to the conservatory that he and John Foxworth had been using after Papa had thrown them and the girls out of his office.

"Mr. John. I did it. They said we could move!"

John grinned at his young charge. He had never known a boy as devoted to learning as Darby was. "So, when do you want to move?"

"I was thinking you and I could move our rooms as soon as possible, then move the school room."

"Do you really want the girls coming out there for their lessons? Or would you prefer to put together a study over there that you and Freddie and I would use, and I can come over here for the girls' lessons?"

"OHHHH. I had not thought about a study for us. Do you think Papa would let us take some books over?"

"I am sure he would. And you are starting to collect quite a library of your own, young sir. Let me talk with the general about furnishings. In the meantime, perhaps you and Freddy would like to start packing up your things?"

"Oh, yes, please."

John sent the young man off to his room. Checking his watch, he had about fifteen minutes before the girls would start their morning lessons. By now, General Charlie would no doubt be in his office.

As John reached the top of the stairs, he ran into Charlie coming down, with Beulah and Reg in tow.

"Ah, John. The very man I wanted. Would you join us as we plan out what will be needed to furnish your new digs?"

"Yes, sir. I was coming to ask you about that, since controlling Darby will be impossible until this move is settled. I sent him to his room to start organizing his things, if you must know, sir."

Charlie laughed. As they strolled over to the carriage house, the two men discussed the things that a proper garçonnière would need, including comfortable and boy-proof chairs, lots of shelves for the book hungry Darby, a well-stocked larder for snacks and midnight attacks of starvation, and a decent study/classroom.

"And for you, John? What would you like?"

"The ability to lock my door. Otherwise I will never get any peace!"

Charlie laughed.

~

In planning the garçonnière, Charlie had shown his

understanding of the needs of young men. Of course, there was his playroom, a huge room that ran the entire width of the building with several tables, two of which had the terrains of famous battles laid out on them. There were specially designed shelves on the walls to display his growing collection of lead and tin soldiers. This huge room had not one, but two fireplaces, both on the inside walls. Built-in shelves rose halfway up the walls on either side of the fireplaces. There were seating areas in front of each fireplace, and plenty of open floor space for whatever the occupants wanted to do. Large windows on each of the three outward facing walls illuminated the room in the day; ceiling-mounted lamps lit it in the evenings.

The door to the rest of the rooms on the top floor led to a central hallway. As you entered the residential area from the playroom, on the left was a nicely appointed pantry, with a small fireplace for heating water or whatever else the residents wanted, a cooling box for the summer that could hold ice and drinks, glasses, plates, utensils, and room for assorted staples to keep hungry boys fed at all hours.

On the other side of the hall was the bathroom. This was Charlie's pride and joy, as it was not only fully plumbed, so that chamber pots were not needed, but it had hot running water to the large tub, which was located opposite the fire place.

The next two rooms were somewhat smaller; they were designed to serve the servants who looked after the gentlemen staying in the space. Both rooms had fireplaces, nicely sized windows to light them, a built-in chest of drawers, and half-high shelving.

There were then four rooms, two on each side, that were designed for young men. The last two rooms were larger still, and stretched across the end opposite Charlie's playroom. One was a large sunny bedroom for John, the other a shelf-lined study that would do well as John's sitting room. Since it was only the three of them who would be living in the garçonnière, the room beside Darby's was to be set up as his study and library. It was the perfect solution for a rapidly maturing young man.

Charlie, John, Reg, and Beulah discussed furnishings for the rooms. Reg promised to have a list of furniture that needed to be acquired after he had taken a look at what was to be brought from Darby's and John's rooms in the main house and what was available in the lumber rooms to make the rooms comfortable by the end of the day.

John was late for the girls' lessons that morning. Fortunately, it was Saturday, and they only had French lessons, rather than the full schedule they had on weekdays.

~

Thursday, December 5, 1867

Rebecca wrung out another cool cloth and placed it on Charlie's forehead. The second day of this year's cold was most definitely having its way with him. His fever was high and the congestion in his chest kept him coughing and choking with nearly every breath. He opened weary, watery eyes and tried to smile.

"Oh, sweetheart." She smiled at him and brushed her fingers through his hair. "If it makes you feel any better, you probably look as bad as you feel."

The laugh caused him to cough, to the point that she had to place a basin under his chin. She held him gently until the fit passed and he managed to spit a glob of greenish-yellow mucus in the basin, and then helped him lie back on the pillows that kept him propped up. Rebecca was worried enough she had already sent for Elizabeth or Rex. She did not care which doctor arrived as long as one of them got there soon.

It was that damn barn fire. She shook her head with her ruminations as she wiped down his face and neck. His lungs had been hurt in that fire even if he did not want to admit it. She watched as his breathing eased, his head relaxed and he dozed off.

Neither one of them had gotten much sleep in the last couple of days. She was grateful he was finally resting and she decided to take advantage of it and lie down on the sofa by the fire. She had barely dozed off when there was a knock on the door. As she sat up, Rex entered the room with his black case.

"I am so glad you are here." She rose to greet him and he could see she was exhausted. "He has a horrible cold. He can barely breathe."

Rex smiled and nodded. The first thing he did was fix her a tincture and make her sit down and drink it. "You rest. I will take care of Charlie." After settling her with a pillow and blanket on the sofa in front of the fire, he turned his attention to the man in the bed.

Two hours later when Rebecca awoke, she found Rex sitting quietly in the chair across from her reading a book and sipping a cup of tea. As she sat up, she looked to the bed and found Charlie to be sleeping peacefully without the hacking and coughing he had been doing. "Thank you," she offered quietly as she stood and crossed the room to check on him anyway. "I was worried about that fever."

"I used some peppermint, black elder and white willow to get his fever down and help him with the other symptoms. He should sleep the night through, I would think, and will probably feel much better tomorrow."

"You are a miracle worker, Rex. My family is forever indebted."

"Nonsense." He rose with a smile and began gathering his things. "You and your family have given Edgar and me a place in the world after so many years of wandering it. You are family and I will always do everything I can for you and yours." He leaned in and gave her a peck on the cheek. "Get some rest. He will sleep the rest of the night." And with that he was gone.

CHAPTER 18

Saturday, December 21, 1867

Reg stood in the hall with Beulah. They had brought in the Christmas tree and set it up in the hall, in its traditional place. Even though the family was planning for a relatively small, quiet Christmas celebration, because of the New Year's party, they had gone all out in decorating the house for the season.

The tree was magnificent, mistletoe was hung over several doorways, garlands festooned the stairs and were hung in the ballroom, there were candles with red ribbons in every window, and the whole house was redolent with the smell of fresh pine and cedar. A smaller tree had been set up in Charlie's playroom, and there were wreaths on every door at the main house and the garçonnière. The two family retainers looked at one another and grinned, very satisfied with their handiwork.

Rebecca had finished wrapping her gifts to the family.

Charlie was getting a smoking jacket in rich maroon velvet, a new humidor for his cigars, and a bright red Union suit made of the finest cashmere for those really cold days.

Charlie's primary gifts to Rebecca were smaller, but no less luxurious. He had visited at one of Washington's premier jewelers, one Alexander Isaac, and had a locket made specifically for her. In the center was an intaglio cameo under an ornate cover set with a flat cut sapphire. Around the filigreed edge were good sized stones, one for each child, mounted in a pentagram. He had selected the most elegant brilliant cuts of each child's birthstone. The whole thing was mounted in fine gold work with a rather heavy chain, so that the locket hung to the cleft in Rebecca's décolletage. To go with this collection of stones, he had commissioned a pair of sapphire and diamond dangle earrings in matching filigree mounts.

Charlie's gifts for the children were all from Schwarz's Toy Bazaar. He had gone overboard, as one would expect given that General Redmond was that store's best customer, but it was well worth it. Of course, Darby got another army of lead and tin soldiers. Well, Darby and Charlie got another army.

For the two little boys, he had gotten matching sets of large wooden soldiers, with a decent collection of cannons, wagons, and horses. He was preparing them for partaking in his and Darby's war games in the future. He also got them a life sized, plush baby elephant for their bed room. It was large enough for them to climb on and ride. He hoped it would give Feighlí and Peri now that he was getting big enough, a break from being prospective mounts for his littlest troopers.

For Suzanne and Emily, he got the makings for realistic dioramas – a stable yard, barn, and a goodly collection of farm animals, mostly of horses, and an elaborate Egyptian scene. It was certainly different, but the two girls interests were diverging quite noticeably as they grew older. The dolls that he had so enjoyed buying for them were now relegated to shelves as trophies rather than playthings. Suzanne had started reading Rebecca's breeding books for fun, and Emily vacillated between history and geology books.

He had also made a major investment in books for his brood. History, science, geography, and the latest in children's and adventure literature were all in the mix. Mrs. Redmond was properly appalled that Charlie had gotten Darby a copy of *The History of the Decline and Fall of the Roman Empire*. They had had something of a row over letting the boy read Mr. Gibbon's sometimes racy descriptions of the decadence of the later Roman rulers, but his father pointed out that Darby's worldliness far outpaced most of his peers, and after all, it was no worse than some of the descriptions of things in the Old Testament, which he had read in its totality. She gave in; it was not worth the fight.

Gifts were gotten for Jocko and Esther, Elizabeth, Richard and Dickon, who would be joining them for Christmas dinner. Edgar, Charlotte and Rex chose to stay home that day, as Edgar had three major services to conduct and did not need the further strain of hauling the twins out to the Redmond house and back.

In addition to giving the house staff their usual Christmas bonus, Charlie wanted to acknowledge the devotion and loyalty that people like Reg, Sarah, Beulah, Lizbet, Freddie and Louis had shown during the strain of the past year. So he had gotten practical and useful gifts for each of them, according to their personal needs. Tomas came home for the holidays, and Charlie gifted him not only with all of his text books for the coming year, but with his own articulated human skeleton, a rare and valued gift for a physician to be.

He sat in his office, smiling gently at the beautiful locket in his hand contemplating how lovely it would look around Rebecca's neck. On the desk was a piece of paper, a gift he was sure she would truly appreciate, but one that was likely to get him a playful swat as well. Knowing how sensitive his wife was to the issue of financial security, he had acquired a life insurance policy.

In the event of his death, regardless of the cause, she would receive a benefit of half a million dollars, cash. It should give her a greater sense of security, in the event that someone else came along and erroneously charged him with murder.

~

Wednesday, December 25, 1867

The morning was bright, clear and bitterly cold. Richard and Elizabeth had wrapped little Dickon up in layers of blankets and put a warm brick in the bottom of his baby basket. Richard made better time than he usually did, knowing that Reg and the staff at Redmond would take proper care of his horse when he got there.

Esther and Jocko we a bit more leisurely in their travels, as they did not have an eighteen month old baby to care for, but still made good time.

They all knew that if they did not get there in time for breakfast, the children would drive Charlie and Rebecca insane.

Sarah laid a beautiful, but simple buffet for breakfast. Eggs, bacon, ham biscuits, grits, and a bowl of what she called ambrosia were set out, along with tea and coffee. Sarah had placed a special order with Mr. Cooper for the oranges, grapefruits, and pineapples she used. She had carefully canned some cherries in sugar syrup that fall to add color and sweetness to the fruit mix. With the meal that she had planned for later, a fairly light breakfast by farm standards was in order. The same breakfast had been provided for the house staff in the kitchen downstairs. General Charlie had made sure that everyone would enjoy the benefits of a Christmas feast.

Suzanne and Emily could not help themselves. They were bouncing in anticipation of the packages wrapped and under the tree. Darby was probably just as excited, but far more subdued, knowing that it would not do to drive his parents to distraction. So the three children who were old enough to understand what was coming were doing their best to be polite and restrained, but if the adults did not move a little faster, they were going to burst.

Finally, the family moved into the hall, where Darby was given the responsibility of handing out the gifts, which he did with alacrity. What followed was a flurry of wrappings and ribbons being cast aside and appropriate oohhhing and aaaahhhing over the gifts received.

While the children spent time examining their gifts in detail, the adults adjourned to the back parlor for more coffee, and to admire young Dickon's growth before he was sent upstairs to join the boys in the nursery.

Shortly after noon, Reg came to announce dinner. They gathered the children and they settled into the dining room to gorge themselves on the turkey, ham, vegetables, spoon bread and other goodies that Sarah had prepared for the Christmas dinner. Charlie particularly savored it; just two months before, he had not expected to sit with his friends and family for any feasts again.

~

Ro had risen early that day. She moved as quietly as she could as she went about her morning chores of stoking the fires in the living room and the kitchen, then tending to the dogs, providing breakfast to her pack.

She came back into the kitchen and prepared a light breakfast for herself and Allison. Eggs, toast, fruit compote and tea were all arranged on a tray, which she then carried into Allison's room.

"Good morning, sleepy head. I've brought you a little something to start the day. Merry Christmas, dear lady."

Allison rolled over and smiled. "Merry Christmas to you," she mumbled. "Oh, my, am I getting breakfast in bed?"

"So it seems. Unless you would like to come out and sit in front of the fire."

"Is there enough for two there?"

"Well, yes, I suppose."

"Then come and sit beside me."

Allison sat up and arranged the pillows to provide back rests for both of them. Ro moved a little awkwardly to sit herself and the tray on the bed.

"This is nice and cozy," whispered Allison as she poured tea for herself. "But you need a cup."

"I'll go get one."

"Not necessary. We take our tea the same way. We can share." With that, she picked up the fork and speared a piece of scrambled egg, which she offered to her companion. "You cooked it; you get to sample the first bite."

They continued to eat, feeding one another and gently playing. Allison had come to realize that Ro was the person she wanted to be with, and that if their relationship was to move forward, it was she who needed to make the next move.

So this playful, tender morning was an opportunity that she was not about to let go by. As they finished their breakfast, but before Ro had a chance to gather up the tray and make her escape, Allison caught her hand. She looked into her eyes and with her other hand, reached out to gently stroke her cheek. "Thank you, dear." With that, she leaned forward and very gently kissed her on the lips.

Ro was surprised, but then melted into the gentle caress, responding and extending the kiss to something a little more assertive. As the kiss ended, Ro drew back to look deep into her eyes. "Is this what you really want?"

"You know it is, dear. You have known since I moved out here."

Ro moved the tray to the floor, getting it out of their way, then turned back to Allison and took her into her arms. "It is certainly what I want. Have wanted since the day I met you."

It was the best Christmas present either of them had ever received.

~

Thursday, December 26, 1867

Breakfast brought an interesting development, at least interesting to Darby. As the family was gathering for their morning sustenance, Beulah bustled into the room and in a clear voice told Rebecca that the furnishings for the garçonnière were completed and Mr. John and Mr. Darby could move over whenever they wanted. It was not the news Rebecca wanted to hear.

"Oh, Mama, can we go? Please?" Darby looked like he was about to drop to his knees.

John grinned at the Redmond matriarch. "Miss Rebecca, I think he and I can get along rather nicely. So if you say so, we can get our stuff and get out of your hair."

She looked from Darby to John to Charlie, who was just standing back, and watching, his hand over his mouth to hide the grin that was threatening to break out, a grin that she would not easily forgive him for.

She turned to Beulah, hoping for a small reprieve. "Well, now with preparing for the New Year's party, do you and Reg have the time or resources to help them get moved?"

"Why, Miz 'Becca, Reg and the boys have finished decorating the ball room, the hall, the parlor and the rest of the house. All of the guest rooms are in good shape. They just need a quick dusting and fires built up in them for the folks staying over. Actually, we could use the extra bedrooms, with Mr. Jerome and his family coming down for the New Year. I took the liberty of setting up the extra rooms out in the carriage house as guest rooms when I was fitting out Mr. John's and Mr. Darby's rooms. So we have plenty of space and I think Reg's boys have the time to haul their things over."

"Excellent, Beulah." Rebecca frowned. The housekeeper was clearly going to be no help. Charlie was certainly not being of any assistance either. As much it went against every protective instinct in her heart and body, it was time to let her oldest child take another step toward adulthood. He had turned twelve, though they had not celebrated since his father was scheduled to be hanged the next day. This was the best she could do to acknowledge his maturity.

She turned to the boy, whose shining face was alight with the excitement of escaping from his younger siblings. "You have to do what Mr. John tells you, young man. Eat your breakfast, and then you can go and arrange your new rooms." She turned to the tutor. "John, it is in your hands. If you find him to be getting out of line, be sure to come tell me. And I expect to see the two of you at lunch and dinner."

After breakfast, Charlie wisely retreated to his office. Rebecca chose to spend the morning with Lizbet putting the finishing touches on her costume for the New Year's party. The dress was a complex creation, made of heavy dark red brocade stiffened with whalebone stays and trimmed with extensive gold braiding. The bodice was tight, showing off Rebecca's slim figure beautifully, with a low, square cut neckline that gave her plenty of room to show off her jewelry against her fair skin.

The bodice was so tight that it made the tops of her breasts bulge out, and so low that her décolletage was quite clearly defined. A stiffened lace half-collar rose from the shoulders and formed a fan behind her head. The full skirt, though not as awkward as the old hoop skirts of pre-war fashion, was still heavy, supported by reinforcing stays along the edge, so that it flared out from her legs nicely.

All in all, the dress weighed almost twenty pounds. Her hair was to be put up and held by a golden crown decorated with pearls. She and Lizbet had contrived it from a simple tiara and hat pins with mother of pearl ends. The whole costume, accessorized with pretty much all of her jewelry collection, should cause quite a stir.

Charlie had been very elusive about his choice of costume, so Rebecca returned the favor. She and Lizbet had been working in one of the unused guest rooms, making sure that entry was limited and the dress was always draped with a length of muslin when they were not working on it.

Tuesday, December 31, 1867

The day of the New Year's Eve party was chaotic. Not only had Sarah gotten every member of her staff up early that day, she had also brought in several of her cousins to help out in the kitchen. First, they had to get the family and their guests fed breakfast and a mid-day dinner, and then there was the exceptionally fancy supper to be served to the party guests, for which Sarah had pulled out all of her culinary bag of tricks.

Jerome Lord and his family had arrived the day before. Their arrival had more than doubled the number of people who needed to be served breakfast. He and his wife Amelia had their eight children with them, all between the ages of five and fifteen. It was quite a horde. With Darby's and John's agreement, the older Lord children had all been housed out in the carriage house. Beulah had sent an extra man-servant to bunk with Freddie and two maids out to stay with them, providing some degree of chaperonage to the girls and sheer numbers to herd the crowd.

The rooms in the main house had started filling up shortly after breakfast. People were arriving in time for the mid-day dinner, knowing that Sarah would treat them well. If they stayed over, they knew they would get some of her famous hoppin' john on New Year's Day. It was a symbol of luck for the year to start the year with hoppin' john eaten before noon. No one would pass it up.

Dinner that day was served at 1:00. Sarah recruited Reg's men to carry up a large number of trays, platters, and hot dishes and lay them out on tables set in the conservatory. From there, people could either sit at small café tables set in the conservatory or wander off to one of the parlors. The main dining room and the ball room were off-limits until the party.

After dinner, most people retreated to their rooms to take a nap and then prepare for the ball that evening. The Redmonds' parties always went late, and the pageantry, music and food were always worth it.

~

Charlie had been extremely secretive about his choice of costume for the party. He was hoping to give Rebecca a pause or two when she saw him. Most everything for his costume had been kept in a locked trunk in the carriage house, and the rest had been brought down by his friend, who was helping him pull off the great deception. Now he sat in a chair in the bathing room of the carriage house, with his eyes closed as his friend began applying theatrical makeup.

"I do appreciate you coming down for this, Hugh."

Hugh Stevens was one of Charlie's few nonmilitary friends. He was carefully applying the makeup. The two had met when Charlie was stationed on desk duty in Washington as a light colonel in 1859.

He had found going to the theater regularly alleviated the boredom of being stuck riding a chair instead of a horse. He had done the duty because it was his turn to do this particular kind of torture and everyone had to do it at one point or another, but he hated every day of the ten months he had been trapped in the city.

He had become friends with several of the people in the theater crowd, actors and the people who made the productions possible, like Hugh, a master makeup artist. They had always managed to maintain their friendship after Charlie had gone back into the field.

"Oh, it is my pleasure. I think your wife will be truly surprised."

"I hope so. It is difficult to catch her off guard or unaware. I hope maybe this will do it."

The younger man smiled as he began preparing Charlie's face to accept the false beard and mustache. "William the Conqueror was a brilliant choice for you. You have the height to carry it off."

"Thank you in your assistance with that as well. I was lost as to where to get that kind of costume."

"I brought one of our theatrical pieces for you. It is very impressive. I also have a special pair of knee britches for you to put on under the costume. It is actual chainmail, Charlie. I was worried about your leg. This will provide a bit more padding and protection."

"Am I going to be able to dance? My wife will be very put out if…."

"Well, as long as you do not plan to dance every reel, I don't see why not. The costume has a bit of heft to it, but it's not horribly heavy." Charlie nodded. Hugh slapped his shoulder. "Hold still, damn it."

"Sorry."

"What costume did Rebecca pick?"

"I have no idea. I want to be surprised. I did not ask and she did not offer. She pestered the hell out of me over mine."

Hugh laughed as he pressed the mustache into place. "I'm sure it will be wonderful. I happen to know that this party has cleaned out most of the costume stock between Richmond and Baltimore. When you throw a party, you throw a party."

"It is pointless otherwise."

"You always did enjoy a good party. I remember that one you threw at the Willard when you got your orders to leave Washington."

"I am glad you remember that party, because I do not. I woke up three days later on a train to Texas with Jocko standing over me with his arms crossed, shaking his head and making that damn little clicking noise with his mouth he always made when was being smug about my hung over condition."

After the beard was put into place, Hugh brought out a small pair of scissors to trim it up properly. "You have done really well for yourself, Charlie. I'm glad you found your bliss."

Charlie smiled in spite of himself and tried to hold still. Anytime he thought of Rebecca, he smiled. It was sappy and romantic, but it was true. Charlie Redmond loved his wife and he was not ashamed or embarrassed by that fact. "I am still amazed every day that she loves me, but until the day she tells me she does not love me anymore and she wants me to leave I will be by her side making sure the world does not hurt her any further."

"Oh, she has you, lock, stock and barrel."

"Her and the children. I breathe for them. My heart beats for them. They are everything I ever wanted. My beautiful wife is also smart and damned fierce in her own right. She has it all. The children could not have a better mother. My children are growing up happy and healthy, learning to be good people and productive citizens. My boy Darby is just a little tornado. Whatever he decides to do, he will master it in no time. I suspect he may need to experiment to find what is right for him. He gets bored very quickly."

"Like his father." Hugh laughed as he began applying the makeup to blend the facial hair into Charlie's own skin.

"I have been accused of that a time or two, yes."

Once the make-up was on and Hugh was happy with it, he let Charlie take a look at what he had done. The mirror showed his face framed with a short, thin line of beard that travelled down his jaw line and ended in a somewhat fuller, forked decoration on his chin. This was topped with a full moustache that covered his upper lip and met the beard on either side of his mouth.

"It is called a French fork. I looked up some drawings of William over at the Library of Congress. In his early years, he only wore the moustache, but as he grew older, he grew the beard. As long as he was fighting, he kept it short, probably so that he could not be grabbed by it, but as he got older, he let it grow longer. I think that this is about what he wore at the height of his power. And it very much suits the shape of your face."

Charlie looked at Hugh's handiwork, admiring himself in a beard from various angles. Finally, he was ready to don the rest of the costume.

Hugh brought the costume out. Charlie took the under things he had brought and headed to behind the dressing screen in one corner of the washroom. He took off the robe he had been wearing and slipped the knee breeches on over his regular knitted underclothes. He was confident enough in Rebecca's undergarments that he stepped out from behind the screen to let Hugh help him into the rest of the costume.

First, there was a pair of chainmail trousers or chausses. It was a theatrical set and was lighter than one would expect, but still had a certain weight that only linked metal rings could have. Hugh decided it would be easier to get him into the soft black leather ankle boots he had chosen for the evening. Dancing would not have been possible in anything else appropriate to the period.

Once the boots were tugged into place, Charlie stood as his friend bought the habergeon, the short chainmail shirt. It slid into place quickly and then a brilliant royal purple tabard with a bright red shield in the center and emblazoned upon that, two golden lions with emerald blue tongue and claws.

Then came the sashes and belts. Once those were properly

fitted and adjusted Hugh tucked a small dirk in Charlie's waist on the left. He moved to one of the big cases he had brought with him. "Now, I did bring this if you want it, but it is heavy, awkward and honestly a huge pain in the ass." He pulled a broadsword and shoulder scabbard from the box. It would require the tall man to carry ten pounds around on his right shoulder.

It was really beautiful and would have added to the costume, but Charlie knew right away and shook his head. "Thank you, but no. I could not possibly carry that around all night."

"I thought as much, but did not want to short change you if you wanted it for the proper effect."

"I think the beard will get the effect I want. You are staying for the party?"

"Of course. I brought my Cupid costume."

"You always did have the legs for that sort of thing."

"And you were always a little bit of a smart ass," Hugh told him as he settled the faux gold and jewel encrusted circlet on the tall man's head.

Charlie, in full costume, walked up toward the house. He had arranged to 'make an entrance' and it was going to be a good one.

Darby had been over the moon when he had been shown his costume for the party and told he was going to be allowed to attend. His father had explained that no proper king could be seen without his faithful page. The young man would be allowed to stand in the front hall and greet the guest in his father's stead. It was a huge responsibility and Darby had butterflies the size of eagles in his stomach as he headed up to the house. Charlie wanted to give the guests the opportunity to arrive and get settled before he made his entrance.

As he was leaving the carriage house, Tess and Ginnie were bringing the younger children up to the playroom. Charlie and Rebecca had arranged for the smaller children to have their own party away from the main house, where they would be taken care of, fed snacks, and bedded down at a reasonable hour, using the sofas in the playroom to provide sleeping space for the Redmond children and putting the Lord children to bed in their assigned rooms.

Apparently, Darby had done a splendid job of greeting the guests, because Charlie could hear people laughing and carrying on as he took the first steps up to the veranda and to the ballroom doors. If it were a summer party, the doors would be open to help cool the room, but as it was winter and cold as hell, the doors were firmly closed and properly covered with heavy drapes. This meant that no one would see him until the doors were opened to allow him entrance.

Two footmen stood outside, dressing in long heavy coats to ward of the cold, waiting to pull the doors open for him. When he was in place, a signal was given to Darby, who would then in turn ask the musicians to play the proper cue for the doors to be opened.

The room was filled with a gentle rumble. It was the sound caused when a group of people who knew each other well splintered into their regular cliques and engaged in vivacious conversation. People were laughing and teasing, joking and playing. It was a brilliant stroke on Charlie's part to add the masked costume aspect to this year's ball.

The costumes and masks properly allowed the attendees to play and flirt with each other without the normal social constraints. While there was no doubt that couples and in one very rare case, threesomes would leave with each other at the end of the night, the party was a bit of a Hellfire Club moment in time at Redmond Stables.

Reg was standing at the main doors to the ballroom, announcing the identity of each guest as they arrived. Jocko was announced as His Imperial Highness, the Emperor of France Napoleon Bonaparte. He was clean shaven, his hair cut short and dyed dark brown, causing quite a stir. Esther came as Jeanne Antoinette Poisson, Marquise de Pompadour, showing more cleavage than anyone suspected.

Duncan arrived as Robert the Bruce, while Samantha entered as Margaret Tudor, Queen of Scotland. Edgar and Charlotte came in as Robin Hood and Maid Marion, looking dashing in matching greens and browns.

Then Rex appeared at the door, alone, and stunning. Reg sonorously announced, “Julius Caesar, Emperor of Rome.” The transition from his usual black or dark green to the blazing white toga trimmed in purple was amazing.

Charlie adjusted the black silk mask tied around his eyes as he awaited his cue. He was hoping it would be soon; metal rings got very cold in thirty degree weather, even with two layers of under clothes.

The room had been filled when Rebecca made her entrance. It was a good thing the entrance doors to the ballroom were double, as her skirt completely filled the entry way. The rich maroon velvet and gold braid that covered her body stood out in the candle and fire light, but not as much as the jewelry she had adorned her ears, throat and breasts, and wrists with. It looked like she was wearing every single ornament she owned.

Reg cleared his throat and tapped his major domo’s staff three times. “Her Royal Majesty Catherine de’ Medici, Queen of France.” There was a chorus of gasps, then a shuffling and rustling as the gentlemen in the room hurriedly looked for an appropriately throne-like chair for the Queen.

She processed across the ballroom floor to the seat the gentlemen had set for her, taking her place to preside over the party in front of the fireplace at the far end of the room. Rex managed to place himself at her shoulder, where he would stay for most of the evening. The ladies and gentlemen of the party formed a proper line to pay tribute to the queen, their hostess.

The door in front of him cracked, but was then held to just a crack. "Papa, it will be a few moments. Mama just came in and she has caused quite a stir."

A moment later, the door cracked open again. A hand with a mug of hot mulled cider emerged. "Thought you would need this, Papa." Then Darby was gone again.

Standing in the dark, in the cold, in freezing cold metal, he could hear the ooohhhs and aaahhhs over what must have been Rebecca's entrance as he managed to sip from the mug without spilling it down his front. There was a strange scuffling sound coming from the room. *What the hell is going on in there?*

Finally things calmed down. Darby gave the signal to the band. The trumpeters stood up and played the old English "Fanfare for a Warrior." The footmen pulled the doors open and Charlie strode in as Reg intoned, "William, Duke of Normandy, known as The Conqueror."

Charlie, as a bearded and armored warrior king, was a proper match for Rebecca's magnificent queen. A gasp went up around the room at the power of his costume. He strode – and jingled – majestically across the room to stand in front of his wife. With a sweeping bow, he greeted her, "Your Majesty." Rebecca extended her hand, which he caught in his and gallantly kissed.

She whispered, "Good God, Charlie. How long have you been out there? Your hand is frozen."

"I know. I had to wait for your admirers to settle back down before I came in," he hissed back.

He extended his arm to his beautiful queen and together they made the circuit of the room, greeting their guests and complimenting their costumes. Robin Hood made a snarky crack about Normand French invaders who took possession of land from good Englishmen. Charlie threatened to throw him in the dungeon for his impertinence.

Edgar's brows rose. "The closest thing you have to a dungeon is your wine cellar." He put his hands out as if offering himself up. "Take me."

There was a cluster of people around Robert the Bruce, admiring his beautiful kilt and the magnificent bearskin sporran he was wearing. "It w-w-was my gr-gr-great great grandfather's. He c-came over into P-pennsylvania and b-brought it with him."

Queen Elizabeth greeted the Queen of France and the King of England as one would expect royalty to greet one another. The pirate queen standing beside her introduced herself as Gráinne O'Malley. Charlie and Rebecca looked puzzled, so Ro explained, "She was a great pirate queen during the original troubles between England and Ireland. And yes, she actually did meet with Queen Elizabeth to negotiate a truce."

Both of her hosts laughed. Charlie commented, "A great role model for you, ma'am. Seems to be Irish is to be a rebel of one sort of another."

They continue to make the rounds, greeting two George and Martha Washingtons, three Romeo and Juliets, a Master John Dee complete with alchemical symbols, and a Shylock and Portia. Rebecca grinned at them. "If I get my identities right, you two cannot give up your roles as the town's money lenders, can you?" Frank and Eloise laughed.

When they found Jocko, it took someone who knew them

very well to identify them under their costumes. Charlie looked his old friend up and down. "My God, Jocko. I did not know you even had an upper lip. I have never seen you clean shaven before!"

"That as it may be, Charlie. You look good in facial hair. You might think about keeping it."

Rebecca grinned. "Let me see how it works for me, first!"

As soon as they finished making the rounds, Charlie signaled for the first dance tune. He led Rebecca out onto the floor for their waltz. The band had learned Mr. Strauss' latest work for this evening, *By the Beautiful Blue Danube*, and the party was properly underway.

Sarah had laid an assortment of finger foods to sustain the guests in the breakfast room, and had included several of Rex's more savory little treats on the menu. In addition to her learning various recipes from him, she had sent her own right hand cook over to the manse for several weeks to learn more of Rex's recipes and techniques, and the guests were benefiting from this cross-cultural cuisine.

Reg had set up several drink tables with cold fruit punch, chilled wines and champagne, his famous milk punch, and by one of the fireplaces, cauldrons of mulled cider and mulled wine. People wandered in and out to find refreshment as the evening wore on. But the real treat was scheduled for midnight. Sarah and her crew had outdone themselves with a buffet that would have been admired at one of the grand chateaus in France or the most impressive mansion on Park Avenue in New York.

Back in the ballroom, Rebecca found herself assaulted by a line of gentlemen in search of a dance. First in line was the man in the Roman toga. It turned out that Rex was as adept at dancing as he was at self-defense, and she enjoyed the dance with him, an energetic reel that Charlie would never have been able to pull off. She was pressed, given the weight of her dress.

Rex escorted her out onto the dance floor as many times as he could socially get away with, as the two of them were almost as striking a couple as Rebecca was with Charlie. They were of a size, as Rex was only a couple of inches taller than Rebecca. And the Asian man was an amazingly graceful dancer; as graceful on the dance floor as he was when defending himself. They were a pleasure to watch together, at least to all of the attendees except Charlie, who found he was a bit jealous of his friend and physician.

Rebecca had been startled when Ro approached her, bowed and asked for her hand for an exuberant polka. But, she thought, who was she to call a kettle black, and accepted Ro's hand with a gracious smile and a nod of her head.

A little later, Darby approached his mother. She realized with a start that the young page who had been squiring Jerome and Amelia's two oldest daughters that evening was asking her for a waltz. She smiled at her son and realized he was now as tall as she was. She looked up at Charlie, who had approached but stepped back when Darby came up. Charlie smiled and nodded as Darby led his mother out to the floor and managed to lead her through a credible waltz.

"Where did you learn to waltz, Darby?" she inquired gently as not to embarrass him.

"I got Aunt Elizabeth and Uncle Rex to teach me so I could dance tonight," he responded, clearly proud of his inclusion in adult entertainment. "I have danced with a number of our guests, Mama, and especially with Stella Lord. She is really nice, and pretty. She knows lots of history too."

Rebecca blinked. Here was her son, who she had only had for a year and a half, and he was already moving out, pursuing girls and growing like a weed. He was already as tall as she was and showing no signs of stopping. *When he starts shaving, I will die.*

As midnight approached, Rebecca found that she had danced with literally every gentleman attending the party, though most frequently with Rex. His skill as a dance partner was splendid, and she truly enjoyed his company. He had even escorted her out for a waltz, when Charlie had stepped out of the room to have a smoke with the gentlemen, and they were so good together that people had stopped their own dancing to watch Rex expertly swirl Rebecca around the room.

At one point, as Caesar was leading Rebecca in an energetic Schottische, they spun past Charlie standing with Charlotte. Rebecca noticed they were standing very close to one another, and Charlotte was softly caressing the hair on Charlie's face. As they floated past, she called out to Charlotte, "You may look, cousin, but **do not** touch." *Ever again.* She added silently.

Just before midnight, the band played Josef Strauss's *The First and Last Waltz*, timing it so that the dance would finish just at midnight, and the masks would come off. Charlie managed to make it to Rebecca's side for the last dance, as he and she had established their tradition of the first and last waltz.

They were the only couple who were allowed to dance with one another for the unmasking. At the end of the rather long dance, there was a flurry of masks being cast aside, laughter when unexpected individuals found themselves wishing one another happy new year, and a couple of embarrassing moments when one lady realized she had been flirting with Mr. Cooper all night, thinking it was her husband. Mr. Cooper managed to be very gallant about the whole thing.

As couples sorted themselves out, Reg counted down the

last seconds to midnight. With a loud cry of "Happy New Year," the couples exchanged rather chaste, or in some cases not so chaste, kisses to celebrate. Ro snuck a kiss from Allison; Edgar leaned Charlotte back; Richard lifted Elizabeth's face to his own for a tender kiss. Charlie gave Rebecca a taste of moustache framed kiss. She rather liked it, though it did tickle a bit.

Reg gave the guests time to enjoy their various embraces, then cleared his throat again and announced, "Supper is being served in the dining room."

It did not require a second announcement. The word 'supper' had started a mass migration.

As Ro and Allison stood waiting for their turn at the buffet table, Katherine Reynolds, escorted by James Armistead, the younger brother of the town's lumber mill owner, strolled by. Katherine looked Ro up and down, and then turned to Allison. "So Mary Simms, you could not find yourself a proper man, so you settled for this… substitution." Mary Allison Simms flushed a deep red, not in embarrassment, but in anger. James looked embarrassed, hoping he did not have the beginnings of a cat fight in his lap.

Allison looked back at her once-friend, grinding her teeth. She finally found an answer. "I found an honorable companion who is caring and gentle and good to me. That is all I need. You keep looking, my dear. If you are lucky, you may find the same for yourself before you grow too old. If I were you, I would hurry. You are already on your way to being an old maid." Allison then very pointedly turned her back on Katherine. James took Katherine's elbow and led her away.

While many people found seats at the dining room table, more of them wandered around the house, finding corners in the breakfast room, the conservatory, the ball room, and even the smoking room. There were a number of folks who found that a second trip to the buffet was in order.

Finally, Charlie and Rebecca saw the last of the guest either out the door to their waiting carriages and buggies, or up the stairs to their waiting bedrooms. Darby took a lantern and escorted the Lords to the carriage house. John would be back later, after he had escorted Annabelle Calvert, the school teacher, home.

CHAPTER 19

Wednesday, January 1, 1868

The host and hostess finally retreated to their bedroom. They had sent Lizbet and Louis to bed hours before, knowing that if they got to bed before three in the morning, it would be a miracle. They were perfectly capable of assisting one another out of their costumes.

Charlie started by unlacing Rebecca's skin-tight bodice. As her breasts broke free of the very stiff whalebone supports, she breathed a deep sigh of relief. "That is much, much better. I thought my breasts were going to be permanently squashed by that thing." She had to give them a gentle massage to return some blood flow to the now unbound flesh.

As she did that, he tried to pay attention as he undid the various necklaces she was wearing, unhooked her earrings and pulled the pins out of her ears, and dropped the collection of jewelry into her jewelry box. Meanwhile, she stripped the rings off her fingers and they followed the necklaces and earrings into the box.

He untied her skirts and she dropped the three layers into a large puddle in the middle of the floor, stepping out of the hole in the center where her waist had once been. She was standing in her chemise and pantaloons, looking Charlie up and down.

"I believe you, sir, are seriously overdressed."

Getting the tabard off was easy. It was just a matter of dropping his belt and pulling it off over his head. The chain mail was an entirely different story. It was tight and they discovered that trying to get it off by pulling it inside out was not possible.

He sat on a stool while she pulled the top off by the collar. The boots came off easily, and she finally got to the two clips that held the front flap of the metal pants together. The chain mail pants slithered off his legs, leaving the padded underwear that Hugh had provided to peel him out of. Finally, she had managed to strip him down to his usual knitted silk underwear.

He started to pull that off, but she said, "No, I rather like it."

"What about the beard?"

"You can leave that on too."

Charlie blinked. "Oh!" He grinned lasciviously. "All right."

"Let me try another one of those bearded kisses." She grabbed him by the ears and pulled his head to hers. After a couple of very heated exchanges, she started backing up, still pulling him by the ears, until the backs of her legs hit the edge of the bed.

"Come here, big boy. I have missed you… All night long!"

Charlie slid her up the bed, crawling after her. He started at her throat and worked his way down, unbuttoning her chemise and kissing a beard-ruffled trail to her breasts, which he gave extensive attention to so that they could properly recover from the compression they had suffered all evening. It was a little disconcerting that she would periodically start giggling before reverting to the soft moaning he was more used to hearing.

After he had made sure her nipples were so sensitized from his attention that any more would be painful, he started working his way down her ribs to her belly.

That got an unexpected reaction. She started giggling. "Your beard, dear. It tickles. So either use a firmer touch or get rid of it."

He chose the firmer touch. He had absolutely no intention of stopping now to find something to remove the beard. He worked his way down to her navel, spending a fair bit of time nibbling and teasing around it, then dipped lower as she lifted her hips and allowed him to completely divest her of every stitch.

Her legs wrapped around his head. She grabbed him by the ears again, this time to keep him in place, and moaned appreciatively, until her breathing became very ragged indeed, her back arched, and her body shuddered from one end to the other.

Slowly, he crawled back up her body. "Better?" he asked, grinning.

"Oh, yes, very much better."

"Good." He settled himself behind her, holding her close. "Now, sleep, since you have your sample of the benefits of a beard on me."

"Yes, dear," she mumbled, burrowing into his good shoulder.

That was the last thing either of them said or did until the sun was well up into the winter sky.

Breakfast that morning was a chance sort of thing. Reg's men were still finding plates and glasses stashed in various corners all over the first floor. Sarah had the good sense to keep a pitcher of The Cure and a large pitcher of water in the breakfast room. It was welcomed by a number of their guests.

Charlie and Rebecca were not the last people down for breakfast, but it was a close thing between them and Amelia and Jerome Lord. Charlie only had a minute to ask Rebecca if she liked the effect of the beard or not.

"Actually, I prefer you clean shaven, dear. I have a nasty case of beard rash this morning in a place you really do not want to have beard rash."

He laughed as they entered the dining room hand in hand and he escorted her to her seat. Just then Suzanne and Emily came into the breakfast room looking for their parents. Suzanne started. "Mama, may we go down to the carriage house? Please?"

Emily was just staring at her father, her mouth hanging open. She pointed at his face and then broke into tears. Charlie went over to her and tried to pick her up. She would have none of that. Instead she ran to her mother, hiding behind her. "What did you do to my papa? Where is my papa?!"

"Why, I am right here, sweetheart," he said, bending down to her.

"You are **not** my papa!" she wailed. "**My** papa does not have a hairy face." She turned pleading eyes to her mama. "Where is he?"

"I will go and get your papa." Charlie gave Rebecca a helpless look and a shrug before he went off to find Hugh and get the beard removed before it could cause any further rashes in his household.

Later that day, Charlie and Jerome sat down in his office to catch up on the current politics in Washington and share a quiet cup of tea far away from the women and children.

"You know, Congress is talking about impeaching President Johnson. They are furious over his suspension of Stanton and his naming Grant as Secretary of War ad interim. Grant is miserable at being put in the middle of what is essentially a battle between the Radical Republicans and the President. Johnson is saying that the Tenure of Office Act is unconstitutional and they have no right to tell him who should be in his cabinet. It is getting bloody ugly up there."

"I was afraid it would be. Johnson wanted to follow Lincoln's policies, but this Congress and Stanton would not let that happen. I am sure they are saying Johnson is a closet rebel trying to protect his friends in the south and let the rebels off easy for the last four years."

"That is exactly what they are saying. And Johnson's little speaking tour last fall did not help him. If anything, it made the situation worse. Johnson did not have the good sense to keep his mouth shut about his opponents in Congress. Denigrating and insulting Radical Republicans in their home states was not his smartest act, one in a whole string of not smart acts."

"I know why Lincoln had a southern as his vice president. It was a last-ditch effort to prevent the war. But damn, it is making a mess now."

Jerome poured himself another cup of tea. He looked at Charlie thoughtfully. "You know that Grant is going to run for president?"

"I assumed he would be."

"You know your name keeps coming up in his circles. He wants you to come back to either active duty or to his administration."

Charlie shook his head. "I will not go back to active duty.

Good God, Jerome, I got half my ass shot off. I am in no condition to go back to active duty."

"He would put you on a desk job. He wants to keep you close."

"Oh hell. I am about as suited to a desk job as you are to building forts."

"I am just warning you, old man. Grant will come knocking on your door. And I assume it will be sooner than later. The election is just a little over a year away, and I think Grant will start running shortly."

"McClellan is going to hate this."

"I think McClellan has the good sense to just quietly pack up and retire."

Charlie shook his head. "Well, if Grant manages to get this growing movement with the Ku Klux Klan under control, it will go a long way toward electing him. Devil Forrest has started something truly dangerous."

"He is already using the army to try and restrain those bastards, and he has the full support of the Radical Republicans."

"Therein lies the rub for me. Even if I could stand the Washington politics, I do not think I qualify as a Radical Republican."

"Hell, Charlie, you are the victor of Appomattox Station. A war hero, Grant and Sheridan's right hand man. They would fall all over themselves just to be seen with you up there."

"No, no, and again no. I am NOT going to go swimming with those sharks."

"Then you are going to have to find a damned good reason why you will not go and support your general."

Charlie dropped his chin on his chest. Jerome was right. Grant was not beneath wheedling, cajoling, and harassing, and otherwise making his life miserable until he said yes unless he could find a really good excuse.

"You think I am joking?" Jerome raised a brow.

"No."

"Good." The attorney looked to his tea cup and then to his old friend's right hand, where the finger adorned with the West Point ring tapped nervously on the arm of the chair. "Did you ever look inside that ring?"

"What?" Charlie was startled by the change in subject.

"Your ring? The one the cadets gave you during your visit. Have you ever looked at the inscription?"

He shook his head. He had no idea there was an inscription. Other than when he had briefly removed it to leave with Rebecca on execution day, it had not left his finger since she had placed it there in New York.

"My nephew was one of the cadets who helped design it. He graduated this year. He told me he learned more from you in three days than he did in his four years at The Point. And the inscription in that ring is why Grant wants you so close."

Charlie pulled the ring from his finger and held it up to the lamp. Using a magnifying glass from his desk, he peered at the inscription on the interior. To: Iron Man. From USMA, Class of '68. Duty, Honor, Country.

Jerome was right in all of his predictions. Less than two months later, Andrew Johnson was impeached because of his attempt to remove Stanton as Secretary of War and what the Radical Republicans saw as his leniency toward the southerners. A month later, Grant announced his formal candidacy for the presidency.

~

Friday, March 27, 1868

Rebecca looked on in total disbelief. "How could I possibly be married to you for three years and not know this disgusting little tidbit?"

Charlie was reclined back on his elbows, his long legs stretched out and crossed at the ankles, looking out over the pond as the smaller children played on one side and Darby and Jeremiah fished on the other. "We have never been by the pond like this in spring?"

He sat up looking at the ground next to the blanket. With his left hand he made a quick grab and landed a small grasshopper, which he gleefully popped in his mouth. "I will admit they are better roasted or done in a pan with a little bacon grease or butter."

"And I thought oysters were bad. How is it you…" she had to look away when he ate another one, "…eat bugs?"

"I was a soldier. When you are a soldier you learn to eat all manner of things."

She looked back in time to see him pick what she was pretty sure was a leg from his teeth. "Well, you are no longer a soldier. You are now a wealthy gentleman of leisure. I am fairly certain you can strike bugs from your diet. Especially if you intend to put your mouth on any part of my body **ever** again."

The last grasshopper he had captured escaped unharmed as he was tossed toward the high grass. Charlie made a great display of brushing his hands together to show her they were now empty.

"That is what I thought." She laughed and kissed him on the cheek. "So where is our not so little family trip going to take us?"

"Darby and I have discussed it and he would like to see Washington, Boston, and Philadelphia. What do you think?"

"I think we may have gone slightly around the bend. It is not just us, it is also staff and…"

He nodded. "I know. I have already considered that and I think the thing to do is hire an express train. It will simply be easier."

"Our own private train?" She looked at him a bit sideways, her brow going up.

"I think that would be best. That way we are not tied down by schedules and potential delays. If our travelling gets delayed by something, it will not matter." He plucked a wide blade of grass from the ground and began peeling it apart. "We will be able to relax if we do not have to worry about such things and I think since we are going to have the children with us, the less we have to worry about, the better."

"True. Given some of the train trips we have had to make, I think you are probably right, my dear."

"When are you willing to go?"

She looked up into the bright morning sky and sighed happily. "Whenever you want to go. Albert and I have everything ready. He and Brooks are prepared to run the farm for the time we are gone. I am ready at your pleasure, sir."

"Glad to hear it. The train arrives next Friday."

She laughed and gave him a playful shove that knocked him off balance and back to the blanket. Wasting no time or opportunity she stretched out and lay down next to him. She put her fingers on his cheek and turned his head so he would look at her. "I would kiss you but I think you probably have wings between your teeth."

He ran his tongue over his teeth and grinned wide. "No wings. See?"

She shook her head. "No, you ate a bug. Several of them

actually. Lips only on this one, Redmond, and you are lucky you are getting that."

He tried not to laugh as he puckered his lips for the kiss. Hers had barely touched his when they heard the girls giggle and then squeal, "Ewwwww," at the same time. Displays of affection between Mama and Papa were not uncommon, but they always seemed to illicit the same response and it always made him laugh.

~

Monday, March 30, 1868

Rebecca scratched her forehead as she contemplated exactly how they were going to manage getting ready for this trip. The potential for a logistical nightmare was very high. Then she remembered who she was married to and made her way to their office. As she took her seat across from Charlie she folded her hands on top of the desk and smiled sweetly. "You get to do it."

He looked up from his ledger and queried, "What?"

"Organize this family for your little excursion. You moved armies around; I assume you can do the same for us. You tell me what to do and I will do it."

He nodded, seeing her point. "All right, the first thing to do is to get clothing and needed accessories packed up for everyone. Have those trunks and bags put in the front hall and I will have them taken and loaded onto the train. Louis should pack for me and himself. Lizbet for you and herself. Ginnie and Tess for themselves and the children. I will have Louis assist Freddy in preparing for himself and John and Darby. We are expected to be gone at least a month, maybe six weeks. You will want to plan accordingly. And make sure we pack at least one trunk of toys for the children. Darby will be responsible for his own entertainment. I will have Big Ben standing by to hoist the crate of books."

She laughed as she stood, giving him a little salute. "Yes, General. I will go get everyone started. You might want to consider bringing Ben with us."

"Best second in command I ever had," he teased as she left the room.

"I will tell Richard you said that," she tormented as she made her way down the hall.

"Richard knows it," he called back. "He agrees the one who sleeps with me regularly is probably going to by my favorite. He and I only slept together once. All right twice, but it was two nights in a row so I only count it as once."

He knew that would bring her back and he was not disappointed. She leaned against the door jamb and crossed her arms over her chest. "Excuse me?"

He roared with laughter and waved glibly. "Me, Richard, and Jocko. It was a brutally cold winter encampment in '63. Several of us had to double and triple up to keep warm. We were fully clothed and mostly frozen. Everyone was stiff, but not in the way you are thinking."

She just shook her head and turned to go back to the children's rooms. "I am not sure why I still get taken in by those things when you say them." She just continued to mumble to herself, "You would think after all this time, I would know better."

~

Thursday, April 3, 1868

In the afternoon, the entire family was gathered for a combination spring lawn and Bon Voyage party for the

Redmonds. The ladies were in the gazebo, playing with and feeding babies and children while the men loitered around the tables just beyond the steps, picking at the food and laughing among themselves.

Rebecca held her namesake on her lap while the baby sucked her little finger and played with a ribbon on her caregiver's dress. She was enjoying having babies around again, especially since she could love them, spoil them, and then return them to their parents. Her entire brood was now comprised of five very independent little people and she was very glad there was no more need for flats and all the other accessories required for infants. She had been a mother long enough now to her instant family; she was entirely over the infant stage.

She watched with some interest as a small group of the men clustered around Charlie. Edgar, Richard, Jocko, and Duncan were listening with great interest to a story he was telling. Rebecca's brows knitted together as she watched his hand gestures and their reactions. Then they all reached into their pockets and handed him money. Settling back in her chair, carefully shifting the baby in her arm, she looked to her companions.

"Elizabeth, Esther, Samantha? Do any of your husbands eat bugs?"

"What?" Esther looked particularly disgusted.

"Rebecca?" Elizabeth's brows were up at the top of her head. "That is revolting."

Samantha Nailer was laughing so hard she nearly dropped little Sam.

"That is what I thought. Excuse me." She handed little Becky to Charlotte and left the gazebo to join her husband and his troop of troublemaking friends.

"How much?" She asked, crossing her arms over her chest, as she looked at the tall man.

"Dear?"

"Do not "dear" me, Charles Huger Redmond. How much did you win with your little bug eating bet?"

He looked down at her with a shamefaced grin. She noticed the other men were suddenly looking for either birds or God. She poked her husband in the chest. "How much?"

"Forty dollars."

She put her hand out. "Give."

He took the bills from his pocket and put them in her hand.

"Thank you. Just so you know," she offered as she turned to rejoin the ladies, "I hate you all."

The men laughed and patted him on the back as she retook her seat to the amusement of the ladies.

"He does not get anything over on you, does he?" Elizabeth asked, impressed with how well Rebecca actually handled Charlie on a daily basis.

"Occasionally I have to let him think he does, but he has done nothing but torment me today and this was just so far up the tree I had to call him on it."

~

Friday, April 3, 1868

Rebecca looked down the track at the train. Silently, she counted cars and shook her head. It was becoming quite clear she was married to a lunatic. "Did you rent Mr. Pullman's entire stock?"

Her husband chuckled and shook his head. "Hardly. However, we did get one of his newest cars, called The President, for ourselves and the girls at night. It cost eighteen thousand dollars just to build one. It is the most modern car he has. He has not even officially launched it yet; we get to give it a trial run and…."

She held up her hand in an attempt to stop his adolescent-like running of the mouth. "Please, tell me we did not buy a train car."

He laughed heartily. "No, dear. And the company was happy to specially refit the other cars for the children and our staff."

"And what are the others for?"

"The railcar behind the coal car has our luggage in it. Then there is our car. The parlor car is for daily use. Then there are the cars for the children and our staff. After that there is the kitchen car, where the Pullman staff will be fixing our meals when we need that service. Then there is a car for Pullman staff, and a railcar for supplies."

"Well, this is quite the menagerie. Are you trying to give that Barnum fellow a run for his money?"

He just smiled and shook his head as he led her to the car they would be using. The Pullman porter was immediately there to help them board.

"General Redmond, sir. My name is George. I am your personal porter for your trip. We do hope that you and your family will be able to enjoy your holiday. Mr. Pullman has sent his best staff for this trip, sir."

"Thank you, George. Mrs. Redmond and I are looking forward to it. If you could please make sure that my children and staff are being properly settled, we will be along shortly."

"Yes, sir, right away."

By lunch time, the family, staff and crew were all well settled into both their work and living spaces, prepared to depart Culpeper for what Darby was sure would be exciting points north. The other children could not care less about destinations; they were just excited to be on a trip with Mama and Papa. The family was gathered in the parlor car for lunch as the train slowly pulled out of the station in route for the first destination of Washington D.C.

Buddy and Andy each sat contentedly on a parent's lap. Andy was happily chomping down a small bowl of grapes as he sat on Rebecca's knee. He would look at her with the sweetest little smile as he sucked the juice from each piece of fruit before opening his mouth each time to show her he had indeed eaten the cool, sweet treat.

His elder brother, by a mere six weeks, rocked back and forth on Charlie's good leg as he quickly swallowed apple slices as fast as his father could cut them away from the core with his penknife. "Easy there, Buddy. You are going to choke."

The little boy, who looked exactly like the man who held him, smiled and nodded and tried to chew with a bit more caution. Charlie could only shake his head as the third piece of apple went in right after the second. "This one is going to be trouble," he told his wife as he kissed the top of his son's head.

"I am certainly glad you figured that out. It took me about a year. As soon as he started walking, I started praying to God. Your son there may be the death of me. I do not like what the future holds with him; he is going to be a heller."

"Darling, he is three. I am sure you do not need to start worrying already."

"You say that now. Let us see what you say at the end of this trip." She nodded knowingly. He was going to get to know all his children and all their own little habits by the end of this journey. "If you are not ready to send him off to one of Rex's monasteries at the end of it, I will be surprised. I have already considered it twice." She pulled more grapes from a bunch in the center of the table for Andy.

Charlie just shook his head as he looked around the table at his little family. Darby and Em were bent over a geography book. Normally, a book would not be allowed at the table, but as it was a family holiday, normal rules had been left at home so everyone could relax. Suzanne watched everything that was going on at the table. He mused to himself that she was so much like Rebecca, taking in every little detail of the world around her. Someday she would be a challenging spouse for anyone lucky enough to capture her heart. He was extremely proud of the family he and Rebecca had brought together and he had high hopes for each of them.

Duncan had sent Jeremiah to watch at the train yard so he could let all of the workmen know when the Redmonds' train pulled out of the station and rounded the curve in the tracks north of town. As soon as it did, even while the plume of smoke from the locomotive was still visible, Jeremiah thundered down the street from the station toward his stepfather's shop. As he ran past Mr. Hudnut's shop, he yelled, "They are gone!"

He did the same as he charged past Mr. Armistead's lumber yard, Mr. Stevenson's copper smithy, Mr. Butler's shop, and the manse, where Rex was prepared to supervise the town's artisans over the coming month. He reached Duncan's shop and jumped up on the seat of the large dray, and Duncan immediately whipped up the horses.

A caravan of wagons and drays started down the road to Redmond Stables, loaded with tools, lumber, copper tubing, bricks, and large objects wrapped in canvas. Workmen were sitting wherever they could find a space on the piles of building supplies. Charlie had been very clear – he did not want Rebecca or the children getting a hint of what was going on at the house while they were gone, and the sight of this parade of men and supplies would have been a dead giveaway.

The heavy carts and wagons moved to the side to let Rex's pony cart pass to the head of the line. Rex was Charlie's official representative in this remodeling adventure. Reg, Beulah and Sarah knew what was coming, but no one else among the staff had been informed. The three of them pulled the staff together that morning after the family had left and briefed them on what was coming and what they needed to do to help the construction teams.

The wash rooms were cleared. The winter kitchen was stripped and emptied of all the supplies, plates, and cooking implements. The summer kitchen was completely emptied, with the movable supplies and tools stowed in the playroom of the carriage house.

By sundown, the summer kitchen had been demolished and half the roof was torn off the main house so they could get the reservoirs into the attic.

They arrived in Washington in the early afternoon. Darby was so full of energy at the thought of seeing the city, Charlie and Rebecca had no choice but to give him a bit of pocket money and issue a request to Mr. Foxworth that he have Darby and Freddy back to the train yard by sundown, so they could be tucked into bed at a reasonable time. The tutor assured his employers that he would do his best and the young men were off to explore the city.

Rebecca was no fool. She knew exactly why her clever husband had placed Freddy and Darby together. The young Negro man would get a good, formal education while simply doing his 'job' as their son's valet. "How much money did you give them?" she asked as she considered which hat to wear out to dinner.

"Twenty dollars to Darby. Ten dollars to Freddy. John will submit expenses." He chuckled.

"We may not see them until it is time to leave for Philadelphia." She held up two hats for his opinion, and he looked at them both and gestured to the one that matched her dress.

"I still have a hard time remembering he is only twelve."

"Twelve going on thirty." She sighed as she set the bonnet aside with her coat and reticule, and then appraised her appearance in the full length mirror near the bed.

He chuckled as he looked in a small oak box that held the studs and cufflinks required to fasten the stiffly starched white shirt of his dinner clothes. "Gold, silver, or onyx studs and cufflinks?

"The silver studs I think, darling. Always safe. However," she took a moment and fished a small box from one of her trunks, "I do hope you like these."

"What is this?" He smiled as he took the box from her.

"A little something."

"For?"

"I do not know, Charlie." She sounded a bit exasperated. "It is Friday." She smiled and shook her head. "Just open it."

He cracked the little box to find a striking pair of sapphire and diamond cufflinks set in a stunning and delicate silver setting. "Oh, sweetheart, they are beautiful. Thank you."

"They match your eyes. I could not resist them when I saw them."

He held up his wrists. "Give me a hand? I am a little short." He grinned and wiggled the fingers of his right hand.

"Always, you lunatic." She quickly took the jewelry from the box and got his cuffs squared away just as Louis came into their car with Charlie's black evening coat. He had needed to give it a quick pressing before the general and Miss Rebecca left for supper.

"Perfect timing as usual, Louis." Charlie efficiently got his shirt studs in place, then Louis assisted him with his vest and bow tie before helping him slip into the black dinner coat. As he adjusted his sleeves and shrugged to settle the coat over his shoulders, his valet carefully inspected him and brushed away any lint or dust. He knelt down and scrutinized Charlie's shoes, using a soft cloth pulled from his trouser pocket to wipe away a smudge that had made it to the toe of the left one.

The general reached to the dresser and picked up his prosthetic fingers, fastening them into place before plucking his white gloves from the top of the dresser. With his cane and gloves clutched in his left hand, he guided Rebecca to the door of their car where Lizbet waited, holding Rebecca's hat, coat, and reticule. Louis helped him into his overcoat, then handed him his top hat. With a smile and orders not to wait up for them, the couple left for a romantic dinner in town.

Rebecca discovered one advantage of her husband being part owner in a livery stable was that when they stepped out to the street, they were greeted quickly by a chipper young man who introduced himself as Mr. Galloway's nephew Geoffrey. He opened the door to one of the largest and most luxurious coaches she had ever laid eyes on.

It could have easily held six adults in its large leather seats. There was even a small folding table that could come down between them. This was a coach built for long range travel, not generally used for short trips around town, but Rebecca surmised that William had sent it because it would be extremely comfortable and would offer the smoothest ride possible.

Geoffrey handed Rebecca into the coach and stood by as Charlie climbed in. As he shut the door, he paused and asked, "Where would you like to go, General Redmond?"

"Ebbit House, please. I am looking forward to a quiet evening with Mrs. Redmond."

"As you wish, sir. Uncle William asks that you please just tell me anything you require. I will see to it. I know the city very well."

"Thank you, Geoffrey. We do appreciate it," Rebecca said with a warm smile as she took Charlie's hand and threaded her fingers through his and she pulled it into her lap for safe keeping, as if he could not be trusted with it. "Please, take your time going through the city."

"Yes, ma'am. As you request." He tugged the brim of his hat and jumped up to the top of the coach, using a long willowy whip to snap the four horses into motion.

"We are not going to the Willard?" she asked as she watched the city move by through the window.

"No, darling. The Willard tends to be the core of political beings, and since I have no desire for any of my business associates to know I am in town, I thought someplace with less "traffic" would be nice. Ebbit House is not terribly fancy, but they have a wonderful chef and the atmosphere would be more relaxed."

"Perfect." She placed a lingering kiss to his cheek as she continued to look out the window. "You are really embracing this vacation theme, yes?"

He nodded, bringing her hand to his lips for a quick kiss. "Absolutely. I only want to be with you and the children. I have not time nor patience for fools on this trip."

"We probably should have avoided Washington all together," she offered dryly.

"Probably." He agreed with a nod as he lit a cigar. "Tomorrow, I was contemplating a – I cannot believe I am saying this –shopping trip."

"General Redmond, you live with a wife and two growing daughters. Of course there will be shopping on this trip. A lot of it, if I have my way."

"Wonderful," he said as genuinely as humanly possible. "Do you want cash or the checkbook?"

"I want **you** to bring the checkbook."

"Oh, joy." He gestured aimlessly in the air. "Absolutely. Am I also allowed to bring a regular book? For the purposes of keeping myself occupied while you," he paused and looked at her seriously, "do whatever it is you do at a dress shop."

"I get naked."

He swallowed hard. "You do not!"

"I do. A proper dressmaker needs to take the right measurements. That cannot be accomplished in layers of fabric and a corset."

"I want to go with you to the dressmakers," he said as he nodded sincerely.

"You, sir, are a mischief-maker." She gave him a playful poke in the ribs as he settled his arm around her shoulders and pulled her close.

CHAPTER 20

Friday, April 3, 1868

They arrived at Ebbit House to find, much to Charlie's dismay, practically every high ranking Army and Navy man in Washington now camped out there. He groaned and shook his head as he looked around at the faces. Many of them he knew and they would certainly know him. His plans for a quiet evening with his wife just went out the window. "I am sorry. Last time I was here, it was not like this."

"It is all right, Charlie." She looped her arm through his as they were led to a reasonably quiet table at the back of the restaurant. "We are together; everything else is unimportant."

They had time to have a drink before a seemingly endless line of men started coming by the table to shake his hand and say hello. Rebecca just sat quietly with a smile on her face as she watched him diplomatically cut short every conversation. When they had a moment between visitors, she commented, “You military men are a thick bunch.”

“What?”

She laughed, gesturing to him. “See? It should be very clear to every man in here you do not want to be disturbed, but yet, they persist.”

He signed and nodded. “Sometimes we can be a tad dense.”

Once their entrées were served, they were left in peace to enjoy their dinner. As dessert was served, a bottle of Cristal champagne, vintage 1845 arrived at the table. Charlie’s brows drew together as he questioned the sommelier who was preparing to open the bottle. “I believe there has been a mistake; we did not order…”

“Oh no, sir.” The man smiled as he removed the cover and then prepared the cork. “From General Sheridan.” He lifted his chin to the other side of the room where Phil Sheridan sat at a table by himself. He lifted a glass in their direction when eye contact was made.

“Go ask him to join us,” Rebecca encouraged her husband as the cork was popped.

“Absolutely. Excuse me, darling.” He rose and crossed the room. She watched as they exchanged greetings and then walked back to the table together.

“Rebecca.” Sheridan leaned in and gave her a peck on the cheek as she stood to greet him. “It is so good to see you again. You look wonderful.”

“Thank you, Philip. It is good to see you under happier circumstances.”

“Indeed.” Charlie gestured to a chair as he held Rebecca’s chair for her. “Let us enjoy this wonderful bottle together. Please.”

“I did not want to intrude,” Sheridan started to protest.

"Nonsense. You could never intrude." Rebecca waved off his concern. "Please?"

He settled himself and the champagne was poured.

Sheridan gave them a sly grin after taking a sip. "How long are you in town for?"

"We leave Tuesday morning." Charlie knew that look and he wanted to stop whatever was about to start.

"That is good. Grant is still in New York. You will most likely miss each other."

"Why should we want to avoid General Grant?" Rebecca was truly confused.

Sheridan sat back and looked at them. "You do not know?"

"Philip, please." She placed her hand on his. "Charlie and I have been through too much; what is going on? Do not keep us in the dark."

"Rest assured, my dear, General Grant and now presidential candidate Grant, does not want anything that would be harmful to your family, but he does have his mind set on who he would like to have for a couple positions here. He needs his right hand back."

"Sorry, I no longer qualify. I am retired, remember?"

"He does not think that counts for someone he wants to reactivate, put another star on your shoulder and put you over in the War Department, or perhaps even a cabinet position. There is an outside chance he may need an ambassador somewhere."

Charlie groaned. "I already sent him a campaign donation; what more does he want?"

"That is simple." Sheridan shrugged. "You. Heart, mind and soul."

"Well then." Rebecca lifted her glass and tipped it at Philip. "General Grant will have to learn to live with disappointment because those things are already spoken for and well claimed."

Philip quirked a brow. "And if he is actually elected president? One does not usually tell their president no when he asks you to serve your nation."

~

Rebecca checked on the girls, who were bedded down at the far end of their parents' train car. The boys could be happily left together in a car with John and Louis to keep a watchful eye; however, a single car for two little girls would have been a bit much, even by Charlie's standards.

It was decided the girls would sleep in a fold out trundle bed at the far end of the car while their parents would enjoy a specially installed, stand-alone feather bed, like the one they shared at home. A curtain pulled across each sleeping space would provide the appropriate privacy for all concerned.

He slid under the covers, quickly kicking his feet to warm the sheets before she joined him. He also took a moment to rub his hands together to make sure they were nice and warm as well. The train was a perfectly acceptable temperature, but he always preferred to greet her in their bed with warm hands.

By the time she slipped under the covers, he had done an outstanding job of creating a nice warm little nook for her to curl into, which she immediately did. There were a few minutes of mutual squirming and resettling before they happily curled into one another.

Charlie's breath caught when he felt her hands beginning to wander. "No," he whispered, softly giving her a kiss on the top of her blonde head.

"No? What do you mean no?" In the three years they had been together, she was reasonably sure she had never heard him say no when she was being affectionate.

"Darling." He pulled her to his chest. "The girls are just across the room. We really should not risk…"

She managed to pull back and look at him in the low light of the car. "You mean to tell me that you intend to be…" She nearly choked on the word. "Celibate. For the next month?"

He looked at her, his brows rising in a questioning manner. "What else? I nearly broke my neck when Buddy intruded, and he had a door to open we did not hear. What about your tendency to…you know…"

"Moan?" The word was offered as his stomach clenched painfully and his skin broke out in goose flesh. She took the opportunity to push him back and kiss him thoroughly. Once she knew he was completely breathless she pulled back and looked into his eyes. "You are sure? No?"

Nothing in his life had ever been this hard before. He nodded and quietly cleared his throat. "Yes, dear."

She sighed dejectedly and rolled over, curling into him, his arm immediately encompassing her. "All right then, General Redmond, we shall see how long this little strike lasts."

Charlie tried to placate Rebeca by nuzzling her hair and holding her tight. "It is not a strike, but an attempt to preserve modesty for all involved."

She just growled and grabbed his wrist as she pulled it tight to her. "You call it what you want. I am calling it a strike."

~

Saturday, April 4, 1868

Breakfast was taken in the parlor car. The older children excitedly talked about what they would like to see and do in the magnificent capital city. The boys sat on a blanket on the floor where Tess and Ginnie cleaned up the inevitable mess as they tried and failed to eat their breakfast. Charlie cleared his throat and the room went completely silent. Even Buddy and Andy sat quietly, waiting for what their papa had to say.

He looked to each child in turn. "Today, Mama has asked to go shopping." He tried not to smile when he saw Darby roll his eyes. "So this is my suggestion. I think that Darby, John and Freddy should go out today, explore the city and put together an appropriate tour for the family that Darby will guide tomorrow. I will take Mrs. Redmond and the girls to the dressmaker this morning." He smiled at Lizbet and winked, "Perhaps you would like to see if Tomas is available for lunch or dinner?"

"Yes, sir. I would like that very much." Lizbet smiled shyly. She had hoped she would have some free time to seek her husband out while they were in the city.

"I think that is a perfectly reasonable way for you to spend your day." Charlie stood and crossed to the young black woman. He dug in his pocket and pressed a ten dollar gold piece into her hand. "Have a wonderful time. I will tend to Miss Rebecca tonight. Do not worry about getting back."

Once Andy and Buddy were squared away with Tess and Ginnie, Charlie informed the women who took such loving care of his children that they were being treated to a special lunch because they were formally 'trapped' on the train with the little ones. He had asked the Pullman staff to make sure that the caregivers and the children were given anything they asked for.

Once the women in his life were properly prepared, he escorted them outside, where he once again found Geoffrey and the beautiful family coach ready to convey his ladies in style and comfort. He quickly lifted Em and Sue into the coach and then handed Rebecca up. He waited for dresses to be properly settled before he climbed in. Once again, Geoffrey's smiling face was in the window. "Where to, sir?"

Charlie looked to Rebecca, who smiled and offered, "To Madam Gaston's, if you please, Geoffrey. I believe she is on 8th between…"

"Pennsylvania and D Street. Yes, Mrs. Redmond, I know right where to go." He smiled playfully and waved at the girls before taking his seat on the box.

"This sounds like it is going to be expensive and painful," Charlie commented as the coach lurched forward, carrying him closer to purgatory.

She patted his leg. "After last night, you had better believe it. I intend to get satisfaction in one manner or another."

When they returned to the train in the afternoon, the girls were giddy with excitement after having spent a whole day with Mama and Papa all by themselves. They had been treated to two new dresses each from the dressmaker and then Papa had taken them to a real, honest ice cream parlor where they had enjoyed lunch and a special treat of the creamy, frozen concoction. After that, it had been a bit of a chore to settle them down for even a short nap in the parlor car.

Charlie, on the other hand, was more than happy to collapse on the sofa in their car. His wife entered after settling the girls and checking on the boys to find her husband sprawled along the length of the sofa.

"What is wrong, Charlie? Did we wear you out?" She smiled indulgently.

"Yes," came a truly dry response with a nod.

She chuckled and took a seat on the floor near him, brushing her fingers through his hair as she had done almost from the moment they met. "Is it tougher to be a husband and father than a military commander?"

"Yes. My soldiers did not cry if something went wrong in their lives. I thought Sue was going to combust when they told her they did not have the dress she wanted in blue like yours."

She laughed and patted his hand. "We sorted it out."

"You sorted it out. I hid until it was time to write the check."

"Which you did, with great bravery. There must be some kind of millinery medal somewhere we can pin on your chest. "

"Thank you." He was more than happy to accept her kiss as payment for his job well done. He hummed and licked his lips when hers left his. "What would you like to do for supper tonight?"

"I would very much like a quiet evening with you, dear husband, but I am afraid with our current accommodations…"

"Which you are entirely unhappy about."

"That is neither here nor there…"

"Actually, I have solved that problem as well." He pulled his pocket watch from his vest and gave it a glance. "A small car for the girls, Lizbet, Tess and Ginnie should arrive in the next thirty to sixty minutes. The children may dine in the parlor car and we shall do so here. Together. Alone. I know when I have made a logistical error. I fixed it."

"I love you!" She pushed herself up and kissed him soundly.

He laughed and wrapped his arms around her as she laid her head on his chest. "I love you, too, my darling. I want us all to be able to relax while the house is being remodeled and renovated and it was clear to me that having the girls occupy space with us was not going to work for you."

"House remodeled and renovated? When were you going to tell me?"

"Um, I planned to show you when we got home. I know you

will love it, dear."

"Um-huh. We shall see. For now, let us go and enjoy our privacy, shall we?"

Charlie sighed with relief. He had expected Rebecca to have a more vehement response. Little did he know, she was already plotting her revenge.

~

He lay back in the bed, a satisfied smile on his face as Rebecca mewed happily, completely and thankfully sated. He pulled her close and kissed the crown of her head. "Better?"

"Oh, yes." She nodded happily. "Thank you."

"I told you. No need to thank me. I enjoy doing that."

She laughed and got as close as she could without actually getting into his skin with him. "You are a wonderful husband and father, do you know that?"

"I like to think I am."

"I assure you. If all men treated their wives and children as you do, there would be no divorce."

"Or spousal murder."

She laughed and gave his stomach a pinch. "True. It may run in the family. We are fairly certain that my great grandmother on my mother's side murdered her first husband."

"First? How many did she end up having?"

"Four, and what happened to numbers two and three is sketchy at best."

He lay there for a moment, not sure if she was kidding him or not, then he felt her giggle. He began laughing with her, pulling her close. "You scared me."

"Good."

"So what would you like to do in Philadelphia?"

"As long as I do not have to watch you eat oysters, I do not care what we do."

~

Tuesday, April 7, 1868

As the train made its way to Philadelphia, bypassing Baltimore in favor of visiting there on the way back, Rebecca was grateful for the canvas barriers that had been installed between the train cars to make passing between them easier and safer for everyone. She and Charlie had agreed that dresses were too damn dangerous to move between them, so she was dressed in her normal farm clothes. She now understood why he dressed the girls like this when they traveled.

She stepped through the door of the parlor car and smiled when she saw him sitting there reading the newspaper propped up in front of his face, legs crossed, his booted right foot bouncing with the movement of the train.

She poured herself a cup of coffee and moved toward him. "You look relaxed, darling." She nearly dropped her cup when the paper fell and Darby was behind it. "Thank you, Mama, but if you are looking for Papa, he is with the girls."

She peered at the paper. "And you are reading the Financial Times. Of course you are." She sat down at the table and sighed as she fixed her coffee.

Darby was not sure, but he thought he heard her mumble something about shaving. "I am trying to learn the concepts of the stock market, but I think it is a bit beyond me yet. However, I am anxious to diversify some of my holdings."

His mother sat there, slack jawed. "Holdings? You have holdings? You are twelve."

"Yes, ma'am." Like the gentleman he was, he put the paper

down because it was obvious Mama now wanted to talk about his situation. He leaned forward and smiled. "Would you like to hear about them?"

"Please."

"Of course there is the property that Suzanne and I own. I collect fifteen dollars a month in rent on that. Now, those monies are split equally between me and Suzanne. We each have our own accounts at the bank. Papa made sure to see to that so she would always have a source of income."

Of course he did, she mused.

Her eldest son continued, "Some of that money I used to help support a recent expansion Jeremiah wanted to make to his business. He has discovered that there are a lot of men who can use special things like he makes for Papa. So we bought a couple of new saddle forms and a new set of tools, because the ones he had were second hand and not in very good shape. He was also able to take on an apprentice."

Jeremiah is not yet thirteen, and he has an apprentice? Oh, dear Lord. Her head was starting to reel at the rate at which these young men were growing up.

"I have also considered investing in Miss Ro's kennels. She sells her pups as fast as she can breed them. They are even over in West Virginia now! It seems a good, solid investment. I am also working with a few of the younger fellows around town, trying to organize a new delivery service. Mr. Randall uses a couple of boys to deliver telegrams. I do not see why we cannot use more boys for more businesses, and put more people to work."

At this moment, Charlie came into the car. Sliding the door closed, he made his way over and joined his wife and son. "Well, what are you talking about that has you both so engaged?"

"I am sitting here listening to the next business tycoon in the

United States." Rebecca just shook her head. "Have you two been talking or is he absorbing this by osmosis?"

Charlie nodded and poured his own coffee from the service. "Young Master Darby does occasionally ask my thoughts on his plans, but for the most part, he makes his own business decisions."

"Are you aware he has gone into partnership with Jeremiah?"

"Oh, yes!" His father nodded proudly. "He beat me to it. He is also contemplating a larger investment than I have with Ro Jackson that would make him a senior partner in what would then be our shared business venture."

Rebecca could only smile at both of them. With these two looking after the family fortune, it was in extremely good hands.

Wednesday, April 8, 1868

Charlie made a rather startling admission on their first day in Philadelphia. "I am afraid it is time for me to invest in a pair of reading glasses. My eyes are not what they used to be."

"I think you will look very dapper in glasses," Rebecca tried to reassure him. Her husband could still be a tad vain and she knew the thought of needing glasses must be irritating him to no end.

"I think I will look positively ridiculous, but I must have them. I am getting headaches when I read for more than an hour or so."

"It seems that Philadelphia, home of Franklin, would be the place to have it done. They must have some of the finest opticians in the country."

"That was sort of my logic. If I leave now, I might be able to meet you back here for lunch. There is a shop I was planning on taking Darby to this morning. A clothing store, Rockhill and Wilson, over on Chestnut. Perhaps you can get your shopping lust for this leg of our journey out with our sons? They all need new trousers and boots. They seem to have grown an inch on the trip already."

She smiled and patted his hand. "Yes, dear. You go get your glasses. I will tend to getting the boys properly outfitted."

"Thank you. And please, make sure Freddy gets a couple of new outfits as well. I noticed the tops of his boots were starting to peek out from his trousers last week."

"Of course." She smiled lovingly at him.

Making it official would have caused quite the scandal, but she knew in her already overly protective, motherly heart, that her husband had adopted this boy too. Regardless of race, he was as much loved and respected as any of the other children who slumbered under their roof and protection. Freddy would be given every opportunity and advantage the general and Mrs. Redmond could manage without tearing apart the social fabric that held the community together.

Mama had taken the children shopping, as promised. That gave Darby, Freddy, and John the freedom to go and discover the features of the planned family tour the next day. Charlie rejoined Rebecca and the younger members of the family that afternoon.

"So, dear, did you get your glasses?"

"Yes," he mumbled.

"Reading glasses?"

"Yes." This time the reply was outright sullen.

"So, may I see them?"

He pulled a simple clam shell case out of his inner pocket,

opened it and pulled out a pair of steel framed, half moon glasses with wires that wrapped around his ears to keep them in place. He tried to hand them to her for inspection but she smiled and gestured.

With a grumble, he put them on and looked at her rather sheepishly. "They said I would probably need glasses all the time in the next few years, but this would do for now."

"Darling, they make you look distinguished."

"Darling, they make me look old."

Thursday, April 9, 1868

Darby ferreted out the location of several key sites in old Philadelphia, starting with Independence Hall and the cracked Liberty Bell, Christ Church, where many of the founding fathers had attended church, Benjamin Franklin's print shop, and the first post office in Philadelphia. He even booked a table for lunch for them at the City Tavern, where many of the founding fathers had stayed when in Philadelphia, and where Thomas Jefferson, with Benjamin Franklin, Roger Sherman, John Adams and Robert Livingstone had written the Declaration of Independence.

He scheduled the whole afternoon for a visit to the Franklin Institute, founded almost 50 years before, to celebrate Franklin's devotion to science and mechanics. There were a number of exhibits, mostly demonstrating the work that the Franklin Institute's scientific fellows were pursuing. As they strolled through the building, somewhere between the steam train exhibit and the electricity exhibit, they lost Emily.

Darby, Charlie, and John split up, leaving the younger boys with Rebecca and Suzanne, to search the exhibits for her. Darby headed for the earth sciences exhibit, which they had passed but had not explored, as rocks had little attraction for most of the family. There he found her, moving from exhibit to exhibit, staring at the rocks and fossilized shells and shark teeth with intense fascination. It took some serious persuading to get her to come back and rejoin the family.

When she did, Mama was decidedly upset with her. "Do you know how much you frightened me by wandering off? You have to stay with the family, little one."

"But Mama, they have rocks. Lots of rocks. Beautiful rocks, and lots of old shells and bones and things. I **NEEDED** to see them."

Rebecca did not know it yet, but she would hear that repeated over and over whenever they visited a science museum over the next few years.

~

Monday, April 13, 1868

They arrived in New York early in the morning, having travelled overnight from Philadelphia. Darby and John set off to plan their tour of the city. Tess and Lizbet took the boys to play in Central Park, and Rebecca, Emily, and Suzanne set off to shop for new furnishings for the house. Charlie and his checkbook were required to accompany them. Rebecca's response to his surprise remodeling and renovation of the house was in full flight.

They started at the Cooper Institute Carpet Store, where the owner, Mr. Hyatt, was more than happy to provide Mrs. Redmond with a new Turkish carpet for the office, another for the bedroom, a third for the sitting room, and two very large ones for the front and rear parlor. Charlie wrote the check and gave Mr. Hyatt shipping instructions.

She then took a collection of color samples with her to the next stop, so she could match the colors to the wall paper she wanted to get. Mr. Paul Vacquerel greeted them at the door, as Mr. Hyatt had sent a runner over to warn him of the Redmonds' impending arrival. New wall paper and complimentary borders were acquired for the front and rear parlor, the dining room, and Charlie and Rebecca's bedroom and sitting room.

He handled the payment and logistics there, too, then escorted the ladies in his life to the workshop of Mr. W. H. Sackett, Jr., the manufacturer of the best bed frames in New York. Rebecca selected a beautiful serpentine mahogany bedstead for their bedroom, and acquired two new beds for the girls in matching black walnut. New beds for the boys were also acquired because their cribs could simply no longer contain them. He played his role, though he paled a bit at the size of the check.

~

Tuesday, April 14, 1868

New York offered so many options that Darby, Freddy and John continued their exploring and tour planning into their second day in the city. Rebecca and the girls continued their shopping to redecorate the house. Charlie plodded along behind.

At Doring & Abel, Mrs. Redmond selected complete suites of new furnishings for the front and back parlor, choosing rosewood for the more intimate back parlor and mahogany for the formal front parlor. She bought sofas, armchairs, side tables, and lamps for both rooms. And for the back parlor, she bought a card table and four matching chairs. He thought he was done as he wrote this check, but no; she had two more stops to make.

At Ebbinghousen & Co, she selected new furnishings for

their private sitting room and bedroom. She selected two new wardrobes, one for each of them, as well as chairs, a loveseat for in front of their bedroom fireplace in mahogany to match the new bed, a new and very soft sofa for their sitting room, and miscellaneous other tables and chairs. Charlie smiled wanly, wrote the check and provided the shipping information.

The last stop was at Mr. Joseph Loader's, an upholsterer who had a brilliant array of window treatments to provide a new look and feel to all of the rooms in the house. Here she went absolutely mad with the joy of selecting new draperies for every public room in the house – the ball room, the dining room, the front and back parlors, as well as for their bedroom, sitting room, and office. The gentleman of the house had no idea that basically strips of material could cost so much.

By the time they were done, Charlie and the girls were exhausted. They staggered back to the train, where Tess and Lizbet had the boys back from the park, fed and to bed. Darby, Freddy and John were relaxing in the parlor car having already eaten.

The Pullman staff had a nice dinner waiting for them. Charlie, Rebecca and the girls ate hastily, then the girls were settled down, and he collapsed on the sofa in their car, too tired to pull his own boots off.

Louis appeared and helped him strip out of his outer clothes, down to his shirt, britches and socks, and then Charlie sent him on his way. He finished undressing and collapsed into bed, still in his knitted underwear that his wife had so lovingly made for him. He barely moved when she crawled in beside him, simply rolling onto his side and throwing his arm around her. His snoring did not even falter.

~

Rex walked through the winter kitchen, stepping carefully around the piles of fire bricks that had been brought in to serve as the bases for the new stoves. Stevenson and his crew were standing beside the sinks, beaming with pride. They had laid the pipe for both the hot and cold water.

"So, Stevenson, how goes the installation of the reservoirs?"

"They are in place, Mr. Rex, and we should have the heating pipes finished within the next two days, so we can hook them up. We have run the cold water pipes to the attic and they are in place."

"So we should be able to test the system within the week?"

"Yes, sir. And the water closet for the general's washroom came in. We are finishing up the drainage pipes now, and should be ready to install it and the tub and sinks this week as well."

"Excellent, Stevenson. Excellent. Have you laid the pipes out to the summer kitchen as well?"

"Yes, sir."

"Well, then shall we go see how that is coming?"

The two men walked down the half-finished walkway between the winter kitchen in the house and the summer kitchen beside the vegetable garden. Duncan's men were still working on the roof that would protect the staff from foul weather.

The new summer kitchen was partially brick and partially wood, with large levered windows that could be adjusted to catch the breeze from any direction, and help keep the kitchen as cool as possible.

Duncan saw Rex strolling through the construction site and came over to report on his progress. "Good morning, Rex. Have you been upstairs yet?"

"No, I was going there next."

"Then let me walk with you. I am rather proud of what we have done."

As the two men walked back to the house, Rex noticed a whole row of cabinets sitting on the back porch, ready to be installed and painted in the winter kitchen. "Very nice cabinetry, Duncan."

"Wait until you see the washroom."

Duncan was as good as his word. The tile work was impeccable, the wooden cabinets for the sinks were beautiful, and the water closet was perfect. Duncan was grinning with pride. "We will have it all done by the time they get home."

~

Wednesday, April 15, 1868

Darby and John Foxworth had decided the night before to divide and conquer. They had discovered a genuine archeological dig on Manhattan Island that was open to visitors. Darby was going to take the family on an historical tour of the city while John would take Emily to the archeological dig.

Rebecca was a little distressed about having her daughter go off without her, but Charlie grinned at her. "Darling, you know Em needs to dig in the dirt or she is simply not happy. This gives her that all-important dose of dirt."

Mama surrendered. Em was ecstatic.

Darby took the rest of the family to see some of New York's more notable places, including the Federal Hall National Memorial at the US Custom House, which sat on the site of the first capitol of the country, and was where George Washington was sworn in to office. The memorial included the bible that was used by Washington to swear his oath of office. They then went to Wall Street and watched the trading on the New York Stock Exchange from the visitor's gallery. That was rather intense, so the next stop on Darby's agenda was lunch at the oldest continuously operating restaurant in New York, the Empire House.

After a very satisfying lunch, they went down to the Battery, where American Forces and British gunships had faced off during the Revolution. They enjoyed the view from that lovely park out over the great waterway that defined New York harbor and across to Governor's Island, where both American and British Forces had controlled the waterways at various times during the Revolution. Most recently, Governor's Island had been used as a prison for confederate prisoners of war during the recent rebellion.

The last stop was at the great construction site in mid-town, where the Cathedral of St. Patrick was being built. It was a marvel in the neo-gothic style, and at this point, visitors could see the great flying buttresses used to support the soaring weight of the building being put together.

The family returned to their train just in time to meet Emily, who returned dirty and happy from the architectural dig at Ward's Point. She had to tell them all about how they had discovered ancient artifacts from the Indians who had once lived there, and how they let her use the tiny pick and brushes they employed to protect the artifacts from damage as they dug them up.

That evening as Charlie and Rebecca were preparing for bed, Charlie looked at his wife with a speculative eye. "You know, dear, with all of the renovations that I am having done and all of the new furnishings that you have ordered, we will be returning to a new house. What do you think about giving the house a new name as well? I know there are people who still think of the house as 'the old Gaines place,' even though the horse breeding program is from Redmond Stables. I think I would like to change that."

"Oh, Charlie, that is a lovely idea. All the refurbishing I have been doing is specifically to get rid of anything that was left from the Gaines family." She smiled and wrapped her arms around his neck. "So, General Redmond, what would you like to call our home?"

"I was thinking of something like Mountain View. We do have a great view of the Blue Ridge."

"Yes, we do. Then Mountain View it is."

The next morning, Charlie handed George a note to have a telegram sent to Rex. He requested a brass plaque be made to go beside the front door.

~

Thursday, April 16, 1868

Thursday was spent rambling around the city, exploring the many mansions along Fifth Avenue, which were notable for their magnificent architecture and outrageous ostentatious arrogance. The names of the owners were as well known as the most popular actors, including Carnegie, Frick, Astor, Vanderbilt, and others. Farther down the avenue was the exclusive shopping area of the city, built no doubt to meet the needs of the millionaires who lived up the street. There were jewelers, haberdashers, art and sculpture studios, shoe makers, and knick knack shops all along the street. It was a bit overwhelming, even for Rebecca Redmond, Mistress Extraordinary of most shopping districts.

When they returned to the train, John and Tess took the children off to get cleaned up and have supper, while Charlie and Rebecca prepared for an adult evening out on the town. First was an early supper at the famous restaurant, Delmonico's, where Rebecca had the courage to try their Lobster Newburg. It was good, for seafood.

Then Charlie had gotten tickets to Wood's Museum and Metropolitan Theatre, where Miss Lydia Thompson had brought the famous – or rather infamous – British burlesque performance of *Ixion – or The Man at the Wheel*, an Original Extravaganza by F. C. Burnand. It was a great deal of fun, a parody of classical Greek tragedy that was more than a little salacious. The two of them had a wonderful time.

When they returned to the train, they were both grateful for the privacy of their own car and took full advantage of it to exercise their libidos, which had been titillated by the outrageous stage performance.

~

Sunday, April 12, 1868

The following Sunday, Darby led the family to services at St. Paul's Chapel, lovingly called the Little Chapel that Stood because it had survived the fire that burned over a quarter of New York that was the result of the Battle of Long Island. St. Paul's had been Washington's church when he was in New York for two years after his inauguration, and was the oldest church building in Manhattan. After church, Darby had their driver give them a tour of some of the more beautiful churches in Manhattan, including Trinity Church, Grace Church and St. George's. Darby had become interested in various building styles, and was showing off his knowledge of architecture to his parents.

CHAPTER 21

Monday, April 20, 1868

They pulled into Hartford, Connecticut in time for lunch, having left New York early that morning. Rebecca looked out the windows as they came into the town, which at that time was a major manufacturing center. All she could see was large brick buildings, smokestacks, and a haze of smoke over the whole city. "Why are we stopping here, dear?"

"Because the Colt factory is here, and I wanted to see how they do what they do to make the repeating pistols and rifles. When I started in the army, we were using single-load weapons; the revolving pistols and rifles were a godsend during the war. And Winchester is making the new lever action repeating rifle that I want to see as well, but that is over in New Haven. I am hoping that Colt will have an example of the competition's product."

"You may want to have a look at the Weed sewing machine

factory. I understand they are making some very attractive new models that you would like. I really do not think we will be here for more than just a day, dear. Do you mind?"

"Not at all. The girls and I will go look at sewing machines while you look at guns. Are you taking the boys?"

"I will take Darby, Freddy and John, I think. Tess and Ginnie can handle Andy and Buddy. We will be back in time for dinner."

"Oh, no. You will be back before then. I expect you to come and collect the girls and me before you come back."

"Yes, dear." He knew that meant he needed to bring his checkbook. "Shall we go?"

~

Wednesday, April 22, 1868

They travelled overnight so that they arrived in Boston in the morning. Darby was chomping at the bit to get out and start putting together a tour of another city redolent with Revolutionary War history.

Rebecca looked over her girls and decided that some exposure to art and literature was in order, so after breakfast, she packed them up and headed to the Boston Athenaeum, which had a spectacular collection of fine art, as well as a grand collection of literature. Emily looked bored even before they left. Suzanne was ready to go; it was something Mama was interested in, therefore it was something she was interested in.

Emily looked at her sister and hissed, "Mama's girl."

Suzanne whispered back, "Mud puppy Papa's girl."

Tess, Ginnie, Lizbet and Louis packed Andy and Buddy up and headed to the Boston Commons. The little boys needed some running room.

Charlie retired to the parlor car. He settled in with a fresh pot of coffee and a plate of sweet rolls that George brought him, and a pile of newspapers that Darby had read but for which he had not had time. It was the first day of real relaxation that he had enjoyed since they started on this vacation trip. He settled his new glasses on his nose, ordered the papers by date, and started in on catching up with the news.

The papers were full of Congress's effort to impeach President Johnson. The full transcripts of the trial in the Senate took Charlie almost four hours to read through. In his opinion, the Radical Republicans were fools. Their plans to punish the southern whites were vicious, and Johnson recognized that.

But as long as Stanton was Secretary of War, and the southern states were under military control, that punitive approach would go unmitigated. Lincoln's plans to return the Union to a whole were totally unimportant to the Radicals. Thank God, they were one vote short of impeachment. He knew they would be back for more. Johnson was not out of the woods yet.

Tess, Lizbet and Louis returned with the boys first. The boys were dirty, tired and happy as bugs in rugs. Tess recruited George to help her get them fed and cleaned up, and tucked them away for an early bed time.

Rebecca and the girls returned next. Mama was thrilled with the day; they had seen some beautiful works of art. Suzanne was dutiful in reporting what she had learned. Emily was miserable, bored, and uninformed. She sat in the corner and sulked until Papa told her he was taking the whole family out for dinner that evening, but not to a fancy restaurant, so they did not have to get dressed up in evening clothes.

Finally, Darby and John appeared. They were both a bit windblown, and John was limping, as he had turned his ankle on one of the old cobblestones that lined many of Boston's streets. Darby had a pile of notes in his pocket from which he would assemble his plans for the family's outings. Both professed themselves to be starving.

Charlie inquired of the group, "So, dear family, how do you feel about having a traditional New England dinner at a restaurant where you will be sassed and insulted by the waiters and enjoy a lot of good food?"

Rebecca looked confused. "Insulted and sassed by the waiters?"

"Yes, dear. If you are not properly sassed by them, you have not had the full experience and they will not have earned their keep for the night. It is an old tradition at Durgin Park. But you will get to sample the traditional dish here – Boston Baked Beans. They are delicious, I promise you. And they serve a fish dish they call scrod that I think you will like. And no, you do not have to watch me eat oysters – at least not tonight."

"So what is scrod?"

"Some say it stands for 'seaman's catch received on deck,' others for 'small cod remaining on deck.' Whichever it is, it is a small, tender white fish, boned and lightly dried – just for the day – then broiled with lemon juice and butter, and I assure you it is delicious."

Rebecca shook her head, but said, "I am starving and so are the girls. Let us go and be sassed and fed."

The sassing started when they walked through the door. The host met them, looked at the family, and then addressed Charlie. "Such lovely ladies. How is it that they are with you? You must be rich." He escorted them to a table and the waiter approached them.

"Good evening. What would you be drinking? I assume you, sir, will be drinking some of our best whiskey; any man with this many children needs it."

Emily piped up. "Mister, my two little brothers are not with us."

The waiter looked at Rebecca. "You must like him a lot! Or is it the money?"

She could not help but snicker. "I do – and the money is not bad either."

The evening went on like that, gentle jibes with Rebecca in particular giving as good as she got. The food was good too.

~

Friday, April 24, 1868

Darby had laid out a lovely tour of the historic city, focusing on the Revolutionary War history that Boston represented. At breakfast that morning, Charlie and John had talked and the two men decided that it was time to take Buddy and Andy with them, giving Tess, Ginnie, Lizbet, and Louis the day off – a reprieve from the boys and the constraints of the train.

So with the youngest of the Redmond troops in tow, they set off to discover the town.

They started at Faneuil Hall, where the Declaration of Independence had been signed, and proceeded to visit many of the major sites of the revolutionary period – Old North Church, Old South Meeting House, Old City Hall, the Old State House and the site across the street where the Boston Massacre occurred, the Paul Revere House, and the Granary Burial Ground, where Paul Revere, John Hancock, and Samuel Adams, among others of the founding fathers, were buried.

By then, it was lunch time. Darby had booked a table at The

Green Dragon Tavern. It had been open since 1654. The site of many meetings to plan the revolution, from the Boston Tea Party to the recruitment and training of the firsts Colonial troops, it was unofficially called 'the Headquarters of the Revolution.'

After lunch, they headed out to Breed's Hill, the actual site of the first battle, which many mistakenly called Bunker Hill. The boys were let loose to run, while Emily exercised her new skills at conducting archaeological digs to discover a number of spent bullets that were obviously from revolutionary era muskets. She was over the moon when she discovered something her father could identify as a piece of buckle. What kind of buckle he could not tell her, but that did not matter--it was something different.

Late in the afternoon, Rebecca and Charlie took the children home. Tess, Ginnie, Lizbet and Louis had returned before them, and were ready to herd the children to their various meals, after dinner activities and bed. Charlie and Rebecca dressed for dinner and a concert afterwards. John was given the evening off and went to explore the more adult aspects of the town on his own.

Charlie took Rebecca to Parker's Restaurant, one of the modern restaurants in the city. The room was magnificent, all dark wood paneling, crystal chandeliers, gleaming white linens and fresh flowers. The staff provided impeccable service. Dinner for Charlie started with New England clam chowder, followed by his beloved oysters on the half shell. Rebecca opted for English pea and mint soup, followed by a delicate plate of foie gras and fruit compote. She just shook her head as he slurped his oysters and washed them down with a crisp champagne.

Their entrées were salmon for him and a lovely rack of lamb with asparagus for her. The dinner rolls they served were unique, light, very buttery and delicious. But the real treat was the dessert. They called it Boston Cream Pie, but it was not really a pie. Instead, it was a wondrous combination of yellow cake, vanilla custard and a chocolate topping that was not quite a frosting but thicker than a sauce. It was delicious.

After dinner, they hailed a cab to take them out to Cambridge and Harvard University, where the classical guitarist and composer José Ferrer Esteve de Fujadas was giving a performance of his own compositions and classical Spanish guitar pieces. His playing was brilliant; his compositions were evocative of the Spanish culture. Charlie was enthralled, so when the concert was finished, the couple approached the musician to chat with him.

His English was broken, their Spanish was non-existent, but all three of them spoke French fluently. Charlie told Senior Ferrer of his physician assigning him the guitar as a therapy for his hand. The musician was fascinated by the use of his instrument as a medical prescription. He was also curious about the work of the guitar maker Christian Martin, of whom he had heard good things. They immediately invited him to come back to their train and meet a Martin guitar. He agreed with alacrity.

When they returned to the train, Charlie excused himself while Rebecca rang for coffee and brandy. A few moments later, he returned to the parlor car carrying his guitar case and a small card. "Senior Ferrer, I will happily let you play my guitar, but I would ask a favor. Would you please note your name, the date, and what piece or pieces you play on my guitar and sign the card? I would like to keep a memento of our private concert."

Ferrer agreed with a grin, and lovingly extracted the Martin from its case. He carefully inspected the guitar, then tuned it and started playing. He played a movement from his own *Recuerdos de Montgri,* a celebration of the capture from the Saracens of the island of Majorca by King James I of Aragon in the 1200s. He then played several short songs from Catalonia.

As the hour grew late, he smiled at them, handing back the

Martin. "It is a beautiful instrument. Thank you for giving me the opportunity to play it, and for providing me with a wonderful way to relax after a concert. I hope your travels continue to be enjoyable." He dropped the card in the guitar case, donned his coat and bid them good night. The hack that had brought them from Cambridge was still waiting for him. Charlie walked him out and tipped the driver liberally.

~

Saturday, April 25, 1868

Darby had one more place to visit before they left Boston, so the next morning the whole family assembled and traveled up to the ship yards on the north side of Boston Harbor. There, they found all kinds of boats and ships being built or refitted. It made the shipyards in Richmond look tiny.

Sitting at a dock in the midst of all of this activity was a magnificent frigate, the USS Constitution. Charlie's status as a line officer opened doors for them, and the first officer provided a personal tour of the 17 gun ship of war that had been so successful during the War of 1812, and continued to ply the waters off the coast of the United States to protect her shores.

After the tour, Darby led them back to Faneuil Hall, and then across the street to the oldest restaurant in the United States. Ye Olde Union Oyster House opened in 1826 and was modeled on the French style restaurant, instead of the taverns that had been the primary eating places in the colonies and early United States.

Rebecca drew a deep breath, girding her loins, as it were, to watch Charlie eat disgusting things again. She was correct in her preparations.

They started the meal by ordering clam chowder for the

children and onion soup for Rebecca. He ordered a dozen oysters on the half shell for himself.

The starters arrived and Emily looked at her father's plate with interest. He picked up the first oyster, doused it with a little squeeze of lemon, and slurped it down.

"Papa," she said. "Those look good. What are they?"

"Oysters, Em. And I think they are very good."

Rebecca mumbled, "They look good? They look like slimy gray blobs."

Suzanne heard her mother and muttered back to her, "Yes, but Piglet over there eats dirt."

Em asked, "May I have one, Papa?"

"Certainly, child." He squeezed a little lemon juice on the next oyster and handed it to his daughter. "Just slurp it down."

Rebecca dropped her head into her hand.

Em slurped. She chewed for a moment, swallowed, and proclaimed. "Oh, yes, they **are** good. May I have another, please?"

He prepared and handed her another oyster. Mama looked pained. The rest of the children looked interested. If Em liked them, they thought they might like them too.

Rebecca heaved a shaky sigh. Suzanne and Darby both asked at the same time to try one as well. Buddy and Andy wanted to be part of what their older siblings were doing and piped up too.

Papa squeezed lemon over all of the remaining oysters, then passed them around to his children. He hailed a waiter and ordered another dozen for himself.

There was a chorus of, "Papa, these are really good," "Yummmm," and "more please."

John had ordered a bowl of steamed mussels. The children turned on him. Darby started this round with, "What are you eating, Mr. John?"

"They are mussels, steamed with butter and garlic."

"May we try them too?"

John looked at Charlie, who smiled and shrugged, then passed his bowl around the table.

Their father admonished the children, "Just take one. You have soup coming."

"Yes, sir," they chorused.

Charlie added another bowl of mussels to his order. He glanced over at Rebecca, who was looking slightly pea green. "Clearly, they have inherited this atrocious taste in slimy sea things from you, sir."

He was about to make it worse. When the additional oysters and mussels were brought to the table, along with the chowder for the children and the onion soup for Rebecca, he ordered fried oysters, clams, scallops, and shrimp, along with crab cakes and lobster cakes, with baked beans and coleslaw served family style for the children, himself, and John, and broiled chicken with vegetables and rice for Rebecca.

She ate her chicken quietly, staring at her plate, trying to avoid watching the other members of her family voraciously gobbling down sea creatures she was convinced were repellent.

As they left the restaurant, Charlie whispered to Rebecca, "Darling, I promise I will not subject you to that again in Baltimore. John and I will take the children to a seafood shop after dropping you at a ladies only tearoom for lunch. Perhaps Mr. Schwarz's wife would like to join you?"

She nodded, and mumbled faintly, "Oh, God. Mr. Schwarz's? No, I cannot do that to myself."

As they were returning to the train that had become their mobile home, Charlie took a few minutes to send a quick telegram to Mr. Schwarz, telling him they would be in town on the following Monday and explaining that his wife needed the quiet company of a mature woman to go shopping, have lunch, and **not** have to keep track of their children. He expressed his hope that Mr. Schwarz could help, and telling him they would be at the Toy Bazaar at 10:00 in the morning on Monday.

The work at the house was finished. Sarah, with Rex's permission, decided the proper thing to do was to provide a festive meal for the workmen. They would celebrate the long, hard hours they had put in to make sure that all of the work was done, done properly, and ready for the Redmonds when they returned. She cooked in the summer kitchen and served a proper feast in the patio behind it. There was enough food so that every worker took home some leftovers to share with their families.

Sunday, April 26, 1868

Sunday was a quiet day. They attended services at the Old North Church and then returned to the train for a quiet family day together. Charlie released their staff with a bit of extra money and cautioned them to be back by supper time as the train would be leaving then.

He and Rebecca took all the children to the parlor car, where then spent the entire day playing games, reading books, playing blocks and generally being a great big, happy group of silly people.

Mama and Papa were happy and the children were completely delirious. Time spent like this was rare. Charlie and Rebecca did their best by the children every day and were very attentive parents, but hours upon hours of undivided attention was a rare and precious thing.

The only incident to mar the day was just before nap time when little boys tend to be the grumpiest. Buddy managed to bite Andy, which then resulted in the three-year-olds engaging in a fist fight and rolling half way across the car before Papa could get each one by the scruff and pull them apart.

Mama had to get into the fray and grab Buddy because Charlie had snagged him with his weak hand and the bigger boy was about to get loose. "Enough!" she commanded and the entire room went silent and still. Mama had spoken.

~

Monday, April 27, 1868

They arrived on schedule, had breakfast in the parlor car, and set out to Mr. Schwarz's establishment. Charlie had received a telegram from the shopkeeper when they arrived, saying that his wife would be pleased to escort Mrs. Redmond around Baltimore and he would make his carriage available to them as well. As they arrived promptly at ten as promised, he saw Mr. Schwarz and a tall graceful lady standing in front of the store waiting for them.

As they pulled up, Charlie turned to Rebecca. "Darling, you have had nothing but children to deal with for days. I thought you would enjoy a day of shopping and sightseeing with a woman of your own age and interests, so Mr. Schwarz's wife has offered to escort you around town today. Mr. Schwarz has also offered his carriage and his driver, John – you remember John?"

The idea of a day without the children and not having to watch the entire family eat disgusting things for lunch was very attractive. As she dismounted from the carriage they had taken from the train station, she smiled her best smile at the woman who had agreed to be her cohort for the day. "It is a pleasure to meet you, Mrs. Schwarz."

She smiled as broadly as Rebecca had. "The pleasure is mine, Mrs. Redmond. Please, call me Caroline. You have given me the opportunity for an unlimited shopping trip and lunch with a pleasant companion."

"I am Rebecca. You, ma'am, have bought me a reprieve from chasing five children, six if you count my oldest boy's valet, and him," she pointed at Charlie, "all day long! He is the biggest child I have. Not to mention the fact that it saves me from watching them eat slimy things from the ocean for lunch."

Caroline laughed. "My dear, you are in Baltimore. We all eat slimy things that come from the ocean and take great pride in it! However, I think I can find a tearoom that goes against the Baltimore traditions, just for you."

While the ladies chatted, the children, herded by John and Louis, had disembarked from the carriage. They were looking into the windows of Mr. Schwarz's shop, fascinated with the contents. John and Louis lined them up to be introduced to Mr. Schwarz and to hear what their father had to say. Freddy stood quietly behind them.

Just then, the driver arrived with Mr. Schwarz's town carriage. Caroline looked at Rebecca and beamed. "Shall we make our escape – quickly?"

She grinned back, nodded, and the two women waved to their spouses and climbed into the carriage, with Caroline giving John instructions on where to go first. As they drove off, Rebecca said, "I am so grateful to you."

"Oh, la. Do not be that grateful. Your husband is my husband's biggest client. My whole family would do much more for your family than just escort you around town for a day, dear."

Charlie stepped forward. "Mr. Schwarz, these are my children. Darby, Emily, Suzanne, and the twins, Buddy and Andy. Children, make your bows to Mr. Schwarz."

The children dutifully bowed or curtseyed to the host.

"Now, children, we will let you go in, but before you go, there are some rules. This is Mr. Schwarz's shop. You will be courteous at all times to him and to his staff. You will be careful; I do not want you to break things. Anyone under the age of thirteen may have their choice of three items. If they are small, you will be able to take them back to the train with you. If they are large, Mr. Schwarz will ship them to us at home, and they will arrive within a few days. Am I perfectly clear? Three items only."

He smiled at Mr. Schwarz, who opened the door to his shop. His staff was waiting inside, one for each child. The Toy Bazaar was open for one customer and one customer only today – Charlie Redmond and his family.

The general turned to John. "Please, you may select anything you feel will add to our classroom at home as well."

"Thank you, sir."

Charlie, John, Louis, and Freddy followed the family inside. The four of them stood in a line, watching the Redmond children as they explored the store. It was a wonderland for children, with more toys than even the Redmonds had ever imagined. Freddy looked around, his eyes as round as saucers, but made no movement toward any of the many things Mr. Schwarz had displayed. After a few minutes, Charlie noticed the boy's lack of movement. He stepped behind John and Louis, and laid a hand on the boy's shoulder.

"Freddy, how old are you?"

"I am twelve, sir. Just like Master Darby."

"Did I not say anyone under the age of thirteen should choose three things?"

"Yes, sir, but that is not for me. I am a servant."

"Freddy, you are a twelve year old boy. Go. Find your three items."

He blushed, a deep purplish blush. "Yes, sir. Thank you, sir!" He sprinted off, gravitating to a display of telescopes and books on astronomy.

He came back just a few minutes later, with a large astronomy book, a small telescope, and a huge stuffed bear that had been crafted in Germany. It was almost as big as he was.

Charlie looked at the items, smiling gently. "I think you need a larger telescope." He beckoned one of Schwarz's employees over. "Could you please get me the largest telescope you have for this young fellow?" The clerk took the small scope and scurried off, returning a moment later with a very large telescope indeed. "There. This will do for you, Freddy. But tell me, lad. Why the bear?"

"Well, General Charlie, I got no family, you know. And it gets kinda lonely at night sometimes. I just need a hug sometimes."

He looked at this boy who had been so hard working for so long and smiled. He reached out and wrapped his arms around him drawing him in close. "You can have a hug any time you need one, lad."

The boy was startled at first, then gave in and allowed himself to enjoy the embrace for a moment, even tentatively returning it. The general pulled back and smiled. "Now I must excuse myself for a few minutes."

With Rebecca's birthday coming soon, he had been looking for a proper gift for her. He had noticed a jewelry store across the street as they came in. He nodded to John and excused himself to see if the jeweler would be able to do anything for him.

He walked across the street and into a small but beautiful store. It was obviously the shop of a custom jeweler who took pride in his designs. A small man came out from the back room, wiping his hands on a chamois and smiling.

"Good morning, sir. How may I help you?"

Charlie smiled. "Mr. Nelson?" He had seen the name on the sign outside the door.

"Yes, sir. And you are?"

"My name is Charles Redmond." He dropped his card on the counter. "I am looking for a birthday gift for my wife. I could not help but notice the beautiful ruby pendant and earrings in your display there."

Mr. Nelson glanced at the card as he responded. "Why, thank you, sir. I am very proud of those pieces; I created them when I was awarded my title of master jeweler by the Jewelers Guild in London."

"It is worthy of the rank of master, sir. Would you consider selling it?"

The jeweler looked a little startled. The main ruby alone was a great deal of money. The whole set was worth a small fortune. "Well, yes, sir. But I have to warn you, it is very pricy."

"Price is no object. And if you need an endorsement, Mr. Schwarz across the street will vouch for me. So how much would you like?"

"Sir, the set is valued at ten thousand dollars!"

Charlie did not even blink, but pulled his checkbook from his breast pocket. He laid the checkbook on the counter and opened his fountain pen. "How shall I make it out?"

"Um, Adam Nelson, please, sir." The jeweler blinked several

times and then dove under the counter for a case lined with velvet to box up the gift.

Charlie made out the check and handed it to the jeweler. Mr. Nelson polished the necklace and earrings and reverentially placed them in the case. "Thank you, General Redmond. If there is anything else I can do for you, please do not hesitate to call on me."

"Thank you, Mr. Nelson." He slid the jewelry case into his inside pocket, waved at the man, and re-crossed the street to ride herd on his troopers.

The children selected items that were fairly predictable if you knew their personalities. Em chose a set of digging tools, including a small hand pick, brushes, a specialized trowel, and other tools, a book on geology and fossils, and a microscope.

Darby raided the sets of lead soldiers, selecting a revolutionary war period army of British soldiers and a comparable set of colonial troops, and a new world globe with elevations in full relief. Suzanne found a book on horse breeds, a set of beautifully formed model horses, and a book on modern farming.

The twins raided together. They found two hobby horses they could ride and be pushed around on instead of being stuffed into the rolling baby seats their mother had been putting them in. They found some wooden toy soldiers and each took one set. They also found a set of building blocks in all sorts of shapes and colors and sizes, and a wooden toy train set with real tracks, depots, and little towns, which they agreed to share.

John had found several books he wanted, a small chemistry set, and a stereoscope with over 100 scenes of the great sites of the world, including the pyramids in Egypt, the Coliseum and St. Peter's Basilica in Rome, Stonehenge, the Great Wall of China, and a number of other important sites.

By the time Charlie got back from the jewelers, Mr. Schwarz was starting to tally the Redmond family bill. Mrs. Redmond's oldest child threw in some more lead soldiers and additional terrain features for the playroom as well.

When Mr. Schwarz presented the final tab, it was not quite as bad as the check he had written for the jeweler. He asked that all of the items made it over to his train before the end of the day tomorrow, especially the stuffed bear.

By the time they got out of the Toy Bazaar it was past lunch time and everyone was hungry. He gathered his little troopers, loaded them into the large carriage they were using, and headed down toward the harbor. There were plenty of places down there where he could buy his horde more oysters, clams, crab cakes, and fried fish. Personally, he was starving.

Later that afternoon, they had managed to get the children back to the train, get their smaller items unloaded, and get the twins settled down for their afternoon naps. Charlie had arranged with their porter, George, to have dinner for the whole party served by the Pullman staff that evening. Tomorrow was another big day.

Rebecca came in shortly before dinner time, with the carriage driver following dutifully behind hauling a number of hat boxes and bags in for her. "Thank you, John. It was a lovely day." She handed him a ten dollar note.

Charlie was sitting in their private parlor reading a paper. He looked up over his half-moon glasses and smiled at his wife. "Hello, darling. Did you and Mrs. Schwarz have a good day?"

"Oh, yes. She introduced me to the most darling hat maker. Simply brilliant."

"I am so glad, love. You needed a break from the children."

"I see you survived them."

"It was a most enlightening and productive day."

"I am so glad. Did you clean out Mr. Schwarz's shop?"

"No, dear. I limited them to three things each."

"I did not ask if the children had cleaned him out; I asked if **you** had cleaned him out."

"No, I only got a few things, mostly things to help John in teaching."

"Well, I am amazed!"

"There is something I did that you need to know about. I let Freddy get some things too. He got a telescope, a book on astronomy, and a huge stuffed bear. He said he got the bear because, without family, he gets lonely sometimes and needed something to give him a hug at night. So I gave him a hug, and I will keep on giving him hugs when he needs them. He is a good boy."

Rebecca looked at her husband and smiled gently. "If he will accept them from me, I will too."

With that, they left to join the children in the parlor car for dinner.

~

Wednesday, April 29, 1868

The last day of their vacation dawned clear and bright. They had spent the previous day wandering around Baltimore, and particularly through the harbor region where the oldest buildings in the town were located.

They spent the afternoon exploring around the shipyards, which were busy building a number of boats and ships, especially the specialized sail boats called Skipjacks that were unique to the Chesapeake Bay oyster fishermen.

Charlie had used his connections to create a wonderful adventure for his troopers. He had arranged a custom tour of Fort McHenry with an officer who could tell the whole story of the War of 1812 and the writing of the 'Star Spangled Banner.' They piled into the big carriage and rode around the harbor to the entrance to the fort.

They ate lunch in the Officers' mess, an honor that the children found to be fantastic as they got to see how Papa was respected and treated by the other men present. Most of the children had been too young to remember his days in the service, and of course Darby and Suzanne had joined the family well after.

They sat quietly and respectfully as they watched man after man come up to salute him and shake their papa's hand and thank him for his service and final, heroic actions at Appomattox Station. By the end of lunch every one of them wore a proud smile and Darby was at risk of losing the buttons from his vest.

Rebecca, who generally tried to tolerate military surroundings with a polite smile, really did find herself smiling when she realized that their children were seeing for the first time a very important part of what made their father the man he was.

After lunch, they completed the tour. Around mid-afternoon they crossed back to the town side of the harbor on one of the steam powered harbor taxi boats, which was also an adventure for the children. They strolled around the harbor for a while, looking at the various ships and boats in the bustling port, then had dinner at one of the water-side taverns. The children enjoyed the seafood, Charlie ate grilled sea bass, and Rebecca did not watch them too closely and enjoyed her grilled lamb chops.

When they finally returned to the train, they were all tired. After the children were tucked in, Charlie sank into one of the chairs in their private car. “My God, I am tired. I will need to rest after this vacation, dear.”

“That is the way it is, I think, love. Did you have a good time?”

“I did. Did you?”

“Oh, yes, it was lovely. And the new furnishings for the house will be wonderful.”

CHAPTER 22

Thursday, April 30, 1868

The entire household was on hand to welcome the family home. They were waiting on the front portico as the family drove up. Rebecca was especially struck immediately by the brass plaque above the front door, 'Mountain View at Redmond Stables.' Beulah and Reg were grinning broadly.

After greetings and welcome homes were exchanged, it was time to unpack. Charlie stood in the front hall watching as the footmen and various staff began dragging trunks and boxes of every possible shape and size inside. It would take weeks to sort all of it.

Rebecca's New York shopping trip had ended up costing him a small fortune. It was her revenge, executed when she found out he was using the time away to have the house remodeled to include two new washrooms with plumbing, particularly with running hot water. She had determined it was time to redecorate the house too. He had started the war, but she was going to finish it and she would only accept an unconditional surrender.

As the children were sent off to their rooms to get cleaned up and start unpacking their things, Rebecca stripped off her hat and gloves, dropping them on top of her cloak. "So, show me these renovations."

"Yes, dear." He nodded and took her arm, leading her to the kitchen. When the door was opened, she actually gasped.

This was a room the likes of which she had never seen before. She imagined that the great restaurants in New York or Boston had kitchens like this, but not private homes.

The kitchen was a huge new room, with fire places at both ends, and a large, open double fireplace in the center. It looked out onto the back lawn, the stables and the pond, with windows and doors leading onto the back porch. From one door, a path led to the kitchen garden with its herbs and vegetables; the other toward the summer kitchen. The windows made the room bright and sunny, and there were large lanterns hung from the ceiling to provide light on dark days and at night.

On the inside wall, across from the big double fireplace, there were now not one but two of the largest iron wood burning stoves on the market. The Our Maine stoves were the height of modern technology, and to have two of them was amazing. On one side of each was a large wood bin; on the other was a marble topped work surface with storage underneath. But these were not the only cooking appliances in the room.

Charlie had asked Rex to obtain one of the special cook stations for the large, flattened pans he called woks and used to prepare his oriental specialties. This was installed on the back wall on the other side of one of the doors into the back hall, and had its own work surface and wood bin. At the other end of the room, also on the inside wall, were two large sinks with drain boards and work surfaces, and, of course, hot and cold running water. The old water boiler had been replaced with a larger reservoir next to the fireplace at the end of the room.

All three fireplaces had been fully refitted, with built in ovens with steel doors on either side of the fireplace, and mountings for spits and spiders that would make a small ship yard owner envious.

In the middle of the room, between the fireplaces at the ends of the room and the big central fire pit, there were long, wide tables with alternating chopping block wooden tops and marble tops to support preparations and serving activities. Beneath each table was additional storage, and running above them were racks that held utensils, pots, pans and lids on hooks. They were high enough to be out of the way, and low enough to be easily accessed.

In each front corner of the room, there were two of the largest ice boxes Rebecca had ever seen. Every other open wall surface was lined with shelves and glass fronted cabinets to store food stuffs, china, and serving pieces. There was even room in front of a window for a decent sized table and chairs for staff and visitors to stop and have a cuppa when they wanted. Of course, the children's table and chairs sat in front of one of the other windows.

Sarah stood in the middle of the room, smiling so broadly she was at risk of breaking her face in half. "Miss 'Becca, it is wonderful! I can cook for any size party you may want – and make fancier things than I ever could before. And the running water – oh, ma'am, it makes things so much easier. Mr. Hudnut even made it so the water from the sinks runs out to water the kitchen garden, so no more hauling water either way!"

"And you cain't believe it, but they built a covered walk out to the summer kitchen so we don' get wet in the rain and they did the same thing out there! They put in louvers to catch the breeze and keep it cool in the heat. There's even a porch with a roof and trestle tables for the help to eat at in the summer, a new brick grill and a stone lined pit for Big Ben's barbeque. It is so wonderful! I think I died and went to cook's heaven."

Rebecca walked out to the summer kitchen with Charlie trailing quietly behind. It was as well equipped, including running hot and cold water at the sinks, as the winter kitchen in the house. Her mouth fell a little open at the extensive renovations to the summer kitchen. It was literally a new building. She was speechless.

Once that unveiling was complete, they adjourned upstairs to see the new washrooms. She was pleased to find the one that would be shared among the children and guests was a nice, modest room with a little tub at one side with Charlie's precious running hot and cold taps. A small sink, also with running water sat along another wall next to two lovely little dressing tables, one at a regular height for grown ladies and right next to it a smaller identical one for little ladies. She could identify Duncan's work right away.

Now, their wash room was another thing all together. Their huge tub was now fully plumbed with the taps and it also had waterproof canvas curtains strung all the way round it. Charlie pulled them back to reveal that not only did water run into the tub, but there was also now a tall pipe with a special fitted head that provided a shower as well.

The sink was a huge double basin thing with a marble base and top, trimmed in gold leaf. It was a work of art. On the left side sat a small dresser where his toiletries were neatly set out. On the right an extremely ornate dressing table for her. It had a large mirror in the center with oak leaf scroll work at the top and two smaller mirrors off each side that were identical in design. To each side there were three large drawers and in the center a place for her brushes and hairpins and other accessories. It was ivory in color, also trimmed in gold leaf. It was truly spectacular and she could not go on being upset with him as she sat down on the stool. "Thank you, Charlie. It is beautiful."

"You are welcome, darling, but there is one more thing." He grinned and moved to a corner where a small room had been added; she had assumed it was a linen closet. He pulled open the door. "No more chamber pots or outhouse trips for us."

"You did not!" She was on her feet looking at the new water closet. "How is that possible?"

"It helps that we know a clever Chinaman who happens to know about the technology they have in England. He helped acquire all the hardware. They are rare, but they do exist."

She wrapped her arms around his neck and kissed him thoroughly. "Thank you. You do know the children will want to use this?"

"That will be up to you, my dear. I am looking into having one put in downstairs, but the remodel on that will take some extra design work. Not to mention the chances of coming across the proper hardware again anytime soon is negligible. Now the only thing you must remember and we have to make sure to teach the children, you need to turn the cold water on first and then slowly begin adding the hot. There is no regulator for the temperature. It comes from a tank in the attic through a copper pipe coiled around a chimney stack. It is always very hot."

She nodded, making a mental note to make sure the children were always supervised in their father's new playgrounds. She noticed in the corner of the room, well placed between two windows on each side, her husband had treated himself to a bit of an upgrade as well. She walked over and took a seat in the new barber's chair, running her hand over the rich red leather. "Very nice."

He smiled a bit sheepishly and shrugged. "Lying back for a shave is always more comfortable than sitting upright, especially for me."

"Darling, you do not have to explain yourself to me. You have made it very clear you intend to enjoy your life and I am not going to try and stop you. You have more than earned the right to live any way you desire."

He moved to the chair and pulled the handle that made it recline, taking Rebecca with it. He leaned over and kissed her. She wrapped her arms around him, happily accepting his affection.

She nipped at his earlobe as she whispered, "We may have found another use for your chair, General."

He was contemplating what she might be thinking when there was a knock on the door. "Gen'l Charlie, sir," Reg called through the door. "Colonel Polk, Mr. Jackson and Mr. Cooper are downstairs."

He helped her from the chair and they immediately went to the door. "I had expected to be home for a couple of days before people started calling." He was truly puzzled. "There must be something wrong."

At the top of the stairs, the pair waved the men up and into his office. Reg excused himself to go get a coffee tray for the unexpected visitors.

"Well, firstly, welcome home." Richard greeted them, shaking Charlie's hand and giving Rebecca a kiss on the cheek.

"We are damn glad you are back!" Cooper was far more enthusiastic with his handshake.

"Aye, Charlie boy." Jocko kissed Rebecca's cheek and looked to his old friend. "We are glad you're back. Culpeper needs you."

"What has happened?" Charlie lit a cigar and looked at each man.

"Horace Frazier died ten days ago."

"What!?" Rebecca immediately turned to her husband. "I have to go to Missy."

"Of course, darling. You go see to her while the gentlemen fill me in."

She was gone in a flash and the men settled into chairs to tell him everything that had happened in the last week and a half.

Richard began, "Horace had a massive heart attack. He was dead before he hit the floor."

"Oh, dear God." Charlie shook his head. "Is Missy all right?"

Cooper nodded. "She is fine. Horace had a heart condition for years. The problem we now have with his unexpected passing is that since he had just been reelected last month in the municipal election, there is a special election scheduled and only one person running for mayor."

"Harold Kirtley," Jocko spat.

"Horace beat him by a wide margin last month," Edward continued. "But now…"

"Now Kirtley is going to be elected mayor." Charlie sighed.

"Yes. Unless we find someone to run against him." Richard gave him a look his old commander knew well.

He straightened immediately. "Oh, no! No way."

Jocko shook his head. "You cannot leave the town to the likes of that man. You know he rode with Raeburn."

"What about you, Edward?"

"No, I cannot. I do not have time to run my store and the town. You are the only reasonable option."

He buried his face in his hands. "Oh, God."

~

Rebecca had no clue what to say to someone she actually cared about. The platitudes required to leave her lips were for Margaret Williams and had been a very bitter pill to swallow. In this case, she truly respected Horace and considered Missy a dear friend. This was a truly difficult call to make, but as a friend, she had to do so.

She pulled her trap up in front of the Frazier home and tied Shannon to the hitching rail there. She walked hesitantly to the door, still at a loss as to what to say. Maribel, their housekeeper, let her in and quietly pointed to what Rebecca knew had been Horace's den.

Missy was standing in the middle of the room, turning round slowly, staring with a look of mixed bewilderment and horror at the piles of papers stacked and crammed onto and into every surface and nook. She saw the younger woman standing there and beckoned her friend to come in. "Oh, there you are, dear. I rather expected you would show up as soon as you heard."

"Of course I did, Missy. I came as soon as I could. We only arrived home this morning. How are you holding up?"

"Oh, I am doing as well as can be expected. Horace had a heart condition for years. He could have gone at any time. I am just grateful I was with him for as long as I was."

"I had no idea." She had moved to Missy's side and slid her arm around her friend's shoulders.

"Oh, no. No one did. We felt it was better to just go along, day by day until the inevitable happened. The children are grown and off on their own, and the finances are in as decent an order as they can be; I am taken care of that way."

She looked around the room again. "But one of the things Horace chose to let go by the boards was filing his papers – obviously. He thought spending time together was more important. Now I am left with this. What the HELL am I supposed to do with all this, Rebecca? Most of this are papers and ledgers the town should have."

Rebecca looked from her friend to the room and its piles of papers to her friend again. This was not the reception that she had expected. There was no wailing or sobbing. Indeed, Missy was very matter of fact about Horace's passing and seemed to be grateful for the time she did get with her husband.

The challenge was a pragmatic one; how to transition the administration of the town from her house to wherever it should go. Looking at the piles of paper, and knowing that Horace's office at the courthouse was no better, the task seemed insurmountable, even for someone with the organizational skills that both Missy and Rebecca had.

"And then there is the matter of what is in the attic. You think this is a mess? Wait until I get the boxes and boxes of stuff out of there. And then there is the question of to whom it will go? That awful man, Harold Kirtley, is running in the special election. He will be the only candidate for mayor, and I would rather burn all of this stuff than hand it over to him. Hell, I would burn the house with it if it meant I could keep him from being mayor."

"The first thing we need to do is just box it up and get it out of here. I am sure Richard will find someone or some way to handle it. I know a couple of boys who can come and pack it up for you. My boy Darby will be a godsend for this." She thought her son and his delivery boys would be more than happy to do the work, though she would have to warn him he could NOT stop and read all of this. It was not the time for him to learn how the town government worked; it was time to get the papers out of Mrs. Frazier's house.

"Oh, the paper is not the worst problem. We have to find someone to run the town. Harold Kirtley is, both Horace and I agreed, the worst possible option for someone to take Culpeper into the next decade. The only person I know who can fix **this** problem is you."

"Me? What do you mean me? Women cannot even vote, let alone be mayor, you know that."

"Who do you think has been the de facto mayor of this town for the last two years, you silly girl? But that is not what I meant. You need to get Charlie to run. This town needs him. Horace and I were in absolute agreement about that, and the only person who can get him to run is you."

At the same time that Missy was trying to convince Rebecca to get Charlie to run for mayor, he was sitting in his office, surrounded by Edward Cooper, Jocko Jackson and Richard Polk, all trying to convince him of the same thing.

"No, no, no, and no! How many times do I have to say it to you, fellows?

"Charlie boy, you do not have a choice. It is you or Kirtley, and if Kirtley gets into office, Esther and I are going to move. Where, I don't know, but my family will not stay, not in a Culpeper run by that pig."

"Jocko, not six months ago, half of this town wanted to hang me."

"And the other half did not."

Edward joined in. "And even those who thought you killed Raeburn do **not** want Kirtley as mayor. Even old Armistead, who was part of Raeburn's crowd, wants you as mayor."

Richard added, "And the Freedman's Bureau already thinks things are going to get hot around here – they have given me 100 more men from the 18th to guard the courthouse and ride the district circuits. We all need you."

"Oh, my God, men. All right. I will think on it. And I will talk with Rebecca. But right now, I can tell you, I think the answer is still going to be no."

Edward dropped an envelope on Charlie's desk. "Please do."

Missy had taken Rebecca into the parlor and asked Maribel to bring them a pot of tea. The two women talked for quite a while. Well, actually, Missy talked and Rebecca listened. She came to realize that Missy had loved her crotchety old husband as much as she loved hers, and how hard it had been for her to live with the idea that he could die at any time. Hard and yet a blessing that he had survived with his bad heart for so many years after he had been diagnosed and told he could drop dead at any moment.

Missy finally came back to the subject of the mayor's job. Rebecca smiled and suggested, "Why, I think that you should come out to the house tomorrow for lunch. You can make your argument directly to him. I think that will be best."

The older woman smiled. "And it would give you an opportunity to show off your new kitchens and wash rooms. The whole town knows about what was going on out at your house while you were on holiday, dear. I would love to see it, and see if I can twist Charlie's arm."

"Then it is settled. Shall we say around eleven? Is there anyone else you would like to see?"

"No, no. Just a small, informal visit. I know what I am supposed to be doing as the mourning widow, and I do not want to offend the more appropriate members of the community, but we do have to keep going, do we not?"

So with hugs and promises for the morrow, Rebecca took herself back home, intent on having a serious conversation with

Charlie. She passed Richard, Edward and Jocko on the way home. She smiled and waved; they all looked like someone had just killed their best foxhound.

When she arrived home she found Charlie sitting at their desk, his forehead resting on his hands.

"Hello, Mr. Mayor."

He looked up over his glasses with flashing eyes. "Oh, do not tell me they have recruited you to this little scheme?"

She took her seat across from him and sighed. "No, darling, the gentlemen had nothing to do with it. Missy on the other hand…" She gestured somewhat aimlessly. "I know you do not like it, but they are right. The town needs you to do this. If Kirtley becomes mayor we will be no better off than we were before the war."

"You do remember last October?"

She nodded, but she refused to respond verbally to such an obviously rhetorical question.

"Rebecca, do you want me to be mayor?"

"No," she answered honestly as she shook her head. "But I did not want you to be a solider either and we survived that, so I suspect we will survive this as well. Think of it, love, if Kirtley is elected, everything that you have worked for, hell, everything everyone has worked for, will be at risk. He will do everything in his power to make you and the rest of the town miserable."

"Jocko said he and Esther would leave town if he gets in." He sighed, tossing his glasses down on a set of papers that Edward had left with him.

"Seems like that would be tipping the scales in your decision making process."

He nodded. He hated the thought of them leaving, not only because they had worked so hard to create a successful business, but because he and Jocko had been together for so long he would feel like another piece of him would be missing.

"Missy wants you to do it. She threatened to burn down her house to keep Harold from laying hands on Horace's papers. She is coming out here tomorrow, in her words, not mine, "to twist Charlie's arm."

"I do not feel like I have a choice." He tapped the papers. "Richard and Edward took it upon themselves to fill out the registration paperwork. All I have to do is sign it."

"There is another potential benefit." She looked thoughtful.

"Yes?" He would take anything that looked like a silver lining in this situation.

"It will probably put the brakes on whatever it is that General Grant is plotting in your direction. Surely, he would rather have you at the local level where you have some influence in Richmond as Virginia prepares to be reinstated to the Union."

"That," he nodded and shook a finger, "has actual merit, darling. I had not considered that. Thank you. I would much rather deal with the scoundrels in Richmond than the scoundrels in Washington."

She smiled and nodded. "You are welcome. Now I will leave you to think while I go see how the unpacking is going."

They both rose and met half way across the desk for a peck of a kiss before she departed. He looked down, sighed, and signed his name.

Jocko, Cooper, and Richard returned to the bar when they got back from seeing Charlie. A number of the businessmen in

Culpeper had seen them returning, and within five minutes, the tavern was filled with men.

There were the ones that were expected, including Duncan, Hudnut, Stevenson, Halliburton, and Johnstone. But there were also some who were not so predictable, as they had been part of the crowd that ran with Raeburn. Henry Armistead and James Granville were two of the first men to show up, eager to find out if General Redmond had been willing to run for mayor. They, more than many, knew what kind of a man Harold Kirtley was, and although they may have agreed with him about southern traditions, as businessmen, they knew that Charlie was a far better choice for mayor than Kirtley was.

When it appeared that the crowd was not going to grow any larger, Esther helped Jocko serve all of the men with coffee, as he was sure it was not a time or a subject where the bar should be open. He cleared his throat to get everyone's attention.

"Well, gentlemen. We have explained the situation to him. He is not thrilled at the idea, but I suspect that part of it is that he is not sure that the town will support him. After all, many of you wanted him hung just six months ago."

There was some mumbling, and a number of men looked at their boots, still ashamed of their response to Raeburn's killing and their willingness to jump to conclusions, not to mention their willingness to act as a mob.

Jocko gave them a few minutes to consider their own actions and then spoke again. "I believe that if we can show the general that we truly do support him, that we want him to lead our town into the future, he will accede to running for mayor."

Armistead spoke up. "So what do you think we need to do?"

A soft voice spoke from the back of the room. Standing in the shadows, where they had quietly slipped in after the white men had settled, were several of the black businessmen from

Sweetwater. Miles Tolliver, the printer who served both blacks and whites in the community, spoke. "If we could put something in our windows, nothing blatant, but something that would show our support without having to say anything, it might help. A small poster or something?"

Henry Armistead, like all of the other men in the room, had turned to stare at the Negro man. "What are you doing here? What do you care who wins the election? You cannot even vote."

"Mr. Armistead, we know how hard things will be on our people if Mr. Kirtley is elected. General Redmond has been good to us. He has opened his bank to support us; he has helped clean up the colored towns – at least as much as he can. He has created jobs for a lot of people, both whites and coloreds. We do not think Mr. Kirtley will do anything but make things harder – for all of us. So we want to help." He smiled, rather hesitantly. "You know as well as I do, we black men will be able to vote in the next election. Congress will not reinstate Virginia in the Union until we have the vote."

Armistead looked uncomfortable at the idea of black men getting the vote, but he was enough of a pragmatist to know Tolliver was right. He turned to the white men in the room, pointedly turning his back on the printer. "What do you gentlemen suggest?"

Richard spoke up. "Well, there is one symbol that no one else in this town is associated with--General Redmond's star. I suppose if we do something…" He trailed off, at a little bit of a loss.

Frank Halliburton picked up on the idea. "I know that sometimes a simple image can convey a lot of information. Think about what a dollar sign can say? Or Jocko's picture of a beer with a frothy top outside. People recognize symbols quickly. Why not simply make an image of the general's star and put it in our windows? It would tell him we support him, without being obvious."

Richard and Jocko, as the two men in the room who best knew Charlie, thought for a moment, and then Jocko started nodding. "Yes, yes, that might do it. A simple image that could be displayed to let him know we are behind him. Yes, I think that will do it."

Richard nodded his agreement, then looked to Tolliver, who was smiling eagerly. "Can you, will you, do it for us? Make a small poster that can be put in the window?"

The young Negro man looked to his fellow black businessmen, who were all nodding agreement. "Yes, Colonel Polk. We can make a nice little poster; say about six by six, with a single large gold star in the middle. To show we are serious, the black business community will pay for the materials and labor to make them, but you have to figure out a way to distribute them."

Richard smiled and looked at Duncan, who nodded. Between Jeremiah and Darby, distribution was not going to be a problem. He did not realize it, but he had also just created the opportunity for Darby to get his delivery service started.

Friday, May 1, 1868

Missy was delighted when Charlie immediately showed her the properly executed documents that would put him on the special election ballot for mayor against Harold Kirtley. She wrapped her arms around his neck and gave him a kiss on the cheek.

He was a bit startled, but the amused look on his wife's face helped him relax and accept the affection and appreciation the older woman was showing. With the business aspect of the luncheon out of the way, the three of them sat down to one of Sarah's amazing meals.

"Thank you again, Charlie." Missy shook her head as she patted his hand. "I was afraid I was going to have to come out here and beg you."

He shook his head and smiled at her gently. "No, my dear. After Rebecca and I talked, I realized that I am the only person who can offer Harold a bit of a challenge. Now that does not mean I will win the election…"

"You will win." She nodded knowingly. "I have yet to meet one person who wants Kirtley."

"I understand that." He looked at the ladies. "However, you must both realize there is always the chance I will lose. What people say and what they do at the ballot box can be two entirely different things. But I will try."

Rebecca patted his hand as well. "That is all we are asking, darling."

He looked to their guest. "Is there anything you need? Anything at all?"

"No, I am fine. I do appreciate your concern though."

"If anything arises, will you let us know?" Rebecca poured another cup of tea for all of them. "You know that Charlie and I will always be available to you."

"Of course I do, dear. Horace knew that too." She turned to the general and took his hand. "We were always very grateful you chose to come back here. Horace always said it was good to know there was another honest, honorable gentleman to step up if the community needed it. He knew you would do it."

Sunday, May 3, 1868

After church services that Sunday, a number of people wanted to welcome the Redmonds back home and to hear about their trip. Charlie and Rebecca were rather mobbed by well wishers waiting for them in the churchyard. People jostling and milling around gave Richard the perfect opportunity to pull Darby aside and explain the need for a distribution service.

Darby just grinned. "Uncle Richard, you have given me a great idea. I will come by tomorrow and talk about the best way to get this done. I assume you would prefer I not tell Papa about your little plan?"

"Smart lad. If you tell him about it, it would spoil the impact, would it not?"

"Absolutely. I think Papa will make a great mayor. With him in office, it will be good for business. Mr. Kirtley would be a disaster. Let me go talk to some of my friends."

Richard watched as Darby slid off into the crowd. A minute later, he noticed the boy with Jeremiah. The two of them quickly rounded up a small group of youths who retreated to a tree as far away from Charlie as they could get, and circled around Darby.

Monday, May 4, 1868

Charlie's first stop Monday morning was the courthouse to file the paperwork. The clerk did not even blink as he processed the documents and gave him an official receipt.

"Good luck, General Redmond."

"Thank you." He nodded. "I think."

Then he was off to the bank. He gestured and Frank and Eloise followed him dutifully to the office. Once he pulled his coat off, he got straight to the point. "I suppose by now you have heard about Horace?"

They both nodded.

"I am not sure exactly how it happened, but within an hour of my return Thursday, I was shanghaied into running for mayor."

They both smiled. He looked disgusted.

"To that end, I have decided that I need to resign from my position as president of the bank. I cannot be seen as having any conflicts of interest. So, Frank, my man, you are now the Vice President and Chief Executive Officer of the bank. If by some miracle I am saved the aggravation of actually winning this election, I will resume my position as president and of course I will retain my seat on the Board."

He looked to his secretary. "And please, please, find a replacement for yourself here, because if I win this ridiculous thing, I will need your help. I will be taking you away from all this and burying you under a ton of misplaced and misfiled government documents that I am fairly certain go back through Culpeper's entire history."

They both agreed with him and his plans as he outwardly groused about the current state of affairs, but they could also see that bit of a charge in the way he was standing and presenting the situation to them. General Redmond might seem perturbed on the outside, but inside he was preparing just like he always did and would face this challenge head on, because he did not know how to do anything else.

Darby waited a few minutes for his father to be well on the way to town before he, too, set out. He dropped Tucker behind Duncan's shop and headed to Uncle Richard's office, staying in the alleys to avoid being seen by his father.

Richard looked up as he slid in the door. "Good morning."

"Good morning, Uncle Richard. I have a solution for your distribution problem. Since we only want to give stars to people who want them, you tell me or Jeremiah who wants one. We will send one of our runners over to Mr. Tolliver's print shop to pick up just the stars that are needed. That way, we can keep a list of people who ask for stars at the print shop. Our guys will deliver the stars to whoever you tell us to. That way, we have two lists, which I can compare so I know if we missed anyone or if someone got a star that you or Mr. Jocko did not authorize."

"Actually, Darby, I think you should get your direction from Mr. Cooper or Jocko. They see more people than I do."

"We can do that."

"Why do you want two lists that you can compare?"

"Oh, well, I will be giving the runners a penny for each star they deliver, so I want to be able to run a control check on them."

"Hummm… a penny apiece. I think I can do that."

"Oh, you do not have to, Uncle Richard. Consider it my contribution to Papa's campaign."

When he entered the bar, Jocko was smiling like the cat that ate the canary.

"I hope you are happy," Charlie groused as he took a seat. "I am now the biggest toad in the puddle."

"Aye, we heard you filed your paperwork this morning."

Charlie pulled his watch from his pocket and glowered across the bar. "I was there only thirty minutes ago." He snapped it shut and put it back. "Telegraph system could learn a thing or two from this town. May I please have a cup of coffee?"

"Of course. I will even buy this one for you."

"How generous of you, but no. Now that I have been thrust

into the political arena I cannot be accepting anything from anyone. Not even a cup of coffee." He tossed a nickel on the bar. His voice softened with his next words, "But thank you for the offer."

Jocko poured the coffee and placed it in front of his friend. "Thank you for doing what needs to be done."

The general nodded. "You are welcome. I suppose by now everyone in town knows."

At that moment the door burst open and a horde of gentlemen practically tripped all over themselves to get inside to congratulate and thank him.

~

"Yes, it is official. I have lost my mind." He lifted her hand to his and kissed her fingers as they sat in the gazebo watching the sun set. "I cannot believe I have been talked into this."

"Darling," she gave his hand a gentle squeeze. "You did not 'get talked' into anything. You did it because you knew it needed to happen and you always do what is right and needs to be done. Believe it or not, it is one of the many things I love about you."

He smiled and leaned in for a tender kiss, whispering against her lips at the end. "Would you care to share something else you love about me?"

She drew back, a playful smile on her face, as she considered his question. She leaned forward and crooked her finger, inviting him closer. As he leaned in she whispered in his ear.

As he listened to her, he felt all the blood in his body rush south. His breathing grew ragged and harsh. His mouth went dry as the Sahara. Then he actually began to shake a little as she alternated between whispering her erotic and borderline obscene suggestions and blowing in his ear, while her fingers traced a path between his thigh and groin on the inside of his leg.

She stood and smiled down sweetly. “Is that what you meant?”

His eyes wide, he nodded, planning to get up and sweep her into the house and up the stairs to their room as quickly as humanly possible. He stood, his eyes flashing with need and desire as he moved toward her, a lecherous grin alighting his lips.

He was practically panting when she placed a hand in the center of his chest. “Maybe later. I have to go check the horses.”

He whimpered.

She moved closer and caressed his cheek. “Maybe next time you will reconsider before saying ‘no’ when your wife is desirous for your touch, General.”

With that she turned and headed for the barn and stables, leaving her shaking husband with a seriously inflamed libido.

He contemplated a dip in the pond, but headed for his first cold shower in the new wash room instead.

CHAPTER 23

Tuesday, May 5, 1868

Charlie walked slowly down the street. He had been to the bank to cash a check. He then went over to Cooper's to place an order for kitchen supplies such as salt, sugar, and flour. Stopping by Duncan's, he discovered the carpenter up to his eyeballs in workmen needing direction and customers wanting attention. The general decided not to wait. As he turned to go to Jocko's to meet Rebecca for lunch he noticed in the corner of the window of Duncan's shop a poster of a single, five pointed gold star.

Thinking on it, he realized that he had seen the same thing in several other windows, and as he made his way to Jocko's, he paid special attention. As he walked, he counted. A majority of businesses in town had the same poster in the window, even the new dressmaker, Miss Hunter, who had not officially opened her doors yet, much to Rebecca's chagrin.

When he arrived at Jocko's, he could see his lovely wife

awaiting him at their favorite table, but he also knew his old batman would have the answers he sought because, there in his window, was the same symbol.

When he entered, he dropped his hat and cane with his wife, giving her a brief greeting, a peck on the cheek and begging her pardon as he went to the bar. He leaned over and crooked his finger at his old friend.

"Yes, Charlie-boy, what can I be doing for ya?"

"Tell me about the star, Jocko," he whispered, thinking he had an idea, but wanting confirmation.

The Irishman failed any attempt at denial. "All right, it is our own little code."

"For?"

"What do you think it means, you hard headed bastard? How many people around here have stars on their shoulders?"

"Oh, my God!" The general groaned and returned to the table where his wife sat looking puzzled. He simply shook his head.

"Charlie?" She ducked her head, searching his face as she waited for an answer.

He tossed his hands up in frustration, letting them fall to his thighs with a slap. "The entire town has lost its collective mind."

She sighed, lightly scratching her brow in frustration at his ability to be obtuse. "I am sorry, I do not understand."

Taking a deep breath he shook his head apologetically. "No, I am sorry darling. However, I have a feeling you had better be prepared to be married to the mayor."

She smiled and relaxed back in her chair. "Already there, my dear. I have no doubt about the fact that you will be elected. I suspect by a landslide. And in other news, I have the first appointment with the new seamstress next week."

He could only laugh. "It is so good to see you have your priorities straight."

"Obviously, I will need a new dress for your swearing in."

"Not one of the six or seven you bought on the trip will do?"

"No."

"Why not?"

"Because they will all have been seen by then."

"Silly me."

"Indeed, General Redmond, I do not know what you were thinking."

Harold Kirtley stomped into Mrs. Allen's common room looking for Henry Armistead and James Granville. He found the two of them sitting quietly in a corner having an after work drink before they headed home for supper.

"Good. I found both of you. What the hell do you think you are doing putting those damned stars in your shop windows? I thought you were loyal?"

The men looked at one another rather sheepishly. They knew that as soon as they put the posters in their windows, this confrontation would inevitably happen. It just happened sooner than either of them was ready for.

Granville cleared his throat. "Well, you see, Harold, um, well, the mayor has to support Culpeper businesses, and keep things organized, and, well, er, you are not exactly known for being particularly organized."

Armistead added, "And you certainly are not a businessman, so…"

They both petered out, and sat there, heads bowed in front of the glaring Kirtley. "So you two decided that your wallets were more important than our traditions?" he ranted. "Well, see if you get any more of my business!"

He stomped back out of the small building. As he did, he passed a boy making a delivery to Mrs. Allen. He did not notice it when she placed her star in the window.

The blacksmith looked at his friend. “Well, losing Kirtley’s business is not going to be any strain on my income. He even shoes his own horses, since he cannot afford to have me do it.”

Armistead laughed. “Nor is it any strain on mine. And can you imagine him representing Culpeper in having Virginia reinstated in the Union? My God, the man would sooner try to secede again.”

Ro and Allison had finished their work for the day. The dogs had been bedded down for the night and their feed for the next morning had been prepared. Supper had been eaten, the kitchen cleaned up and the main fire properly stoked and backlogged to burn through the night.

Ro had washed up from her rather sweaty work day and changed into a night shirt that did not smell of wet canine or anything else associated with their dogs. Allison had changed into a lovely blue night gown. Both were in robes and slippers, having a last cup of tea before they headed for bed.

Ro looked at her companion. “Do you know what that idiot Kirtley has promised if he is elected mayor? He has promised to make Irish wolfhounds illegal in Culpeper County because they are so dangerous. If he has his way, he will have all of our dogs put down.”

“He cannot do that, can he?” Allison was stunned.

“If he gets elected, yes, he can.”

“So we need to do something to help make sure he does not get elected.”

"You know, Mr. Cooper is giving posters with stars on them to people who support General Charlie. We should make sure to get one."

"Really? Well, then, tomorrow, I will go into town, get a stack of stars, and go and call on everyone who has bought a dog from us!"

"Everyone except the Redmonds." Ro laughed. "It is supposed to be a clandestine movement! But that is one of the things I love about you, my dear. You will always jump into the fray!"

Allison smiled at her partner. "Well, dear, tomorrow I will jump into the fray for General Charlie. Tonight, I would prefer to jump into bed with you."

Ro gave her lover a lewd leer, swallowed the last of her tea, and held out her hand. "That is an invitation I cannot turn down."

~

Wednesday, May 6, 1868

The next morning, Allison hurried through her morning chores. She dressed carefully in a dove gray walking skirt and matching jacket, white shirtwaist, and straw hat. The only color in her ensemble was a yellow ribbon around her neck and a sunflower attached to her hat. While she dressed, Ro groomed their horse until its coat shone and hitched it to Allison's basket cart. She was waiting at Mr. Cooper's door when he came downstairs and opened his shop.

"Good morning, Mr. Cooper."

"Good morning, Miss Simms. What can I do for you today?"

"I understand that people who are supporting General Redmond for mayor are showing gold stars in their windows, as you have, sir. I was wondering if I could get some so that those people who have purchased Irish wolfhounds and do not want to have them declared dangerous and put down can display their support for the general."

"Why, yes, Miss Simms, of course. How many do you need?"

"Well, Mr. Cooper, I know I need at least forty, but I would like to have fifty. I would rather have them and not need them, than need them but not have them."

"Fifty?" The shopkeeper asked incredulously.

"Well, yes, sir. We have sold forty dogs in the past year or so, and then there are my friends who have met our other dogs and know what gentle creatures they are."

"Oh, well, of course." He reached under the counter and pulled out a stack of cards. He counted out fifty for her, which left him a half dozen. "If you do not use them all, please bring them back. Otherwise, I will need to send for more cards."

She grinned at him. "If I were you, sir, I would send for more."

Her first stop was to see Charlotte. The two of them had become close after Allison had started using her middle name and living with Ro. Some of her old friends from the more 'appropriate' members of the community had distanced themselves from her when she had chosen to associate with an Irish immigrant, even though Ro had decided to join her in attending the Episcopalian church rather than the Catholic church of her childhood.

Charlotte was surprised to see her on her doorstep so early in the morning. "My goodness, what can I do for you today?"

"Have you heard what Mr. Kirtley wants to do to our dogs if he is elected mayor? I am going to all of my friends and Ro's clients to convince them to support General Charlie for mayor."

"I do not know what I can do. I certainly cannot vote."

"Neither can I, but if we can convince the men of this town that the general is the best choice, then we will have done our part. And if we can show General Charlie that we support him, so much the better."

"So what would you have me do?"

"Put one of these cards in your front window. That is all I am asking."

"Of course I support Cousin Charlie. I would be glad to do so."

"Thank you, Charlotte. I must be going, as I have a number of calls to make today."

She called on every single person who had purchased a dog from Ro, and on those of her friends who had stayed close after she had moved. By the end of the day, she had one and only one star left.

"Mr. Cooper?" She called as she entered his store shortly before sundown. "I brought you back what I have left. I hope you sent for more, as I only have one." She thought for a moment. "Oh, no, I do not have any left. I need this one for **my** house!"

Cooper laughed. "You certainly cannot ask someone to do something you would not do yourself. Thank you, Miss Simms, for your support."

"Thank you, Mr. Cooper. Good evening."

She returned home, where Ro had supper waiting for her. "Long day, dear?"

"Very long. Very productive. Thank you for supper, sweetheart."

Allison set her card in the front window of their house. "There. We cannot ask others to do this unless we do it ourselves."

"Of course. General Charlie supported me and then us in getting started. We can do no less."

"My thought exactly."

~

Sunday, May 17, 1868

Over the past ten days, Charlie had been busy putting his affairs in order, handing off his activities at the bank to Frank, and communicating back and forth with Jerome to make sure none of his investments could be construed as a conflict of interest, or simply turning over those investments to Jerome to manage without his involvement.

The family drove into church that morning with the last of the paperwork for Jerome packed in a portfolio that Charlie intended to hand over to George Randall, the station master, for courier shipment to Washington on the train the following day.

As the service ended and Charlie and the family walked out into the churchyard, Harold Kirtley was standing in the middle of the path from the door to the road.

"Redmond! Say, Redmond!"

"Yes, Mr. Kirtley? How may I help you?"

"You are running for mayor. I am running for mayor. I think the people of this town ought to know what they are getting if they elect you. So I challenge you to a debate."

"A debate, uh? When and where, sir? I will meet you whenever you want."

"Shall we say the steps of the courthouse two Saturdays from now?"

"Saturday, May 30th? What time, sir?

Kirtley was grabbing for straws. He had not expected him to agree to the debate. "Um, shall we say 4:00? As it is a Saturday, that way most people will be done with their work for the day and be able to attend."

"4:00 it is, sir. I will see you then."

Kirtley nodded brusquely, then turned on his heel and strode away.

Richard, Edward Cooper, and Edgar all clustered around Charlie. Richard spoke first. "A debate? My God, Charlie, what are you going to say?"

He looked at his friends and supporters and spoke very calmly. "At the moment, I have no idea, but within two weeks, I suppose I will have to figure it out. I also suppose it will depend quite a bit on what Mr. Kirtley has to say."

On the way home, he stopped at the train station and dropped off the portfolio for Jerome. Yesterday's newspapers had arrived on the 10:00 train, and he picked one up. The headline read, "Johnson Acquitted by 1 Vote."

On the way home, he sat there shaking his head over the report in the paper.

Rebecca looked confused. "I thought he was acquitted in May?"

"He was, but they did not drop the charges, and brought it up again in the Senate. It looks like he just squeaked by. Stanton's supporters have a death grip on the members of the House of Representatives, but it looks like he is not quite as well supported in the Senate."

"One vote certainly does not make an outstanding lead for the more moderate senators."

"No. And it means that Grant will win the presidency in the next election."

"Then you need to win this election, dear. I think it is the only thing that will keep Grant from calling you to Washington."

His shoulders slumped. "I am afraid you are right. You know I do **not** want Kirtley to run this town into the ground. But…" He looked rueful. "I suppose it is the best of a bad set of choices."

Saturday, May 30, 1868

At 4:00, Richard mounted the steps of the courthouse. Two podiums had been set, one on each side of the landing at the top of the steps. Charlie sat behind the right hand podium; Kirtley behind the one on the left. Richard stood halfway between them.

Richard began the proceedings. "Thirty three days ago, our beloved mayor, Horace Frazier, passed away suddenly. We announced the need for a special election on the 29th of April. Yesterday, the thirty day period for individuals who wished to run for the office to file their submission closed. There are two declared candidates for the office, Mr. Harold Kirtley and General Charles Redmond. Today, these gentlemen come to you to present their positions and to debate the issues."

"Each candidate will have up to ten minutes to present his opening statement. At that time, they will be allowed to exchange questions, or to take questions from me as moderator or from you as members of the community. The debate will end in one hour."

"Mr. Kirtley will be the first to present, as he was the first to submit his application as a candidate. Mr. Kirtley?"

Harold stepped to the podium. He looked out over the crowd. It had driven him to distraction to see all the gold stars that had been displayed all over town – in shops and in private homes. Surely there were still good southern men here in Culpeper who would want to see things run the way they should be. Today would be critical in finding out if there were still true southerners in this, his home town.

"Good afternoon. As you know, I am Harold Kirtley. I grew up with most of you, went to school with you, fought for our southern beliefs and hopes with many of you. I am one of you.

Today, I ask you to remember that as you consider and select the man who will lead this community into the coming days, weeks, months and years of change, when the Northern unionists try to force their beliefs on us."

"As your mayor, I will do whatever must be done to protect our rights, to preserve our traditions, to keep our people safe and secure. If you elect me as your mayor, I will see to it that jobs are reserved for white southerners, that the coloreds and the Yankees and the foreigners do not take jobs away from good southern men. If you elect me as your mayor, I will see to it that these dangerous dogs that have started spreading across our county will be destroyed and that no more of these vicious animals are allowed in Culpeper County. If you elect me as your mayor, I will work to ensure that businesses that come to Culpeper are owned by good southern men, and that the carpetbaggers who are taking over our community," he stared pointedly at Richard, "no longer have power over us."

"If you elect me as your mayor, I will see to it that Culpeper retains its traditions and remains a traditional, southern town. Thank you."

Kirtley looked at his audience. He was surprised that no one had applauded his little speech. Had they all lost their sense of what was right and proper?

Kirtley sat down. Richard introduced Charlie.

"Good afternoon. You all know me; in fact, not six months ago, some of you wanted me to hang for a crime I did not commit. Now, however, many of you have asked me to step forward and lead Culpeper during the coming time of change." He allowed his Charleston accent to come through strong and clear.

Making sure to make eye contact with as many people as possible, especially the ladies for this bit, he continued. "Like you, I am a southerner, married to a fine, dignified, southern lady, and father to a troop of good, obedient southern children. Like you, I want what is best for all of the residents of Culpeper, white and colored, families who have been here for generations and new comers, unionists and secessionists. The time for separation is over; now is a time to recover, to reconstruct our community, our economy and our country."

"I believe strongly in the need to do whatever we can to return Culpeper to the thriving community it was before the war. You know I have done many things since I came home, to do just that. I have created a bank committed to supporting farmers and merchants. I have helped many of you start new businesses or put the businesses you had before the war back on their feet. I have directly or indirectly created jobs and opportunities of all sorts for both white and colored people. If you elect me as your mayor, I will continue to work to help Culpeper rebuild and grow, so that we can look forward to a time of economic prosperity for our future and for our children's future."

"It is critical to the well-being of Culpeper, and indeed, all of Virginia, that we be re-instated as a fully recognized state within the federal Union. Until Virginia is again a full member of the community of states in these United States, we will be controlled by the vindictive actions of the Radical Republicans. Indeed, President Johnson, a good Tennessee man, barely survived the attempt to impeach him because he did not agree with the Radical Republicans' desire to continue to punish the south. I will serve this community by contributing in any way I can to the re-admission of Virginia as a full state, so that our voice can be heard again in the halls of power in Washington. In this way, the great traditions of Virginia, the legacy of Jefferson, Washington, Madison, and Monroe, will be remembered and honored."

"And last, but not least, if you would like to see just how

dangerous and vicious Irish wolfhounds are, then I will invite you to meet me tomorrow afternoon at 2:00 at Miss Jackson's kennels. I do not think it will serve anyone to order the wholesale destruction of a beautiful breed of dog because Mr. Kirtley does not like them."

"Thank you for your time and for your consideration."

The crowd's response to Charlie's speech was very different than their reaction to Kirtley's. There was a rousing round of applause followed by several protestations of belief in Charlie's innocence in the matter of Alex Raeburn's murder.

There were no questions from the audience. Richard stepped forward and asked if either candidate had any questions for the other. Kirtley looked like he was ready to explode, but chose not to put forth any further opportunity for the audience to disregard him or for Redmond to diminish and insult what he thought was important. Charlie simply looked bored at the idea of questioning Kirtley about anything. After a final request for questions from the audience that resulted in silence, Richard thanked all of the participants – the candidates and the audience – and ended the event.

Jocko was standing at the foot of the stairs as Charlie came down. "Ro is over at the tavern. I think you had best go talk to her, since you just invited all of Culpeper to visit her tomorrow afternoon."

He gave a rueful grimace. The idea of killing off the Irish wolfhounds because Kirtley did not like them was simply offensive.

As he walked into the tearoom side of the tavern, Ro and Allison were waiting for him. Ro grinned at him. "We heard. We will be ready for you, with all the dogs clean and groomed. Feiglí will be thrilled to see you and the family." Feiglí was visiting at Ro's to be bred.

"Thank you so much. I know I should have checked with you first, but Kirtley had simply grated me the wrong way with his arrogant declarations."

"You think he irritated you!" Allison spoke up. "He annoyed me so much I have gone to everyone who bought one of our dogs to convince them to support you. They all did, by the way."

"Um, thank you, I think." He grinned at her.

Just then a large group of his supporters came into the tavern and any further personal conversation was impossible.

~

Sunday, May 31, 1868

Edgar kept the Sunday sermon as short and crisp as possible. He was perfectly aware that at least half the town wanted to see the general, Ro, and Allison demonstrate just how gentle the huge Irish wolfhounds actually were.

Ro and Allison had attended the service, and like the Redmonds, left immediately after to prepare for the impending invasion of curious people at their home. Allison whispered to Rebecca as they were leaving, "Honestly, it is the best endorsement and advertising we could ever hope for."

As soon as the Redmonds got home, they grabbed a quick lunch that Sarah had ready and then they all changed out of their Sunday best and into day-to-day work clothes. Rebecca acceded to social mores, especially on a Sunday, by wearing a walking skirt, shirt, and vest, along with her work boots. Charlie collected Peri, Buddy, and Andy, and, with Rebecca, loaded them into the small trap. Darby, wanting to see the circus that he was sure this would be, followed riding Tucker. The girls opted to stay home.

They arrived at Ro and Allison's at about half past one. The kennels were immaculate, and the dogs were all groomed and looking elegant. As soon as Rebecca came near the kennels, Feiglí started alternately barking and whining, wanting to fling herself at her beloved mistress's feet. Ro opened the gate into the run and Rebecca entered, sitting on a bench at the side and petting and scratching her dog. Peri followed Rebecca, and he tried and failed to get Feiglí's attention.

People started arriving around 2:00. They watched Rebecca sitting in the run, cuddling her huge dog and being ignored by the fifteen other dogs in the enclosure. By half past, Charlie estimated that all the people who were going to come had arrived. There were about fifty people ranged around the large pen, looking and pointing at Rebecca and her dog.

He stepped up and got their attention. "Ladies and gentlemen, you see how gentle and loving these dogs are. Indeed, my wife is in absolutely no danger from these animals, but that is not the most compelling evidence of their gentleness that I can offer."

He stepped to one side and collected Andy and Buddy from Allison, who had been watching them while Rebecca was in with her dog. He opened the gate into the dog run and ushered the boys in. At the same time, he beckoned to Rebecca to join him. He then shut the gate, leaving the boys in with the dogs and with no adult supervision or protection. Feiglí and Peri immediately went to check on their boys.

Charlie called, "Mount up, boys!"

"Really, Mama?" The boys chorused.

"Go ahead. Just this once." She understood, even though she did not approve of riding the dogs.

The boys led the two dogs over to the bench, jumped up, and threw their legs over their backs, grabbing on fluffy scruffs. They giggled and laughed as the two dogs carefully walked them around the run. The other dogs came up to them, sniffing and curious, but were very gentle with the two little boys riding on the canines that were almost as large as small ponies.

After a while, the boys got bored with riding and slid off to run around chasing the other dogs, rolling on the ground with them, petting them, pulling on ears and tails, and generally being three-year-old hooligans. The wolfhounds treated them as they would unruly puppies, nudging them when they got out of line, but mostly playing and licking their hands and faces.

Charlie looked at the crowd, who had been laughing as the boys played with the dogs, which were easily four times their size. "Ladies and gentlemen, I admit these dogs would defend the boys against anyone who **threatened** them, but otherwise, Irish wolfhounds are big, gentle, friendly animals, not the vicious beasts that Mr. Kirtley portrayed. Do you have any questions? I am sure Miss Simms and Miss Jackson would be happy to answer them." With that, he opened the gate, walked into the midst of the pack and retrieved his sons and his dog.

After loading the boys and Peri into the cart, the Redmonds left. Ro and Allison were surrounded by people asking questions.

Rebecca grinned. "I would be willing to wager they are going to be dealing with extensive demand for their animals for quite a while after this."

He laughed. "I hope so."

~

Tuesday, July 7, 1868

Rebecca sat across the breakfast table from her beloved spouse and waited. He had spoken to every child, and consulted with Reg, Beulah, and Sarah about deliveries and supplies. Having eaten his breakfast, he had consumed three cups of coffee and read the paper twice.

Finally, she could stand it no longer. "So?" She tapped her spoon against her coffee cup, more or less to get his attention from his fourth cup of coffee and third go round with the paper.

"So? What?" He looked to her, dropping the paper in his lap.

"You are going to vote?"

"Eventually."

She sat back and carefully weighed her next words. "How dare you take it for granted?"

"What?" He looked to her again, truly surprised by her outburst.

"You have voted in every election since you were twenty-one, correct?"

He nodded. "Yes."

"Because you are a free, white," she paused, sighing heavily, "man. How dare you take for granted the fact that you are allowed to exercise a right so many others would willingly die to have? Who have died for it! I seem to remember a little war not so long ago…"

"That was not about the right to vote," he defended.

"It might as well have been. With freedom come certain rights. So let me ask you, husband, I am a free white woman. Why am I not allowed to vote?"

His brows nearly launched off his head. "I have no…"

"You have no good answer, because there is no good answer. You can carry the weight of this one on your shoulders, General Redmond. You taught me about partnership and equality and you can damn well bet I will make sure to pass the message on to our daughters. It may be too late for ladies like me, but I hope **my** girls rule the world."

He smiled gently. "With a mother like you, how could they fail?" Taking his napkin from his lap, he placed it on the table. *Where is the Rebecca who thought her daughters did not need to go to college because their future was having a husband and children?* He stood and moved to her side of the table, kissing her on the crown of her head. "I will go vote now."

"You do that." She dropped her napkin to the table, irritated that he had managed once again to stop her before she got a good start. "And make sure you vote for the correct gentleman," she said over her shoulder as he started to leave the room.

"Yes, dear." He returned, kissed her once again and retreated to the barn to get Jack.

He arrived at the courthouse and dropped from Jack's back, tying him under the shade of a large oak tree. He watched as several men entered and then exited the side of the building where the polling place for the special election had been set up. He also noticed several uniformed troopers around the building. He knew they were part of the contingent of over 100 soldiers under Lieutenant W. S. Chase, sent in to make sure that Culpeper came through this election as well as supporting disarmament of the local blacks as part of the District Four policing policy.

He stood there under the tree and smoked a cigar as Jack grazed on the grass and snorted his displeasure at the offering. The horse was accustomed to nice, long sweet grass; this was almost so bad he doubted a sheep would eat it.

Charlie finally found a lull in the crowd and made his way inside. Richard was leaning against one wall, keeping a watchful eye. Edward Cooper and Rafe Johnstone sat at a table with the registration book and ballot box.

Cooper grinned and dipped a pen in ink, offering it to Charlie. "Please, sign the register before you cast your vote, General."

With a nod, he took the pen and signed the book. Rafe handed him a ballot and gestured to a spot where he could mark it off in private if he wished. Charlie just sighed, shook his head, marked his ballot, and dropped it in the box. "Thank you, gentlemen. I am sure you will let me know how it comes out."

"Count on it." Edward nodded. "Probably sometime tomorrow morning. Turn out is very heavy. It will take most of the evening to count them."

~

Thursday, July 9, 1868

It was almost noon before Cooper and Johnstone finished counting the ballots, with Richard and Lieutenant Chase looking on to verify the count.

"Well, Charlie won, as we all knew he would." Cooper was looking pleased, though tired.

"By how much?" Richard was curious.

Johnstone scribbled a few numbers on a scratch pad beside him. "By eighty-two percent."

"Excellent. Who is going out to tell him?"

"Well, Colonel Polk, since you are his friend…"

"Oh, no. Not me. You two, as the election officials, should have the honor."

Cooper did not look thrilled. "Telling General Redmond the election results is one thing. Telling Mr. Kirtley is entirely another problem."

"Perhaps Lieutenant Chase will be willing to accompany you. It is his job, after all."

Chase looked unhappy, but acquiesced. "Let me get an escort troop together and then we can go."

Polk grinned. “Excellent idea, Lieutenant. Now, if you will excuse me, I have some telegrams to send.”

As Chase, Cooper, and Johnstone tromped off to find horses and an escort, Richard took himself off to the telegraph office. “Hello, George. I need to send the following telegram to several people.”

“Let me guess, Colonel Polk. Generals Grant and Sheridan, General Lee, Mr. Lord, and who else?”

“Oh, I think to Montgomery Blair, Robert Todd Lincoln, Morrison Waite, Oliver Wendell Holmes, General Alfonse Mayberry, Colonels Constantine Douglas, George Allenby, Everett Salton, and Trevor Veriton, and Captains Jason Bailton and Randall Lightborne. Let them know what happened to the man they tried just a few months ago for murder.”

George Randall started chuckling. “Anyone else you want to rub their noses in this?”

“No, I think that will do. One message for all, I think. Charles Redmond elected mayor of Culpeper in special election by eighty-two percent margin. Stop.”

George and Richard looked at one another and broke into gales of laughter. Richard gasped, “Serves them right, what?”

While George and Richard were having their little joke on men in power, Cooper, Johnstone, and Chase had mounted up and, with their escort of five mounted and armed troopers, headed out to Redmond Stables. Fifteen minutes later, they were knocking on the door to be greeted by Reg, who was looking eager and expectant.

Cooper cleared his throat. “May we see General Redmond?”

“Oh, yes, sir. He is up in his office. May I take your coats?”

“No, thank you, Reg. We will only be here a few minutes. And we know the way; you need not show us up.”

Chase and the troopers remained outside, holding the horses for Cooper and Johnstone.

Cooper knocked on Charlie's office door frame. They could see Charlie sitting at his desk. Charlie called from within, "Come."

The two men walked in, stopping just inside the door. Charlie looked up at them. "Well?"

Cooper coughed, then said, "Charlie, you won. Swearing in is tomorrow at noon."

"By how much?"

"Eighty-two per cent."

"Bet Kirtley is thrilled. Thank you, gentlemen. I will be there tomorrow. Tonight I will enjoy my last day as a free man."

"Thank you, Charlie. Until tomorrow." They knew they had been dismissed.

As they backed out the door, Johnstone moved to close it.

Charlie called, "No, please, leave it open. I do not like closed doors."

Johnstone pushed the door back open, then both men hurried down the stairs and back outside to their horses. Kirtley was next.

Kirtley was sitting on his front porch, a half empty bottle on the table beside him, a glass in his hand. He rose as the delegation rode up. "Gentlemen?"

"Good day, Mr. Kirtley." Cooper was being especially polite.

"Is it a good day, Mr. Cooper? Am I to show up in town tomorrow for a swearing in?"

"No, sir. I am afraid not."

"No surprise there, Cooper. All those yellow stars you and your friends spread around town were a bit of a clue, if you know what I mean." Kirtley took a healthy swig of whatever was in his glass. "So how bad was it?"

"Eighty-two to eighteen percent, sir."

Kirtley nodded and sucked on his bottom lip. "So a large majority of the town would basically just as soon see my back as my face?" He took another swig, then threw the empty glass at Cooper's feet. "Well, then you and your fellow scallywag lovers can have the town, have your darling general, and to hell with you all." He turned around and entered the house, slamming the door behind him.

Cooper wiped his brow with his handkerchief and grinned at Johnstone. "Well, that went well, do you not agree?"

CHAPTER 24

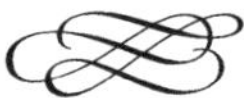

Friday, July 10, 1868

Charlie, followed by Rebecca, mounted the steps of the courthouse promptly at noon that day. Edgar, wearing his official ministerial robes, was waiting for him, holding a rather large bible in one hand and a piece of paper in the other.

"What are you doing here?" Charlie was startled at Edgar's presence, having expected one of the town elders to be the one to swear him in.

"I am your minister. Who better to make you take an oath I know perfectly well you do not want to take?"

"So, before you, God, and the people of Culpeper, I get to subject myself to four years of bureaucratic hell?" He gave Edgar a rather rueful grin.

"Three years and seven months. Horace survived a month of his term and we had a ninety day hiatus until the special election. But yes, that is exactly what you get to do."

"Oh, thank you so much. Those months are precious. Shall we get this over with?"

Charlie turned to Rebecca, who had been side-tracked by several of the women of the town who wanted to admire her new dress and hat, acquired during their time in New York and Baltimore. "Darling, you need to come and hold the bible for me."

She hurried up the stairs and took her place between Charlie and Edgar, holding the bible and looking rather determined. Charlie wondered exactly who was about to become the de facto mayor.

He placed his left hand on the bible and raised what was left of his right hand, and Edgar read the oath, phrase by phrase, with Charlie repeating each line, and finishing with, "So help me, God." *You better help me, God. Otherwise I will not get through this.*

After the pomp and circumstance of the swearing in was over, they invited everyone to Jocko's, where lunch would be served.

Charlie offered Rebecca his arm and they began the slow stroll towards the tavern. As they walked, a number of people nodded and said hello, with a few stopping him to shake his hand. Just as they made their way to Main Street, one of Darby's runners brought him a stack of envelopes.

"These came in for you this morning, General Redmond."

He nodded and took the bundle, pitching the boy a dime. As they continued walking he thumbed through the telegrams, stopping with one particular one that also stopped their forward movement.

"Darling?" Rebecca questioned as she watched his face.

Without a word, he plucked his knife from his pocket and slit open the envelope. After reading it, he smiled and handed it to her.

CONGRATULATIONS MR MAYOR STOP
ASSUME YOU TALKED WITH SHERIDAN STOP
CLEVER VERY CLEVER STOP
EXPECT YOUR SUPPORT IN RICHMOND STOP
USG

Rebecca nodded, satisfied. "It worked."

"So it would seem."

Rebecca smiled sweetly as she began unbuttoning Charlie's vest. He had already been reverently divested of his jacket and tie, and now she was happy to work on the remaining layers. "I must say, I have never had so many firsts in my life before I met you."

"Is that so?" He could only smile as she pushed the material from his shoulders.

"Yes." She nodded, tossing his vest onto the pile over the back of the sofa. "Until you came along, I had never made love to a Yankee before…"

"I am not a Yankee."

She nodded. "Yes, of course. All right then, I had never made love to a Union officer before. Or a banker, or a general, or a..."

"Mayor?"

She laughed, crinkling her eyes and nose in a manner he found positively adorable. "Yes."

"Then another first for you my dear." He caught her up in his arms and guided her to the bed.

But as they approached the bed, she caught him by the wrist and spun him around, pushing him back so that his knees caught against the edge of the bed and he fell back into it. She pounced on top of him and started crawling up his body, nibbling her way up to his neck and ears. He laughed at her aggressive approach, and caught her wrists in his hands.

"Where do you think you are going, madam?"

"Exactly where you want me, Mr. Mayor. Exactly where I want to be."

~

Monday, July 13, 1868

Charlie and Eloise met on the steps of the courthouse at exactly 9:00 that morning. They looked at one another and each took a deep breath. Then they marched up the steps, entered the building and made their way to the mayor's office at the southwestern corner of the building.

Cautiously, Charlie opened the door. Darby had warned him after having his boys haul the boxes of papers from Mrs. Frazier's house to the office. It was worse than Darby had said.

Eloise looked at the mountains of paper. There was not a single surface in the room that did not hold a pile of paper at least a foot high. There were piles along the walls, so that there were simply paths through the piles to get to the various areas of the room. Charlie worked his way to the windows, planning to open them to relieve the stifling summer heat, but Eloise cried out.

"Oh, no! If you open the windows, there will be a breeze and it will blow these papers all over the place."

"Eloise, we cannot work in this heat."

"May I suggest that we find an empty room, make it our work space, and take a couple of piles at a time?"

"Do you think Frazier had some sort of system?"

"I honestly do not know. Give me a couple of hours to

conduct a quick review and I will see if I can figure it out. That is, if he had any system at all."

"You are braver than I am. There must be twenty years' worth of paper in here!"

"The entire time he was mayor." She looked around the room. "Maybe it is by year. Or by type of document. Or… something. If there is a system, I will figure it out. You go meet with your constituents, or they will start driving you insane."

"Yes, ma'am. I will start organizing that meeting I promised the businessmen. I think a personal invitation would be a good thing. And I need to talk with Richard and that Lt. Chase about getting the number of military patrols down to something reasonable. It feels like a damned prisoner of war camp around here sometimes."

Eloise rolled her sleeves up and pulled a large white apron out of the small carpet bag she had carried in with her. "You go. I will see if I can make heads or tails of this mess."

"I will see you at lunch at Esther's. My treat."

"You have a date, sir."

He stepped out into the hall and dusted himself off before he headed to Richard's office on the floor below him and at the other end of the courthouse. It was not a room he was fond of entering, having spent far too many hours in the small cell behind the office, but doing something about the number of troops in Culpeper and the surrounding county was important.

He stuck his head in the door and found Richard just going through the reports from the previous night. "Hello, Mr. Provost. Want a cup of coffee with your new mayor?"

Richard looked at the pile of paper, then back at Charlie. "It would be my pleasure, sir."

The two men walked over to Jocko's, where they knew a fresh pot of Esther's outstanding coffee would be waiting. Once they settled into chairs at a corner table, Charlie looked at Richard and asked, "So, are we really prisoners of war camp, or can you get rid of some of the excess troopers?"

Richard laughed, but then swiped his hand over his face, looking rueful.

"It is a matter of making sure the Negroes are not armed while trying to keep control of these vigilantes that are taking after Devil Forrest's organization. It is a very delicate balance that the officers in the First Military District think can be solved with the only tool they know – force." Richard sighed and shook his head. "The good news is that they are talking about rescinding the disarmament order. The geniuses at the Freedmen's Bureau pointed out that farmers cannot protect their herds without guns, nor can the coloreds hunt to put food on their tables, both of which are necessary."

"Is there anything I can do as mayor to speed this along?"

"Well, you could write to the powers that be and request a couple more deputy provosts for me in exchange for getting the troops out of here. You know damned well I will not enforce the disarmament issue and I am certain that it will be lifted soon."

"You have it. A reasonable force of deputies to enforce the law, keep the Saturday night drunks under control, and do what we must to deal with the fellows in the silly robes with the fiery crosses seems like a good idea."

"Thank you. You know, I think you and I will be able to work together quite effectively." Both men started guffawing at that jab.

They finished their coffee and each set off on their respective tasks.

Richard returned to his office and his reports. Charlie started by asking Jocko if he would be able to host a meeting of the businessmen in the town on Thursday night. Then he methodically called on every business along Main Street, from Spring Street to Piedmont Street. Where it would normally have taken him no more than ten minutes to walk the thirteen blocks of the main business district, it took him over two hours, stopping to chat for a few minutes and invite the business owners to come to a meeting with him to discuss ways to make things more attractive for business in Culpeper on Thursday night.

He was ten minutes late to lunch with Eloise, and hot, dusty and sweaty. She had already ordered their lunch and had a large, icy lemonade waiting for him. Somehow she knew he would need it.

"So, have you organized your businessmen's meeting?"

"I think so. I have them coming here to Jocko's at 7:00 in the evening on Thursday."

"What are you doing about the black businessmen?"

He blinked a couple of times. The black businessmen had not even crossed his mind.

"Are there enough colored businessmen to justify another meeting?"

"The bank has twenty five different business accounts with various colored businesses. There are printers, draymen, smiths, dry goods merchants, food shops, including one of these best barbeque shacks I have ever had food from. One of the men who handles the drays is talking about a livery service, which we desperately need."

"Well, I guess I need to put together a meeting with the colored businessmen."

"Yes. Yes, you do."

"You think the Methodist minister will let me use their facilities?"

"You certainly can ask him. I suspect they will be so

surprised that someone other than the Freedman's Bureau wants to talk with them, they will fall over themselves to be there."

He took a deep breath as the server brought them their lunch of a cold chicken salad, fruit, and big drop biscuits. They ate in silence for a few minutes. Charlie asked the question that had been floating in the space between them.

"So, was there a system?"

The secretary heaved a sigh. "No. It was just drop it into the closest pile. When than pile got too big, move it to the floor and start a new one. At least it is sort of in chronological order."

He shook his head, before scratching his chin, "How long do you think it will take us to sort it out?"

She blinked a couple of times, then stared at the ceiling, and finally looked at the mayor. "Months," she declared flatly.

"And if I got you some help?"

"Still months, but fewer."

"How many people do you want?"

"Shall we start with five? And we need to set up a clerk's office."

"Do you want to be the clerk?"

"No." She shivered, despite the heat. "I am your secretary. I want to supervise the clerk."

"Then, as my secretary, your first assignment is to go hire a clerk and five people to assist with the piles of paper."

"Mr. Mayor, who is going to pay for these people? Culpeper does not have any money. I think the town has about three hundred dollars in the bank."

"Obviously, I am. Otherwise you and I have hell to face in the form of twenty years' worth of undone filing."

They ate in companionable silence for a few minutes. Then Eloise asked the next disconcerting question. "What about the businesswomen in town? There are not many, but there are some, like Mrs. Allen and Dr. Walker – and your own wife has the best horse breeding stables in the area. As we get Culpeper back on its feet, there will be more – dress makers, hat makers, boarding houses, things like that."

He sighed. "Next week? Maybe a luncheon here at Esther's? Damn, this job is going to be bloody expensive."

Saturday, July 18, 1868

It had been well after midnight before Charlie managed to get home. He took his boots off in the hall to avoid waking the entire house as he made his way up the steps. He slipped into the washroom, stripped off his clothes, and wiped down with a warm cloth. He changed into fresh small clothes and then headed into the bedroom.

He had barely managed to lie down and pull the covers over himself before Rebecca rolled into him. He smiled, kissed her forehead, and wrapped his arm around her waist. He had no time to consider anything else before he was sound asleep.

When Rebecca awoke that morning, she was still tucked into his chest, warm and content. She lay there for quite a while then, trying not to wake him, and then began extracting herself from his embrace.

He groaned and rolled onto his back, his eyes barely cracking open. "That was a very short night."

She smiled and sat on his side of the bed, brushing her fingers through his hair. "I think you should go back to sleep. It is Saturday and you need to rest. What time did you get in last night?"

"I have no idea. I know it was after midnight. The meeting with the colored businessmen was a **long** one. And that horse's ass from the Freedman's Bureau did not make things easier."

"You are exhausted." She continued stroking his dark locks,

combing her fingers slowly through, barely grazing his scalp with her nails. "Go back to sleep."

"You are sure?" His eyes dropped closed despite his efforts to keep them open.

"I am positive. Get a couple more hours. We will keep a breakfast plate warm for you."

"Thank you, my love."

She kissed him and covered him when he rolled over to slumber for a bit longer. "I love you, Charlie." She doubted he heard her, as he was already snoring again.

She was quick to pull the curtains, making the room as dark as possible, then she retreated to the wash room, where Lizbet was waiting to help her with her morning routine.

Charlie was up and about by nine. He quickly gobbled down the breakfast plate Sarah had carefully kept warm in one of her new ovens, happily telling him how easy it was to keep everything nice and fresh until he was ready for it.

After breakfast, he rounded up Darby and Sue and they headed off on a ride together. Rebecca laughed as she listened to Charlie admonish Darby to remember that they had his sister with them and that since she was on her little pony, they would have to make sure to keep a special eye on her.

He made sure to ride slowly, and even Jack understood, because he was keeping a close eye on the little Shetland and if it looked like it was going to throw any temper at all, the big stallion would snort, whinny or stomp and put a stop to it right away.

Once they reached their favorite meadow, Papa stopped and helped his little lady down from her mount and they walked hand in hand through the field, talking about all sorts of things that fascinated a six-year-old girl while Darby rode Tucker in wide, fast circles.

They returned in time for lunch, which the family took together out in the gazebo. After lunch, Papa adjourned to the edge of the pond with Emily, where she showed him her now carefully staked out 'archeological dig.' The child had absorbed absolutely everything she had learned on their trip and even scolded her papa when he inadvertently stepped over into one of her carefully roped off little squares. He apologized profusely as she spent ten minutes making sure his "big clumsy feet" had not disturbed her precious dig site.

Once the little archeologist was happy that her dig was still intact, she was content to take her trough and brushes and begin her 'work.' Papa sat down and diligently waited as she handed him shell after shell and rock after rock. He was particularly impressed when she pulled out a pair of shark teeth. Not so much that she had found them, but he really watched just how careful she was to extract them, clean them, and place them on the canvas with the best of her finds. That was when he realized she considered the handful of things he had, the 'junk.' After she became so engrossed in her efforts that she had forgotten he was there, he kissed her on her head and returned to the house.

He had just enough time to wash his hands, face and neck when the boys came barreling into the kitchen. The moment they saw him he was the target of their attentions. The position of mayor had already started to take its toll on his children, who were accustomed to their papa being available to them most days.

Now it was down to just one or two days a week. They had been told all day that they would get their turn with Papa and now they wrapped themselves around him, making it nearly impossible for him to move.

"All right, my miniature fellows." He brushed his fingers through their hair, noticing it needed trimming; he would have to mention that to Tess. "Would you please go over there and ask Sarah if perhaps she might have a snack we can share? And remember your manners, my little gentlemen, or I shall take you to the woodshed."

The boys giggled at the empty threat. Their papa would threaten them with trips to this supposed woodshed, but they had never seen it. The worst punishment either boy had ever seen from Papa was a slap to the hand and that had been when Andy had been reaching for a hot kettle on the hob in their parents' room one morning last winter. Now, Mama was another story. Mama would spank. They had felt her hand on their little rumps more than once. They learned fairly quickly not to irritate her to that point.

They turned in unison and marched over to the cook, who was already trying not to smile.

"Miss Sarah?" They both asked.

"Yes, my young sirs?"

Charlie watched with a grin as Sarah put the boys through their paces.

"May we have snack? For Papa?"

"Just one snack? For your papa?"

The boys looked at each other, and then shook their heads. "No, ma'am. For all," Buddy said, sticking out his little chest.

"Please?" Andy smiled his big, infectious smile.

Sarah nodded and gestured for them to take their seats at their little table. Charlie snatched a chair from the big table and settled it near his boys. They were all served. Papa got lemon cake and coffee, and the boys were happy with apple slices, a small piece of cake like Papa had and a glass of milk. He sat there, eating as best as he could while making sure that cups did not get spilled and as much food as possible made it to the intended targets.

The wonderful thing about the boys at this age was they were happy with the half hour or forty minutes he could offer them. Once the snack was complete, Tess took them off for afternoon stories and naps.

Charlie was relieved and even took the time for a second cup of coffee. He was still seated in the big chair at the little table when his wife entered the kitchen. "Have you been naughty?" she managed to get out around her guffaws. "Is that why you are at the children's table?"

"Oh, very funny." He took his chair back to the big table and joined her. "I was occupying our sons during snack time."

"Oh, I know." She nodded and took her seat with her cup. "I heard all about it as Tess and I tucked them in for their nap. They were very happy boys."

"I am glad. I think I have managed to make most of the house happy today."

She nodded. "Most of it."

He chuckled, placing his hand over hers. "What do I need to do to make the entire house happy?"

"Go play poker tonight."

That was not the answer he was expecting. The one he thought he would get had to do with being unclothed and up to something truly 'naughty' with his lovely wife. This particular answer gave him great pause. "All right…"

"You need an evening off. You have been working yourself to exhaustion. We have not had a night out with our friends in months. Let us go into town, have some of Esther's wonderful pub food, a drink or two too many, and a few hours of relaxation with our friends." She shrugged. "Besides, Rex owes me the chance to recoup some of my losses during our last game and I know Jocko thinks your pockets are far too full at the moment."

He sipped his coffee and nodded. "I think that is a wonderful idea."

"And I will make you a private side wager."

"Yes?"

"Yes." She leaned over and smiled, her thumb caressing the back of his hand. "Whoever wins the most money…"

"Or loses the least?" He perked up and grinned.

"Or loses the least," she agreed. "Gets to pick tonight."

His libido immediately hit a hard gallop, knowing exactly what she meant by that. He grinned wide and nodded enthusiastically, "Agreed!"

She laughed out loud. He was so easy. "I am glad, my dear. Now, might I suggest a nap and perhaps a bath before we go out this evening?"

"Together?" He wiggled his brows, hoping he was right.

"Oh, yes." She stood and took him by the tie, giving it a gentle tug as she pulled it from his vest. "Come, husband."

Sarah laughed out loud as the lady of the house led the gentleman from the room by the strand of silk material.

Yes, indeed. He was going to manage to make the whole house happy today.

Jocko was damn quick to pour Charlie a coffee topped with brandy when he and Rebecca walked through the door. She laughed and peeled off to join Rex and the ladies as they congregated in the tea room for mah jong and whatever alcoholic libation they decided to pour in tea cups to maintain social proprieties for anyone peering in the windows.

Rebecca had considered more than once the idea of just lifting one of the big mugs of beer Jocko offered, but she decided the other ladies would not be amused, so she drank her brandy out of a tea cup too. Besides, the mere smell of beer made her sick to her stomach.

As the ladies settled, while awaiting Rex and Charlotte, and on the gentlemen's side, Edgar, Esther was quick to offer a particularly good red wine. She and Jocko had managed to lay hands on several cases at a ridiculously good price. It was not often that she got to indulge the ladies, with her husband preferring to spend resources on whiskies, brandies and other libations on the more profitable gentlemen's side.

Charlie took his normal seat at the poker table and awaited the arrival of Edgar, Richard, and Edward. He and Jocko sat, just enjoying their drinks and sorting the chips and cards. Before too long, a couple of gentlemen not known to the regular poker crowd managed to find their way in to order a quick drink and have a word with the mayor.

By the time Edgar, Rex, and Charlotte had arrived, having been delayed by grumpy twins who had no desire to let the adults in their lives leave the manse, Charlie was surrounded three deep by men who just needed a 'moment of his time.'

The ladies and Rex had been seated and drawn their tiles in preparation to start their game. Rebecca knew that by this time, the men should be well into theirs as well, with Jocko complaining loudly about the quality of his cards.

She tried to pay attention to her own tiles, but kept one ear cocked on the room next door. She finally sighed and lifted her hand to her tablemates. "Please, excuse me for just one moment."

She stood and brushed a wrinkle from the skirts of her dress as she made her way to the large archway that separated the two sides of Jocko and Esther's business.

She watched as Charlie sat at the table surrounded by men. He alternated between nodding toward one or shaking his head at another. It was clear he could not in any way understand anything any one man was saying because they were all talking at once and he was doing his best, but he looked like a tree being whipped in a heavy wind as his head snapped back and forth.

“**ENOUGH!**”

The bellow stopped every last noise on both sides and every head turned to Mrs. Redmond, standing in the door between the rooms and looking like she was going to blow the roof off both sides of the building.

“If you are not here to eat Mrs. Jackson’s fine food or drink Mr. Jackson’s equally fine liquor or to even play poker, get out!” She moved into the bar side, her hands planted firmly on her hips.

Charlie started to get up, only to have Edgar from one side and Richard from the other take him by the arms and set him back down. “Stay,” they both said.

“And be quiet.” Jocko shook his finger from across the table. “Let her go.”

“Seems to be a common theme in your life,” Edgar joked as he let go of his friend’s arm.

Every man standing in the bar who had been trying to get a word in edgewise with the mayor now stared slack jawed at the woman raging before them.

“He has been mayor less than two weeks and you are already wearing him out! He will never survive the next six months if you do not allow him time to breathe! Where were you at midnight? Were you happily sleeping in your bed? My husband was not! He was coming home after having left before 8:00 in the morning. For the love of God, all we want is a couple of hours to relax! Is that too damn much to ask?”

Several of the men looked properly abashed, but Rebecca was not yet done with them. "If he is fortunate, he will get to have a little food and a few drinks. He might even share a laugh or two with his friends. If he is very lucky, I shall take him home later tonight and drain his coffers dry!"

Charlie choked on his coffee. Edgar patted him on the back and quietly congratulated him on not only having a wife brave enough to do it, but say it out loud.

The rant continued, "But for Christ's sake! None of that will be possible if you do not leave him alone!

Charlie cleared his throat and whispered to Edgar, "She enjoys the shock factor."

"No doubt." The minister nodded, noticing all the particular shades of pink and red in the room as the men tried to make their way to the door.

Rebecca stood there, daring them to say a word. Most of them only made slight bows and scooted backward out the door. The rest simply bolted as soon as an opening was available. She looked quite satisfied as she smiled and said, "Enjoy your game, gentlemen." Then she turned and rejoined her companions as if nothing had happened.

~

Sunday, July 19, 1868

While Charlie had not been mobbed after church, as the men of the town would not dare given Rebecca's explosion the previous evening, a number of them stopped to have a word with him. There were several themes in their comments--the need for recruiting additional businesses to the town and what kind of businesses they thought were needed. These were expected issues and Charlie was prepared to respond. With the meetings he had held the previous week, he had started to plan a campaign to attract new businesses. This was a bit of a challenge, as the demand for labor in Northern Virginia had drained the area of much of its excess labor force. To put Culpeper back on the commercial map, he would have to find ways to attract new residents.

But the one issue that Charlie had not expected was the desire to establish a lodge and reinstate the role of the masons in the community. Like virtually all of the officers in the Union army, Charlie and Richard were both masons. He was surprised to discover that a number of the businessmen in the community were also members of that society. He and Rebecca had property in town that could be used temporarily as a meeting place until a proper lodge could be built, but before he made that commitment, he wanted to talk with his wife because she was a part owner.

That evening after dinner, Charlie looked over the rim of his brandy snifter and grinned at Rebecca. "Would you like to know what they are calling you in town now?"

"If it is anything less than bitch, I shall be disappointed."

He laughed. "They would not dare. No, my dear, you are now Mrs. Mayor and the gentlemen have decided they would rather lie on a bed of nails than get on your bad side again."

"Good, then my work there is done. I assume this means you will be home in time for supper every evening from now on."

"No doubt, or at least more often than I have been. I do believe the gentlemen were just being enthusiastic because they finally feel like they have someone who will listen and talk to them. Poor Horace could not do much for them, and every time someone came to him with a problem he basically threw his hands up and told them he was doing everything he could."

"Which was the truth," she agreed.

"Absolutely. The man was well and truly caught between a rock and a hard place. Fortunately, I have a bit of grease in both Richmond and Washington that should keep me from the same fate."

"Is that grease doing anything about the number of federal troops that keep riding over everyone in the county?"

"I have approached the First District Government about it. General Schofield has his hands full with the results of the Underwood Constitutional Convention. They are still arguing about ratifying it, but if they do, as written, it will disenfranchise over half of the town because they supported the southern cause. And it will give colored men the right to vote. Schofield is trying to juggle all of the different issues and still manage to govern, sort of. As far as I can tell, Governor Pierpont is useless in all of this, paralyzed by the conflict between the Radicals and the old-school conservatives."

"Well, paralysis seems to be common, both here in Virginia and with that mess going on up in Washington."

"Revenge is a nasty political motivator, dear. I think that we are very fortunate that we have less of it here in Culpeper than some communities are dealing with."

"We still have our share of it. Consider what Kirtley and his friends want. If they had their way, we would go back to the pre-war social conditions."

"If they had their way, every colored man would be forced to work or arrested as a vagrant and put into work gangs."

"Well, the roads would be in better shape, but I fear that the social situation would not."

"By the way, talking about the social situation. There are a number of men here in town who are masons. They have asked me if there is something I could do about getting a lodge started up here. What would you say to letting them use one of our properties in town as a meeting space until they can build their own lodge?"

"You mean using either Mrs. Williams's or Miss Simms's old houses as a meeting site?'

"Yes. What do you say?"

"Are you a mason?"

"Yes, yes, I am. Most officers in the army are, you know."

"That explains the embroidered apron in the back of your wardrobe. Who did the embroidery for you?"

"Thank you very much, I did. It is one of those things you have to do as a mason."

"You, sir, are a dab hand with a needle. So why is it again that I have to do your darning?"

"Um, because it is what a good wife does?"

"Harumph. Well, if you boys want to play in a secret society, by all means. I think it is a matter of divine justice that you use Mrs. Williams's old house."

"Yes, dear. I will let the gentlemen know, and contact the master lodge to start the process of putting together a formal organization here in Culpeper."

"Please do. You know, my father was a mason."

"It is a good organization, and I think it will be good for Culpeper – help to bring the community together."

She nodded her agreement. Masons were a quiet organization, and no woman was supposed to know what went on behind closed doors, but it certainly brought men together, and that was not a bad thing.

"How is construction going on the school for coloreds in Sweetwater?"

"It is going well. The school will open this fall, as scheduled. Culpeper is ahead of the rest of the state, with the school you opened last year and the colored school this year."

"Good. Education is critical, I think. And not just for children like ours. I think all children should at least be able to read a newspaper, write their names, and do simple ciphers."

"As do I, dear. As do I."

"If you had your way, all children would go to college."

"That is not true. For example, I think apprenticeship is just as good a solution as college for many children. Can you see Jeremiah going to a university? That boy is already more proficient at leatherworking than many grown men. I see a great future for him as an artisan. I do not think there is a university course available for smiths or brick layers, or any of those kinds of trades, but I do not want an apothecary who does not understand the properties of the drugs they blend or a physician who has not been properly educated. So if our girls want to go to university, you are no longer opposed."

"No. I see your point about that. I have come to realize, thanks to you, darling, that the future for our girls offers far more opportunities than just marriage and children. I fear that Em is going to spend her life digging in the dirt, and not because she wants to grow things. Suzanne is on her way to being a far better breeder than I am already. Perhaps a course in animal husbandry will be useful for her."

Charlie looked at his wife and just smiled.

CHAPTER 25

Friday, November 13, 1868

Charlie sat by the fire in the sitting room next to their bedroom, his feet propped up on a small stool near the flames. Rebecca had commanded he do his best to keep himself nice and warm. He had been fighting a cold all week and was doing everything he could to stop it before it went any farther. At first sign of this year's cold, Rex had even prepared a foul tasting concoction reminiscent of The Cure, but it had indeed healed his sore throat and helped clear his chest before the congestion set in too badly.

He was reading the paper when the door opened and his lovely wife entered with a tea tray. She had practically been forcing liquids down his throat for two days. He was very grateful for the inside water closet in the next room.

She poured him a cup of tea, handing him that first, then a telegram from the tray. "This came about twenty minutes ago."

He popped the seal and smiled as she fussed with the shawl over his shoulders. "It is from the president elect. A personal, informal invitation to his inauguration."

"He is rubbing it in."

"Yes, he is." He laughed as he tossed the paper down. "The Republicans were worried right up to the end. They thought Seymour had a bit more than a little chance. Jerome mentioned that Washington was in a right mess with people running around as late as October trying to figure out what the hell was going on. It did not help that Grant refused to campaign."

"I thought he took a campaign trip with Generals Sherman and Sheridan."

Charlie laughed heartily, his head going back in amusement. "If you call standing on the back of the train and waving without saying a word a campaign trip."

"When will it be?" She took her seat across from him, making him give up some of the territory on the stool for her feet.

"Oh, I would think that the ratification of the election will take a few weeks. It is a damn complicated thing this time round with the reconstruction. You know there will be challenges made along the way. The actual inauguration is in March." He nodded knowingly. "It gives you plenty of time to have a new dress made."

She smiled and pushed his foot with hers. "Are you feeling better?"

"Yes, my dear, I am, thank you. I do believe we managed to get this one before it got me."

~

Friday, December 25, 1868

Ro was up and out early. She wanted to get the dogs squared away for the duration while she and Allison would be off to the Redmonds for Christmas celebrations. She dressed quietly, doing her best not to disturb her better half, who still slumbered quietly in their bed.

She managed to slip out of the bedroom without disturbing her partner. A quick cup of yesterday's coffee warmed over the fire place hob, and then she was out the back door to the kennels.

As it was bitterly cold out just before false dawn with a fresh blanket of thin snow on the ground, the dogs merely raised sleepy heads when their mistress entered the building where they stayed warm and safe through the night. She was swift to check the belly of the stove and get it reheating quickly. Once that was done, she saw to water, food and the ability to get out into the yard if they desired.

She stomped around to the front of the house, intending to leave her snow and mud caked boots under the protection of the front porch until she could get them cleaned properly. It took her a moment; the second look happened after she sat down on the bench to catch the heels of her boots in the jack.

In front of the door was a basket. A large basket covered in blankets. She swallowed hard as she looked at it, afraid to move from her spot. Taking a deep breath, she moved in socked feet toward the bundle. With one finger, she caught the edge of the blanket and pulled it back.

"Sweet Jesus!" She yelped, taking a step backward when she saw the face of the sleeping baby. "Allison!"

It did not take long for the door to be yanked open, a panicky Allison pulling her robe tight around her as she looked for her companion. She stopped suddenly at Ro's frantic waving and pointing to the ground. Looking down, she gasped.

"Oh, my God!" She quickly grabbed the basket up and

hurried inside with her panicky partner following quickly, slamming the door. The loud bang startled the sleeping baby, who immediately began wailing. "It is all right…" the young woman soothed as she lifted the child from the basket and took a seat by the hearth.

Ro was quick to build the fire up as her mate took the time to inspect the baby. "It is a little boy. He seems healthy enough. Well fed."

"Where do you think he came from?"

"As if I have a clue! Perhaps, my dear, he fell from the sky with the snow. Maybe there is something in his basket to give us a clue."

"What should we do with it?"

"**It,** as you say, is a helpless child. We shall do what is required to see to his needs."

"Ahhh…" Ro thought she might pass out. "You…you mean to keep it?"

"What else should we do?"

"Certainly, there are other people more suited to this sort of thing. The Redmonds for example! They have…"

"Already taken in more than their fair share of orphaned children." She cuddled the little boy and he quieted instantly against her shoulder, sliding back into slumber. "Though we will have to sort out a method of feeding him."

Ro looked stricken. Instant parenthood to a little human had never been in her plans. Dogs and puppies, yes. Little people, no. She started pacing back and forth, from the fireplace where Allison and the little person were sitting to the pantry beside their cook stove. "I have some goat milk that I got from the general for the new puppies just in case. Could we use that?"

"Excellent, dear. If you could warm it and get me a soft rag…"

"But if we feed it, won't it stay? Does it mean we have to keep it?"

Allison laughed. She laid the baby back in his basket. She caught her partner's waist and pulled her backward. "Darling, it takes a while for them to be able to get around on their own."

"But Allison! A baby? I never thought about children!"

Allison slipped her hands up Ro's belly, then cupped her breasts, pulling their bodies close together. "I believe you were saying just last night that we were destined to be together for the rest of our lives, darling. For most couples, that usually includes children."

"But, but, we are not like most couples." Those roaming hands were distracting her, but not enough to forget what was lying in the basket in front of the fire.

Allison tweaked Ro's nipples through her flannel shirt. "My love, we are exactly like most couples. We live together, we work together, we sleep together, and we make love on a very regular, and need I say thrilling, basis?"

"Eh, uh, yes, of course, my heart. But a child? Where will we put it? What will it do to our life? And how can we bring up a baby?"

Allison stretched up to nibble on the base of Ro's neck. "We will figure it out, my love."

"Yes, dear," Ro said, rather breathily.

"Now, let us go and celebrate Christmas between the two of us while the little one sleeps. Then we can figure how to properly feed him. Perhaps the Redmonds have something we can use."

Ro followed dutifully as she was led back into their bedroom, being careful to leave the door open so they could hear if the baby started fussing.

Allison slipped out of her robe and then pulled her nightgown over her head. She stood in front of her lover, resplendent in her nudity, with the chill of the morning making her nipples hard and beckoning. Ro simply stood there, gazing at the vision before her.

"Um, darling. You are definitely overdressed." Allison laughed.

While Ro hurriedly stripped off her shirt, britches, socks and underwear, Allison slid under the still rumpled covers on their bed. She pulled the comforter up to her waist, sitting in the middle of the bed, then cupped her breasts in her hands, offering them to Ro. "They are cold and are missing your attentions, dear."

Ro moved quickly to place herself beside her lady love. "Let me warm them," she murmured as she leaned over and softly breathed warm air onto the exposed skin, then looked to admire the way they had gotten even harder, even though they were no longer cold.

Forty five minutes later, both women were lying, arms and legs entwined, relaxed and warm. Then Allison sat up suddenly. "The Redmonds! We need to get dressed and go or we will be late for breakfast!"

They jumped up from their bed, not bothering to make it as they usually did, and pulled on their clothes. Ro ran out to the small barn to hitch up the horse and buggy while Allison hastily offered the baby boy some warm goat milk on a twist of soft, lint-free cotton. He took some, and promptly wet himself. Fortunately, whoever had left him had included some clean, dry flats in the basket so she could change him before they left.

By the time they arrived at Redmond Stables, Ro was well and truly ready for a drink while her partner seemed to have settled immediately into a motherhood role to the abandoned infant.

As soon as they were through the door of the parlor where everyone was awaiting the announcement of breakfast, the women were on their feet seemingly drawn to the little bundle of blankets. Immediate 'oooing' and 'awwing' commenced as Dr. Walker took the boy and gave him a quick but complete examination.

She declared he seemed quite healthy and had indeed been well fed. She also concluded he was about eight weeks old. Much fuss was made over the mounds of red hair and the beautiful blue eyes the little fellow had. Rebecca mentioned they looked like Charlie's and hoped they stayed that way. As far as she was concerned, her husband had the most beautiful, striking eyes she had ever seen. Not quite blue, not quite white or silver, unless his mood changed.

Charlie handed Ro a mug of coffee with a shot of his best brandy. "Where did you find him?"

"On our front porch! What kind of person leaves a baby on a porch? In weather like this?"

"Someone who is desperate to find the help he needs? What are you going to name him?" The general asked, knowing perfectly well he was only adding to her apprehension. Sometimes Charlie Redmond could be a real ass.

"Na…na…name him? Why should we name him?"

"Because trust me, in the time I have been a father, I have discovered they respond better to their own names. 'Hey you' stops being effective after about the age of three."

Ro stood there, shaking her head and mumbling 'no' over and over.

Charlie looked across the room at the women clustered around the newest member of the extended family and simply nodded before saying. "Yes."

"Surely one of the churches…"

The general shook his head, taking a place in front of the panicky young woman, placing gentle, calming hands on her shoulders as he looked her directly in the eye. "It will be fine."

She shook her head. "General C, with all due respect, I am not ready to take on a baby."

"Well, it seems the partner you were ready to take on is. So now what? You cannot be thinking of changing your plans, because your plans have changed. Trust me. I did not plan to have a wife and five children in less than five years. You must adjust accordingly. Especially if you love that woman. If you truly love her, then you must be prepared for anything and willing to do everything, even if you were not expecting it."

"I…I…"

"I promise you it will be fine. Everyone here will make sure that you, Allison and **your** boy have everything **you all** need. So now you need to be thinking about names. I think John is a good one to consider."

"Jesus, Mary, and Joseph!"

Her host nodded. "Or one of those. Though I would not vote for Mary. I think it will get him beat up. A lot."

Charlie man slapped Ro on the shoulder and made his way over to inspect the newest member of the clan as his wife made her way to various storage rooms to fetch left over items from when their boys were babies.

There were bottles in the kitchen and other things including clothes that would have to be fetched from the attic. He was fairly certain that before they left, the young couple would have everything they needed for their newly delivered son.

~

Monday, February 1, 1869

Marine Sergeant Joshua Tompkins tied the reins of the nag he had acquired from the provost's office to the post in front of the imposing house he had been sent to. Making the deliveries for the inauguration committee was a miserable assignment, especially given how cold, damp and windy the weather was being. He mounted the steps and knocked on the front door. It was quickly answered by a well dressed colored man, who quickly invited him into the entrance hall.

"Good day, sir. I assumc you are here to see General Redmond. If you would like, let me take your coat, then I will tell the general you are here. May I give him your name?"

The marine shed his coat and looked at the man. "No, I am here to deliver a message to Mrs. Rebecca Redmond, if you please. Could you inform her that Sergeant Tompkins of the President's Own is here to see her?"

"Certainly, sir. Would you care for something hot? A coffee or tea?"

"No, thank you. I have a number of places to be today and need to be back in town to catch the next train."

"Certainly. One moment then, sir."

Tompkins looked around the hall while he waited. It was a very nicely appointed place and the grounds were well tended. Obviously, the general, whoever he was, had done well for himself.

Reg scurried up to the office, where both Rebecca and Charlie had holed up against the cold, each pursuing their individual interests. He was studying financial reports; she was studying breeding records. "Miz 'Becca, there is a marine sergeant asking for you."

"For me? Whatever for? Well, show him up, please, Reg."

A minute later the sergeant was standing just inside of the office door. “Mrs. Redmond? I am Sergeant Joshua Tompkins, ma’am. I have a message for you from the Office of the President, Inaugural Committee.”

The man presented a very ornate looking envelope, thick, made of heavy parchment, with a large red seal and a gold ribbon, and addressed to “The Honorable Mrs. Rebecca Redmond and That Man, whom she took pity on and married.”

She snickered as she read the address. Before she opened it, she looked at the sergeant and asked, “Sir, are you needing a reply?”

“No, ma’am. If I may be excused? I need to get back to town to catch the next train.”

“Certainly, but if you have a moment, I have some hot tea or coffee; it is bitter cold out there.”

“Thank you, ma’am, but no, I had best be going.”

Rebecca rose to show him out while Charlie reached across the desk for the envelope. At the door, she turned and looked at him. “That is for me and you will keep your hands off of it until I get back.” He dropped it, causing the thick packet to land with a little thump.

She walked the sergeant to the top of the stairs, where he politely took his leave of the lady and let himself out to return the nag and catch the train.

Walking back into the office, she looked to Charlie and smiled. “Who do you think is sending **me** official looking messages by military courier?”

“It is obvious. That is Grant’s handwriting; I would recognize it anywhere.”

Rebecca picked up the envelope and opened it. Inside was a heavy card, imprinted with the seal of the inauguration committee at the top. The invitation, printed in ornate copperplate text, read:

The Inaugural Committee
requests the honor of your presence
to attend and participate in the Inauguration of
Ulysses S. Grant
As President of the United States of America
and
Schuyler Colfax
As Vice President of the United States of America
on Thursday, the fourth of March
one thousand eight hundred and sixty-nine
in the City of Washington

There were two cards included in the envelope, one granting admission to the swearing in ceremony, the other providing entrance to the inaugural ball. Both were made out, appropriately, to "Brigadier General and Mrs. Charles H. Redmond." There was also a hand-written note. *"Tell That Man to wear his full dress uniform to the ball – USG."*

Charlie sucked air through his teeth. "What do you think I did to offend the powers that be?"

"You mean other than outsmarting him by becoming the mayor of Culpeper? Nothing, dear."

"Oh, well, there is that." Charlie looked at the cards. "At least you have plenty of time to get a new day dress and a ball gown."

"You are fortunate. You only have to wear one of your usual suits and your dress uniform."

"Yes, dear. Fortunate." *My ass,* he thought to himself.

~

Thursday, March 4, 1869

The morning started wet, cold, and dreary. As neither of them was being sworn in as president at noon, the Redmonds decided to spend a warm and luxurious morning wrapped entirely around each other before rising at about nine in the morning to start preparing for President Elect Grant's swearing in at the capitol. Happy, relaxed, and sated, they rose in a most leisurely fashion.

Mrs. Galloway made sure there was plenty of hot water and made herself available to help Rebecca with her preparations. Charlie simply put on his best suit and adjourned to the front parlor to read the paper while the ladies fussed.

Rebecca was not thrilled with the idea of him standing in the rain in forty degree weather. She made sure he had his hat, heaviest coat, a muffler, and gloves. She was extremely irritated to discover they had no proper umbrella, only a small parasol, which she knew would do no good against the nasty spring weather. She hoped it would either stop raining or that they would be able to find some shelter at the event.

William was there to personally drive them to the capitol. He warned them that the combination of muddy streets and crowds was going to make it a slow trip, so that what normally took about fifteen minutes took over half an hour.

He grinned and wished them well, promising to be waiting for them at 1:00, after the speeches and other formalities in the capitol rotunda. They were not planning to accompany the president on his trip to the White House. It was bad enough to have to join the crowd at the inaugural ball that evening at the Treasury Building.

The sky was iron gray, and a light rain was still falling when William pulled into the line of carriages in the driveway in front of the east portico of the capitol building. Drivers were moving along as quickly as they could, given the number of people who had passes to the capitol steps. There were marines standing at the foot of the steps, holding umbrellas, checking tickets, and escorting people to their proper places.

They were fortunate to find a place beside one of the columns on the House side of the building. While their view was not splendid, as mostly what they would see was the backs of peoples' heads, it was somewhat protected from the wind and rain.

At exactly noon, Chief Justice Salmon P. Chase stepped up to the podium that had been placed at the top of the stairs. Grant and Colfax followed him, each accompanied by their families. Mrs. Grant stepped forward to stand between Justice Chase and her husband, holding the bible that he was swearing on. The oath of office was administered, and Grant and Mrs. Grant stepped back to allow Mr. and Mrs. Colfax to take their places while the oath of office for the vice president was administered.

Grant's first speech as president was not particularly stirring, nor was it inspiring. Fortunately, it was not long either. In essence, he promised to do his best to help put the country back together and to help it recover from the economic damage of the war. He bowed, was politely applauded, then stepped back into the rotunda to shake hands and speak with each member of Congress. The crowd moved toward the Senate chamber, for which Charlie and Rebecca also had tickets, where a smaller, more elite group of supporters were able to express their congratulations.

They were standing in line to approach the newly minted president and express their pleasure at his election and their commitment to supporting him however they could in Virginia when Phil Sheridan slipped up beside Rebecca and whispered in her ear, "He is still miffed with Charlie, you know. He wanted him in his cabinet."

She looked over her shoulder and said, “Hello, Philip. Fancy running into you here. And of course he is still miffed, but Charlie can do more for getting Virginia reinstated from Culpeper and his links to Richmond than he ever could from here. And neither of us wants to live in this nest of vipers.”

Charlie looked around to see who Rebecca was chatting with. “Sheridan. Good to see you again. Will you be at the ball this evening?”

“Oh, I would not miss it for all the tea in China.” He turned to Rebecca. “May I claim a dance with you this evening?”

“Of course you may, Philip. But not too many. We would not want people to talk, now would we?”

“What are you planning to do for dinner, dear lady?”

“We have rooms with a lovely lady over off of K Street and she does a very good pot roast.” She smiled. “Unfortunately, she does not prepare enough for us to have guests.”

“Well, perhaps I could convince you and your companion there to join me? Same place as last time?”

Charlie grinned but deferred to Rebecca. “Your choice, dear.”

“Then, Philip, what time would you like us to join you?”

“Shall we say around seven?”

“Lovely. We will see you then.”

Sheridan left to circulate with the guests. Charlie and Rebecca only had three other parties before they were standing before President and Mrs. Grant.

Rebecca and Julia, having met several times before, exchanged the obligatory air kisses. The president shook Charlie’s hand and grinned. “So, you figured out how to stay in Culpeper – at least for a while. But wait. I am sure to think of something when your term as mayor is up.” He turned to Rebecca. “Mrs. Redmond, I would love a dance with you this evening, but I fear that the obligations of office may prevent me from dancing with anyone except my lovely Julia."

"Mr. President, should you find your circumstances allow, I would be honored to share a dance with you. And may I commend you on your courage to face this jungle of political ambitions to realize your goal of completing the re-union of our country?"

"Oh, a jungle is an apt description. There are still many people who want me to punish the south for the rebellion. The southerners, my dear, are not doing anything to help themselves. This movement that bloody Devil Forrest has started is giving us nightmares in several states. I hope you and your husband can help us bring Virginia back into the fold without more trouble."

Charlie cleared his throat and then inserted himself into the conversation. "I will do my best, Mr. President. I believe I can do more to support your current agenda from where I am now, far more than I could if I were up here in Washington."

Grant turned to Charlie. "I fear, sir, I must disagree with you, but I will bow to your current political situation. Just be warned, Charles Redmond. You will not be mayor of Culpeper forever, and when your term is over, I and your country will be waiting."

Charlie sighed inwardly. *Oh, God! I am so screwed.*

The Redmonds moved on, turning the President and his wife over to the next people in the receiving line, and made their escape to William and the waiting carriage. Charlie was perfectly aware that it would take Rebecca a while to rest up from the day's activities and prepare properly for the evening. He was not looking forward to it.

When they got back to Mrs. Galloway's, they discovered that she had thoughtfully laid out a tray with a cold luncheon of roast beef, baked chicken, cheeses and a nice French bread with a few sliced apples on it. She knew that they would get nothing to eat at the swearing in and that they had a long afternoon and evening ahead of them. Within minutes of their return to the house, she knocked on their door to let them know that the washing room was waiting for them and that there was plenty of hot water ready for their use.

"Thank you so much, Mrs. Galloway. I swear I am chilled to the bone from the weather and standing out in the wind and rain. A hot bath and a lovely luncheon are just the thing," Rebecca effused gratefully.

"Mrs. Redmond, I have lived in Washington all my life. I know just how miserable the weather and the big social events can make one. But I have never had a guest who was invited to the inauguration ball. I almost feel like I was invited myself. Please, enjoy yourself." She turned to go, then thought to ask, "Will you be in for dinner?"

"No, thank you, ma'am. We are dining with General Sheridan at Ebbit's."

"Oh, lovely. From what I hear, General Sheridan is quite a socialite, especially for a single gentleman."

Charlie smiled. "Well, for me, he is a good friend. He was my commanding officer during the war, you know."

She smiled. "Well, you children have a lovely evening. I will leave the front door unlocked; there is no telling how late you will be. Why, you might be in after 10:00. And promise me you will tell me all about it at breakfast tomorrow."

As she left, they broke into giggles, which they were both trying to suppress while she was present. If this ball followed the pattern of other events they were familiar with, they might get home by one, if they were lucky.

Charlie wanted to relax. His leg was bothering him and he needed one of Rex's special cigars, so he helped Rebecca get undressed, then went out to the porch overlooking the garden to smoke. Rebecca got her bath and then, while Charlie bathed, she lay down for a nap so she would be rested for the ball this evening.

Mrs. Galloway knocked on the door at around 5:00, as she had promised. Charlie was already up, and was mostly dressed. Rebecca had a complex process in front of her; preparing for a ball was an act of engineering as much as it was one of fashion. With the new bustles, instead of the old hoops of pre-war dresses, dressing was slightly less cumbersome, but the framework for the bustle was more elaborate to get into.

Charlie had the good sense to grab his vest, coat, dress sash, and sword and beat a retreat to the front parlor. He was standing in the front hall, fully dressed, promptly at half past six, holding Rebecca's cloak.

As she came down the hall, his jaw dropped. He knew his wife was a beauty, but the exquisite robin's egg blue silk off the shoulder evening gown, trimmed with off-white lace roses and ribbons, set her figure and her coloring off perfectly. She was breathtaking.

He remembered himself and wrapped her cloak around her shoulders, giving her a very tender kiss on the cheek. Then he helped her, her bustle, and the train of her dress into the carriage. They set off to meet Sheridan at Ebbit House.

He was standing just inside the entrance to the dining room, with the host standing beside him. They were obviously waiting for his guests. The room was filled with dozens of gentlemen, most of them in full dress uniforms, and their ladies looking like escapees from a flower garden.

The bustles and trains that were part of ladies evening dress made it necessary for the staff at the restaurant to make additional space between the tables so the ladies could get through. The host quickly escorted them to the table they had held for them.

After getting settled and ordering dinner and a good wine to wash it down, Rebecca noticed the additional star on Sheridan's shoulder. "So, Philip, I see you got your promotion! Congratulations."

"Yes, thank you. They gave me the third star for the work I have done out in Missouri the past couple of years. I have been running back and forth between Washington and St. Louis like a damned idiot. At least I can do it by train, so it only takes a couple of days."

Charlie grinned. "Could not have happened to a better man."

"Speaking of better men. You know that Grant sees you as one of his golden boys after what you went through at Appomattox Station. He had a plan to put you over at the Department of Interior before you went and got yourself elected mayor. He wanted you to be undersecretary, you know."

"Now he is planning on having you as one of his key points of contact in getting Virginia readmitted to the Union. He is hoping to have it done early next year. He has given me a list of senators and representatives he wants me to introduce you to tonight. Please, keep yourself available to me tonight."

"Oh, hell! I knew this was a political circus, but hoped I would be able to keep a low profile."

"Oh, no." Sheridan shook his head at Charlie, and then grinned at Rebecca. "Neither of you will be able to keep a low profile. We have the Union Army hero of Appomattox Station and his magnificently beautiful 'rebel' wife, building successful businesses, a home, and a family together in Virginia, after the rebellion? Of course he wants to show you both off. You are the standard by which he measures the reconstruction and expects everyone else to do so. He also wants you to tell them about how things are going in Virginia and, with the coloreds having the vote now, that the state is ready to return to the Union."

They both groaned. Their soups appeared just then and the conversation turned to Sheridan's adventures in dealing with the Lakota and Cheyenne Indians over the past two years.

As dessert was served, Charlie looked thoughtful for a moment. "Did you happen to see Gould at the reception this afternoon?"

"No," said Sheridan. "But wherever that man is, I tend to look for the knives, as I am sure that if I am not careful, one will end up in my back."

Charlie snorted. "Well, it looks like he has a new target. He had Grant's brother-in-law, Corbin, cornered and was talking very intensely with him. I assume Gould is going to try to use the president's family as a wedge to get his pet projects approved."

"Oh, Lord. And one cannot say a thing to Grant about his family. As far as he is concerned, every member of his family is as pure as the driven snow and walks on water."

"Phil, we need to keep an eye out. There is not much I can do from Culpeper, but you are up here, and you know who to talk with."

"I will do what I can."

When they finished dinner, they stepped outside, where William was waiting to convey the three of them to the Department of the Treasury building. For the first time in American history, and in part as an acknowledgement of Grant's position as a national hero, a public building was being used as the site of the inaugural celebrations.

Just as they had in the morning, they had to wait in a long line of carriages to reach the door of the Treasury. As they drew up to the steps of the building, Charlie suggested to Rebecca that she leave her cloak in the carriage, as he was leaving his greatcoat. "I have been to these Washington events before, and let me warn you that the horde at the coat room is enough to make Attila the Hun blanch." Rebecca dropped her cloak beside Charlie's and grinned.

"Lucky you." Sheridan laughed, throwing his coat over Rebecca's shoulders. "I have to take mine, since I am sure the president is going to send me off to do something or other tonight."

She stepped down from the carriage and moved up the stairs and into the warmth of the building as quickly as possible. The entrance hall was crowded as they waited for Sheridan to check his overcoat, but then with two generals in full dress uniforms, including their swords, escorting her, somehow an easy path to the door opened for her.

They were greeted by a marine sergeant major in full dress holding a parade baton. He took the invitation card from Sheridan, pounded the floor three times and announced in stentorian tones, "Lieutenant General Philip H. Sheridan." He took the card from Charlie and repeated his pounding. "Brigadier General and Mrs. Charles H. Redmond."

As they stepped forward, heads all around the room turned to look at them. Announcements of arrivals were only given if the guest was especially important to the new president. Again, a path opened for them, and the room grew quiet for a moment as the crowd looked at and obviously admired the vision that Charlie and Rebecca presented. Grant's plan to show off one of his favored was in full bloom. Charlie felt like a goose voting for an early Christmas. Thankfully, the individual conversations resumed swiftly.

Sheridan escorted them around the room, stopping to introduce them to various members of Congress, or to have a word or two with officers that both men had served with over the years. The Marine Band was providing the music, and as the evening wore on, the conversations wandered to the edge of the room, while the center was devoted to whirling couples.

Charlie ended up pinned in the corner by several congressmen who wanted to talk about how reconstruction was going in Virginia and to discover if the people were really ready to return to the status of statehood. Rebecca was rarely at his side, as half of the congressmen and a large number of military officers kept coming to ask her to dance.

She finally managed to offer Charlie an escape when she was returned to his side by her latest dance partner and she charmingly requested that he take her to find something to drink.

"Oh, my God, bless you, woman!" He managed to neatly snatch two glasses of champagne off a tray carried by a waiter as he walked by. "I thought they were going to talk my ear off, and I swear, they were far more interested in hearing their own voices than they were on discovering my experience and opinions on the subject."

"And all of my dance partners wanted to know how a beat up old war horse like you ended up with me! I think they are jealous."

"Good. They should be. Do you think we can slip out soon? I would love nothing more than to return to Mrs. Galloway's and explore our bed together."

"Not until after I have my dance with Philip and one with the president." She smiled. "He let me know a few minutes ago his circumstances had changed."

"Looks like you get to be shown off as well." He laughed.

"I did not realize I would be a target of his machinations."

"Nor did I, dear. I am so sorry."

"It is because he knows," she said confidently in her place as Charlie's wife and partner.

"Knows what?"

"That we are equal spouses, and without my support for whatever it is he is plotting, you will fight him. By placing me firmly in the middle…"

He nodded, agreeing as he tossed back the glass of champagne. She finished her drink and Charlie offered her his arm, leading her back into the lion's den.

~

Friday, March 5, 1869

Charlie nearly snorted coffee through his nose as he read the morning paper. They were enjoying a quiet breakfast in their room. He was trying to get his choking and laughing under control while his wife sat in her chair across from him wondering if he had lost his mind. He folded the paper over and pointed to a small article about the inaugural ball.

He finally managed to draw a clear breath. "Seems as if we left just in time last night. Apparently, things got very ugly."

Rebecca laughed aloud as she read the article. "I wonder who will be looking for a job today?"

"The person who thought it was a wise idea to hire illiterate people to handle the coat check?"

She continued reading, laughing as she did. "I wonder if Philip got his coat back. It says here there were fist fights among the men!"

He nodded, beginning to chuckle again as he poured another cup of coffee. "Apparently, the ladies were in tears."

"It is not funny. I would have been devastated," she said sternly before snickering.

"I told you it would be the most dangerous part of the evening."

"Did you see this bit, here at the bottom?"

"Where it says that some people simply abandoned their coats?" He burst out laughing again, causing his laugh lines to stand out in relief. "I wonder if the president will set up a lost and found at the White House."

CHAPTER 26

April 20, 1869

Buddy and Andy were reveling in their newfound freedom. That winter, they had both celebrated their fourth birthdays, and with that momentous event, they had finally shed the leading strings that had kept them tied, literally, to their nursemaid.

Four-year-old boys can be very, very sneaky. Today, on this bright spring day, they had been plotting together since the moment they got up; whispering in corners when they thought no one was listening. They were going to escape out to the big yard all by themselves and go exploring.

"Buddy, watch for Tess. I can get the door." The latch on the door was very high for a small boy to reach, but Andy was long and lean and very inventive. Standing on tiptoe, propped against the wall, he stretched one arm up and snagged the lever on the latch, then leaned back. The door swung open slowly; Andy hit the floor with much less grace.

Buddy kept peeking around the door into the bedroom behind them, where Tess was making the beds. At the sound of Andy's thump, he looked a little panicked, but manfully carried on with the charade. "Andy, you are so clumsy. Falling over your own shoes."

Andy feigned a sniffle, and then stuck his head through the door to check the hall. It was empty. He waved his brother over, and the two little boys slipped into the hall and over to the back stairs. Moving with all the grace and stealth of any pair of four-year-olds, they stumbled and bumped their way down the steep stairs, finally settling on sitting on the steps and ooching down them one at a time on their bottoms, the best padded part of them. Halfway down the second flight, on their way to the kitchen door, Buddy caught his britches on a nail head that had worked its way a little loose on the stairs. As he slipped down to the next step, he left a chunk of his pants behind.

Finally, at the bottom of the stairs, the two watched as Sarah bustled around the kitchen. She was packing up her spices, as today was the day she moved out to the summer kitchen. She picked up a big basket and hauled it out the back door, leaving it open, since her hands were full. Right behind her, like two little grinning shadows, Buddy and Andy slipped the bounds of four-year-old imprisonment.

They scampered across the kitchen yard, through the gate and into the stable yards. Moving carefully, and staying in the shadow of the big stone barn, they started exploring.

Tess came out of the boy's bedroom expecting to find them playing with any one of the many toys that Charlie had accumulated for them over the years. But there was no sign of them – anywhere. Tess panicked, running into the hall, calling Ginnie from the girls' room to help her look. Frantically, the two women went from room to room on the second floor, calling the boys' names, looking under beds, in armoires, and behind chairs.

"My god," Tess moaned. "If anything happens to those imps, Miz 'Becca will have my hide."

At the far end of the stone barn, two rather muddy and very happy little boys stopped to check their haul of mysterious treasure. Several rocks, a piece of dried horse dung, a crushed early daffodil, and several entirely unidentifiable objects coated in spring mud were produced and compared. Then the two heard a new and interesting sound. Coming from a very heavily boarded pen ahead of them, the two heard the sounds of rambunctious young goats playing in the sun after several days of rain.

Like iron filings to a magnet, the two little boys flew to the pen, fascinated by the new sounds. Andy slipped the latch on the gate and there they were… a whole pen full of animals that the boys had only seen in their picture books. Goats. Little goats. Goats that were actually shorter than the boys. Goats that were just the right size for two big, strong four-year-old boys to play with.

History began to repeat itself, though the boys decided that playing Indians circling the goat wagon train was far more fun than their sisters' game of ring around the rosie. The first time the goats fell down, the boys were startled. They crouched over the nearest kid and poked and pulled at it, trying to get it to stand up, terrified that their father would be very unhappy that they killed his goats. But once the herd regained their feet, the boys realized this was the best game of all – goats who would play with them.

Tess knocked on the office door, then let herself in when she heard a distracted acknowledgement. Rebecca was hunched over her breed books, her most common occupation on a spring morning. "Miz 'Becca?"

"Yes," she answered distractedly.

"Um, Miz ''Becca, I think the boys managed to get out of the house. I found a piece of Buddy's britches on the back stairs and Ginnie and I have looked everywhere."

Rebecca stood immediately, leaving the books open on her desk, which is something she never did. "Have you looked in the yard? Get every available body and start looking for them. As a matter of fact," she commanded as she slipped her jacket on. "Get everybody who is not available to begin looking for them."

"Yes'm, Miz 'Becca. Sarah and Beulah are looking in the kitchen yard and summer kitchen. Reg has already run down to the barns to tell Mr. Brooks. Ginnie went out front to see if they slipped out the front door."

"Then I suppose we should begin our search as well. Where are Louis, Freddy, and Darby? They can certainly help."

"Um, Louis, Freddy, and Master Darby went into town with Gen'l Charlie, ma'am."

"Of course they did," she growled as she left the room in search of her children. "Come along, Tess, it is hard telling what they have gotten themselves into."

The boys were having a wonderful time. The goats made the best wagon train, and they had even found a couple of feathers from a jaybird that they stuck in their now muddy and matted hair. The older goats were not that much fun; they just huddled by the wall of the pen so that when they went all stiff, they just leaned against the wall till they could walk again. But the two-month-old kids stuck together in a cluster in the middle of the pen, and fell down very satisfyingly every time the boys let loose with a resounding war whoop.

Rebecca, after so many years, had developed a keen sense of

mother's hearing, and almost as soon as she stepped out on the back porch she heard the unmistakable sounds of rowdy boys. "Half Indian they must be with all that whooping and hollering they do."

She stepped off the porch and headed directly for the pen, shaking her head, knowing from experience what was going on. “Charlie’s damn goats.”

The truth was, as much as the general liked them, as much as the children enjoyed them and as much as she was fond of the roasts that came off their furry little bodies, Rebecca had never found a place in her heart for Charlie’s damn goats.

Andy saw her first and froze in place, fixed by her motherly stare that he knew in his four-year-old heart meant that he was in serious trouble. Buddy let loose with another war cry and fell over giggling when the goats collapsed. Slowly, he realized that his brother had not joined him in this round of defeating the wagon train and he looked around from his position on the ground with the immobilized goats. In his best contrite voice, he acknowledged the avenging angel that stood over him. “Hello, Mama.”

“Hello indeed. Get up.” She was not yelling and that for the boys was far more frightening than if she were having a full-blown fit. They had learned early that Mama could yell. “What exactly do you think you are doing?”

Little Charlie stood up and tried to brush some of the mud off his shirt and pants. He succeeded in simply making a bigger mess, but he stood up manfully. “Andy and I were playing with the goats. We are big boys now – you said we were, Mama.”

“Yes, I know I said you were big boys.” She knelt next to them, angry they had slipped out but relieved they were not hurt. “But you are not big enough to be out by yourself. There are a lot of things on the farm that could hurt you. If you want to see

Papa's silly goats, you must ask. You must always have an adult with you."

Andy hung his head and shuffled over to stand beside Buddy. Together, the two boys mumbled the words that would come to define their lives for the next few years. "Yes, Mama."

"Good." She hugged them both with a relieved sigh and placed kisses to their temples. "Now, if you want to play with Papa's silly goats for a few more minutes, I will stay with you, but it must be our secret. Do not tell Papa."

Charlie had never been pleased with Rebecca allowing the children to tease the goats, but in all the years they had been on the farm, none had died. Rebecca believed that the goats actually seemed to enjoy it on some level.

Tess and Ginnie waited in the kitchen, knowing that Miz 'Becca would be back shortly and that they would probably be the object of her ire. It was not a pleasant prospect. "But," Tess mumbled to herself, "keeping track of those two little rascals is harder than holding on to a Jack Russell puppy during fox hunt season." If she were lucky, maybe Miz Becca would understand.

They were surprised as Rebecca entered the kitchen, herding her two mud puppies in front of her. "I think these two need cleaning up a bit. It is clear to me that we are all in for a challenging time keeping track of them." With that, she handed the children over to their attendants and trooped off to her room to change.

As lunchtime approached, Rebecca set a trap for her loving husband and his annoying goats. She was dressed in her best day dress, and Lizbet had spent extra time on her hair. In fact,

Rebecca was at her most charming, gracious and lovely best as she waited for Charlie in the small parlor.

He rode up to the front door. Louis and Darby were following in the new pony trap, going slowly as Darby struggled to master the art of driving. Reg was on the steps, waiting to take his horse. "Miz 'Becca's waiting for you in the back parlor, Gen'l Charlie."

"Thank you, Reg." He entered and hung his hat on the rack inside the door. *Hummm. If Rebecca's waiting in the parlor instead of the morning room, something is amiss.* Cautiously, he approached the door, tapped lightly and then entered. "Good afternoon, darling. You look particularly lovely today."

"Thank you. I thought it would be best to look presentable when I broke the bad news."

"Bad news, dear?" Charlie sat beside her and took her hand in his. "Oh, dear. What is the matter?" Solicitous usually worked with her.

"We were invaded by Indians." She tried desperately to keep the smile from her face, deciding to hide it behind her brandy glass instead.

He blinked a couple of times, then a slow grin spread over his face. "Indians, you say. My, my! Perhaps very short Indians?"

"Hmm." She nodded. "About so high." She indicated with her hand. "Runs With The Goats and his brother, Follows Runs With The Goats."

He nodded sagely, trying very hard to suppress the snicker that was burbling up. "I see. And would these two be members of the little known Mud-foot tribe?"

"I think they are members of the local mud everywhere tribe. They were having a delightful time playing with the goats. Slipped out of their room. Andy has discovered he can turn the knob."

Charlie stood up and paced across the room. "So they went

and terrorized my goats – and just a couple of months after they dropped seven fine new kids?" He shook his head. "It is a miracle that those goats have not died from your children's hijinks."

"My children?" She snickered as she poured another brandy for herself and one for him. "Do you mean to tell me that after all this time you have not figured out that when they are bad they are your children?"

"Not at all, dear. When they are bad, they are yours." He lifted the snifter out of Rebecca's hand and kissed her cheek. "I hear Darby in the hall. Shall we go have lunch and discuss what we must do about our two little redskins?"

"I suppose so." She took his hand and let him guide her out of the room.

~

Friday, May 14, 1869

Edgar stood in the parlor looking at the expectant faces in the room. Charlotte was clearly curious and even Rex's normally placid features showed a tad of anxiety. The twins played at the feet of their mother and godfather while their father tried to find exactly the right words.

"Well, dear family." He sighed and pulled a letter from his pocket. "We have been recalled to England. A new minister will arrive in Culpeper in a month and we leave in two."

Charlotte straightened in her chair, a look of disbelief on her face. "Well, we have much to do then. Should we be prepared to vacate the manse in a month?"

"I think so, darling. From my understanding, the new minister is a young man with a wife and two children. I am hoping that our generous cousins will allow us to stay with them again until we depart."

She laughed and nodded. "Rex and I will start packing. **You** get to speak with Cousin Charlie."

~

Later that afternoon, Rex and Edgar had a few moments together privately. "Rex, do you think we could get Darby into Eton?"

"Even if he does not pass the entrance tests for King's Scholar, he will certainly qualify as an Oppidan Scholar. With the fact that he is the son of a United States war hero, your family connections and my money, they will be falling over themselves to accept him."

"So when I go to let Charlie know about what is going on, I may suggest that we take Darby with us?"

"Absolutely. I think it will do the boy good. The biggest question is, will his mother let him go? And of course you will have to consult Charlotte."

"One of the advantages of being a minister. I can make sure Rebecca will feel so guilty about denying him this opportunity that she will not be able to say no. Aunt Charlotte is already on board with this idea." He grinned.

"You have always been a sly one. Where are we going this time?"

"You will be happy to hear they have given me the small parish in Eton Wick."

Rex laughed. "We have already spent some time there, have we not?"

"Yes, my dear friend. I'll have the old church again--St. John the Baptist."

Both men grinned at each other. After being so harshly cast

out by the Monarch of Great Britain, something had changed. Now, obviously, their banishment was over. They were going home.

~

Saturday, May 15, 1869

Charlie and Rebecca were sitting in front of the fire in their private sitting room. They were ready for bed, dressed in their nightclothes and robes, and enjoying a last brandy before they retired for the night.

"Edgar came by today. He has some news that we all knew would come someday, though I am surprised it has come so soon. He has been recalled by the Church of England to take over a parish near his parents' home, a little place called Eton Wick. They will be leaving in July. Since the new minister will arrive before he leaves, he wanted to know if they could stay with us in the month before they depart."

"Why, of course, dear. Where else would they stay? They are family!"

He took a sip of his brandy and a deep draw on the cigar he was smoking – one of Rex's special blends. "He had another request, or should I say a suggestion."

"Whatever he needs. What he and Rex have done for us, and especially what Rex has done for you, can never be repaid."

"Well, dear, he made an offer that I do not think we can turn down. They will be living just two miles from Eton, probably the best boys' schools in the world. There is nothing in the United States that even begins to compare to it. The students at Eton tend to go on to university at Cambridge or Oxford, which you must admit are the two finest universities in the world."

"What does this have to do with his offer?" She was

suspicious that she already knew, but needed to hear him put it into words.

"Since Edgar is a graduate of Eton and his family has been attending that school for multiple generations, he believes it will not be a problem to get Darby in."

"But Darby is only fourteen. Is that not a little young?"

"Not at all. Eton students are between the ages of thirteen and eighteen. Darby will be fifteen this fall."

Rebecca took a deep breath. Her first instinct was to not even want to talk about it.

Breaking into the silence, Charlie added, "At fifteen, we should be preparing for him to go away to school soon anyway."

"Yes. School here – say down in Charlottesville at Mr. Jefferson's school – where he will have his family close so that we can care for him if he is sick or hurt."

Charlie looked at Rebecca out of the corner of his eye. He knew better than to look straight at her right then. "So what are Edgar, Rex, and Charlotte to him? They are family, and Eton Wick is only a couple of miles from the school, not the almost fifty miles from here to Charlottesville. If anything happens, Rex can be there in a matter of minutes, and no one is better qualified to take care of him than Rex."

Rebecca hated it that he was being so damned logical.

"If we let him go with them, how are they going to get there?"

"By ship, dear."

"So he would have to travel from here to New York to catch the ship?"

"Yes, dear. He has made that trip before."

"And then how long would he be on the ship?"

"The trip should only take eight or nine days. Two weeks at the most."

"On a ship? At sea? In the middle of the ocean?"

"Yes, dear. That is where ships are most useful."

"Where they could get caught in a terrible storm and sink?"

"That is not likely, love. The hurricane season does not start until late September, and they will be safely established in England long before then."

"What if he gets washed over by a rogue wave? Or falls overboard because he was climbing somewhere he was not supposed to be?"

Charlie, who was feeling a little silly from the cigar anyway, blew a blast of air through pursed lips. At least it was not an outright guffaw, which was still brewing in his chest and belly. "Dear, washed overboard? Washed overboard?"

He took a deep breath. Finding an answer to her less than reasonable objections was being a challenge. "I do not think any of the adults among the passengers or crew will allow Darby to go climbing the railings or the rigging or be outside in a storm. Even if he were, by some EXTREMELY unlikely chance, to fall overboard, they have life preservers and boats. He would be fished out of the water immediately."

"What if he fell in and got eaten by a shark before they could get him out?"

Charlie had been struggling for control. At this point, he completely lost it. He started laughing so hard that he could neither talk nor breathe. Tears of laughter were running down his cheeks.

"Charles Huger Redmond, how dare you laugh at me!" She kicked him in the foot. "How dare you think putting our young son at risk on a ship at sea, and sending him off to a school where we will not be able see him for **years** is a good thing. Why, if you send him off to England, what will he think? That we have thrown him out? He may never come home again."

"Ahhh." He finally managed to get his laughter under control. "Our son, who wants nothing more than to learn everything possible? Who knows about the school because he learned about its founding by Henry the Sixth when he was studying history? He will not think we are throwing him out; he will think we are giving him the best gift we possibly could by sending him to one of the best schools in the world. He will be with family. You said yourself that Edgar, Rex, and Charlotte were family."

"He will be gone for years, Charlie. Years. Next time you see him, he will be shaving. Next time he may have an English wife and children, for all we know."

"Next time we see him, he may have a beard. He has been shaving for six months."

"But, Charlie. He is our boy!"

"Yes, Rebecca, he is our boy. And we want what is best for him. This **is** best for him. So, dear, you need to acknowledge that he is growing up and put aside what you want for what he wants and needs. We are not going to make him go if he does not want to, but if he does, we are going to smile, and encourage him and wish him God speed."

Rebecca looked at the fire for a while. She drew a deep sigh, then said, in a very subdued voice, "Yes, dear, but he has to promise to write me at least once a week."

~

Monday, June 14, 1869

Big Ben, with help from George and Jimmy, the local teamsters, had moved the Vile family's personal belongings to the Redmond house over the weekend, and loaded the cases they were shipping directly to England in the storage shed at the railroad station.

Charlotte and Rex busied themselves settling their possessions in the same rooms they had stayed in when both had first come to the Redmond household, with the major exception being that Rex had the room he and Edgar had originally shared to himself and Charlotte and Edgar shared the one that she had used in those harrowing first days of her move to Culpeper. The twins were established in the nursery, which still had the cribs that Buddy and Andy had used, though the boys had outgrown their baby beds and now had rooms of their own as 'big' boys of four.

They had left the household staff at the manse, to serve the incoming minister and his family, including their nursery maid, since the Addisons had two children of their own and would need the help. Rex had seen to it that the servants' salaries were covered until the end of the year, and had further established a trust to keep paying for them over time. Mr. Cooper would be able to draw on the account to not only pay the staff, but to also pay for maintenance on the manse should it be needed.

Edgar had gone to the train station to meet the incoming minister and escort them to the manse. He had George and Jimmy, along with their largest wagon, waiting to load and convey the Addisons' possessions to their new home.

Promptly at 11:30, the train pulled into Culpeper station. Edgar stood waiting for the passengers to debark. Several gentlemen, mostly tradesmen coming to sell their wares, stepped onto the platform. Finally, a rather slender young man with light brown hair and a somewhat out of date suit climbed down, holding a young child in one arm and a carpet bag in the other. He dropped the bag on the platform and reached back to offer his hand to a slight woman with mousy blonde hair and a slightly harried look on her face, who was carrying another small child.

The new minister and his family had arrived.

Edgar strode forward, his hand extended. "Good morning. You must be Warburton Addison?" The young man nodded. "I am Edgar Vile. Welcome to Culpeper."

The young man extended his hand in return. "Good morning, Reverend Vile. Let me introduce my wife, Ariel, and my children, Ainslie and Leslie."

Edgar politely greeted Ariel Addison and smiled benignly at the two boys fussing in their parents' arms. "I have some men unloading your baggage; they will bring it to the manse shortly. Until then, can I escort you to your new home?"

He loaded the new minister and his family into the small trap. It was a tight fit, but fortunately the trip was not very long. Edgar knew he had four people to transport, and so took the reins himself.

They pulled up to the manse and Edgar's houseman, Japheth, caught the reins. The rest of the servants were waiting in line at the door; Deborah, the housekeeper; Zipporah the cook, and Leah, the nursery maid. Introductions were made and Edgar led what was now a small parade into the house.

Ariel looked around with an expression of wonder on her face. "Oh, my, it is beautiful." Her husband's first assignment had been in a community that had not recovered as well as Culpeper had, and the housing for the minister and his family had more closely resembled what this house had been like before Edgar, Charlotte, and Rex took it over, replete with the ancient flocked wallpaper, than this piece of modern elegance.

Edgar went on as if she had not expressed wonder at the house. "I am afraid that because we are being sent back to England, we had to leave the furnishings, but I assume over time you will replace them with your own." *Like hell they will*, he thought. "Shall we let Leah take the babies up to the nursery while I show you around?"

Ariel nodded, wordless at the luxury she was entering.

Edgar led them into the front parlor, furnished in the French style. They looked around, an expression of amazement on both faces. From there, he led them into the rear parlor, which he, Rex, and Charlotte usually used as their private parlor. It was comfortably furnished in traditional English country house style. Across the hall was the dining room, with a mahogany table that would seat twelve comfortably, and in front of that was the office and library, with its massive desk, book-lined walls, and comfortable lounge under the windows.

But the real shock to the Addisons came when he showed them the winter kitchen. The walls on one side of the room were lined with glass fronted cabinets and held the glasses and plate, while on the other wall was the great caste iron stove, the wok heater, the sink, the ice box and the work surfaces. Ariel looked closely at the taps over the sink. "Hot and cold running water?"

"Yes. We have it out in the summer kitchen and in the wash room upstairs too."

"Oh, my," came her breathless reply.

She looked at the wok burner. "Pardon me, but what is that?"

Edgar looked at it. "Oh, that. Well, we are rather fond of oriental style cooking, and that is a specialized burner that gets particularly hot to handle. Zipporah knows how to use it. I think you will enjoy some of the things she has learned to make."

Warburton's and Ariel's eyes continued to grow larger and larger. The concept of having a cook who could make exotic dishes was stunning, especially since Ariel had done all of the cooking for the family and their guests at the last assignment. She was not sure she knew what to do with real servants.

Edgar continued to add to the amazement. "The summer kitchen out back is similarly equipped. I hope you like it." He turned and led them back into the hall. "Let me show you the upstairs."

Just as they started upstairs, they heard a commotion on the front steps. Jimmy and George had arrived with the Addisons' baggage, and with Japheth, were unloading it. Deborah came bustling down the stairs to help organize and disburse the luggage.

Upstairs was just as overwhelming. The wash room was the most impressive, with its black and white marble tiles and the huge tub with its hot and cold running water. They looked at the toilet with its pull chain and realized that hauling slop jars was a thing of the past.

They stuck their heads into the nursery, where there were two cribs that the Addison boys had already been settled into for naps. Leah had gotten a light lunch down them while their parents were touring the house and the two little boys had been exhausted by the travelling and the many changes they were undergoing.

Edgar walked back down stairs, and said, "I will leave you to unpack. You have been invited to dinner at the congregation's primary benefactor this evening – just a quiet dinner; I will subject you to meeting the rest of the congregation after you have had a chance to get settled. I will call for you around five?"

"Uh, yes, thank you." Warburton spoke for the first time since they had begun the house tour. "Um, may I ask where you and your family are staying, since it is clear you have already moved out of here?"

"Oh, well, my wife is the cousin of General Redmond, with whom we are dining this evening, so we are staying with them."

"Oh. I see. Well, then, until this evening?"

Edgar turned to leave.

"Oh, excuse me, but what about the servants?"

Warburton Addison was very sure he could not afford house servants on his ministerial salary.

"Oh, that. They come with the house, not out of your salary. A trust was established by the same benefactor who renovated the manse to see to it that the building and grounds were properly maintained."

"Oh," Warburton and Ariel breathed together. This might be the best assignment in the entire diocese.

Promptly at 5:00, a town coach drawn by a matched pair of thoroughbreds drew up in front of the manse. A footman jumped down from beside the driver and went to the door, where he knocked.

When Japheth opened the door, he asked, "Are Reverend and Mrs. Addison ready to go to dinner? Gen'l Charlie sent us to retrieve them."

"I will get them for you."

The two Addisons looked at the beautiful town coach and the even more beautiful horses drawing it as they came out of the house. The footman opened the door for them, and handed them into the coach, then jumped up on the box. They had never been in a conveyance quite this elegant. The drive out to the Redmonds house was beautiful, travelling through the country in high summer, where the fields were lush with growing wheat, corn, and grass for the horses. The brick and wrought iron gates into the Redmonds' home were impressive, as was the long tree-lined drive up to one of the largest houses that the Addisons had ever seen. What in the world were they getting into with this new posting?

Reg met them at the door and showed them into the back parlor. Edgar had warned the family that the new minister and his wife were not exactly the most socially experienced couple he had ever met, so Charlotte and Rebecca decided to keep things very casual. It was a good thing. While the Addisons were wearing their best, his suit was at least five years out of date and slightly worn at the cuffs and elbows, and her dress was equally out of fashion. Charlotte and Rebecca had stayed in day dresses, and Charlie was simply dressed in shirt, vest and tweed jacket, not his usual dinner dress. Rex and Edgar were also casually dressed.

The people in the back parlor all rose when Reg opened the door and showed the Addisons into the room.

Charlie spoke first. He extended his hand. "Welcome to Mountain View. I am Charles Redmond, Charlie to my friends." He turned to Rebecca and then to the other individuals in the room. "This is my wife, Rebecca; my cousin, Charlotte Vile; our friend, Tongzhi Xiang. We call him Rex." He turned to the seven children, five of them lined up side by side, the sixth and seventh being held by two nursemaids. "And these five are our children, Darby, Suzanne, Emily, Andy and Buddy. The other two are the Vile twins, Edgar and Becky."

The Addisons blinked. This house was fantastic. They had never been in a place like this. These people, so casual and easy with one another, were of a social class they had no experience with. What **had** they gotten into?

The children were dismissed to their various locations and polite conversation started the process of getting to know one another until Reg announced that supper was ready. Rebecca led the way to the breakfast room. She was fairly sure that the formal dining room was just a little much for her new minister and his wife.

CHAPTER 27

Monday, July 12, 1869

Rebecca was sitting in the rear parlor waiting for Charlie to get home for supper. She was not happy that he was late as this would be the last supper the family would have together. In the morning, the Vile family would leave for England, taking Darby with them. Yesterday, the congregation had descended on Mountain View to throw the Viles a memorable going-away party. Tonight was just for the family.

Darby had been so excited when he was asked if he would like to go that her natural instincts as a mother had kicked in and she found herself happy he was looking forward to it. They had spent the last month working with both Rex and Edgar to get the things he would need packed and ready to go.

Then came the question of what to do with Freddy. Darby would no longer be able to use his services at school. Charlie immediately reassured the boy they would find him another spot in the house, but Rex shook his head, raising his hand. "I will be in need of a good man to help me take care of the house and the children. Edgar and Charlotte will be very busy when we arrive. Darby will have some time before his first term will start and we would not think of breaking them up. It will be nice for Darby to have a friend that he has known for a while as he gets settled."

Charlie grinned at Freddy, who looked like he was going to faint. "Looks as you are going to England as well. If you want to, that is. No one will force you."

The boy just grinned and nodded before dashing into Darby's room to help him pack. "Hey, Darb! Guess what!"

A knock on the parlor door brought Rebecca back from her thoughts of her son's departure. "Come in!"

Rex slipped in and gently closed the door behind him. He had tucked under his arm a box she knew well. It was the chest that held his beautiful ivory mah jong tiles. She rose and gave him a kiss on the cheek as they made their way back to the chairs by the empty fireplace.

"Allow me to apologize for that louse of a husband of mine. I asked him…"

Rex just smiled and shook his head. "Do not be concerned. We are perfectly happy to wait for Charlie. In the meantime, I wanted to take a moment to give you this."

He placed the box in her lap. As her hands rubbed over the ornate carvings on the top, tears came to her eyes. "I cannot possibly take this."

"Yes." He took her hand and gently brought it to his lips. "My dear Rebecca, you most certainly will. I can think of no one else in the world I would prefer to have it. Besides, you must keep up our traditional Saturday night games. You cannot do that without a proper set." He grinned. "You've always had very good luck with these."

She smiled and caressed his cheek. “Thank you. I will treasure them.”

“I’m sure you will.” He stood and gave her a little bow. “Now, madam, if you will excuse me, I drew bathing duty for the twins tonight and we want them down before that louse you married gets home. Then we intend to drink a great deal of his best wine.”

~

Tuesday, July 13, 1869

Edgar and his family were already in the carriage. They watched patiently and indulgently as Charlie and, most importantly, Rebecca said good-bye to their eldest son. Edgar had expected it would take some time and put his family on schedule to leave an hour earlier than needed.

Darby stood there in one of his best suits, looking tall and handsome, even at fourteen. Charlie winked, shook his son’s hand and handed him an envelope. “You may need this.”

The young man only sighed and nodded as he tucked the money-filled packet into his pocket. “Thank you. I love you, Papa.”

“I love you too, son. You be good.”

“I will.”

They fell into each other. Rebecca watched as both men hugged and patted each other firmly on the back before standing apart. Charlie sniffed once and stepped back, allowing her to have her moment.

“A letter a week, Darby Redmond. No excuses.”

He smiled and shook his head gently. “No excuses, Mama. I promise.”

She palmed his cheek and smiled, fighting tears. “I am so

proud of you. You are a fine young man. You know I love you just as if you were my own?"

He smiled again, feeling his own tears as he touched his mama's face. "I AM yours. I have been since the day I came for the milk."

Now she really smiled, even as her tears spilled down her cheeks. "You be good or I will come tan your hide."

"Yes, ma'am." He reached into his pocket and pulled out an envelope. "My first letter." He pressed it into her hands and kissed her cheek. "I love you, Mama. I will be home before you know it."

~

Monday, September 20, 1869

Charlie settled into his desk chair and started scanning the financial sections of the paper. Something there caught his eye. The prices of metal ores – gold, silver, iron, copper – were fluctuating far more than usual. He frowned. It looked like someone was playing with the market. The price of gold alone had gone from $37 an ounce to over $140. Something was very wrong, especially since Treasury Secretary Boutwell had been selling about $1,000,000 worth of gold a month to stabilize the market and finance government expenses. He made a note to himself to tell Frank to make sure there was plenty of gold coin on hand at the bank.

He went back to reading the news and smiled. Petroleum was doing well; the market for kerosene continued to expand. And the timber market was strong and steady. His decision to diversify the family's holdings seemed to be working.

~

Friday, September 24, 1869

Charlie looked across the breakfast table and felt his heart sink. Rebecca was nearly on the verge of tears again. He took a deep breath and offered, "Darling, come into town with me this morning."

"Why?"

"Why not? Perhaps you could see Elizabeth, or pay a visit to the new dress maker."

"You are trying to distract me."

"Yes, I am. I do hate seeing you like this."

"I miss him."

"I do too, but you know he is fine with Edgar and Charlotte."

"But he is not with them. He is all alone at that school."

"That school is the finest boys' school in the world. Our son goes home to Charlotte and Edgar every weekend and every holiday. He is less than five miles away from them."

"But he is not with us."

"No, he is not, but he is growing into a fine young man and this is important for him."

She nodded. "I know."

"You are his mother and you want to wrap him in cotton batting and keep him tied to your skirts."

"Yes, damn it."

Now he could not help but laugh. "Come into town with me. I have a light schedule today. You visit with Elizabeth and we will have lunch and then come home."

She nodded, agreeing to his plan. She knew he was right. She would be better off spending the morning socializing rather than sitting at home, moping over Darby.

An hour later, Charlie drove one of their little buggies into town, and as they came upon the bank, Frank came out gripping a thick stack of papers in one hand. He stepped into the middle of the street and waved Charlie down.

"General Redmond, I know you are not an officer anymore, but you are still on the board. You need to see these, sir. All hell is breaking loose in New York."

"What is it?" He trapped the reins under his foot as the buggy stopped. Frank thrust the stack of telegrams at him.

"It smells like Fisk and Gould!"

Charlie's eyes snapped shut and he groaned. "So much for my short day." He began flipping through the telegrams, quickly sorting out what seemed to be happening. "Trying to corner the gold market?"

"So it would seem. Should I open the bank?"

"Absolutely." He nodded before turning to his wife. "Darling, I am sorry but I really should try to sort this mess out."

"You go." She reached down and took the reins. "I will go see if Elizabeth is in."

"If you see Richard or any of the deputies, please send them my way."

"Charlie, what is happening?"

He climbed down from the buggy and sighed as he placed his hand tenderly on her cheek. "Greedy men trying to do stupid things to make themselves more money while risking the financial ruin of the rest of the country. I will make sure to let you know everything as soon as I sort out how bad it is."

"Are we at risk?"

"We will see some losses, yes. Jerome and I did everything we could to get a good solid foundation under us. We should be able to ride it out and come out the other side alright."

"Well then, let me go find you a provost or two. Seems like the bank will be a good place for them to be today."

"Thank you, darling." He stepped back and she snapped the

reins making her way toward the courthouse and the provost's office.

~

Charlie made his way up to Frank's office. He no longer kept an office at the bank, but used the conference room when there were board meetings. Frank was standing at the desk, his coat off, his shirt sleeves rolled up, and looking rather harried.

"Thank God you are here and can make the decisions. Take a look at this." Frank handed him a piece of ticker tape. They had installed a stock ticker earlier in the year and now it was reflecting the minute by minute activities on the market. And they were **not** good.

It was apparent that someone was trying to corner the gold market, driving the price of gold up and up. "It was a good thing you told me to stock up on gold coin. Otherwise we would be in terrible trouble. With all of this going on, do you still want me to open the bank?"

Charlie had a grim look on his face. "Yes. The worst thing we could do right now is shut down. People need to have faith in our bank, and I have enough investments in other commodities and industries, so we will survive this."

Frank nodded. Just then, one of the errand boys who delivered telegrams for George Randall, the telegraph operator, came in the door. "Miss Eloise told me to come in," he said breathlessly. "Mr. George told me to run fast with this."

Absently, Charlie tossed the boy a nickel. It was a telegram from Jerome.

FISK AND GOULD TRYING TO CORNER GOLD MARKET STOP

GRANT'S BROTHER-IN-LAW ABEL CORBIN HAS BEEN ARGUING FOR THE GOVERNMENT TO STOP SELLING GOLD ON THE OPEN

MARKET THAT IT WILL HURT RAILROADS AND GRAIN SALES OVERSEAS STOP

GOLD PRICES GOING THROUGH THE ROOF STOP

BOUTWELL IS RELEASING MORE GOLD TO THE MARKET TO HALT THIS RIDICULOUSNESS STOP

SIT TIGHT STOP

THE PRICE OF GOLD WILL CRASH SOON AND ALL HELL MAY BREAK LOSE STOP

JEROME

Charlie sat in the office all day, watching the stock ticker like an eagle watches a trout. At noon, Boutwell's offering of four million dollars worth of gold hit the market. The bottom dropped out of the price, dropping from $160 an ounce to just over $130 per ounce and it continued to fall. But it was not just the price of gold that fell through the floor. The price of many stocks fell. So did the price of agricultural good – wheat, corn, pork. With the prices falling just as the fall harvest was starting, the farmers were going to be facing a very lean year.

He called to Frank. "I think the farmers are going to be in trouble this year. This mess that Fisk and Gould and Corbin have created is going to hurt them horribly. Can you take a look at our debt load and let me know how bad suspending interest for the farmers will affect our profit for the year?"

"Yes, sir. If the bank holds up, then we can hold the farmers up – at least for a while."

"It will be a tough year because of this stupidity. I knew that trouble was brewing as soon as I saw Gould corner Corbin at the inauguration."

"We will get through. You and I have both been damned careful to make sure the bank was on sound footing. With the diversification of the portfolio, we have made good money. We have the reserves."

"And if I have to, I will prop the bank up personally."

"Let us see how bad the damage is."

Charlie and Frank, with Eloise's help, went over the books that afternoon. By the time they were done, they looked at one another and smiled tired smiles. "Well, if we do not have a bank run, we should be able to weather the storm."

Just then Rebecca walked in. "All right, General Redmond. I have visited with Elizabeth, Samantha, and Esther, who fed me a lovely lunch. What the hell is going on?"

He looked up and smiled wanly. "Well, dear wife, Fisk, Gould, Corbin and President Grant have managed to completely mess up the economy out of greed and stupidity."

"Oh, my God, Charlie. Are we going to be all right?"

"Well, it may be a little tight, but we should be able to ride this out. More importantly, with the wise investments Frank has made, the bank, and therefore Culpeper, will be able to ride it out. Belts may have to be tightened, but we will survive."

Rebecca drew a deep breath. "We have survived worse, husband. And I have a little something that may help."

"Then let us go home. I am exhausted and Monday morning is going to be difficult."

As they rode home, both were quiet, both considering the implications of an economic emergency. They trudged into the house, and Rebecca said, "Dear, come up to the office for a few minutes before we go in for supper. I need to show you something."

Charlie looked a bit confused, but followed her up the stairs.

Once in the office, Rebecca sat down on her side of their desk. She opened the right bottom drawer and reached into the back of the drawer with both hands. She pulled out an iron strong box and tried to lift it to the desktop but failed. Charlie reached over with his left hand, grabbed the handle on the top of the box, and together they hauled it up.

Rebecca reached deep into her décolletage and withdrew a key on a silver chain, then unlocked the box and flipped the lid back. The box was full. As far as Charlie could tell, it was all ten dollar gold eagles and twenty dollar gold double eagles. There was also a chamois bag. "How much is there, dear? And what is in the bag?"

"There is about five thousand in coins, and another three in unset sapphires and rubies. I know the bank is reliable, but I wanted to be sure we had enough on hand for an emergency."

~

Monday, September 27, 1869

Charlie made sure to be at the bank well before opening time. He knew that the news of the stock market crash would have gotten out, and people would be worried about the security of their money.

He was right. Forty five minutes before the bank normally opened, people started gathering in front of the building. A few minutes before opening time, Charlie straightened his coat and walked out to the front steps.

"Good morning. I know that by now you have heard all of the news about the market crash. I assume you are here to pull your money out of the bank for fear the bank will fail, but let me tell you a few things first. This mess is going to hurt every farmer in the area, regardless of what we do. Secretary Boutwell has stopped the bleeding in the gold market, so we should see things settle down in the next few days in that area, but with the fall in food prices right at harvest time, it is going to be a lean year. If you pull your money out of the bank, it is going to be even leaner."

"More importantly, Mr. Halliburton has been very, very careful about investing our money, and the bank's investments are sound and secure. If you pull your money out of the bank right now, you will make it very hard for us to support you through the winter."

"I personally guarantee that every single person's money is safe in the Farmers and Merchants Bank of Culpeper. You all know that I am a man of my word, and if I tell you that your money is safe and that I personally guarantee your deposits, you know you can depend on it. If you are unsure, I will gladly write you a personal letter of guarantee. If you are still unsure, we have enough gold on hand that we can clear your account, less anything you may owe the bank."

"If you want that letter, please come up and see me. If you still want to withdraw your money, please see Mr. Halliburton and he will clear your accounts."

With that, Charlie turned and walked inside. Frank opened the doors for business.

Charlie and Frank spent the day talking with people who were still worried. At the end of the day, the two men looked at one another.

"So, Frank. How many people closed their accounts?"

"Only four of them, and none of the big accounts. I think the total was less than 200 dollars."

"Not bad. I only wrote six letters of personal guarantee."

"General, we got off a lot easier than we could have. A bank run would have killed us."

~

Over the next three months, Charlie spent a great deal of his time running between Culpeper, Richmond, and Washington. Whenever possible, he took Rebecca with him. He was doing everything within his power to see to it that Virginia was readmitted to the Union as quickly as possible.

It was an uphill battle, with the more radical Republicans still wanting to punish the south and Virginia in particular because of Virginia's role in the rebellion. Rebecca had become quite skilled at managing politically charged social events, as they both realized that ladies indeed had the ears of their husbands. In this way, they worked together to reinstate Virginia.

When he was not trying to lobby the various participants in the statehood issue, Charlie was doing his best to negotiate beneficial deals for the farmers from Culpeper County, so they could overcome the impact of the fall in food prices following Black Friday. He had been particularly successful in negotiating premium prices for Culpeper wheat and corn with the British trade envoy, which had minimized the impact of the overall fall in food prices. The farmers were very appreciative.

On the 26th of January, 1870, Congress finally agreed to readmit Virginia to the Union, effective July 15th of that year. This gave the citizens of the state time to elect representatives and senators to be seated on July 16th. Charlie and Rebecca were in Washington for the vote. They beat a path back to Mrs. Galloway's, where they ate a light supper in their room and celebrated by messing up the sheets to an impressive level.

~

Friday, July 15, 1870

The party had started at noon and was planned to carry on through the day and into the evening. All the businesses, black and white, had come together to supply the community everything it needed to properly celebrate this momentous day.

Virginia was being readmitted to the Union and a statehood party was a must. It had been a long time in coming and no one more than Charlie was excited to have it happening. He was proud of how Culpeper had come together in the last two years he had been mayor.

He had seen several new businesses open, including three owned by women and seven more owned by prosperous blacks. He was both startled and pleased to discover that George and Jimmy had managed to open their own freight business and no longer worked as day workers for others.

As he strolled down the closed off Main Street, he had no idea where his wife or children were. They had been swarmed and swallowed up into the crowd almost immediately upon arriving. He and Rebecca had already made plans for just such an issue and planned to meet at Jocko's at 2:00.

He stopped to shake several hands and have a word here or there. No one was particularly interested in talking business today. Everyone seemed happy to take the day off and relax. Most of the shops like Duncan's and Jeremiah's were outright closed, giving everyone the day off.

Businesses that were going to make a coin or two were open. Mr. Cooper even managed to have a tub of shaved ice that he was happy to sell for a penny a scoop. He was going through it faster than one of Darby's boys could shave more.

All the restaurants and cook shacks were open. That barbeque place that Eloise was so fond of had managed to work a deal with Jocko and he let them set up out behind his place, where they would have access to the kitchen and the water supply, and he did it nearly out of the kindness of his heart, taking only a half penny a plate.

The family stood together in the center of the small park that surrounded the courthouse, smiling and chatting with people as they came up to thank Charlie and Rebecca for their efforts on their behalf.

During a lull in the parade of people, Charlie looked at Rebecca. “Do you think we can take a break and become the lady and gentleman of leisure we keep hoping to become?”

“Yes, my love. I think we can. In fact, I insist on it, darling.”

“Yes, dear.”

THE END

Thank you for taking the time to read **Enemies In The Gates** If you enjoyed it, please consider telling your friends or posting a short review. Word of mouth is an author's best friend and much appreciated.

Thank you,
T. Novan & Taylor Rickard

Also By T. Novan and Taylor Rickard

Redmond Civil War Romance Series

- Words Heard in Silence
- Paths of Peace
- Enemies In The Gates
- Honor They Father

Other Fiction by T. Novan

- Madam President (with Advocate)
- First Lady (with Advocate)
- The Claiming of Ford

About AUSXIP Publishing

AUSXIP Publishing came about as a natural evolution to the expansion of the AUSXIP Network (Originally came online in 1996) and the Publishing arm was activated in 2015.

We strive to bring readers quality stories with strong female characters that inspire, strengthen and enrich the soul– to build you up, to create a sense of achievement and most importantly to entertain. We love reading about strong women who change their world.

All the hallmarks that made AUSXIP Network a place where people want to congregate is what we want to replicate. AUSXIP Publishing is the company that produces the books we want to read if were were not writing or publishing them ourselves.

Come with us on our journey and lose yourself in our books and grow with us

Where Can You Find Us?

Official Site: www.ausxippublishing.com
Tw tter: http://twitter.com/ausxippub
Facebook: http://facebook.com/ausxippublishing

Made in the USA
Monee, IL
30 April 2020

27074732R00334